School Tales

a novel

Sharon Myrick

SHE WRITES PRESS

Published 2018
Printed in the United States of America
ISBN: 978-1-63152-423-3 paperback
978-1-63152-424-0 ebook

Library of Congress Control Number: 2018932734

For information, address:
She Writes Press
1563 Solano Ave #546
Berkeley, CA 94707

Cover and interior design by Tabitha Lahr

She Writes Press is a division of SparkPoint Studio, LLC.

All company and/or product names may be trade names, logos, trademarks,
and/or registered trademarks and are the property of their respective owners.

School Tales is a work of fiction. Names, characters, places, and incidents are either the
product of the author's imagination or are used fictitiously, with one exception. One
character, Joel Salatin, is widely known in the public sphere as a national leader in the
practice of sustainable agriculture. The incident in *School Tales* where Salatin assists
a young person to become educated in progressive farming is fictitious but consistent
with his actions in real life. For all other characters, any resemblance to actual
persons, living or dead, is entirely coincidental.

Dedicated to all people of youthful spirit who speak, write, create, and live their story of meaning in our world.

Contents

Chapter 1: Fog of School

Once upon a time, I was not like the walking dead. I was young then, but without a fairy godmother to nurture my discovering spirit . . . Now, so much of me is buried that I don't know how to find my way.

I rush down the dark hallway to homeroom, music blaring from the speakers and assaulting me with the high school anthem for seniors, "Time of Your Life." This fairy tale version of high school is way different from the reality of seeing my classmates sprawled lifelessly across the top of their hard desktop beds. Even the loud clang of the too-familiar bell doesn't disturb disengaged souls. We serve time, to-the-second aware of how long it will be till the end of each class and each day in our teenage home base, school.

Laying my head on the box of graduation announcements I just picked up, I also disappear into daydreaming. Four more months till my diploma and then escape to the freedom of college. Wish these announcements foretold who I am, what I can do, and if I'm prepared for life on my own.

The girl in the next row shakes me and hisses, "Listen!"

Still in the fog of my daydreaming, I mutter, annoyed, "I'm tired of listening all day to stuff shoved down our throats, disconnected from what I need to know."

But I give in and refocus, back to the land of discontent I call "Not-ness school." Not life, not freedom, not happiness. Instead, disengagement, disappearance, etc. My little protest: don't "dis" me. Startled by my homeroom's sudden transformation—from sleep to excited, nervous chatter—I strain to hear what people around me are saying.

Our drama-inclined classmate says, "My father heard at work a kid brought a gun to school."

Another student says, "Yeah, this morning it was all over Facebook. I saw a lot of other crazy stuff about how we're all running wild here."

"What a joke that is. We're kept on such a tight leash here, we're not even allowed to *think* about wild stuff, much less *do* anything."

"Yeah, the gun thing is probably just another Facebook rumor."

Right on cue, we hear the principal droning the morning announcements: ". . . Student backpacks will be searched each morning . . ."

Stunned silence from everyone.

One guy quietly says, "Facebook accounts say the gun incident happened two weeks ago and was kept a secret."

Then everyone looks at me, by habit, and someone asks me what I think. *So what's inside my backpack is important, but not what's inside me?* I think. *No me, no person, just the student role. What disrespect.* But what I say is, "I don't know. Why would someone bring a gun to school? Who would do that?"

They look surprised, even worried, that I have no analysis.

Attention shifts back to the principal, who speaks in a voice reeking of power and position: ". . . rules to ensure safety of the school community."

"Really?" I say to the group. "He doesn't know what to do so he makes up another rule, this time about backpack searches? He should confront the real problem, whatever it is. How is this new rule supposed to make us feel safe?"

"Yeah, next it will be strip searches."

Announcements complete, homeroom over, first period begins. Our History of Government teacher displays odd movements like a twitchy snake, looking desperately at the door. I imagine him saying, "Don't tread on me."

The second the bell rings, all twenty-three of us in the class pounce on him at once, asking about his perspective:

"What's up?"

"Why did the Principal come up with this new backpack search policy?"

"What is he *not* telling us?"

Many of us have our arms folded in distrust, trying to create an armor of protection against . . . what? Our incompetence in dealing with this threat? The only threat we've been asked to deal with before now is that of bad grades.

Our teacher mumbles a response that definitely sounds scripted and includes words like "not at liberty to say," "confidentiality," and "due process rights."

That's not him talking. He's usually honest with us. Has he not been told the whole story? This is getting really scary; it seems like not even the teachers know what's going on.

Wildly waving his hand in the air, a guy in front of me blurts out, "I heard a student brought a gun to school a few weeks ago. Is that true?"

The teacher doesn't answer; he looks like he doesn't know what to say. I honestly feel sorry for him. He's changed since he was my teacher in ninth grade. He once told me being forced to shift to a standardized college prep curriculum, with constant testing, took the life out of him. He and other teachers fought the switch but lost. Now they act beaten down.

People in the class continue to throw out comments, revealing mounting uncertainty.

"Why is this whole thing so hush-hush? If somebody really brought a gun to school, deal with it. This is life-or-death stuff."

"Not telling us the truth just makes us feel more unsafe."

Whispered in the back row, inaudible to the teacher, "I don't want the creepy principal going through things in my backpack."

"My mom told me this morning to stay in sight of an adult at school," another kid pipes up.

The class goofy guy says, "What if I need to go to the bathroom?"

Jumping on that immature comment, the teacher says, "This discussion has deteriorated. I wish you cared as much about how our government solves problems as you do a minor change in your daily routine."

His "disappointed-in-you" tone silences us. Then, predictably, he asserts his authority and herds us back into routine, saying, "Everyone take out a pen for the daily quiz on last night's reading assignment from the textbook."

Our response, also predictable, is generalized groaning, shuffling, and 100 percent compliance. Back to predictable routine, we take comfort in the certainty of knowing what to do, letting go of any expectation of thinking about real life. That will have to wait until lunch, the only time we are free to talk or check our phones for messages from the outside world.

I notice a girl on the other side of the classroom wearing a T-shirt that reads, "Freedom . . . is there an app for that?" It's a violation of the dress code. I'm surprised no one's made her change yet.

Post-quiz, we continue class with a documentary film, not part of the approved curriculum—maybe this teacher hasn't completely given up after all—called *Fog of War*. Former Secretary of Defense Robert McNamara talks about WWII, the Cuban Missile Crisis, and the Vietnam War. McNamara rambles and jumps around, but he raises important questions, I think, like whether the firebombing and destruction of sixty-seven Japanese cities, plus Hiroshima and Nagasaki, was a proportional response or simply done out of anger. With the Vietnam War, he says our anticommunist fog prevented us from seeing that the Vietnamese people wanted freedom from all superpowers and would fight to the death to get it.

It's kind of like all us students in high school: We want freedom from the superpowers controlling our life. But the anger and fight in us has given way to—well, it's evident now, looking around the room as the movie ends. Almost everyone around me is asleep. We can't see through the fog we're in to learn from these old conflicts. Plus, the truth is, with no fluorescent, artificial lights stimulating us like mega-doses of caffeine, zoning out will happen during a film. Especially since there's no natural light in here either; windows, after all, might encourage unrestricted imagining—a distraction from school.

The main thing we know is that the film won't be on the test. We only care about learning the least acceptable amount of not-ness tidbits that will be on the test—and even those will quickly be forgotten. I'm supposed to be a passive receptacle, absorbing factoids spoon-fed to us by teachers and then regurgitated on tests. The message this sends me is that I possess nothing of value already inside.

The student assessment of high school I hear all the time: "It's boring." Maybe we contribute to the nothingness by not taking control of things. Maybe I should try to do something about the backpack search thing rather than make my usual escape into dreams of a future.

Bell rings, piercing reality. No time to discuss the film. We file out the classroom door in our "fog of school." My definition: *uncertainty about the purpose of school and my ability to affect anything.*

The walk to second period is a rush of splintered conversations, most with the word "gun" in them. The rush of blood is comforting, clearing my foggy state of mind and warming me up. School is always, always, forever cold and indifferent to the temperature outside. Think frozen bodies in cryonic suspension, considered dead, waiting to be awakened at a later time. "Cryo," freezing, is close to "cry"—as in "for help," for the needs of my body. Wool socks and my Birkenstock sandals admittedly make me look a bit geeky, but they're my primary defense against shivering.

Another human need, to move, runs up against classroom rules to sit still for an hour at a time, six times a day, five days a week, one hundred and eighty days a year. I sigh as I slide into my seat in English class.

All twenty-four of us seniors are in the same classes through-out the day. There's one difference in this classroom, though: the desks are in a circle to promote class discussions. It's not much, but it's something.

Our English teacher is more peppy than usual. Quick to size up the reason for our gloom, she responds with super-happy comments like, "Don't let this spoil your last months before graduation."

I raise my hand and start talking all at the same time: "But we are being treated like infants, not almost-adults. And if the threat is real, it's our lives at stake. Who can think about a diploma as being more important?"

Silence. No other students jump in to say things like they did in government class. My "diploma" comment probably reminded them what's at stake during this season of waiting to hear from colleges. We all know the story of the kid last year who got in trouble at the prom and the school withdrew recommendations for him to an Ivy League college. Also, the English teacher is pretty cautious. She is new so she's closely watched, pressured to "cover the material" and make sure we all do well on standardized tests. I've seen the fire in her withering over the course of this one year.

While I can understand where our teachers are coming from, in the end there's nothing worse than being ignored, feeling like an outcast. I can answer test questions and make good grades, but who will answer my questions? Like what kind of democracy treats students as if we're at the bottom of a pyramid of power? And how the way our school is structured doesn't seem to meet the needs of humans. The only response from teachers, both times: a smile. Then back to the supposed real stuff. My school constructs our world as right or wrong, not questions; us or them, not we; black or white, not colors; back then or later, not now.

Our English teacher fills the silence by reminding us of our next deadline, telling us we need to turn in our project proposal tomorrow. Not used to choices, I've been struggling for weeks to come up with a simple idea for an English project. The obvious of the day jumps out: I'll do something related to the backpack search policy. Like, a survey of what students think. Maybe I can make our voices heard for a change.

I turn this idea over in my head for the rest of class, and when the bell rings, I ask my teacher for approval of my project. Looking sheepish, and I think trying to make up for what happened in class, she says okay. She also says, "Coming up with enough information may be hard since none of us, including teachers, know much about what is actually happening or why."

Off to my last morning class, Spanish. Again the walking-dead aura of zombie routine permeates the halls. True, there's also a bit of joking between those who can rapidly switch into life gear. But nobody walks with a sense of purpose. This project idea has given me a new sense of purpose, but now I need to translate my inner spark to action out there in the world.

Finally, lunch, among a sea of about a hundred students in grades nine through twelve. I sit with my usual cafeteria group. Conversation is a repeat of everything I've heard all day—mostly, the unknown circumstances of the gun incident, though everyone switches to the topic of a fight that took place at the community basketball game last night.

Barely listening, I scan the cafeteria looking for underclass students who might know what's behind the backpack search thing. The cafeteria tables are markers of cliques: jocks and cheerleaders from the community teams, the beautiful people, minority students, skaters, computer geeks. Here, the locus of student power, power to decide who fits where in the status hierarchy, not unlike their parents' views. Anyone not fitting in the tight social structure chooses a life cast aside.

Lunch social time, the only thing we control in school, reinforces the stereotype of "all teenagers care about is social life." That's mixed up. We care about what we are allowed to be in charge of. Like, who enjoys homework, busywork assignments? Instead, we gravitate to all kinds of social media, while adults watch TV, check work e-mail messages, or are glued to Facebook.

I spot the kid from California—a new student this year, a sophomore—sitting on the low window ledge. He must be missing California sun to choose sitting by himself just to catch a few rays. I can relate to seeking out light and warmth as a slice of life in the dead of winter. This is February, after all. I decide to see what he knows about all this.

As I walk toward the window, I notice the fog covering the Virginia Blue Ridge and Allegheny mountain summits has lifted. School is like artificial fog, preventing our view of those mountain anchors.

The new boy always stands out with his outrageous dress— today, a purple bow tie with bright yellow polka dots. Every day, even winter, he wears neon flip-flops, often of mixed colors, with the required coat and tie. Another always is the "QUESTION AUTHORITY" button on his coat lapel. He's a definite contrast to my totally average appearance; only my sandals and wool socks make me stand out.

I smile as I walk up. "What's up?"

"Nothing," he says, returning the smile and taking his ear buds out.

"You're called Surfer Boy, right?"

He grimaces. "Unfortunately. I call you Listener Girl. You don't say much, but it seems like lots of people want to talk things over with you."

Pretty observant guy. He seems way comfortable being alone. I guess I appear comfortable, but I'm not. There's a lot of anger and insecurity I keep in.

"They call me Country Girl. I've known these mostly city kids since ninth grade, but they've all been together since preschool, learning every button to push in each other for high drama. Getting conflict going relieves boredom. So I listen to their gripes and provide some perspective. The focus stays on them. They aren't too interested in hearing about me."

Hope that didn't come out whiny. I've never told anyone here how I really feel about being invisible. "You don't eat?" I say, trying to take the focus off me.

"Nah, I wait till I get home," he says with a shrug. "So how does this naming thing work, anyway?"

The collective splattering of words off concrete cafeteria walls assaults my ears, competing with his easy-going stream of words. I slide in closer to him, not because I can't hear but because I'm attracted to his deep voice, the way it floats effortlessly.

"The top of the student food chain uses their power by granting nicknames and everyone else goes along," I explain. "I don't eat here either. Hey, you hear the backpack announcement this morning? I'm in the dark about it. I want to do a student survey about the policy, for my English project, but I need more background info. What do people in the sophomore class say?" Man, I am a chatty one today. My school conversations are usually one, maybe two sentences tops.

"First I heard about it was homeroom. I heard a student brought a gun to school." Dropping his voice down another octave, signaling importance, he says, "Crazy. What is this school, Columbine revisited?"

My spine tenses up. My stance of outrage had pushed the fear of the morning away, but now I instinctively look around for a shooter. I needn't worry. It's just the usual zipping of backpacks, carrying lunch trays to the window, and couples storing up hugs to get them through the afternoon. "Hope not," I say with a little shudder.

After a pause, he says, "Sophomores didn't seem to know much else, really. I have one junior class since I took sophomore science in California, but juniors don't really talk to me. Just one guy does, another person on the outs from the crowd."

"What's his name?"

"Real name, I dunno. They call him Hiker."

Searching the tables, I look for dark hair framing an Italian-featured face, including dark eyes. "Where is he? I don't see him."

The lunch table social categories have become ingrained habit after all these years. It's like sitting at the same desk in class every day, or eating fast food—it's easy, predictable, feels safe. Although lunch tables, unlike fast food, aren't cheap. You pay through unchangeable identity sunk in concrete by the force of the judgments of others. I am what they think, "they" being a narrow range of friends.

"Hiker eats up in the main office for some reason. Anyway, he's not here today. Probably off hiking. Wish I was."

I perk up. "You a hiker?"

"Not really. I'm a biker."

"Cool. Racing bike?"

"No, a hybrid. Better for exploring country roads."

Another example of him doing things alone, being curious, an explorer. And now I have a new name for him: Biker.

"You'll have to check out where I live," I say. "Country Girl, y'know." Can't believe I actually invited him to my house. And yet I can believe it. He is so easy to talk to.

Brushing long hair out of his eyes, the tips of which are still sun-bleached, Biker says, "Last time I saw Hiker he said something strange to me—'I feel empty inside.' I didn't know what to say. It didn't matter, though, because he walked away before I could come up with something."

Man, this guy really cares about other people.

"I think that is part of the name thing," I say—"'Take a hike.' Now he beats everybody to the punch by leaving before being told to, walking away from what's not good for him. At least that's how it seems from a distance."

"You ever talk with Hiker?" Biker asks.

I've never had a conversation with him in our three years together here. Weird, since there are only a hundred of us. "No, not really," I admit, "but one time I saw him in town standing in front of Gelato Café and I thought, *He looks like an ancient Roman statue.* In ninth grade he won a big deal national Latin award that was on the announcements for days. That's all I know about him." It's so pathetic how little I can offer I can't even look Biker in the eye when I say it.

"I could count on one hand the number of Hilltop students who've actually reached out to have a real conversation with me," he says. "They're sitting at the skater table. Add to them a few girls teasing me about my supposed good looks." He makes a silly face, sticks his tongue sideways out of his mouth.

"Why don't you sit with the skaters anymore?"

"Got boring. Besides, got to keep up my tan." He stretches out, hands behind his head, legs extended, and crosses his flip-flopped feet.

I laugh. "Fair enough. See ya around, Biker."

"See ya, Listener."

Interesting guy. Most people need a social group to hang on to. I'd rather stay and talk to him than go to my afternoon classes—math, science, and arts appreciation—a mish-mash of dull routine and no opportunity to pursue thinking through my English project. But I don't have much of a choice, do I?

Leaving through the school's massive, solid oak front door, the sharp, cold air injects my spirit with hope and energy.

It's a quick walk to my car, down the steep hill from the top where my school sits, appropriately named Hilltop Academy. The "academy" part relates to the college prep focus and the school's location in between our small town's two colleges. This private high school, comprised mostly by kids from the faculty of the two colleges, is distinctly visible to all the other city and county dwellers below.

I wave to a couple of seniors headed to swim practice at the town's indoor pool—we don't have any of our own facilities, and our sports teams are run by a community-wide organization rather than the school.

A Hilltopper whose car is parked next to mine is throwing her backpack into her trunk and retrieving her dance gear for a class at a nearby studio.

"Don't know where you get all your energy," I say.

"Frankly, at the end of the school day, I'm exhausted," she says. "But dance revives me."

I know exactly what she means. My revival starts with driving home, a ten-mile becoming-me-again ritual. No stoplights, little traffic. Good thinking time.

It doesn't really bother me that everyone calls me Country Girl. Living out there is a gift. For my parents, it was a financial thing; the price of city real estate had shot up, and they wanted to buy. For me, it's a sense of freedom to be me, alive like everything else around me, without the evaluating eyes of others. I feel at home among the creeks and rivers and mountains that define our part of the county.

My driving home ritual includes peeling, while driving, my armor off; the leggings go last, and then I'm down to my cotton teddy, the wind from the car windows blowing life back into my body. Only my dogs see my revealed, free self.

At the end of Blue Heron Creek—I saw three of its namesakes on today's drive—I turn onto my gravel road. Machine Cemetery Farm—my joking name for the neighbor's place—grows to my right. Jake lives there with his dad, who knows a gazillion stories of local people and history, telling them with his local accent and in great detail.

Every time I drive past Jake's house, I feel a knot of sadness inside me. I miss him. For three years before I went to middle school, we were inseparable. Our favorite activity was exploring the miles and miles of open space—woods, creeks, caves, and fields of wildlife—and talking to each other non-stop. Jake set the standard for me of what it feels like to have someone truly listen to me and care what I'm talking about.

Before Jake, I played on my own, digging with my hands to build dirt villages and invent happily-ever-after stories of the ancient people I imagined lived on this land long ago. Then Jake came along, and I didn't have to play alone anymore—but as we drew closer, my parents showed a growing feeling of unease. Not that we did anything wrong. We didn't. But I got a strange sense that they thought we cared about each other too much. Like it wasn't right for me to care about a boy who loved farming. Like they were ashamed of me, or for me. Like *I* should feel shame.

When I think about it now, I do feel shame—shame that I didn't stand up to my parents killing our relationship. I often wonder if Jake thinks about those good times we had. He goes to

Stone Creek, the public high school for county kids, so we never see each other anymore.

Now I go exploring with my dogs on no-destination hikes, wandering "expotitions," Pooh Bear style. On cue, here they are at the end of my mile-long gravel road. The dogs are racing and bumping each other, tails set on extreme wag. Honestly, I feel closer to Ayla and Lily these days than I do to any human being.

Our house is a modern log cabin, up high on Hawk Ridge, with great views in all directions. The best thing this time of year is the huge windows all along the south side of the house. The sun they let in keeps the rooms warm and cozy.

I grab my tablet, snuggle into the down sofa with the dogs, and message my best friend, Cora. This is our daily ritual, sharing what happened at school. Compared to her interesting stories from Stone Creek, mine usually suck. But not today! I tell her about the new backpack search policy and my project.

I can say anything to Cora. We only see each other, live, once a week at church. Actually, we sneak away from church to walk and walk around town, talking a mile a minute and returning just in time to appear as if we were there all along. We call ourselves the Free Will Baptists.

Cora opened up to me early on about her big struggle over being mixed race. Her mom, who is white, was treated meanly by women of the largest black church in the area when they first moved here, so Cora and her parents left and came to our church. Cora told me she adores her mom, and her dad too, but sometimes she feels awkward in public with her mom. Cora is somewhere between light skinned and dark skinned—black in the eyes of many.

"Okay," Cora messages me back, "so I'm two years younger than you and my school is terrific, what am I missing? How could someone be so unhappy they would bring a gun to school and NOBODY would know that?"

I don't know how to respond to Cora, and trying to think about it makes me feel all unsettled, so I turn to developing my project proposal. I propose to interview three seniors from Hilltop and three seniors from Stone Creek. Since the two schools are very different in size and student backgrounds, asking questions about a backpack search policy might show contrasting points of view. My write-up will describe what I learn from the interviews. I hear my parents' Prius crackling up the gravel road. I meet them in the kitchen, and my mood improves with the smell of barbecue take-out.

Dinner is usually a rehash of their workdays, like a ten-mile drive home together isn't enough time to be done with that. As college professors, the academic world is all they care about. Even the parties they go to are for things like connecting with people on the tenure committee. I honestly have no idea why they had a child. Fun, excitement, and emotion are not visibly hard-wired into their makeup. I feel like an add-on to their life schedule. As an only child, I've always taken personally the not being seen or known.

But tonight is different. They want to know what I think of the new backpack search policy at school.

"Us kids have a million questions about why we have this new policy and what happened," I say. "But nobody at school tells us anything. Some kids are saying they heard a student brought a gun to school. What have you heard?"

My mom nods. "Yes, we heard about the gun too. Apparently the student who brought the gun to school claims he has been bullied for years and is afraid." She flips a hand to wipe away that last word, as in *how ridiculous.*

"So he was going to shoot other students?" I'm one-upping them with my distant disbelief.

"Who knows?" Mom says. "The point is a gun shouldn't be in school under any circumstances."

They have both perfected their lecture voices after all these years of college teaching.

"So all parents support this backpack search policy?" I demand.

"Probably not 'all' other parents support it, but we think it's a good idea," Mom says.

"That sucks. Why hasn't anyone asked us kids what's going on?"

"I see your vocabulary hasn't improved much lately."

Nice putdown, Dad.

Mom pushes on. "It is our job, and the school's job, to protect you."

"I can't even . . . How can you protect me if you don't understand what is behind all this, what's really going on?"

"The backpack searches are for your protection. So you can focus on getting good grades and into a good college."

It always comes back to the college script. "I already make good grades," I say. "But am I supposed to have blinders on about real life stuff, like someone bringing a gun to school?"

"It's not your job to worry about that. It's being handled by the principal."

"I have approval from my English teacher to do a survey of what students think about the backpack search policy."

Mom frowns. "You stirring things up won't help resolve the problem and could very well get you in trouble. High school recommendations are critical to colleges."

"Did y'all think this way when you were bored out of your minds in high school?" I don't wait for an answer; I storm out of the room before they explicitly forbid me from doing the project.

I've gotten pretty good at avoiding direct power plays from my parents, since I know I will always lose. The current big standoff is all about college. I have two applications in to colleges. My parents feel confident in winning the battle because my grades from "prestigious" Hilltop Academy are good enough to get in to their choice, the "prestigious" state university, UVA. But I want to go to a small, liberal arts college: Oberlin. It's in Ohio, far enough away to put some distance between us. And it is close to my grandparents, who have a large college fund for me—large enough to pay for the more expensive Oberlin. They say my parents should help me decide what is best for me and not use cost as a factor.

My parents have been planning all this out for years. Hilltop Academy, as college prep, fits their requirements. Besides the fact that all college faculty kids get free tuition there, they love the full schedule of required courses every student has to take, the teachers with advanced degrees, and the outrageously strict dress code (coats and ties for guys and similar professional dress for girls) that makes all us students of similar backgrounds look even more alike.

The only thing parents have to pay for at Hilltop is the after-school tutoring in preparation for SATs. We are already familiar with the content of the questions because we get it all the time, repeated ad nauseam, from our teachers' tests, which are supposedly aligned with the SATs. But the review through SAT practice tests helps us re-memorize information. One time I asked a girl in my SAT class why her answer was right and she said, "I don't know, it just is."

My parents also like it that our principal seems to run a tight ship—or at least that they don't usually hear of any problems. Parents don't hear from teachers much either, because the teachers are only there part time—there aren't enough classes in their subject areas for full-time work. Come to think of it, how did my parents even hear about a gun at school? I bet through gossip, and not any official notification. I've never seen any college administrators at Hilltop, even though they fund the high school and the principal supposedly reports to them.

The way I see things, college is my ticket out from under, a ray of hope to control my own life. I don't trust my parents to decide on a college for me, based on what I'm about, instead of their script for my future. The decision where I go should be mine but my parents have the power to enforce, "for your own good." I just need to be smart about the conflict so I don't lose the power struggle. I'm a deer, keeping still, listening intently, gauging my actions for escape, preservation.

I drift off to sleep nestled between the dogs and thinking about my visit to Oberlin. The peaceful atmosphere . . . students from many different backgrounds who seem to be tight with each other . . . freedom to select classes and craft a unique major . . .

My survey proposal is—shock—approved by my English teacher and the principal. I think she was covering herself, running my project by him. I'm amazed he approved it with only the condition that he wants to see my report before anyone else does.

Our principal was once quoted in the local paper as saying his major goal for the school is to stay off the front page of newspapers. Maybe he is worried about what could be brewing and needs inside information. Neither students nor teachers talk with him. *Is there real reason to worry about something like a school shooting?*

My back is all tensed up again.

I begin by interviewing Hilltop students, choosing to talk to the people I least know in the senior class, people I hardly ever talk with. I want to be as objective as possible, not making any assumptions like I know what they mean. And I'm keeping it to only three people so we have plenty of time to dig deeper than a typical conversation. To keep each discussion concrete and individual, I plan to ask the person to reveal what they carry in their backpack. Those items will be the jumping-off point for my questions, but they can say whatever they want. I'll tell students that what they show me, or say, will be anonymous. Each conversation is recorded so I can go back and pull out direct quotes. In the notes I take, I use their school nicknames.

Hilltop Academy Interview Notes

North Face Dude—**confident**—**outgoing**—**"perfect" dress**
"The new backpack search policy is no big deal to me. I'll do whatever they ask because I don't want to jeopardize getting into a good college. That's the main thing to me and my parents right now. Success at Hilltop means keeping your head down and mouth shut."

Backpack—the usual textbooks, notebooks, pencils/pens, calculator, and phone. Selected backpack items:

Copy of college application essay:
- "When I get bored in class, I pull this out and read it. I've read it a thousand times, practically have it memorized. It keeps me going, thinking about getting out of here."

- "It will be better in college because of the freedom. Freedom from parents, rules, more time for me to decide what to do."
- "Yeah, freedom to be me. Dress the way I want. Join a fraternity. And, of course, constant parties!"
- "I don't have any particular major in mind. But at the schools I've applied to, I know I'll make good connections with people that can help me in my future. That's the way it works."

Can of Monster Energy

- "This is my lifeline. I couldn't keep going without it."
- "No, I get enough sleep—about six hours. It's hard to get everything done—homework, after-school sports, volunteering—so I'll be well-rounded in colleges' eyes. I'm under a lot of stress, but it will be worth it."
- "I catch up on sleep on the weekends."
- "For fun? I play video games with the guys I've known all my life."

Personal notes from friends written during class

- "The pace is so slow in class, I can take lecture notes and at the same time carry on conversations with friends by writing notes. Passing notes in class is against the rules, so we exchange our notes in between classes. The disconnect in what we say, compared to give and take conversation, is sometimes pretty funny."
- "I get enough of what the teacher is saying to make good grades. But mostly I'm not interested enough to ask questions. And it is hard to get a real conversation going. The teachers just want to draw some 'point' out of me."
- "Yeah, texting would be easier but it's against the rules. And text language is more limiting. We really get into some heavy, personal stuff in the notes. I've known these people a long time, so it's easier to open up a little."

- "Yeah, I feel safe. I'm a big guy and I got friends to stand by me when there's a problem. Even though my buddies tease me all the time about being fat, they've got my back. There are a few bullies, but they pick on the outliers, not me."
- "The outliers are the gay people and the retarded girl."

Glitz Queen—quiet—little eye contact—trendy, sexy dress pushing the requirement of professional dress
"It's none of the school's business what I have in my backpack. It is my personal, private space and should be illegal for them to force us to show them. . . . I'll show you because you have always been nice to me and I've seen you stand up to teachers before. So I believe you won't rat on me. . . . My mother would never stand up to the school authorities to come to my defense. She's all about 'do what everyone else does and don't make waves.'"
Backpack—usual textbooks, etc.

Phone
- "They better not try to confiscate my cell phone. I'll make them get a search warrant first. My whole life is in my phone."
- "My phone is always on, even at night. I want to be there for my boyfriend. I would worry and not be able to sleep if my phone was turned off."

Birth control pills
- "I can't leave these at home. My mother would snoop around in my room and find them. Then all hell would break loose. She already thinks I'm going to ruin my life by hooking up with a loser. A loser in my mother's eyes is someone who is lower class and doesn't care what she thinks."
- "I'll have to figure out a way to disguise these pills because of the school rule against having medications that are not checked in at the office."

- "It would make me feel ashamed for them to be going through my stuff."

Mace

- "Yes, I'm afraid in school. Guys make nasty, sexual remarks to me all day long. My boyfriend goes to Stone Creek, so there's nobody here to stand up for me."
- "You can see how these same bullies treat gay kids in school. Always have, ever since elementary school. Nobody stops them. Teachers and administrators just look the other way."
- "Girls don't feel powerful enough to stand up to guys. Besides, the other girls don't like me. They don't like the way I dress, say I look low class, and my beliefs are 'out there' for them. For one, I'm a Buddhist."

Star Tech—aloof—self-absorbed—nerdy dress

"If they are just looking for weapons, I'm not opposed to backpack searches. But if they start poking around at everything to find violations of other rules, I'm very opposed. They try to regulate too much of a student's life."

Backpack—Very expensive leather. Hidden compartments, and one is locked. None of the usual textbooks, notebooks, etc.

iPad, in the locked compartment

- "I'm trusting that you will not reveal to school administrators what is in my backpack. But, if you do, I'm prepared to fight their policy of no personal computers in school. I use technology for all my learning."
- "I have Internet access through their WiFi connection. They have very lax security setups. Most businesses, even small ones, are light years ahead of this school."
- "Someday soon, I hope, I will have my own business in the computer field. I am getting no assistance from this school in furthering my personal goals. What I am learning is from other geeks online and my father, who is head of technology for the university."

Car keys
- "I have a Mercedes Roadster. I like going for drives on the Blue Ridge Parkway. Sometimes I hike the trails. Once I was chilling at one of the overlooks and saw an eagle streaking toward a triple rainbow. But mostly my adventures are about the driving, with the top down. That clears my head."
- "My car and my computers are my life. I don't care about the boring humdrum of this school."

Picture of friend in iPad
- "We are close friends, we message each other every day. He's a freshman at MIT."
- "We met at a summer program three years ago and really clicked. We see each other in person several times a year, on holidays and vacations."
- "I've applied to MIT."

Listening to these three students blows me away. Even though they have been in all my classes for many years, I've learned intriguing new things about each person just from a simple conversation. They were willing to be so open about what's in their backpack, how they see school, and their life. Between the hardened boundaries around cliques and total classroom focus on academic lectures, so much of who we are is usually invisible in school.

The sad thing about the interviews is that nobody brought up the gun incident. We all seem to focus on our own narrow concerns and kind of act passive, letting time go by, waiting for . . . exit.

Standing in the lunch line after the interviews, I get caught up on the morning gossip. Hilltop students continue puzzling about who brought the gun to school as a novelty for discussion. The general consensus emerging in the rumor circuit focuses on Hiker, who has not been in school since a few days before the new backpack policy was announced. Everyone seems to assume he is hiking the Appalachian Trail, as he does often. According to gossip, his parents allow him to take off school and hike when he is feeling really depressed. At school he is presumed gay and everyone knows he's been bullied over the years. One student allegedly saw him recently enter the office of a psychiatrist.

Lunch with Biker seems way more attractive than lunch listening to gossip reruns. I wander straight over to him when I get to the cafeteria.

"Hey, Biker, can I join you in the window?" I ask. "I won't hog the rays. I actually bought lunch today. Love their chili."

"Hey, Listener, what's up?" He tosses me a couple pieces of saltwater taffy.

"I just finished survey interviews with three students here. Their views of the backpack search policy are interesting. Want to play 'what's in your backpack'?"

He brightens at the prospect of a show-and-tell game. "People actually showed you? Okay, let's see . . ." He reaches in his backpack, past the textbooks and notebooks, to a cloth case. He unzips it and carefully sorts through treasured items till he finds a photo he was obviously looking for. His usual friendly smile becomes a smile of excitement and self-satisfaction. "It's me standing next to my surfboard, the sea in the background." Within moments the smile completely disappears. He continues to stare at the picture, blank-faced. "Not being in California is depressing. Looking at this picture makes it worse, so I don't know why I carry it around."

Biker's usual go-with-the-flow nature turns to numbed paralysis. It bothers me to see him this way. Slowing down my typical speaking pace, I say, "Did you, like, surf all the time, every day?"

"Pretty much," he says, no emotion in his voice. "Since moving here, I started riding my bike every day as a replacement, to help the depression. Now it's too frigging cold, ice and snow everywhere, and I've taken a nose dive."

I don't have the nerve to ask about his depression. "Where do you ride to?"

"All over the county," he says, perking up a little. "Here's a map I keep with me. All the starred spots are places I've stopped and met really cool people. Some amazing old hippies, tucked away in the hills, do unusual things—like one guy smelts ore for sculpting. I met a shoe maker who used to live near my home in California and used to go swimming in the ocean where my friends and I surfed."

His speech reaches a particular sparkle at the word "ocean."

I have an idea. "Hey, want to try something new and come cross-country skiing at my house?" This is the second time I've invited him to come to my house. Am I being too pushy?

But Biker smiles. "My shrink would approve. He says I need a winter hobby. I don't think he gets it that surfing was not a hobby. It was my life."

So now he mentions a shrink. He's got more courage than me.

"I hate it when adults dismiss our feelings, like we aren't people," I say. "That reminds me . . . I wanted to tell you what my parents said last night. They heard the student brought a gun to school because he was constantly bullied and afraid. Everybody's been talking today about Hiker, and he has been bullied for years. Do you think Hiker's the one who brought the gun to school?"

Biker leans closer to me, like he wants more privacy, even though the closest table to us is pretty far away. I've noticed people looking at us today, one even rudely pointing, as if we are a spectacle. I guess that's what happens any time there's a new event in the cafeteria scene, though. People have nothing more important to focus on.

"I don't know," Biker says. "But a few weeks ago I went to the restroom and some seniors were messing with him. I acted like the teacher had sent me to get him. One of the bullies says to Hiker, 'We'll get you next time.' Hiker looks the guy straight in the face and says, 'You guys are just cowards.' As we leave the bathroom, he gives me a high five. I smile at him, having no clue what to say."

Doesn't sound like Hiker was afraid of the bullies. So why would he bring a gun to school?

"Do you think we should do something, like report the bullying?" I ask.

Biker drags the fingers of his left hand through the hair partially covering his eyes, thinking. "Maybe I can get my science teacher to give me Hiker's phone number, saying I want to catch him up on assignments. I bet he'll give it to me . . . He tries hard to be nice to Hiker but gets little response from him."

"That sounds like something we can do," I say, encouraged. "Everyone else is losing interest now they think it's Hiker. They've been dismissing him for years." I'm ashamed to say I have too. Well, not dismissing him so much as just not paying attention to him. My usual shutdown to most everything.

"Why does everyone dismiss him?" Biker looks genuinely confused. "I know he is kinda different, but that's one reason I like him. He sees things in ways I've never thought of, and he stands up for himself."

Refreshing to hear someone think for themself and not just go with what the crowd says. I hope Biker can hang on to his individuality here at Hilltop. He still has two years to go.

I tear a piece of paper out of a notebook and write down my number, then hold the paper out to Biker. "Here's my cell number. Will you let me know if you talk to Hiker?"

"Sure."

Compelled to know more about Hiker, I head to the school office before the bell rings to see if I can find out why he eats lunch there. Through the glass door of the office, I see Ms. Carter, the school secretary. She works all alone, all day, in this office that almost nobody enters. Usually cheerful, today her face projects overwhelming anguish.

The source of pain seems to be an authentic hiker's backpack sitting on a chair outside the principal's office. A picture hangs awkwardly from the zipper: Hiker and his golden retriever next to an "Appalachian Trail" sign.

Confused, but counting on this being misplaced drama—this is my nothing-happens school, after all—I enter and look around for Hiker.

Ms. Carter seems to read my intent. With great effort, she says, "He's gone. They found his body this morning at the bottom of a cliff overhang. They say suicide."

Instantly my leg muscles weaken, my stomach jumps in a fitful spasm, and my mind comes to a dead stop. Our eyes lock, all four begging for some alternative way to grasp what is meant by her words. I have never heard anything more frightening. All I can think is how I want to run back to boring, away from desperation.

"His parents brought in a journal he kept in his backpack for the principal to read," Ms. Carter says. "I know he was working through feelings of being different, with the help of a psychiatrist, but I can't believe he would take his own life."

I can't listen to any more. I failed to see that the backpack searches were *not* the important thing. Why couldn't I dig down deep to understand? I f-ing don't know how. All I've been taught is destructive not-ness. I deaden myself at school through sleep, not caring or thinking, not speaking up, not acting from true desire, afraid to be myself here, my spirit buried.

I take a last look at the backpack, noticing the embroidered name.

I say it aloud: "Adrian."

"Yes, Adrian," Ms. Carter invokes, a tiny footprint of light in her eye.

Chapter 2: An Unwavering Pivot

Once upon a time, I was pulled down deep below. My fight to oppose the force resulted only in greater fear. Relaxing, my inner pivot aligned with the world as it truly is. Now, my journey is to replicate that awareness over and over.

SEAN

Text from Listener: "Biker, Meet me at Java NOW!"

Walking out of math class and school and nobody even notices me. I could feel bad that nobody cares but I'm feeling too good about a summons from Listener. In the middle of the school day, no less.

It's a short walk down the hill where the edge of campus meets downtown. Java, in the first block, is a quiet coffee shop usually frequented by adults, unlike noisy Mountain Mama's Ice Cream Shoppe, where Stone Creek teenagers hang out, or Gelato Café, the after-school spot preferred by Hilltoppers.

Entering Java, a long and narrow shotgun style building, like most of the downtown shops, I can see all the way to the back, but don't see Listener. Waiting for her to arrive, I take in the works by local artists displayed in the cafe. The bay window in front contains a six-inch-high sitting baby doll perched in the center of an altar, a large muted Madonna wood carving behind it. The Madonna's central feature is a disproportionately large tear slipping off her cheek. This art piece reminds me of one artist I met on a bike ride whose studio was in a treehouse. Her appearance clearly identified her as a hippie, like the ones I grew up seeing in California and others living throughout areas of this mountainous county.

More traditional art on the walls are paintings showing scenes, some of which I recognize, like an oversized barn and an antique pickup truck in the field. Farmers I've met on my rides usually have other jobs, too, needed to support their families. But their hearts are still firmly planted in their farms.

Java this time of day attracts only a few college students and professors huddled in deep conversation. The shops in this four-block-by-four-block town cater to the two colleges that sit at the edge of its center, along with tourists who come to indulge in the trendy restaurants and hotels on Main Street.

In a ring out from downtown are city neighborhoods like the one I live in, groceries, a small hospital, and medical offices. Next layer out, which I can get to by car or bike, is strip malls and a few small industries along the two main highways, which cross in the center of town. Beyond is the county, where I do my exploring. People are amazed how much I know about the county, since I'm a townie.

The clock on the church steeple next door chimes, letting me know I've only been waiting for a few minutes. Churches are everywhere in this city and county. After one bike ride I looked up how many; there are more than ninety in all. One is Buddhist, one Quaker, one Unitarian, one Jewish, and one Catholic. The rest are Christian churches, with the greatest number tilting toward fundamentalist.

One of the college students sitting at a table near me is clearly from a large city, wearing and speaking the glamour of a big city. The map I use on my bike rides says the county, including the city, is about 600 square miles—"a lot of nothing to do," people my age say. I've heard Hilltoppers say they feel sorry for locals who don't get to travel, but the locals I've met on my bike expeditions say the global travelers are just full of themselves, on a race to go everywhere, ending up right back here.

Next to churches, schools are a big deal to residents of the community, not just because the kids go there but because they are the largest employers in the county. My dad is a professor, and I know both of Listener's parents are too.

The bell hanging from Java's front door rings in Listener. She has dark circles under her eyes, and her feet are dragging a little as she walks.

I frown. "Listener, you don't look good. Are you okay?"

"My real name is Chelsea," she says, ignoring my question and looking down.

"Oh," I say. "I'm Sean for real. So . . . what's up?" My usually upbeat voice starts to match hers in seriousness.

"Hiker's name was Adrian."

I tense. "Was?"

"He died," she says, her eyes finally meeting mine, unmasking deep shock. "I mean . . . suicide."

What Chelsea knows comes out in jumbled pieces, between tears as big as the Madonna's. With each new bit of information, I become more and more numb, purposely sealing up and putting the emotions away in cold storage.

"It makes me so upset to think how Adrian must have been in so much pain, so depressed, to kill himself," she says. "I want to feel sad for Adrian, and all of us really, stuck in our miserable school. But, I keep fast-forwarding to mad. Why did we all do nothing? I mean—"

I cut her off. "Calm down, Chelsea." *Why am I speaking like my dad, Mr. Rational?*

Chelsea says in a deliberate, slow, and forceful manner, "Someone should have listened to him. Then he wouldn't have been so desperate." Decibels louder: "NOBODY listened."

I take what she's saying personally.

I look around to see if the sprinkling of other people in Java are noticing us. "You don't need to yell, get so emotional. I can hear you."

Chelsea's body slumps and her head drops to her arms on the table so her face is hidden. I can barely hear her muffled words: "If I had been more emotional before, maybe I would have noticed Adrian wasn't doing well. Maybe I could have gotten other people to pay attention, stop the meanness."

Keeping a low, even voice I say, "Do you think this is our fault?" Long pause. Finally, I hear, "I think it's everybody's fault. And I'm exhausted. I just want to go home and feel sad, be alone so I don't have to monitor my feelings."

"Are you okay to drive?" I ask.

She nods. Then, wordless, she gets up and leaves.

Head to toe, inside and out, my body registers beyond normal cool to glacier cold. Hands in my pockets, heavy coat on, hood up, makes no difference. I feel frozen in place, unable to stand up or walk.

Finally I force myself to rise and make it to the door, but as I reach for the doorknob I lose my balance. Leaning against the wall to right myself, I notice the barista behind the latte machine gaping at me. Mr. Cool won't come back here anytime soon.

Walking along the uneven brick sidewalk covered with muddy footprints, I notice that the sky, already cloudy before, has turned greyer. The tingle of blood flowing through my extremities reassures me. After a few blocks, I hang a left and walk another two blocks, landing me at my therapist's office.

Inside, the receptionist's desk looks closed up. Hearing me enter the main door, Dr. Lewis comes out of his office.

"Sean, good to see you. How are you?"

I can't make small talk right now. "Are you busy?"

After a slight hesitation, he says, "No, come on in."

His office has no windows. I asked him the first time I came here how he could stand not seeing out. He answered that his job was about helping people see in, not out, and then connecting the two. That's how he is—always saying things that make me think.

In the middle of telling him about Hiker, I mean Adrian, and my bungled conversation with Chelsea, I blurt out, "It was when Chelsea used the word 'depression.' She said Adrian must have been so depressed to kill himself. The shutdown valve in me clicked on. I became like my dad with his no-emotions work voice."

"I'm glad you can tell me about all this; that you can open up with what is going on for you." Dr. Lewis rocks back and forth in his chair. The motion comforts me, settles my wildly tangled feelings.

"Maybe it's because I'm so afraid. Afraid I'm like Adrian. You know, my depression. That I could get to a desperate place. Also, afraid I'm partly responsible for what Adrian did. And embarrassed I couldn't connect with Chelsea about all this."

Dr. Lewis gently nods his head. "Say more, Sean."

"I keep hearing this voice in my head saying, 'The worst thing you can do to somebody is ignore them, act like they are invisible, like they don't count.' I did that to Adrian. He told me he felt empty inside and I said nothing. I could have told him I understood. Well, not exactly. I don't feel empty so much as I feel like nobody sees me for who I am, just what I am to them."

"What you are to them?"

"I don't know, like son, student, Surfer Boy. Like people's picture of Adrian as gay, an outcast. Is that how people see me? Am I like Adrian?"

"What do you think?"

I've finally warmed up. Pulling the cap off my head, my left hand automatically clears the hair off my forehead. Somehow that reassures me and allows me to try to think.

"Well, I am sort of a loner, at least at lunch. But I kinda choose to separate myself because the cliques and all seem so stupid."

"How do you think Adrian saw you? Did he get it that you wanted to be a friend?"

"Maybe, but a lot of the time I act wrapped up in myself."

Dr. Lewis stops rocking and leans forward toward me, forearms on his knees and fingers laced. "The appearing cool thing? While your insides are screaming you are somebody beyond your surfer boy looks and oddball items of dress? But you don't know exactly what the real you is, what you care about for sure. You just know there is more there."

"Yeah."

Leaning back in the rocker, Dr. Lewis starts the rhythmic motion again. "What do you want to do about that?"

Now I whip my jacket off. "I don't know. I'm confused all the time now. My mind keeps going back to California, me on my surfboard, watching a buoy tilt in response to wind and waves, bouncing back. Wish I had an inner buoy to help me see past what's coming at me to the unwavering part of me."

Dr. Lewis tolerates silence well; he waits for me to say more.

"I guess I do feel kind of like Adrian, searching for something inside to help me feel okay."

Dr. Lewis stops the rocker again. "Not thinking of ending the search, are you? Any thoughts of suicide?"

"*No!*" I say, surprised by him asking.

We look at each other in a no-nonsense manner and he nods slightly, meaning he accepts the truth of what I'm saying.

Dr. Lewis gives me space and silence to think through my feelings. It seems more like getting still and quiet than thinking, until something escapes from my mouth. What pops out is, "It felt good to reach out, have those lunch conversations with Chelsea," I say. "But then I blew it. I'm sure she thinks I'm a freak, all shut down, not knowing what to say."

"Death is a big deal, Sean, very difficult for anyone to sort through. I think if you talk to Chelsea—if you're honest with her, not worrying about whether you sound dumb—she is likely to respond."

On my half-mile walk home from Dr. Lewis's office in the center of downtown, I feel calmer inside but the gloom continues. As Dr. Lewis always tells me, he can provide support, but I'm the one who has to do all the sorting out of the jumble that is me.

Our house is a small Cape, in a family neighborhood, no college student rentals, quiet as a tomb. The neat things about the house are a large stone fireplace and a backyard full of evergreen and maple trees. They slope down to our piece of the creek that runs through the town. Thank goodness the fireplace is roaring when I walk in.

"Hey, Sean, we'll eat in about fifteen. Your dad just left his office to walk home." Mom always wants to have dinner shortly after Dad gets home so he won't have time for more than one scotch on the rocks.

"SEAN," screams Sarah, racing to give me a big bear hug. I know what's coming: she wants to tell me all about her day. Sarah loves preschool; everything about it is "amazing." But today I can't focus, and only pick up a few words.

Dinner dynamics take a particular shape. Mom asks questions; Dad answers at length, constantly interrupted by Sarah talking about her day; and me, I fly below the radar with one-word answers. Tonight, Dad is upset about rapes that have recently taken place on his college's campus. The school, only one step down from an Ivy League college, is divided about how to deal with the problem.

"Administrators care about the school's reputation, students care about grades above everything else, faculty blame the strong role of fraternities on campus, and town people want the student binge drinking and reckless behavior that follows to stop," Dad says.

The events of my day bolster my courage enough for me to ask, "Dad, has anyone asked and really listened to the students who were raped?"

Mom jumps in to divert the discussion away from conflict. "So, Sean, what's happening at school for you? Something more pleasant than our previous topic, I hope."

"A student committed suicide."

She flinches, clearly not expecting this. "What? Why?"

"Beyond being bullied for years at school, I don't know."

"Did you know him?"

"I tried. He was in one of my classes. But he was pretty skittish about trusting anyone. I failed in being a good friend. Nobody, including me, knew how to reach out to him. His suicide makes me wonder, what if I was the one who needed help?"

Mom gasps, stammers, "Sean, don't talk like that! We would be here for you no matter what."

Sarah can no longer stand being excluded from the conversation. "When can we talk about what I learned in preschool? I don't even know what these big words, like suit-side, mean. I learned to make rhymes today, funny ones—zippy, dippy, yippy, hippie, do!"

I excuse myself and retreat to my room. The only good thing about homework is it sets a pattern of legitimate time alone in my room free of expectations, like chores, or command family time, like church. Not that we are religious, but Mom says it is a good way to meet "people of good character" in our new community.

Anger starts rising in me. *We'll be there for you, Sean.* Bullshit. Drag me here from California after announcing we're moving. No warning, no discussion about the decision, just, "It will be good for all of us." Dad gets a higher status job; Mom has more money to spend on the family and a better house; and Sarah truly is "resilient," as they say . . . not like me. The big gift to me was "the opportunity to go to a really good school." Double bullshit.

School eats up my time and energy—while I'm there, at least. Homework is actually not a big deal to me like it is for other students on the grades hunt. I truly don't care. And I learned last year in California, from my surfer buddies, how to easily meet the increased workload of high school. Techniques like how to skim read and quickly find what the teacher is looking for. I found out that tuning into teacher style and way of thinking is key to what will be on tests. That's the main thing, but another tip is to figure out the big-picture concepts in the chapter titles, the bolded section headings, the first and last sentence of each section, and questions at the end. For a decent reader, not even a great one, a thirty-page reading assignment can be done this way in about ten minutes. This totals less than an hour for all homework in exchange for average grades. I sometimes miss details that turn out to be important, but the teacher usually mentions some the next day and I jot them down. My parents aren't happy with "average" but figure Hilltop's reputation will make up the difference when I'm applying to colleges. They are also giving me some space to adjust to a new school.

Maybe I'm depressed because I'm not doing anything that matters to me. Dr. Lewis says depression is anger turned inward. True enough; I've got plenty of anger. To others it comes off as me being a detached critic, though.

Maybe my nightly shower will relax my anger muscles so I can fall asleep. I head down the hall to the bathroom, but as I pass Sarah's room I hear, "Sean?"

She's calling to me from bed. I poke my head in through her door. "You still awake?"

"Can't sleep."

"What up, Sarah Bearah?" I ask, walking toward her.

"That's a rhyme!"

She giggles. Holds her arms out for a hug. I sit on the side of the bed and give her a big old bear hug. "You worried about something?"

Her lower lip sticks out. "I miss Isabella."

"Well that makes sense, she was your best friend in San Diego. What made you think about her today?"

"A new girl in school looks like her."

"Just like Isabella, or she looks Latina?"

"Not *just* like her, but sorta."

"What's her name?"

"Catalina. She's a new student too."

"That is a Latina name, so maybe Isabella and Catalina have a similar background, like maybe their families are descended from the same country in Latin America. Like how you and I both have the same background. People can tell from our Irish names and the way we look—reddish-blond hair, light skin, and freckles—that we're probably related. Did you talk to Catalina?"

Sarah nods yes.

"Did other kids talk to her?"

Sarah shakes her head no.

"Did you speak in Spanish to Catalina?"

Sarah shakes her head no.

"Try that tomorrow. It might make her less scared and feel more like she's at home. Maybe she could be a new friend."

"Okay." Sarah switches gears. "Tell me a story, Sean."

"Was this all a trick to get me to tell you a story?"

More giggles.

"Okay, what should the story be about?"

"Surfing."

"You trying to make me sad, missing surfing?"

"No. It's just you're always happy when you talk about surfing. And you seem sad tonight."

Sarah has a way of coaxing me to open up. "I could tell you about one time when I got scared surfing—I got totally worked."

"Tell me."

"One day I was worried, thinking about the move here, and not paying close attention. I was lined up waiting for a wave, kinda zoned out, and then caught a wave at the last minute. It was a very big wave, and I caught it wrong. I wiped out—got 'worked,' as they say. When I went under, I was thrown around and around by the water and couldn't come up for air. The force of the wave was holding me under. I panicked and struggled until I was exhausted. Then I heard a hearty voice say, 'Relax, you're okay.' I did . . . and I was! I floated up and surfaced next to a buoy. I held on as it swayed back and forth, always coming back to its pivot point."

"Whoa," Sarah murmurs, her eyes closing.

"When I got to shore my surfing buddies said, 'We thought you were a goner.' Weirded out, I said, 'Me too.' I realized then I'd felt a force with me, like a protector, in the water. I had let go of fear and stopped fighting the turmoil. That's when release came."

Sarah is sound asleep.

Deciding to shower in the morning, I head to bed. I haven't thought about that day since it first happened. I didn't tell my folks, afraid they would make me stop surfing. The guys seemed embarrassed for me and dropped the subject. But since then, I've known the sea is there for me. I am part of it and it is part of me. Alive with motion, power and excitement, sea salt supporting me, playground of gulls flying freely, squawking and wave-crashing music, images painted in sunshine, fish tickling my toes, water forever soft. The sea and me, together, is what I want to be. Here?

Now? Maybe my problem has been leaving the sea behind rather than bringing it with me, continuing to live in the ways of the sea. Even if I'm up a mountain without a board. After all, these mountains were once earth under a vast ocean, according to local people I've met.

Hilltop Academy looks different today. With more dread than ever, I climb the forty-eight steps up to the massive marble columns guarding the portraits inside of Neanderthal-looking principals and wealthy alumnae broadcasting their success. Today, the over-bearing presence of these people and their standards seems ancient history. I always knew I somehow didn't fit in here, but before I thought it was my problem. Now I'm free to be . . . who knows?

Ninth grade, last year in California, was the opposite in many ways of Hilltop. San Diego Westside High was a hodgepodge of immigrants, urban blacks, and middle-class suburbanites. There were three academic tracks: poor kids who didn't read or speak English well; hardcore street kids, many with drug money but few hopes for a long life, being courted to stay in school; and middle-class kids who felt life was okay if we all just chilled. The kids in my middle-class track saw school as something you had to do but was no big deal, and like nothing in school really related to our lives anyway. The immigrant kids worked like crazy but always seemed buried. I don't remember any wealthy strivers; those sure-fire success kids who base life on their upper-class inheritances.

I count the minutes till lunch time. When the bell rings I head straight to the cafeteria and hang out by the door until Chelsea comes in, alone for a change. "Hey," I say quickly, "will you sit with me in the window today?"

"Sure," she says. "My so-called friends don't seem to be big fans of me speaking up about Adrian and how we all treated him horribly. It's amazing how quickly you can become unaccepted."

We settle in at the window, neither of us with food.

"People in my classes know about Adrian, but it's just something exciting to talk about, not upsetting to them," I say, shaking my head.

"This is my first day of feeling thrown away by people," Chelsea says. "Imagine how Adrian must have felt—for years."

I want to be more in tune than I showed at Java yesterday. "You look really drained, Chelsea. Like, your eyes are super red."

"I'm so tired," she says. "I cried for hours last night, until no tears were left. Then I got really mad. Somehow I ended up at my computer and started doing research on the name 'Adrian'—as in, of the Adriatic Sea region, a character in Shakespeare's *The Tempest*, about Italic people and others who led the war against Rome in the 4th century BCE. The University of Pennsylvania has organized archaeological digs in that area, now present-day Abruzzi, Italy. They've found unique architecture there, different from that of any other known cultures. I was up most of the night. All my research was really interesting. Adrian's ancestors might go back to that time."

"That's pretty cool, possibly connecting someone from here to more than 2,000 years ago." What a relief to be able to talk with Chelsea again. Maybe she doesn't think I was such a jerk after all.

"Yeah, I've never done any independent research like that, or even cared to," she says. "Last night, though, it seemed important to attach my feelings to something 'out there' and related to Adrian."

"After you told me about Adrian yesterday, I went to talk with Dr. Lewis, my shrink," I admit. "I realized why I reacted so weird, distant and all. Anyway, I'm sorry."

"I was definitely out of it too," Chelsea says.

What a relief. She's the one friend I have here.

She pops up from her seat on the windowsill. "You know what? Why don't we go see Ms. Carter in the office? I bet she's feeling even worse than us."

✧   ✧   ✧

The school secretary's face lights up when we walk in. She gets up and hugs Chelsea.

"Hi, Ms. Carter," I say, extending a hand toward her. "I'm Sean. Sorry we haven't met sooner."

"I'm so glad y'all came to see me," Ms. Carter says. "It's been a long, lonely morning. I've been doing some heavy soul searching since yesterday, going over and over in my head if I did everything I should have to support Adrian and his parents."

"I started off being angry at all the things that are not right at this school," Chelsea says, nodding her agreement. "Like, what is the job of school? It seems like the only point of school is passing us along to the next level of school. Any failure, the school claims it's ours—not theirs. Student lives don't matter. This whole thing is making me want to wake up, get out of the fog, and say what I think it all means. Like Adrian dying is so terribly sad . . . and wrong!"

I say to Ms. Carter, "I could have come up here with Adrian during lunch. I feel bad I didn't reach out to him more."

Two grey-haired men in expensive-looking suits exit the principal's office. Anger is in the air, and they wear determined expressions as they make their way out.

"You two better leave now, but thanks so much for coming," Ms. Carter says softly.

We walk out quickly, and as we head down the hall Chelsea says, "Those guys looked serious. I'm going to tell my parents about what went on for years with Adrian and say they should demand an investigation of the principal's lack of action all that time. If they say they don't want to rock the boat, I'm going to tell them I will."

"I wish I could do the same," I say, looking down. "My parents are new here, and my dad would be afraid of jeopardizing his job. They won't do anything. But I'm going to think of something I can do."

✧   ✧   ✧

Saturday is Adrian's funeral. Chelsea and I sit together. A couple of other students come in, each with their parents, and look like they definitely don't want to be here. During the service, as the priest talks about Adrian's love of hiking, I decide what I want to do to honor Adrian: I'm going to organize a hike on the Appalachian Trail for Hilltop students and faculty in his honor. I'll plan it for Earth Day, which I hope will give me enough organizing time. I've never done anything remotely like this; in fact, I've never been responsible for anything before.

When I tell Chelsea after the service, she agrees it is a perfect idea. Then she invites me (for the third time, so I guess she means it) out to her house to go cross-country skiing.

The next day, she picks me up from my house since I'm not old enough for a driver's license yet—there's an ego downer—and as soon as I get in the car, she starts talking.

"Hey, Sean, look, I'm really sorry I didn't respond to you in the cafeteria Friday when you were talking about your visit with Dr. Lewis," she says. "I've really been off my game the last few days, really zonked from no sleep. So Dr. Lewis was helpful?"

"Yeah, he's a great listener, like you are—usually, anyway," I say, laughing so she knows I'm teasing. "He helps me think things through, like Adrian's death uncovering my fear I might slide back into another deep depression."

"My friend Cora has been my great listener over the years," Chelsea says. "On our Free Will walk today I caught her up with my knotted feelings of anger, sadness, and fear of my future for next year. She said it sounds like I have PTSD, caused by Hilltop as a place of threat."

"Wow, that's heavy."

"Listen to what Cora told me today about Stone Creek High School dealing with the February blahs hitting, like happens at Hilltop," Chelsea says, getting more animated. "They decided to have a week of everyone getting involved in a school-wide Model United Nations. They do this at some point every year, so the seniors are the leaders and the freshmen are the newbies. The topic this year is Ebola. Each team has a junior ambassador who speaks for a designated country in the committee meetings; a sophomore, like Cora, who serves as the negotiator for the team, talking behind the scenes with representatives of other countries; and a freshman team member who's responsible for research on that country's views and situation. The seniors run the different committee meetings to decide things like giving money to affected countries, coordinating medical volunteers from all over the world, helping refugees, and resolving travel issues. Is that not cool?! The Model UN will be over this coming week, but then she said the whole school has a 'theme' each quarter that every class addresses in some way. The fourth quarter theme is, 'Do computers think?' I wouldn't even know where to start with Ebola or computers thinking. They are learning, and DOING, adult things."

"I've never seen you so amped, Chelsea," I say, looking at her beaming face.

She laughs. "You haven't seen me away from Hilltop, except at the funeral. Driving is an upper, too."

"Look at the blue heron in the creek, on the rock covered with snow," I say, sticking my head out in the freezing wind for a better look.

"Good eye!" she says, and turns onto a gravel road. She points to the right. "There's Jake's and his dad's house. Neat cabin, huh?" Further up the road she points again—"Look, here come my girls. Ayla is the black hound type and Lily is the light brown collie-whippet-terrier. Check out those tails welcoming me home."

Chelsea's cross-country skiing plan for the afternoon is another challenge to my ego. "You know," I say, "I've never been cross-country skiing, but it doesn't look too hard on TV."

She laughs. "Let me know what you think when we're done."

For the next half hour, she gives me pointers and I practice. Then we're off, heading into an aged, mixed hardwood forest. It's hard to talk when we're skiing, me gasping for air and Chelsea with a scarf wrapped around her head. She points to a lake in a distant clearing with a questioning expression. I nod my head yes, grumbling under my breath at how far away it looks.

Watching Chelsea and learning from actually doing, I'm

able to get some rhythmic movement going. Finally, I can concentrate on other things—like the amazing silence, only hearing the whoosh-whoosh of the skis.

The edge of the lake is large rock boulders; it looks like a former quarry. Snow is covering the iced-over surface. We pause to take it all in. The dogs scare up a rabbit and it takes off across the ice-covered lake, Ayla right behind. There's a deafening splash and then the sound of paws frantically hitting water.

"Lily, come!" Chelsea cries, trying to keep her other dog back. She takes off her skis and runs for a fallen tree reaching a ways across the frozen lake, trying to get to Ayla. I follow right behind her.

Ayla is paddling in a circle. She looks terrified.

"Take off your skis and wrap your jacket around the end of one," Chelsea says. She is crawling out along the fallen tree trunk and limbs. Ayla is pounding the water with increasingly frenzied paws, the boulder shoreline preventing her exit in that direction.

"Talk to Ayla to calm her," I yell as I slide the front end of one of my skis in the sleeve of my oversized, bulky coat. Californians don't know how to buy winter coats. Chelsea's is a slim, waterproof jacket appropriate for skiing.

"It's okay, Ayla," Chelsea croons. "I'm coming. Swim a little this way." She grabs the ski from me and extends the coat end out to Ayla. Ayla is able to claw into the coat enough to hang on as Chelsea pulls her toward the tree, ice breaking along the way. When she gets close enough, Ayla scrambles up smaller limbs until she reaches the trunk, at which point she jumps over Chelsea, who's still sprawled on her stomach, and sprints back to land.

Chelsea pops up and runs past me. "Come on, Sean!"

When we're all back on shore, Chelsea grabs Ayla's collar and hands it off to me. "Hold on so she doesn't run off," she says. "We've got to get her warm." Chelsea takes off her coat and wraps it tight around Ayla. Hugging the shivering dog, Chelsea grabs her phone and calls Jake. Luckily, he answers right away.

"Jake, this is Chelsea. We're at the quarry and Ayla fell in. Can you bring the four-wheeler up here to get her back to warmth quickly? Thanks." Turning to me, she simply says, "He's coming."

Underneath Chelsea's competent and strong demeanor, I think I detect nervousness. Another trauma for her to deal with?

Jake arrives faster than seems possible. With Ayla wrapped up in Chelsea's coat, we ride in the four-wheeler to his house, where a fire burns in abundance. Just what Ayla needs, and me too—California boy is still not adjusted to winter, and my jacket's soaking wet.

"This place was built in the late 1800s, and Jake's dad has remodeled and added on to it several times since they've lived here," Chelsea tells me as I look around.

We're surrounded entirely by wood, except for the fieldstone fireplace; it's like sitting at a campfire in the woods. The sparse interior decorations seem functional—like, for instance, there's no need for curtains when there's nobody nearby to look in the windows. I admire the antique tools hanging on the living area wall and the cast-iron cook stove at one end of the kitchen.

"My dad is a traditional, but not too tasty, cook," Jake says. "I prefer fresh and local foods, no frying stuff in fat."

Fidgety, Chelsea paces in front of the glowing fire. "I'm still shaking," she tells Jake. "What if something had happened to Ayla? I couldn't take that. I would just fall apart, really."

"But you didn't, Chelsea," I say. "You were amazing, thinking what to do."

"It has been a long time, but I don't remember you as a nervous type," Jake says.

Chelsea, moving her eyes in line with Jake's, says, "Yes, way too long."

An edgy silence hangs in the air between Chelsea and Jake, with me on the outside of the moment, witnessing.

"A student at Hilltop died this past week," Chelsea finally says. "He was bullied for years for being gay, without anyone putting a stop to it."

Jake offers a slow response. "I heard about that. What about the students he was close to?"

"Nobody was close to him," she says.

"How could that go on for years?" he asks. "That would seem so weird and uncomfortable at Stone Creek, almost everybody would do something, anything, to try to fix the situation."

"What would they do?" I ask.

"Talk about it," he says. "Students, teachers, parents would figure out a plan to pursue why someone was bullied and how we could change things."

"Stone Creek sounds like a very odd place, where people really care about each other," I say.

"This is my second year there, and it only seemed strange for about a day. Funny how easy it is to change to what is truly good for you."

Despite the fact that Jake is a muscular country boy a foot taller than me, he speaks softly. He's easygoing, yet he zeroes in on the heart of an issue so quickly.

"Losing someone you love turns life inside out," he says. "I was only three when Mom died. I still cling to the comfort of remembering her rocking me to sleep each night. In the winter, right here in this rocker, in front of the fire."

Just then a man opens the elegant and heavy pine front door with seemingly little effort, even though he is a small-framed guy. He has one of those mountain-man beards. Jake told us earlier how his dad made everything in the cabin, including the stone fireplace, the wood staircase up to the loft, the cathedral ceiling, which is a modification of the original cabin, and the front door.

"Hey Mr. Deacon," Chelsea says, "this is my friend Sean, from California."

Standing up to shake his hand, I say, "From here, now, since August."

"You live in town?" he asks.

"Yes sir. Wish I lived out here. It's beautiful. Back in the fall, I rode my bike all over the county, exploring, and this is the best I've seen yet."

"I grew up outside of Lee Village, in the north part of the

county. Youngest of a pack of ten kids. Dirt poor. Kept my eye on this neck of the woods until I could afford to buy this place."

"I met a woman on a farm outside Lee Village. She makes cheese."

"I know Sue. Good woman. Two high-energy, rascal kids."

"Yeah, they made me play with them for an hour. Great kids."

"Sue was a Tolley from Iron Creek. Married a Turner, William. The farm they live on is the old Turner place from William's grandfather."

Chelsea tells Mr. Deacon about Ayla jumping in the quarry lake as he sits in a shaker-style chair, petting her and drinking sassafras tea made from a tree root he harvested in his field.

Her story done, Chelsea switches gears and asks, "How's farming?"

Mr. Deacon shrugs. "I get by, with Jake's help and some construction work on the side for my neighbors. Jake wants to move us into the future with sustainable farming practices. To me, the ideas sound like the old ways of farming, but with fancy words and higher costs."

"It must be nice to have a sense of past connected to future and all of it wrapped up in this beautiful land." I turn to Jake. "And to know for sure what you want to do."

A big old smile spreads across Jake's face—enough said.

On the way home, Chelsea drives much slower, seemingly still rattled from the Ayla experience. "I liked what you said to Jake," she says after a long silence. "It's so true that he knows what is important for him and is going after it. Me, I don't have a clue. I've thought about college as freedom from my parents, this small town, and our lifeless school. But the past few days I've been thinking, freedom to do what? Where am I going? No clue. And it makes me angry at myself, that I don't know what I'm looking for, who I am really. Lately, probably because of Adrian, I feel everything more deeply. It's both freeing and scary."

"What I cared about, the sea, was taken away from me," I say, nodding. "Like it didn't matter. I didn't count. So I quit caring. I guess because I'm worried that if I care about something again, it will be taken away too. Even if I had the power to make something happen, I'm not sure what I would do. I feel like I'm just existing—way different from Jake's sense of direction."

"My parents took something very important away from me, too," Chelsea says. She pauses to look at me as if deciding whether to continue, then says, "Jake and I were very close in elementary school. We knew each other so well, the listening to each other was effortless. We laughed all the time. I haven't laughed like that since, not with such openness and comfort in my own skin. And now, since Adrian's death, I've wanted to talk with Jake. I don't know why, exactly. Being with him today, I felt that old closeness wasn't entirely dead. I don't know why I didn't stand up to my parents breaking up our friendship. Ever since then, I've kept everyone else at a distance, except Cora—but I only see her once a week."

There's a pause where each of us digests the obvious love she still has for Jake.

Stepping back from the deep emotion in the air, I take my dad's intellectual tack and say, "I've been thinking, Chelsea. Do you think part of the reason we have no direction is that school isn't teaching us to think for ourselves or to work on things that really matter to us?"

"Definitely," she says. "And I know for sure I'm furious with Hilltop right now. Adrian should not have died."

"Stone Creek sounds so different from Hilltop. What Jake was saying about how what happened to Adrian never would have happened there . . ."

"Maybe we should go ahead with the plan to interview Stone Creek seniors," Chelsea says, her face lighting up. "It's all set up by a counselor there. You could do the interviews with me."

I grin, grateful to be included. "Sure! We've got nothing to lose—and I wouldn't feel like a shy little sophomore doing it with you, Chelsea."

Since I have a day off from school—it's a teacher planning day—and my mom has a doctor appointment, it's my job to walk Sarah to preschool.

On the way, she asks, "Why do they call it Sunday school? It's nothing like a school, nothing like my preschool."

I know what she means. I went to my class for Sunday school here only once and balked. Told my parents I wasn't going back to it, but I would go to church. Compromise. What Sarah means is that she has to sit quietly while the teacher in Sunday school reads a long story about people and times Sarah knows nothing about. The real point is not to understand their experiences but to get the moral of the story at the end. This is the church's idea of how to preach to children.

We arrive at the preschool building, and Sarah tugs at my hand. "Come in and see!"

I hesitate. "Will that be okay?"

"Sure, lots of people come and go. We don't care. Some come to play games with us."

When we walk through the preschool doors, Sarah drags me to the teacher, who gives her a big hug.

"Sean is going to stay and play with me!" Sarah says.

I look at the teacher. "Is that okay?"

"Of course," she says.

The classroom looks so different from the ones at Hilltop. There is a library in the corner with a rocking chair for the teacher to sit in to read stories. The children sit on pillows on top of the thick carpet.

"The teacher picks a book to read in the morning, and she lets one of us pick a book to read after nap," Sarah explains eagerly. "We get to look at books we like before going to sleep at nap time, too."

The main action is the learning centers all around the room, which kids can engage with for however long they want. Dress-up is one of the favorites, and not just for girls. One little boy in a fairy princess dress is a riot; some of the girls fix his hair and makeup, and laugh when he falls down trying to walk in heels. There are also centers for computer work, art projects, building blocks, listening to music, and puzzles.

I'm walking by the puzzle table when a girl yanks a puzzle piece away from a boy.

He turns and pleads with a nearby teacher, "Help me. She took my piece."

"Talk to her," the teacher encourages. "Use your words. Say what you want."

The little boy turns to the girl and says. "My piece."

"*I* know where it goes," she says.

He grabs at it, misses. "*I* want to do it."

"Okay, but give me another piece. You're hogging them."

He hands her two other pieces and she gives him his piece back.

Wow! No yelling, shoving, or name-calling. Hilltoppers could learn from these kids. Why is this classroom so different, happy, full of energy?

Of course. Nobody is making them do something they don't want to. The kids are in charge. They decide what they are going to learn. And all these centers are not just play. Kids are problem-solving, measuring, pretending, constructing, and learning to get along with others. No wonder Sarah says preschool is "amazing."

The teachers are also very tuned into each child, helping them deal with their uncertainties and easing the transitions from one exploration activity to another.

I stay longer than I expect to. Just before I go, I join Sarah and some of the other kids on the playground. They chase me until I collapse in the dirt, and then six kids pile on top of me, laughing crazily, until I am laughing uncontrollably myself. When was the last time I felt relaxed enough to laugh like this?

As I dust myself off and say my good-byes, one little boy asks me, "Why are the very tips of your hair yellow and the rest of your long hair red?"

"The yellow bleached out part is what's left of my surfer days in California," I explain.

"You said that so sad," the little guy says, squinting up at me. "Before you were laughing."

I ruffle his hair. "Little man, you are very smart to see all that."

"We learn a lot in our school," he says.

Maybe this preschool's approach is the best design for any school: happy, lively, allowing kids to decide what to do, letting them be creative, helping them learn to get along with others. I know I'd be a lot happier in a school like this.

Chapter 3: Time to Decide

Once upon a time, my wish was to become unstuck. I believed
"out there" could make me right, when actually I needed to find
a new personal direction and become whole.

SEAN

Lately, Chelsea and I have been drifting toward the school office
and Ms. Carter pretty often, like maybe she can help us get to the
bottom of all the upheaval we are experiencing.

Today, as we approach the glass door into the office Chelsea
stops abruptly, then backs up around the last corner.

"What's up?" I ask.

"Ms. Carter is talking with a woman in the office. I've seen
her before—on TV, I think." She taps her lip. "I know; she's a
reporter for Channel 10."

"Channel 10? Wow." That station is based in the biggest city
in the region and covers news in our town. It's kind of a big deal
for them to be here doing a story.

"Do you think it's about Adrian?" Chelsea asks.

"I hope so," I say. And I do. Adrian deserves to have his
story told.

Chelsea squeezes my arm. "Let's come back after school."

In the afternoon classes, there is, as usual, no mention of Adrian. Nothing since his death. I ask a guy in my last class, Science, if he went to the funeral.

He looks at me like I'm an alien and says, "No. Why would I?" Organizing this hike in Adrian's honor will not be easy.

The bell rings, and I head straight to the office. Ms. Carter's alone in here this time reading through a huge stack of papers, and she gives me a big smile as I approach her desk.

"Hey, Ms. Carter, I have this idea of organizing a walk on the Appalachian Trail in Adrian's honor, for Hilltop students and staff," I say. "Could you tell me how to get in touch with Adrian's parents?"

She puts down the stack of papers. "Sure," she says. "But I would wait a few days to talk with them. They have a lot going on right now."

Chelsea arrives in time to hear these last comments. "What's going on, Ms. Carter?" she asks. "We saw you talking to that TV reporter this morning and now you look so . . . I don't know, stirred up."

"I can't really say, Chelsea. But it is a good thing that's finally happening."

Chelsea looks lighthearted for the first time since Adrian died.

"Well, it seems we're getting halfway to the truth anyway," Ms. Carter says. "Now, I've got some work I need to do before I go home."

We take the hint and head out the door.

"I'm definitely going to watch Channel 10 tonight," Chelsea says as we walk down the hall.

Me too.

My folks always watch the national news, but not usually the local news channel. To make sure I won't be overruled in wanting to watch the local news, I make up a story about hearing bad weather might be coming and we should watch the local news.

In the first segment, the reporter I saw in the Hilltop office this afternoon reports about Adrian's death, interviewing his parents. She makes it clear that Adrian was bullied at school for years. Adrian's mom also says he would never have committed suicide or killed his dog, Fella, who was found next to him.

"The administrators from the two colleges, responsible for school oversight, declined to be interviewed and the principal did not return telephone messages," the reporter concludes. "But someone close to events confirmed the parents' charges of bullying and the lack of disciplinary action for those involved. It was common knowledge in the community that the student was bullied and did not want to come to school."

When a new segment begins, I turn to Mom and Dad. "What do you think?" I ask.

"It's awful," Mom says.

"We can't jump to conclusions about any of it," Dad says. "This is a local news station, not the *Washington Post*. I haven't heard anything at the college about all this."

"Could you ask?" I say. I'm not usually snarky, but this time it sure popped out.

Next morning, a follow-up news report is all over TV saying our principal has decided to retire at the end of the year.

At school I ask, "Chelsea, did your parents help make this happen?"

"Are you kidding me?" she asks, her face grim. "They were shocked at both of the news reports, last night and this morning. I point-blank asked if they had talked with anyone. Mom simply shook her head no. No other comment. I was so pissed, I walked out of the room. I was afraid I would lose it."

After catching her breath, Chelsea tells me a volunteer for the community Rescue Squad is in her homeroom and that this morning he whispered to the Government teacher, loud enough for Chelsea to hear, that he was on the call when Adrian's body and his dog's body were found below an overlook. He said they found sneaker footprints up top on the cliff edge. Adrian was wearing hiking boots. The police concluded the footprints could be from any of hundreds of people hiking the Appalachian Trail since the last rain.

We head straight to the office to ask Ms. Carter about the footprints and the police decision to not investigate.

"The city police don't look for trouble when the universities are involved in incidents," she says.

"What can we do?" I ask.

"I don't know," she says, shaking her head. "The college administrators don't come down here anymore. They wouldn't listen to me anyway. They probably figure I'm the 'someone close to events' in the TV news report. All the colleges care about is their image and how an incident might affect recruiting students and faculty for coming years. They'll do what they can to hush up any controversy."

"We can't count on our parents to do anything, either," Chelsea says, trying to control her rage. "If they won't stand up for me, they certainly won't stand up for Adrian. Or jeopardize their jobs, god forbid!"

"I saw Adrian's mother yesterday," Ms. Carter says. "She told me they have been contacted by hotshot lawyers from Richmond that were hired by the colleges. She's so frail right now, I felt like I couldn't ask what that was all about. She and Adrian's father have tried to pressure the police to investigate more but the police have bought into the misguided stereotype of tragic gay guy commits suicide." She sighs. "I told them when they interviewed me he had been confused, talking with a psychiatrist, but he was a strong person getting happier. It breaks my heart every time I hear him portrayed as a pathetic person. He wasn't."

"That's true," I say. "Adrian was strong. He stood up for himself with the bathroom bullies. Something is very wrong with this whole thing. Nobody is listening to us peons."

Chelsea and I are now a regular event at lunch and people have quit staring. Today, she tells me she received acceptance letters yesterday from both UVA and Oberlin.

"The battle with my parents starts," she says. "I don't know if I'm prepared to win. I can't figure out how to handle this. I want to go to Oberlin to escape, go as far away as I can, but I have no real plan of what I would do there. It just seemed so neat when I was there. Everybody was chill and friendly and seemed happy. That's what I want. But my parents will say there are so many more opportunities at UVA, and since I don't know what I want to major in, I should go there."

A fight breaks out by the entrance of the cafeteria, and we turn to look. The only adults around are the cafeteria ladies, average age about sixty. There have been quite a few fights lately, and the teachers are getting really disgusted at being bouncers instead of scholars. It takes quite a while for them to show up and stop the fights. I see three bloody noses.

"This place is getting more and more disgusting," I say, wrinkling my own, blood-free nose. "Back to important matters: how was your visit to UVA?"

"It was like a big Hilltop. I felt like a little fish in a huge pond, with no idea what I wanted to do. It's weird, but since that night researching Adrian's name, I've been thinking it would be so neat to see old history, old art, learn Italian—to go to Italy and really experience the place. UVA has a study abroad program with locations all over, including in Florence and Siena. At Oberlin, I would likely have to organize something on my own, but probably neither school would sponsor me to go until a few years of being there. And I really just want a change now. I'm tired of always having to pay my dues now to *maybe* get something later. How do I know if I want to do something until I try it?"

"Think about poor me, two more years to go in this place," I say with a shudder. "So, you would want to travel now?"

"Yeah, and by myself, but that would never fly with my folks. And I wouldn't want to just travel for a week or so with them, tourist style. I didn't show them the college letters yesterday, so I'll just keep quiet until I can get clearer about how to deal with all this."

Chelsea's preoccupation with college choice sinks into my brain, and when I get home I tune into an article in the local paper. Since things flared up at Hilltop, my parents have subscribed to the local paper and are starting to watch local TV news too. The headline news story in today's paper is still about Adrian—or rather, the college administrators saying that his supposed suicide had nothing to do with Hilltop Academy. But another article about college is the one catching my attention: the principal of Stone Creek High School is quoted about the big increase in the number of Stone Creek seniors who have been accepted to colleges for the coming fall. A community group wrote grants to some foundations to get money and the school counselors worked with the colleges that students applied to, getting a record amount of scholarships and grants for students. This information would definitely impress my dad. Particularly in light of the fact that my Hilltop counselor handed me my schedule on my first day of school and I haven't seen her since. She wouldn't even know who I was if I walked into her office.

Falling into my usual pattern when I need help about something important, I call Dr. Lewis's office to schedule an appointment. When I tell his receptionist, who has always been really nice to me, that I'd like to come in as soon as possible, she says, "Can you be here in twenty minutes? Dr. Lewis had a cancellation."

"I'm on my way."

I leave the newspaper, folded to the Stone Creek story, on the dining room table. Too bad the story's not in the *Washington Post*. He would find it much more impressive.

✧ ✧ ✧

After catching Dr. Lewis up on my life, I tell him I want to transfer to Stone Creek. I want his help to convince my parents.

"Why do you want to transfer, Sean?" he asks.

"I need to find out who I am. I want to do stuff I'm interested in, be involved. Not be so down all the time."

With his usual expressionless face, Dr. Lewis says, "I don't see you as down or depressed these days. I think you've really come out of a slump. A good example is all the work you are doing organizing the walk for Adrian."

"But if I can convince my parents that I'll be happier at Stone Creek, maybe they'll let me. I think they are still shook up from what Adrian did. I know they don't want me to get depressed again."

"I don't think it is right to play with people's emotions, to worry your parents into doing what you want," Dr. Lewis says. "I think you should be honest with them. Focus on the first part of what you said to me. You want to discover things you're interested in, pursue those now, before college."

Excited that he might be on my side, I blurt out, "Will you help me? Will you talk to my parents?"

"I will help you think through what you want to say to them," he says. "You can speak for yourself. And I believe they will decide what they honestly think is best for you."

I deflate. Dr. Lewis assumes the best about everyone. But one, I don't feel prepared to speak for myself, and two, my parents don't have a track record of listening to what I want. For the first time, I feel like Dr. Lewis has let me down.

The last comment Dr. Lewis made during our session, about my parents deciding what is best for me, goes beyond bugging me to making me super tense. Why should all the weight be on their point of view? It's my life. I need to buck up, get my arguments together, and feel confident in my own decision.

Today is the first official day of spring, and I wake up determined to relieve the tension I'm feeling and clear my head. To achieve that, I turn to my old coping mechanism: I decide to get back in the saddle and go for a bike ride.

My early Saturday wakeup prompts a sarcastic comment from my dad: "Is hibernation over already?"

"Whatever," I say, and keep walking toward the garage. He looks surprised when I just let it go. Even doing maintenance work on my bike—a necessary precaution, since it's been sitting in the garage for so long—does not dampen my anticipation. Finally, I pack a big lunch of my favorites: PB&J, Cool Ranch Doritos, and OJ. Sometimes I love still being a kid.

I like my hybrid bike: it gives me a bit of a workout, and frees me from the anxiety of flying down country roads on super skinny tires. I am compliant enough to wear a helmet, but I don't do fancy riding gear, just jeans and a T-shirt.

Minutes after I begin my ride, the freedom of the open road floods me with good feeling. "I'm back!" I shout into the wind.

It's a sunny day, with the bluest of skies, puffy clouds, and that Virginia way the sun rays billow through the clouds.

I head off along Heron Creek toward Chelsea's, but break off in a different direction about five miles out from town. I cross a low water bridge to the other side of Heron Creek and follow a one-lane road along the creek, going I don't know where. This road is at a lower level, with easier access to the creek. Looking for a spot to gaze at the sights, I come upon a perfect rock outcrop. I lean my bike at the bottom and climb on top.

A fisherman is a ways upstream, in the water, fly fishing. I hope he doesn't mind me invading his space. Observing his technique is mesmerizing, how he flicks the line back and forth. There's no sound here except for the water spilling over the jumble of rocks in the creek bed. I can't help comparing this water to the sea, my master teacher about life. The power of the creek water is more gentle, but determined, and obviously effective in forming the creek bed structure. The vastness of the sea is always apparent, while the narrow creek originates high in the mountain to the west. Herons with six-foot wing spans hunt here, quiet, nothing like the gulls with their loud calls. The movement of the water is constant and in one direction, instead of the back and forth pull of the tides.

The sun brightens the depths of the transparent water below me, and also the bank's wild growth. Schools of minnows entice me to dunk my toes for a tickle. My awareness of the creek's character strengthens, rather than diminishes, my memory of the sea. My definition of happiness: feeling alive, a part of all the forms of life around me, soothed as when I would come out of the ocean after a morning of surfing.

Lying in the sun, on my back, my consciousness drifts to a fuzzy place, memory trying to let out long-ago witnessing of . . . can't catch hold of the memory.

Coming to, curiosity leads me on a short walk upstream, and I strike up a conversation with the fly fisherman. Long white hair flying in all directions frames the most peaceful face I've ever seen, welcoming me not with a smile but an openness that states, "This is the way of the world."

He talks to me without taking his concentration from his fly-water-fish moment.

He is retired.

"What did you do?" I ask.

"Serve others. Well." The fly circles around behind his head and lands back in the water in front of him.

"I have no idea about what I will do for work," I say.

"What do you do now?" The fly circles around behind his head and lands back in the water in front of him.

"Tread water," I say.

"Exhausting," he says. "Where does your bike riding take you?" The fly circles around behind his head and lands back in the water in front of him.

"Around the county, exploring."

"What have you experienced, felt, in your explorations?" The fly circles around behind his head and lands back in the water in front of him.

"More relaxed, myself."

"What else?"

"I'm not sure."

"Pay attention," he says. "Your feelings, now, in what you do, will bend your life in the right direction, suited to you. That deference to your experiences, what you learn, is rooting your growth. Stop trying to plan a future. Train your senses to take in your perceptions of now. See the fly, the water, the fish? Right now, that is all and everything for me."

I think of Sarah, the joy of a three-year-old who is being allowed to explore her world with no thoughts of what will come later. I hope she never loses that opportunity to love her life.

Turns out I didn't invade the fisherman's space. He permeated mine.

Retreating back to my rock in the sun, the submerged memory pops out. I see Sarah born in a large tub of water in my parents' bedroom, my mom assisted by a woman in nurses' clothing. Seeing me in the doorway, my dad escorts me back to my room. I'm not sure what I actually saw until he confirms it. My shock is tripled by hearing him say I was born the same way. Dad says it is a family secret. There are no other scenes in the memory. We've never talked about it again. I've never even thought about it again until now.

As I launch the walk for Adrian, I follow the spirit of the fly fisherman. Instead of making energy-numbing to-do lists, I focus on having enthusiastic personal conversations with people at school. During lunch, I invade the table boundary lines. Plopping myself down, I explain my hopes for what I'm now calling EarthWalk on the Appalachian Trail, following Adrian's lead of seeking calm in the awesome mountains surrounding us. I think, but don't say to people, that a higher vision might help us all.

I always ask the kids I talk to what they think would be fun to do on the hike. Unsurprisingly, I get many sarcastic remarks. Like, "Maybe all the boys could walk along holding hands."

Rather than respond with a counter attack, I try to think how to elevate the discussion. "Everybody is free to do what they want," I say. "For example, I'm pretty good at hacky sack. Are you?"

Usually, there's no answer to that kind of question, but sometimes another person jumps in to reduce the tension with something like, "We could see who can hike the trail the longest while dribbling a soccer ball."

I know most of the people I talk with will not show up, but at least putting everyone in the position of making a conscious choice about whether they will attend expands the impact of EarthWalk that much more.

Chelsea is talking it up to people too. She is also trying something new in her Listener role: she listens more for emotions in what people say, and responds to those feelings. Like, she told me the other day that she has been spending a lot of time with a girl whose mother just found out she has cancer. Other people seemed to notice, and now they're also consoling the girl. And a few people she's talked to about EarthWalk have said they will think about it.

Adrian's parents are, of course, inviting their family friends.

It's EarthWalk day today, and I'm stoked to discover that nature has responded with one of those ten perfect weather days we get here each year.

We gather at the trailhead and hang around until everyone arrives. The atmosphere is casual; there's no particular plan or agenda. Many of the Hilltop teachers Chelsea and I reached out to have come, including her government teacher, who says he came for her and to be part of an uplifting event, and my science teacher, who is a big birder. He hands out a flyer of area bird pictures and descriptions to everyone who wants one. And of course Ms. Carter is here.

When it seems like everyone who is going to come has arrived, I say a few quick words.

"Welcome to EarthWalk, a hike in honor of Adrian. Your participation in this walk shows the impact Adrian had on this community. He could not have arranged a more perfect, sunny day for us to enjoy ourselves and remember his lasting spirit. As you walk along, notice the many beautiful rocks along the way and select one to carry up to the top as a remembrance of Adrian."

That speech was more than I thought I would get out. I volunteered to speak down here at the start so I could relax the rest of the day; Chelsea is responsible for speaking at our tribute at the top.

Our milling around transitions to wandering off in groups, up the trail path. Many students who arrive with their parents initially look apprehensive, suggesting that their attendance might have been the adults' idea. I'm surprised the students do not gravitate to their lunch table cliques. The groups include people of all ages, even a few young kids.

As we walk, I hear one group chatting about this year's World Cup. In another group there is a competition for who knows the best joke. A junior I recognize but don't know is playing a ukulele and others are singing along. Sarah, who loves to sing, runs off to be with that group. My parents fall in with Chelsea's parents, who they just met, and some other people from the college they all know.

The sound of human conversation, not the words but the tone, creates a reassuring atmosphere, like we're a tribe with a purpose. My mom kept saying I should plan everything out, but I decided to go with the fly fisherman spirit. I'm glad.

The exclamation point of our two-mile hike is an overlook of the Rockfish Valley. A math teacher passes around her binoculars. Development in the valley is sparse, giving our little town an escalated air of civilization. Everyone pauses to sit on a rock or the soft grass, or to lean on a pitch pine tree. I'm standing, feeling the wind on my face, identical to an ocean breeze—except the smells on the wind here are of sap, dark dirt, and berries.

I share a look with Chelsea, and I know we're both thinking the same thing: this is the time for our prepared remembrance of Adrian. She steps forward and clears her throat.

"Look around at the various rocks in people's hands," she says. "If your rock is on the larger side, will you please come up here and start the stacking? We'd like to build a cairn sculpture in Adrian's honor."

Having selected larger rocks on purpose, Chelsea and I go first. As the structure grows, people are more deliberate in selecting the perfect placement of their rock. It is a quiet, intentional process. By the end, the cairn has grown to a height of about three feet.

When it's complete, there is a natural wave of people looking around at each other, making eye contact and smiling, some hugging and giving each other gentle slaps on the back. Chelsea's government teacher holds up a bottle of water and says, "To Adrian." Water bottles are passed around.

The ukulele player starts "Will the Circle Be Unbroken" and heads back down the trail, others following. New groups of hikers form, even more diverse than on the way up. People are taking selfies with Adrian's monument.

His parents are the last to leave, wobbly but holding each other up. I hear a high-pitched gasp. Turning around, I see Adrian's mother pick up what looks like a piece of an old lanyard kids make at summer camp.

Adrian's father says, "Fella's collar, broken."

So low I can barely hear, Adrian's mother says, "Fella would never have resisted Adrian and broken his collar." She looks at her husband in that older person's way of determined conviction.

I'm the only one to observe this scene; fog surrounds my brain matter and every nerve ending in my body goes on charged alert. Walking on is automatic. I have no idea how much time has passed, when I become aware of Chelsea's voice, which sounds light and lively for the first time since we became friends. She is talking with her English teacher. "Have you ever read *Clan of the Cave Bear*? It's a novel dealing with pre-Neanderthal people and a young girl full of different spirit than the rest of her tribe. One of my favorites."

"Sounds like a book I would enjoy reading, too, Chelsea. Thanks for telling me. And, it's nice to hear this interest of yours."

Chelsea asks, "Will you be staying at Hilltop for another year?"

The answer is a slow, sad headshake—no.

Thank goodness Chelsea did not hear the exchange between Adrian's parents. She deserves a chance to move on in her life. Me too. The uncertainty of what might have happened to Adrian is something I will have to learn to live with. How would he handle this situation? He would walk, move forward, building inner strength.

Knowing Chelsea these past months has opened me up to believe I can learn to connect with others and rely on them for support. I even connected with Adrian, as much as was possible given both our states. He gave me a model of interior confidence. And I think I gave him a sense of acceptance. He kept coming to me with something to say, and I think he knew I never judged him.

My dad comes up behind me, puts his arm around my shoulders, and says, "Sean, I'm proud of you. This was a great day."

I would never have thought praise from Dad would mean so much. But it does. I can't think of what to say so I just smile and punch him on the shoulder.

I walk the last leg of the trail with a senior from the athlete lunch table whose name I don't know. After some warm-up small talk, he says, "A day like this makes you think about the meaning of life. I believe that Earth is a cell in the body of a greater being and humans are just one teeny, tiny speck in that cell."

I am speechless, with no idea how to think about such a statement. Could be, what do I know?

The day after EarthWalk, Sunday, is the usual: off to church in the morning, and then a special meal cooked by Mom when we get home—today my favorite, standing rib. No vegetarians in this household.

When Sarah asks to be excused to play on the tire swing I put up for her last weekend, I seize the opportunity to talk with my parents about Stone Creek High School. I have to remember to go slow and not pressure my parents so much as reach out to them. That was Dr. Lewis's advice, which I think makes sense—a lot more sense than the other stuff about it all being my parents' decision.

"Mom, Dad, I want to transfer to Stone Creek High School this coming fall." I stop and look at each of them, to let the news register. Mom instantly looks alarmed. Dad has what seems to me like a bit of a smirk on his face. I display what I hope is a reassuring smile. I don't otherwise respond to their reactions.

"I know this is a surprise to you," I continue, keeping my voice calm, "but I have been thinking about it for a long time. I need to be more involved in school and take control of my life." I think about mentioning Dr. Lewis here and how he supports me getting more involved in things. But I decide it makes me look more grown up to speak on my own. Besides, Dr. Lewis didn't specifically endorse me transferring to Stone Creek. He did say not to expect them to jump in enthusiastically and say, "Whatever you want, Sean."

Continuing in my slow, almost patronizing, tone, I say, "I'm telling you"—*not asking*, I think—"about wanting to transfer now so you have plenty of time to think it over. I understand it is a big decision." *Mine.* "Mom, I was thinking you could talk with the realtor who sold us our house about Stone Creek. Her son, Daniel, goes to school there. And we could all meet with the principal of Stone Creek so we could ask about any concerns we have."

They don't say anything, so I press ahead. "Also, I will be accompanying Chelsea to interview three Stone Creek seniors this week, and maybe she and I could get a tour at the same time. That will give me even more information to consider before making a decision."

Mom looks both shocked and a little sick. But dad, surprisingly, has lost his smirk.

"I'm impressed by how you've presented this idea," he says. "It shows a maturity I've hoped to see in you one day."

"So you'll let me transfer?" I ask, hopeful.

"We'll *think* about it," he says.

Of course.

✧   ✧   ✧

Next day at lunch, I can't wait to tell Chelsea about my conversation with my parents. She is impressed with the guts I showed in putting myself out there. But she is also consumed with her own news: she finally talked with her parents about her college acceptance letters and had a conversation with them about UVA versus Oberlin last night.

"I told my parents I could see value in both choices, but feel I'd be more comfortable in the smaller, more laid back atmosphere of Oberlin," she says. "And I said another option could be going to Oberlin for two years and then transferring to UVA later, when I know what my major will be. My parents responded that UVA will have countless more careers for me to explore and that transferring is often difficult—sometimes you lose credits from the first school because the second won't honor them. Then I threw out what I really want to do, go to Italy for the summer. I had trouble explaining a reason for Italy; in the end I told them I just feel drawn to explore archaeological digs there, and to learn fluent Italian. I said even if I don't major in a related field, at least I will have the summer experiences to enrich my life right now and build on later in life. The positive experience will give me the boost of enthusiasm I need to be ready for UVA in the fall."

"And what did they say?"

"My dad mumbled something about how I certainly could use a shot of enthusiasm for life before going off to college." Chelsea rolls her eyes. "My parents were of course stunned at my proposal and wanted to know where I thought I would go in Italy and what I would do. I asked my mom if she would be willing to ask my aunt Lucia if I could stay with her in Florence for a couple of months— she's not really my aunt, she's actually my mom's old college friend, but I grew up calling her 'aunt.'"

"That was smart, bringing your mom's friend into it!" I say. I know my parents would be way more likely to let me do something like what Chelsea's talking about if it involved an adult they trusted.

Chelsea smiles. "I thought so. I reminded Mom that Aunt Lucia has invited me to visit many times. I also asked her to remember how important traveling all over Europe was for her after she graduated from high school. I said, 'It's time for me to grow up, Mom'—and Sean, they actually said they would think about it. So I must have been pretty convincing!"

I extend my arms over my head in touchdown pose, and say, "Whoa, Chelsea!"—in a loud enough voice that I attract the curious eyes of the rest of the cafeteria. Lowering my voice, I say, "You're so brave! I just want to go across town and you want to go across the world."

"Yeah, well, I'm not as brave and mature as I made myself out to be to my parents," she says with a guilty look. "But it's true: I have to take the plunge and grow up some time. And I like Aunt Lucia a lot. She is very warm and loving and has always been encouraging to me."

"And the college thing?" I ask, realizing she never told me what she decided.

She looks down. "I don't feel confident about going to UVA. But I've convinced myself that maybe my parents know best in this case. What do I know about how to make a decision like this? What if I make the wrong choice? And this way, I'm sure to get one thing I want: going to Italy."

I don't want to deflate her feeling of success, so I don't tell her how surprising her drop in confidence is. Instead I ask, "What if your parents decide 'no' to your Italy proposal?" From what Chelsea has said about her parents, that seems like it could be a real possibility.

"I have no idea, maybe a deep depression. What if your parents say no about Stone Creek?"

"I'll try to fight back some way," I say.

It feels like growing up is about taking yourself seriously enough to put your deep wants out there, not to seek encouragement from someone else but because it changes you inside.

Chapter 4: Unleashing Energy

Once upon a time, a wise group of scholars turned a pyramid school upside down so students were in charge of their learning.

CHELSEA

Walking into Stone Creek High School with Sean, I can't help comparing it to Hilltop. First, school starts an hour later—at nine—and there's not one red-eyed student in sight. In contrast to Hilltop's entrance sign, with its declaration of a *drug-free school zone*, we are greeted by an artistic, *fear-free school zone* sign when we walk through the doors.

Cora, who's agreed to take us on a tour, appears next to us. "Hi Chelsea," she says, giving me a hug. "And you must be Sean." She offers him her hand. "Welcome."

"Thanks," Sean says. "A *fear-free school zone*, huh?"

Laughing, Cora says, "That's the first of many slogans you're likely to see or hear this morning. Our principal, Chief, encourages all of us to take risks and learn from mistakes."

I say, "You call him Chief?"

"When he came last year he joked he wanted to be seen as the Teacher-in-Chief," Cora explains. "The 'Chief' part stuck."

Sure enough, the front hall has another slogan on a large banner. *"One more thing . . . It's your life. Build it with choices worthy of you."*—Chief

Cora guides us down hallways on the way to our destination, the cafeteria. I poke my head in one classroom: It's quite large, with different areas delineated by computers, small round discussion tables, conference tables, soft reading chairs, thick rugs with floor pillows, and individual work carrels. Student creative work is displayed around every inch of wall space. Several adults are engaged in lively discussions with different individuals or groups of students. All appear radiant, lit up by the natural rays pouring through the room's expansive windows. No hyper-pitched voices. And people are actually touching each other, a signal to me of a high level of comfort. A few of them glance my way with curious eyes.

I realize I've lost Cora and Sean, and I skip down the hall to catch up with them.

"If I went to school here, how I dress wouldn't stick out," Sean is saying. "Lots of differences here. Cool."

The smell of fresh bread signals our arrival at the cafeteria. A tall man and an older woman wearing an apron are standing in the doorway, talking.

"Chief, Ms. Goodbar, meet my friends from Hilltop Academy, Chelsea and Sean, who are touring Stone Creek," Cora says. She turns to us. "The first thing Chief did is partner with Ms. Goodbar so now she and other staff actually cook rather than just heat up frozen food."

"Welcome, Cora and Sean!" Chief says. "Number one request of students when I came was better food. So we're working on it."

"I explained the meaning of *fear-free zone* to them, Chief," Cora says. "What would you say has been your biggest mistake since being here?"

I can't believe Cora is talking with him like they're . . . equals. I've never even talked with Hilltop's principal, much less like this.

"Well, the failure that bothered me the most was not knowing what to say to a student who told me he was a boy living in a girl's body. What I learned was to treat him just like anyone else and ask him to let me know if he ever wanted my help."

Cora gives me that lifting of her eyebrows like she had no idea he was going to say that.

It is all I can do to keep from laughing at Sean's totally freaked expression.

Cora asks Chief how he would, in a word, describe the general changes at Stone Creek over the last year and a half.

"How about two words, Cora. You know how I like to go on and on. My two words would be: unleashing energy."

"Good ones, Chief," she says.

Cora explains to us that the cafeteria is where the junior class meets first period, and today they're performing a scene from a play written by students that she wants to see. They based the play on a book from the 1950s called *Black Like Me*, a true story about a white man who darkened his skin to experience what life as a black man in the Deep South was like. Judging from the scene we see, his conclusion was that life was just as bad as black people had been saying for many years. Cora says that later today, the students will discuss changes from then until today in their English/social studies block classes.

"This place is amazing," Sean says.

I'm still thinking about what Chief said earlier. "I love the expression 'unleashing energy,'" I say. "It perfectly describes the opposite of how I feel at Hilltop: bottled up."

A woman is coming down the hall toward us, and her face lights up when she sees Cora.

"That's Ms. Jordan, who I wanted you guys to meet," Cora says. "She led the school change process last year with planning teams made up of students, teachers, parents, and other community members. Chief decided no big-wigs with power in the schools could participate because change wouldn't work if it came from the top down."

I remember Cora telling me last school year that Ms. Jordan had helped her get past a deep crush on a senior who treated her more like a little sister. I'm glad to put a face to the name.

After a quick hug, Cora introduces us to Ms. Jordan.

"Welcome to Stone Creek," Ms. Jordan says warmly.

"Please tell my friends why you and other teachers wanted to make changes here," Cora prompts her.

"We all had story after story of students who were not getting their needs met," Ms. Jordan says. "One disturbing experience of mine was stumbling upon a girl in the restroom one day who was throwing up; she was pregnant and nobody else knew, including her family." Ms. Jordan's eyes lock onto mine. "I was shocked to think of how alone this young woman must feel. Her schoolwork had crashed, and she was desperately distraught. To this day, I worry what would have happened without that chance encounter."

"Was change hard for you and the other teachers?" Sean asks.

"Change is always hard. But our great discovery was that we teachers agreed with the other people involved—the students, parents, and community—about what young people's needs are. It was a great relief to know we were all on the same page and didn't have to fight for what we believed. The experience fired us up to figure out how to change school to better meet the needs of our students—and we came to realize we would have to grow in some ways, too, which was scary, but also exciting. That's life!"

"I recently moved from California and thought I was the only one going through coping with change," Sean says. "But I'm starting to realize that, like you said, change is life."

Ms. Jordan looks at Sean with kind intensity, nodding in agreement.

"If you're interested to know more about changes here, Sean, I could recruit Daniel to help me explain what the planning groups did," Cora says. "We were in different groups but the experience was pretty similar. You've met Daniel. His mom is the realtor who helped your family buy your house when you moved here."

Even at this larger school of about a thousand, you see the small-town dynamics playing out. People are aware of who knows who.

I put a finger to my temple. "I'm beginning to realize why I've had such a hard time understanding what you tell me about Stone

Creek, Cora," I say. "I always think in terms of school schedule, rules, grades, tests, and things like that, but not people, relationships, and interests. That's the key, isn't it?"

Ms. Hoffmann, a school counselor, has arranged for Sean and me to interview three seniors in their different classrooms.

For the first interview, with a kid named Peter, we settle in at a small table removed from the action of a math/science classroom. Never before has action and math gone together in my head. I see an adjoining room that is a lab. I see students entering from another adjoining classroom and mixing with students from the classroom we're in.

Sean and I have decided to let go of the original focus on bullying, backpack searches, and guns at school. Instead, we want to draw out what is important to each student we meet.

The math/science environment helps us get going with Peter, because his story is all about math. Specifically, he hated math for years. He is vague about why—something about how he was treated in eighth grade. After that, at Stone Creek, Peter would only do the bare minimum of work to pass his math classes, even though he was a whiz at all the tests.

"Then the middle of last year, eleventh grade, big changes started at school and the teachers were different," Peter tells us. "This year, the classes are different; having the math and science block together means we can relax and dive into stuff for two hours. Kids in each class are all different, too—there's no tracking so-called smart kids only and dumb kids only into classes. The main thing, though, is we decide what projects we want to work on, and we can do them either by ourselves or with other people interested in the same thing."

"What project are you working on now?" I ask Peter.

"Let me show you," he says.

Sean and I follow him to a computer and he brings up a design of a skateboard park he created.

"Our computer specialist on this teacher team helped me the most, showing me ways to use this cool software," Peter says. "Last year the school stopped buying textbooks and in exchange we got more computer teachers. A community group got grants to buy more computers. If I get stuck on my design, I get help from the math or science teacher.

"Your design looks like a real challenge—and fun!" Sean says. "I can't believe you figured out how to do all that. You still a skater, Peter?"

"No, and it's mostly 'cause I got bored with the old skateboard park. I designed this for an upgrade. The city council approved paying for the upgrade, and they're going to put up a plaque with my name on it at the park."

A guy sitting at an adjacent computer slaps Peter on the back. "Some day I'll say I knew you when . . ."

Heading to the next interview, we pass a classroom where a girl is standing in front of classmates holding a basketball. Sean motions for me to stand next to the door, where we can hear but not be seen. The girl is presenting her research on the physics of the basketball free throw.

"No way," Sean whispers. "This place can't be for real."

Our next interview takes place in an English/social studies block class. The whole class of about forty students is huddled together as the teachers introduce a writing activity: a letter to someone (real or imaginary) about something you are worried about. To demonstrate how letters are different from e-mails or tweets, a teacher reads an excerpt from a Flannery O'Connor letter sharing her feelings about her disease of lupus. "I'm sure your style of writing will be quite different, as it should be," the teacher says.

On his way over to us, our interview subject—Dave, a hulk of a person—laughs with a short, skinny guy whose static hair stands on end. He's wearing a T-shirt that proclaims, "Nerds of the World Rise Up." What an unlikely pair.

I start by asking about the letters. "What do you think of this assignment?"

"This will be an easy one," Dave says. "What I'm worried about is getting a football scholarship, so I'm going to write a letter to the coach at the college I'm going to."

"What will happen if you don't get the scholarship?" Sean asks.

"Ms. Hoffmann has me applying for other sources of money for college," Dave says, "but I just want to play football, and them giving me a scholarship means I will get to play." He looks at us as if waiting for a sign that we're following what he's saying.

I nod and ask, "You're not interested in the college classes part?"

"Look at these brainiacs I'm in class with," he says. "They're college material. There are some average kids and other dummies like me here, but I miss the slower pace, when it was just my dummy friends."

"Seems like you get along with the brainiacs," Sean says.

"Oh, yeah, we've become good buddies," Dave says. "They help me with my assignments and sometimes I give them ideas. So I been thinking better about myself . . . but it's too late for me to become college material." His bubbly energy seems to fade away after that statement.

Ms. Hoffmann escorts us to the third and final classroom—it's apparently pretty hard to find—and on the walk there we ask her about Dave.

"I helped him find a small college with a good football team not far from here," she says. "What Dave doesn't talk about, even though everyone knows, is he's worried sick about his mother who has cancer. He also doesn't tell strangers what everyone else knows about him: He is great with kids and will be a great coach one day. That will get him through college."

Ms. Hoffmann explains that the last stop is "lunch and club time," so it will be noisy and less formal than the other two classes we visited. We meet Shauna in a classroom that's been converted, for the next forty-five minutes, into a jazz club. Shauna looks for all the world like a beatnik you would see in old movies of 1960s New York City in her black turtleneck and beret. She removes her dark glasses as we approach.

"How do you eat your sandwich and play the saxophone at the same time?" I ask, laughing.

"That's when being versatile and switching to a bass comes in handy," she says.

Sean, still observing every aspect of her cool attire, asks, "So, we've been hearing all these great things about Stone Creek; what is something you don't like?"

"Foreign languages," Shauna says, practically screaming in order to be heard over the music. "We have to take a language class every year, every day for an hour, and my class takes place right when I'm all warmed up to play some jazz."

"You don't have a music class?" Sean asks, as if he's finally found a flaw in Stone Creek.

"Oh, yeah, that's last period," Shauna says. "And most of us stay until late in the afternoon after school so we can play longer."

"What class would I have if I didn't take music last period?" Sean asks.

"Another arts class, like drama or painting; an intramural sport, like ultimate Frisbee; computer technology classes; or a vocational class taught by a community college teacher," Shauna says. "One semester I took a vocational class, robotics, and then I would join my friends in music for the after-school jam sessions."

"That's a lot of choices," Sean says, "but what if I wanted to take a photography class?"

It's like Sean is deliberately trying to find something wrong with the school. Or maybe he's just trying to prepare himself for any objection his parents might make to him transferring here.

"If there were enough people who wanted photography, a class would be formed, or maybe even a half class. If it was pretty much just you or a few students, then you could do independent study with a mentor from the community and get class credit. The computer people set up a whole database of experts in the community on various topics last year, and people add to it all the time, so it's easy to find someone who can be a mentor."

Sean has been outmaneuvered in his gotcha game.

"Are you going to college?" I ask Shauna.

"Oh, yeah," she says, "my portfolio of work, teacher recommendations, and Ms. Hoffmann helping me choose which colleges to apply to helped me get in with a scholarship. Ms. Hoffmann also helped me stay motivated in all my classes by going over my work each quarter with my teachers. Counselors do that for all the students here."

When the interview is over, I notice Sean checking out what other people in the club are wearing. He seems particularly taken with an Afghan pakol hat. Of course, hats of any kind are against the dress code at Hilltop.

Ms. Hoffmann returns to walk us out, and the first thing I ask her is, "How do you have enough time to help each individual student?"

"That was the miracle of Chief," she says. "When he came, he initiated a collaborative effort to move athletics to a community organization. People in the community were dying to be coaches and in charge of sports, and Chief wanted to use the extra money from not paying athletic teachers and coaches to hire new counselors. We now have three counselors for each grade level, and I only have eighty students I'm responsible to."

Interesting she said responsible "to" and not "for." Again, the "students in charge" thing. I wish I'd known about this place sooner.

SEAN

I meet Cora at the city park in town across from Mountain Mama's Ice Cream Shop. She tells me we'll have to drag Daniel away from his element; he's known as Mr. Mayor here, where Stone Creek students gather every day after school. At least, the ones who are not currently on a team run by the community sports organization or don't have special activities like riding show horses or taking a college class or working.

"Daniel comes alive here," Cora says. "He manages to find out things about every single person without sharing anything substantial about himself."

Daniel responds to Cora's gesture to head to Mountain Mama's, which is quiet on this beautiful spring day. She invited both Chelsea and me to hear what happened in the meetings over a year ago to change Stone Creek, but Chelsea declined. Frankly, after today's visit to Stone Creek she seems even more bummed about Hilltop and all the opportunities she has missed by going to school there.

Daniel walks up, flashes me a smile, and raises his hand for a fist bump. We know each other already. His mom brought him along when she was showing us our house so he could tell me about youth in the community here, and I see him around town once in a while.

"How's the pistol named Sarah?" Daniel asks.

"Loving life and everything about her preschool," I say.

First on the agenda, ice cream cones—my treat. While we're gulping down homemade original flavors—I chose pineapple-coconut—Cora and Daniel tell me how the groups got formed, stories of some funny incidents within groups, and about the general excitement people felt to be able to start from scratch with thinking about what schools should aim to do. Teachers facilitated the groups to make sure they didn't end up like a reality TV show, with everybody at each other's throats.

Cora brought a copy of the final report with input from all the planning groups, each of which was made up of students, teachers, parents, and other community members. The report is a list of needs of adolescents, grouped into categories, and then stories told by people in the groups related to each category. Students were in charge of compiling the report.

"Whoa, look at all the emojis in here," I say.

"That's me!" Daniel says.

"True," Cora says. "It was Daniel's solution to bring a boring list to life. And I think his idea worked. Like, look at the fear face emoji next to a discussion of anxiety in teenagers."

Daniel looks uncomfortable and flips the page, pointing to another emoji. "My favorite is this one—the helicopter emoji, as in helicopter parenting. Lots of my friends complain about that."

"Probably the most important emoji," Cora says, "showing a central conclusion of the groups, is the clock."

"What does the clock refer to?" I ask.

"Well, the big new idea is students need to be in charge of their own learning," she says. "And if that is going to really happen, it means students have to be in charge of their time."

"Like in the classroom?"

"Yes, in a big way," she says. "Like, not everyone needs to do the same thing at the same time."

"Or in the same way," Daniel adds. "Like, get creative. Investigate what others have done and then go the next step—or in a whole different direction."

"Exactly!" Cora says, pointing to Daniel.

"Seems from what you say and what I've seen, it's about *doing* things, not sitting, taking in, spitting it back out over and over, wearing down, getting exhausted."

"You know who talked in the groups about being exhausted the most?" Cora asks, looking at me.

"The teachers!" Daniel says. "I was really blown away by their reaction. I thought they'd defend being workaholics based on all the college degrees they have."

"The teachers felt it was too much to do lesson planning that would be fresh and appeal to a variety of interests, then share information in an upbeat way, then develop tests or assignments that would show what students remembered, then grade all that work while paying attention to individual detail, and then start all over again in a week or two."

"One teacher came out and said, 'Teachers are doing all the work and we're treating students like infants,'" Daniel says, looking amazed.

Maybe that's one reason teachers like Chelsea's favorite, her English teacher, don't last long at Hilltop.

"The teachers concluded that they wanted out of the director role and into having more time to get to know kids and what they wanted to learn."

"And is that working now, teachers really knowing students and helping them individually?" I ask, a little skeptical, even after everything I saw today.

"Yes," Cora immediately answers. "With four teachers in a class of forty—two subject teachers, one special needs teacher that floats to another classroom at times, and a computer specialist that also floats—plus 180 days of required school, two hours each day, we really get to know each other well! If I want to know something about the human body, for instance, I'll go to my ninth grade science teacher to get some perspective, because she was an ER nurse before she decided to switch to work with less drama. It doesn't matter that she's not my teacher anymore, she makes herself available."

Daniel starts to stand but then sits back down, his back stretched to the limit of upright. "I'm a traditionalist when it comes to school," he says. "Just give me the content I need for SATs so I can get into a good college. The teachers ask me questions that challenge my traditional approach, but they also accept me for who I am and don't make me feel weird for wanting that. No making me feel threatened."

"One more thing about the planning groups, Sean," Cora says, "there was one super academic teacher who really influenced the thinking of many people involved in this process, young and old." She takes out a piece of paper—unlined typing paper, which I find interesting. When I point to it with a quizzical look, she says, "I don't like being boxed in with lines. Anyway, the guy I'm talking about drew a circle on a whiteboard and put a tiny dot in the circle." Cora draws it. "He said the dot represents what subject matter he could cover in a year in the circle of what is known about human biology. He asked why he should decide which dot is learned. His perspective was, it doesn't matter where anyone starts in the circle. Also, what if people are curious about things outside the circle—all the as yet unknown things about human biology?"

"This is where I start getting lost," Daniel says, pushing his chair back from the table. "Like, what did they mean when they summed it all up by saying young people just need to 'learn to learn' and specific content wasn't so important? I disagree! You have to know answers to questions on the tests."

He is so rattled he spills the last of his ice cream on Cora's drawing.

I'm with Daniel in feeling lost.

"I think they meant focus on *skills*," Cora says. "Like communication, critical thinking, collaboration with others—the stuff employers say they are looking for in employees these days."

Daniel starts bouncing his leg up and down. "Well, I already know what I want to learn: to be a successful business person. And I don't want to waste time on things that won't help me do well in college."

Cora softens her voice. "I think they believe learning those skills *are* the best preparation for college."

"I don't know. The way they're evaluating our progress now seems a lot harder than the way grades used to be done. Colleges look at grades and test scores when they're deciding who to give money to." Daniel's voice is getting quieter and quieter, like he's giving up the argument.

I wouldn't be able to argue against Cora either.

Cora tries the soft approach again, saying, "Colleges are different, I think, and I want to go to one that lets me direct myself."

These guys are my age, but I never think about college or how to learn or what I'm interested in or any of this stuff they're talking about. "Did you guys think about these things before the planning groups or did you learn how to think about schools in the groups?" I look to Daniel to respond, but he is looking off into space.

"Before, I felt things about what was not working for me in school but I thought it was just something wrong with me," Cora says. "The planning groups were very supportive to the students in them and they helped us say what was on our minds." She stands up and, as if she's doing show-and-tell, gestures to her treasured item, the shirt she's wearing. "The adults gave all us kids in the groups these T-shirts." On the front it reads, *Free Range Kids*.

Daniel shuts down in every way except his bouncing leg, and even Cora can't get him engaged anymore.

Cora and Chelsea get the idea to have a debate about whether I should transfer to Stone Creek next year. I will ask questions or express concerns, and one team, Cora and Chelsea, will answer in favor of transferring, while the other team, Daniel and Jake, will be against me transferring. Crazy, but I'm willing to play.

We gather together at the park on Saturday, and Cora tells me to start things off when I'm ready. I take a deep breath, and then dive in.

SEAN: I don't feel confident I can actually work on my own.

CORA: You'll see how others come to it.

JAKE: Maybe nobody else shares your interests. You'll be a loner.

SEAN: I don't like looking dumb.

CORA: It's exciting to not know and discover new ideas. It's like a treasure hunt if you really care about your questions.

DANIEL: But it's scary to feel like you're hanging out there on your own.

CORA: Others will help you.

DANIEL: It's not good for teachers to realize how little you know. They write college recommendations.

CHELSEA: Maybe how much you grow is as important as what they think you should know.

SEAN: Okay, I gotta admit I'm not all that driven by learning things. Where does fun come in? How about meeting girls? Oops, don't mean to be gender rigid. So, what do I say . . . heartmates? That sounds truly stupid.

CORA: I can honestly say that we try to get away from judging others at this school.

DANIEL: I don't always feel comfortable here. Not having to do with sexuality, but just in general.

CHELSEA: What about school makes you feel uncomfortable, Daniel?

DANIEL: Everyone pushing at me all the time: What do you think about this or that? What are your interests? What is your gut telling you? Sometimes it's too much, like just leave me alone.

CORA: I agree, Daniel, sometimes it's overwhelming. But that's just a part of life and part of what we need to learn. Like, who am I on the inside, regardless of black and white stereotypes out there in the world. That's what I'm preoccupied with.

SEAN: Okay, let's get back to the "fun" part of my question. Where's that?

JAKE: I definitely enjoy coming to school every day. Maybe it's because work on the farm is so hard, and it's nice to use your brain muscles some. The fun comes from people I've grown up with who know me well and who I don't have to explain things to. So I can just relax and laugh a lot. And while we do a lot of work in classes, the teachers aren't breathing down your neck and pressuring you.

CHELSEA: Seems like who you are on the inside is in synch with who you are on the outside, Jake.

CORA: Yeah, I'm definitely not there yet, but I do expect school to help me figure out "me" related to the big-picture "out there."

DANIEL: Sometimes I think of school like a stage where I can try out being different people. Everyone calls me Mr. Mayor, and I get that it's kind of a slam against my friendly, on-the-surface ways and liking to know what everyone is up to, but that's okay. It seems like fun to me. It feels comfortable when I know how people will relate to me. Also, I think that role will serve me well in the business world.

SEAN: Here's another concern I have: the obsession with declaring "interests." My main interest is surfing, and there's no ocean here.

DANIEL: Yeah, like there are only a few small businesses around here. Who will I learn from?

CORA: That's a starting point for both of you to figure out. Like, maybe it's not the size of the business, Daniel, but practices like entrepreneurship, which people are good at in both small businesses and large corporations.

CHELSEA: And I don't know, Sean, it seems in addition to surfing you also like biking, cross-country skiing, hiking . . . all these outdoor adventure activities. They seem to represent "fun," which is a big part of you.

JAKE: I want to ask you a question, Sean: What do your parents think about you transferring to Stone Creek?

SEAN: They haven't said much yet. They're "thinking about it."

DANIEL: Sounds like you need to build a case and sell it to them if that's what you want.

JAKE: I don't know about that. I wouldn't want to go against my dad. It's a big responsibility of a parent to know their kid well enough to help guide them to make good decisions.

SEAN: I'm caught between wanting it to be my decision and worrying that I'll make a bad decision.

DANIEL: I can see why, Sean. It could be a bad decision because you are all set to get into college, graduating from a fancy private school like Hilltop.

CHELSEA: But Sean's miserable at Hilltop.

JAKE: Change is hard.

CORA: But change is a lot easier when you do it with other people, like close friends.

DANIEL: You can make close friends anywhere you go. That's easy.

CORA: Really deep friends? Who will support you no matter what?

SEAN: I'm not sure how to do that no matter where I am.

A few days after our "debate," Chelsea volunteers to drive me out to Jake's to hear about a problem Chief had with a group called the Hardee's Eight. Jake's dad is a central character in the group, and Jake keeps up with their activities through dinner table conversations with his dad.

Chelsea drops me off at Jake's, right next door from her house, and tells me to call her for a ride home when we're through talking.

Jake's in the middle of his farm work.

"Hope you don't mind, Sean, following me around while I do my afternoon farm chores," he says when I walk up.

"No problem." I'm glad I wore my hiking boots. I took a cue from Jake, who always wears his work boots.

The first chore is to walk the fences to make sure there are no breaks. Rounding up lost cows is apparently a pain. Jake counts the cows to make sure all are accounted for—particularly the calves, who he says tend to be more adventurous explorers and sometimes get caught in brambles and such.

"The whole controversy started around two things," Jake says as we walk. "One was those planning groups, which were made up largely of professional people in the city and did not include regular folks out in the county who had not been big successes in school. There's always been this divide in the community, with about four out of five students coming from families not considered big economic players. Apparently, Chief, being new to the area, didn't realize this until it was all over. And nobody had realized the groups would be able to make real changes, since groups had been put together in years past to advise the schools but were never listened to. The changes the teachers came up with, based on ideas from the groups, were considered far-out and radical to my dad and his friends."

I'm a little distracted by watching the cows, waiting for one to gore me like I've seen in bullfights. I'm reassured a bit when Jake walks over to one of the calves and scratches its head. The mama cow barely glances at him, but she stares at me like she knows I'm a stranger.

"Nothing much happened at first," Jake goes on. "The Hardee's guys—they're named that because they eat breakfast together there most every day—got their revenge by spreading around their nickname for Chief: 'Greaser,' meaning he could talk a slick line but watch out for his ideas. The city people call him Mr. Shepherd, a few poking fun at the herding the sheep reference."

Uh-oh, trouble. I see a calf on the wrong side of the fence. "Hey, Jake, check it out," I say pointing.

"Good eye," he says. "Let's find the break in the fence so we can guide it back through." He starts walking again. "Then comes the big hoo-ha: After changes started at the school, some kids were caught exploring online porn sites—at home, not at school, but they had learned about the sites from other kids at school."

Laughing, I say, "I bet that didn't go over well in a community filled with fundamentalist churches."

"You got that right. Hey, I found the break!" He's all business now. "Let me tell you how you can help. First, we walk real slow—no fast moves or the calf will get spooked and run who knows where. I'm going to leave this pile of fresh-cut grass I've been carrying on this side of the fence to attract the calf; it'll probably attract other cows too, but that's okay. We'll go around behind the calf to head it in this direction, and when we do, make yourself big by extending both arms up and wide, keeping them that way. Then move very slow and quiet."

Everything happens exactly as Jake said it would, and in no time we have the calf back where it belongs.

"Darn if it doesn't work!" I exclaim as Jake sets to work on the fence break. "I love learning new skills. Now if I ever get stuck on a country road with a cow in the middle, I'll know what to do. Except it would be a lot scarier by myself and with a full-grown, monster-size cow."

"Back to the story," Jake says, not hyped up. I realize this must be a common occurrence for him. "So with the porn thing, the school did the right thing by not evading all responsibility. Instead of claiming it wasn't the school's problem and insisting that teenagers have always traded sex information among themselves, Chief organized first period class meetings, with outside speakers and parent observers, to discuss the implications of porn sites— how they promote risky and illegal sexual behavior and demean women and young children as objects of the porn industry, and what the importance of moral values in society is. The Hardee's group thought the important thing was the discussions on moral values. Chief made friends with some local ministers by asking them to focus on the issue in church, saying that was something they had more practice at than schools did. In general the controversy died down, but the tremendous initial uproar has left a suspicious bent about what goes on at Stone Creek."

We make our way back to the barn, where we start shoveling out cow pies and putting in new hay for tonight. The night temperatures in the spring can still get down in the thirties, so the cows are more comfortable indoors.

Jake wipes his forehead. "Another thing that's come up lately is transgender rights and the issue of bathroom access. The wife of one of the Hardee's crowd, who's a nurse, has been quietly organizing medical people to talk with their neighbors about the awful threats transgender people face. We'll see where that goes."

"Apparently Chief isn't shying away from this subject either. One of the first things he told me and Chelsea about when we visited Stone Creek was his reaching out to one transgender student."

"Really?" Jake smiles. "He's pretty amazing. I hope he can last in this very traditional community. Power over what goes on in schools is about the last thing people still have with the decline in small farms, the big recession a few years ago, and technology taking over so many people's jobs."

"It's really impressive how you see things in a big way but also keep your focus on what you most care about, a small farm," I say. "You're pretty smart to see how what you want relates to everything else that could help or get in the way."

"I feel lucky to be able to stay here and have work I want to do. Many kids graduate from high school and move away, never coming back except to visit, and I've heard a lot of them say how much they miss it. Some could start businesses here, but they say the place is too conservative for them to feel comfortable."

"Hey, Chief," I say, my mouth dry. "Thanks for meeting with us."

My mom and dad exchange handshakes and introductions with Chief. I'm as nervous as I ever remember being. My parents and I look at Chief, expecting him to take charge.

He responds by making it clear authority rests with us. "My understanding, Sean, is you are considering transferring to Stone Creek in the fall. And your parents want to know more about the school to advise you about a possible move. Am I on target for what you-all want out of the meeting?"

We all nod.

"I hope none of you will perceive me as trying to sell you on Stone Creek. I will for sure get enthusiastic when I talk about our school, but by no means am I presuming to know what is best for you, Sean. One other warning is I talk a lot—and I mean *a lot*. So feel free to interrupt at any time. I'm used to it." Chief chuckles. "Let's start with each of you stating concerns or asking questions so the discussion will meet your needs."

Everybody looks at me. I have to act mature if I want this discussion to go well, starting with talking first and with confidence. "If I do transfer here, this will be my third high school," I say. "I worry that I've missed a lot the last two years and it will be hard to catch up. I've already met three other students here, though, and that is three more people who I consider friends than I would have back at Hilltop next year. I don't exactly know how to say it; I just think Stone Creek would be good for me, and I would become involved in a way I haven't at Hilltop. But I will definitely need help."

My dad tells Chief about EarthWalk. Chief broadcasts a big old smile and holds up a hand for a high-five when Dad is through.

I'm surprised, but I reach up and slap his hand without hesitation. There's something about him that makes me feel comfortable doing it.

"Really awesome, Sean," he says.

"Yes, Sean's initiative was very impressive," Dad says. "I am concerned, however, that Stone Creek may present too much of an opportunity for Sean to go back to coasting through life."

"I'm interested to hear more about the values at the foundation of Stone Creek," Mom says. "Where did all this come from? I understand you used to be a math teacher. Maybe you could describe how you motivate students to want to learn math—not Sean's forte, I assure you."

Chief sits in silence, apparently as comfortable with listening as he is with talking at length. "Great questions and concerns," Chief says, while obviously sorting through it all. "If it's okay with everyone, I'll start with the math challenge. Our approach to all classes is learning with assistance, as opposed to teaching. Part of the assistance is challenging people to solve a problem in which they have an interest."

Chief turns to me and I panic, my brain repeating a mantra of, *Please don't ask me anything!*

"If I recall correctly, Sean, you have great interest in surfing and the sea. If I were meeting you for the first time in a math class, I might ask you questions about your surfboard design and how it worked on the waves. If you responded with interest, I could suggest some fundamental design questions for you to explore, offer some ideas for resources, and ask you to get back to me when you get stuck. The point is, students need to be in charge, making decisions constantly about what to explore. Their success along the way creates confidence and desire to keep learning. You with me?"

I look at Mom and Dad for clues to where they're at. Mom is concentrating on following everything Chief is saying and she looks like she is ready to burst with forty million questions, all of them starting with *Yes, but* . . .

Dad, meanwhile, has the blank face he uses a lot when planning a *gotcha* trap question. I know the expression well.

Chief plows ahead. "Sean's forte not being math, we would want him to take some standardized tests for assessment of where he might have gaps from his moving to different schools. This is the only way we use standardized tests: to determine areas of need. We are considered a 'pilot' program with the state of Virginia, giving us lots of flexibility, but we do take the state tests at the end of courses, just like everyone else. The results show our students are doing far better, learning far more, than they did in the past. Even better than tests for assessment is our team of math teachers, which would work with Sean to determine what his skills are and then design an individual plan for him to catch up in some areas if he needs it. We do this kind of thing for all students." Chief turns to me. "Does that reassure you, Sean, that we would assist you in areas where you need help? But the key is, you have to use the initiative your dad says you have—take charge of your own learning. We can't, and won't even try, to *make* you learn something."

"Are there kids who don't make it here?" I ask.

"Only a few, and it's those who refuse to try—those who, for one reason or another, can't do school right now."

Dad jumps in before Mom can get a question formulated. "Why all the emphasis on choice? Wouldn't it be more efficient to just transmit the core information needed?"

Uh-oh. Dad's going to get defensive about his own identity as a teacher.

"Perhaps that would be true in, say, a college situation, where students are able to freely choose what courses they want to take and the professor is responsive to individual students probing areas of their own interest. But when those conditions do not exist, as in a traditional high school, you tend to see a great deal of disinterest among students. We believe high school students need to explore a range of interests before their next stage in life, when they will be expected to make decisions for themselves. Otherwise, they've wasted a lot of time in high school."

Looking directly at Mom, Chief says, "Your intensity bubbles forth in your eyes. How are we doing addressing your concerns?"

Mom takes a long time to collect her thoughts into what she wants to say, but she looks enormously pleased that Chief is willing to wait and she doesn't have to compete for the floor.

"Frankly, I'm fascinated," she finally says. "What you're saying seems to ring true, though I'm not entirely sure why. My high school experience was very traditional."

"I suppose people get to where I've landed in many different ways," Chief says. "For me, it was an experience with hospice a few years ago, when my mother was dying."

"My father died three years ago and hospice was wonderful to him. And also to me," Mom says.

I remember the hospice people, too, when Grandpa was dying. They would come into Grandpa's room at home, and the first thing they did was go over to his bed and touch him in greeting. They would ask how he was doing and listen to him in a very connected way. Then they would ask what he would like from them. Whatever he wanted, they would do. One time a guy brought his guitar and played Beatles songs Grandpa loved.

Chief nods at Mom. "My encounter with hospice was a profound eye-opener for me. I quit my teaching job, both to be with my mom and to end a frustrating job that I was not allowed to do the way I believed it should be done. Hospice gave me perspective, insight into a different approach to people's needs. With hospice the patient is in charge, no exceptions. The compassion and assistance the staff are able to provide comes from that understanding. My translation was that students should be in charge."

Mom looks like she's really contemplating what Chief has just said. For the first time, I think she may support this transfer idea after all.

Dad stands up to leave. "I think we've taken enough of your time, Mr. Shepherd." He walks over and shakes Chief's hand.

Chief turns to me. "You good to go, Sean?"

"Yes, sir."

With that cue, Chief stands. Mom reaches out and takes both of Chief's hands in hers, rather than giving him a handshake. "Thank you for the gift of much to think about," she says.

Dad is reading something written on a napkin that's framed and hanging on Chief's wall. After shaking Chief's hand, I walk up beside Dad to see what it says:

Learning

When inner person meets the outer social and natural world
Your dreams meet history
Your voice meets other voices
Inner longing meets mysteries of nature
Fear of the future is calmed by focusing on now
Events out there open new possibilities by stirring imagination
We all search to answer the question, "Who am I?"

Chapter 5: Change and School

Once upon a time, I was on a road to creating my ideal world, ensuring security, safety, and internal peace.

DANIEL

Chief greets kids coming in the front door of Stone Creek High School every day. On this first day of my junior year, I up my game by greeting each junior coming through the cafeteria doors for our first period class meeting.

Way early, like a newbie, here's Sean.

"Hey, surf's up," I say to him.

"Good to see a friendly face, Daniel," he says, grinning. "So you're not surprised to see me?"

"I make it my business to know what's up, all the street news." I definitely hate surprises.

Sean looks surprisingly cool, calm, and collected for his first day at a new school, though it may be his style of California casual dress—a loose fitting T-shirt and jeans with his trademark flip-flops.

People tell me I act tightly strung. They could be reacting to my perfectionist dress: only the right brands, although they're few in number, since I don't have much money. It's true I have a thing for keeping my Nikes unmarred, in line with my experience that looking right makes me feel right.

"Let me show you the morning check-in routine, Sean," I say. "This way to the computers. You can also print your schedule if you don't have it yet."

While Sean waits to sign in, I do my Mr. Mayor routine, an animated facial expression for everyone, friendly one-liners, zero attachment.

It hits me how much I've missed school the last few months. Not just the comfort of routine and my place in the social scene, but the physical space of Stone Creek as well. It feels like home.

Each first period meeting space is anchored differently in the building. Seniors have the best view: their windows face to the east, allowing them to take in the movement of the newly rising sun from behind the Blue Ridge Mountains—predictably later each day. The Allegheny Mountains, to the west, anchor the view from our junior space, the cafeteria. Their captivating size speaks of origins and possibilities beyond the horizon.

Our cafeteria walls display student artwork, with background walls painted in soft but vibrant colors. Framing the windows are drapes created by the textile arts student club last year. While the cafeteria has no super soft seating like the senior space does, our tables and chairs can be moved around for flexibility of purpose. Ceiling tiles keep the space from being unbearably loud.

Chief says the architecture of this school, especially all the windows, is not typical of high schools, and we are lucky the previous school leaders designed such an open atmosphere. There is a large courtyard between the cafeteria and library, for instance, that allows for easily accessible fresh air and a feeling of openness.

As Sean heads back my way, I home in on what's different now from the last time I saw him in the spring: his hair. "What's with the shorter and totally bleached hair, man?" I ask, nudging him. "New school, new look?"

"I was a lifeguard all summer at the city pool," he says, running his fingers through his hair. "The chlorine and the sun bleached out the usual light red. I've rekindled my surfer image."

"I worked at the country club pool all summer," I say. "They pay much better. I didn't swim in the pool because of the chlorine and what it's in there for." I run my hands through my hair with an effeminate flair. "My naturally blond locks were covered by my cap. Pretty boring job, huh?"

Talking to Sean, I'm missing some spoken greetings to incoming juniors, so I just give a head raise—the non-verbal *what's up?*—to a couple people.

"Not to me," Sean says. "Had some pretty exciting moments, actually. One day a few weeks ago a two-year-old lost her balance walking in the baby pool. Her mom didn't see her go under the water, so, you know . . . Super Sean to the rescue."

"The most exciting thing that happened at my job was a college age girl diving in and her bikini top comes off. Thought I might die from laughing."

Guess you had to be there; Sean's not laughing.

For the school year, I've applied to work after school and weekends at the town newspaper, but I haven't heard back from them yet. The downside of the job would be not having time to go to the park after school. But earning money is more important than just hanging out.

My school counselor helped me with the newspaper job application. She suggested I include my role on the school newspaper this year writing feature stories. My mom suggested including something about the importance of deadlines and my habit of always being on time. I'm pretty compulsive about time, really. Being late makes me wicked uncomfortable.

Mom, as a here-and-there realtor and a budding artist, makes little money. My law professor stepfather makes plenty of money but isn't inclined to share it with a stepson he doesn't like.

"Daniel, I have a blank on my schedule for club time," Sean says.

"You can change that in the computer once you decide," I tell him. "I want to start an Investment Club this year—any interest?"

Sean chuckles.

I tense up a little. "What are you laughing at? It's going to be great. We can get free advice from bank people in town about how investment works and how we could increase whatever money we have saved. I know it would be a risk, I could lose money, but it would be worth it to learn the ropes now, while the investments would be small. And you know, in two years we'll be off to college, and I don't want to have to rely on handouts for going to a good school. I could only do Investment Club twice a week, though, since I have to meet with school newspaper staff three times a week at lunch."

"Investments sound a little over my head," Sean says. "My thing is, this is my first year here, and I feel like I wasted all last year—and the year before that, too, honestly. I want to really throw myself into learning things I'm interested in here. But I'm pretty nervous about not knowing what I'm doing."

"Jumping in head first is the right way to get something out of this school," I say. "It's just that what interests me is, well . . . money."

Cora wanders over. Actually, that's not right. Cora never "wanders." She is extremely purposeful in everything she does.

"Hey Daniel. Good to see you here, Sean. I'm going to miss my Sunday walks with Chelsea."

We all compare schedules. Cora and I are together in the same morning English/social studies block. Sean and I are together in Spanish 3 and the afternoon science/math block. We both also signed up for soccer last period, which is always the largest of the fall intramural classes.

"Sean, you're not in any of my classes," Cora says. "Do you know what lunch club you want to do?"

"Maybe I'll shop around for a bit to see what there is besides 'Investments,'" Sean says, grinning at me.

My response is, hands in the air, "Whatever." People whose families have money can afford to treat it as not important. We'll compare notes in thirty years.

"I'm going to do Math Club," Cora says. "Come check it out, Sean. I scoped out the games they have. New ones, not just traditional ones like chess. It's in Room 202. Try it out. You can switch clubs all you want. For sure I'm going to do forensics later, when it's time to prepare for spring speaking competitions."

"Cora, why don't you do intramural soccer last period with Sean and me?" I ask.

"Nope, I'm going to play golf. Minority girls wanting to enter professional fields need social activity that fits with that goal."

"You know what Chief would say. 'Do what you love, love what you do.'"

"I actually do like golf. And you don't have to get all sweaty and dirty doing it." She waves her hand back and forth under her nose.

"Okay, okay." I give up. "Hey, Sean, I just had a great idea. We could get the other soccer players to divide up into teams by language. Like, we could be the Chilean National Team." I turn to Cora. "Tell him about the junior class sister school in Chile." She doesn't jump in, so I move on. "Plus, using our Spanish during games would be cool, and the non-Latino teams wouldn't know what we were saying. Our team's cheer could be 'Chi-Chi-Chi, le-le-le,' like people did when the Chilean miners were rescued a few years ago."

Cora gives me a friendly shove. "Your enthusiasm abounds, Daniel. Sean, be careful hanging out with him. Daniel is very opinionated and argues a lot to prove he's right."

"I don't argue, I simply inform," I say, grinning.

Usually we decide things about class projects, talk with community people about different topics, learn about college options, and lots of other things in first period, but today it's just about saying hello to people we haven't seen since last spring.

End of first period we walk to our morning block room; Sean splits off with Jake, who has the same English/social studies class he does, and Cora and I walk together to our class.

Entering the room with Cora, I survey the space to see who's in the class. People tell me I always look confident in public settings, but anyone who is really aware, like Cora, knows my self-assured style is only surface deep. In the business world, where I'm headed, projecting confidence is important for success. It's also important to have someone like Cora around; she kindly points out the cracks in my armor so I can learn to patch them.

I've been in classes in previous years with eight of these forty students. Since we spend two hours a day, all year, together, it's nice to have new people to get to know in-depth. Part of what we've learned via the openness creed is that everyone is interesting down deep, and it is worth taking the risk to really get to know people. I try, but it doesn't come easily to me.

After a few minutes of informal circulating, the team of four teachers asks us to sit in a circle. The teachers, who are spread around the circle, introduce themselves first, and then explain that we will explore US history and literature for this block.

The social studies teacher starts a discussion by posing the question, "What, to you, is a particularly fascinating time from US history? Everyone think about it for a few minutes and then we'll share interests. You don't need to know anything in particular about that time, just be curious and maybe have an open-ended question in mind."

If I've learned anything at this school, it's that all learning starts with curiosity and questions, not already formed answers. The teachers always give us time to reflect and think for ourselves before sharing our thoughts. Plus, you can pass in the discussion if you want to without having to justify yourself. But the more experience we get with this approach, where there are no put-downs, the rarer passing becomes.

The first student to share talks about a family trip to New Mexico, visiting an Anasazi site.

What's an Anasazi?? Strange word to me.

As if she's read my mind, the social studies teacher goes to a flip chart, not interrupting, and writes the word. Another teacher asks the student to tell us what she wonders about these earliest Americans.

"I wonder if they were happy. Or if life was too much of a struggle," the student says.

Other students, having been out of school all summer, and

it being this early in a class, are a little shy to jump right in with a response. This will change quickly as we all get to a comfort zone with each other and are encouraged by the lack of judgments from adults in the room.

"I have also visited Chaco Canyon, the historical center of Anasazi," the technology teacher chimes in. "And I went to some of the Pueblo villages where descendants of the Anasazi live today. I look forward to talking with you about our experiences."

Next, Cora says she is interested in the time of slavery in the US, "for obvious reasons."

"What are the obvious reasons?" someone asks.

"Those times in part define who I am," she says. "But only in part."

She chooses not to elaborate, so all eyes move to me.

"I'm interested in the Industrial Revolution," I say.

"Would you tell us more about your interest?" the English teacher asks with a smile.

"I think it was a very exciting time, all those new inventions so people didn't have to work as hard."

"Do you think of yourself as an inventor?" This question is from a student I know from last year.

"No, I'm not too interested in science. More the business end of things, learning how the big tycoons of the day became such a success." I wonder if the teachers remember what each person says. I sure can't. I focus on trying to remember names of people I don't know. People like that, when you remember their name. Then they won't get offended when I ask them to remind me what "interest" they talked about.

When everyone in the circle, including teachers, has had a chance to share an interest, we are asked to get up and circulate, seeking out people we want to talk with about their interest. Teachers join in too, modeling how to focus on listening and sharing honestly, no phony nicey-nice stuff.

As the discussion energy wanes, we are asked to come back to the circle. Many of us sit in a new place, now that everyone has shared something personal and conversation seems easier.

The English teacher tells us we will have lots of opportunity during the year to follow up on our interests through reading at least one book, short story, or article of our choice each week.

"Tomorrow we will meet with the Junior Librarian, who has been following you folks since ninth grade. You can update her, individually, on your interests, and she may already have some book suggestions based on knowing you and what you have read in the past two years. Talking with her now will allow her to order new books she thinks you might enjoy." She looks around the room, making eye contact with as many people as possible. "Another aspect of communication is writing. Your assignment for the rest of class today, to be completed before class tomorrow, is to write a minimum of two pages on a topic we all have in common—what school means to you, or, stated another way, what you want from your school experience. Okay, find a space at the computer desks, tables, or chairs to write and get going so you have no homework tonight."

Most of us complete these types of assignments in school. Our only homework, usually, is reading books we have selected or doing research for projects we have chosen to work on. So both are things based on what I care about, not drudgery. And I can pick the times during the week when I want to work on these. If I didn't have those assignments, I'd probably be bored. I can only do so much schmoozing in the park after school. Of course, if I get a job then my spare time will be filled up with that.

Our classroom environments are chill; we can talk with other students while we work, not like Sean's description of Hilltop, where they aren't allowed to talk in classes and are desperate for time to hang with friends. He says kids there mainly interact at night through social media. Pathetic, I think, compared to being able to talk with a friend in person. I don't always agree with all the teaching methods here at Stone Creek, but I'll take this over Hilltop any day.

✧ ✧ ✧

Our school newspaper was named many years ago, when adults working here were apparently pretty disconnected from youth culture. Students then voted to call it *Stoners Report,* supposedly a reference to the school name, when really it was a joke about students smoking weed.

At today's club meeting, we decide while eating lunch who will do what for the end-of-September edition. I volunteer to cover the first Chautauqua event, specifically the book club discussion Cora is facilitating. Chautauquas are held monthly for our whole community. The name comes from Native Americans and then a town in New York in the early 1900s where people shared things like concerts, recreation, lectures, and discussions of the day.

One of the student editors tells me I also need to be available to do things that come up at the last minute. This kind of structure of being told what to do isn't typical of Stone Creek clubs, and I'm not a fan. I'll have to see how all this goes; maybe I won't end up wanting to be part of the newspaper group after all.

When I arrive at Spanish class in the afternoon, I greet Sean at the door. He went to the Future Farmers of America meeting with Jake last period to check it out, and I can't help but tease him about it a little.

"What's up, Farmer Sean?" I say, grinning, as we walk into class.

"The FFA people were really nice and they know a lot about the county and what goes on here," he says. "I told them about some of my bike rides. They knew all the people I had met."

The Spanish teacher starts speaking a mile a minute, in Spanish, telling us to gather round the tables. I head to one of the tables and motion for Sean to follow.

Sean looks sick. "Are you kidding me? What is she saying?"

"Don't worry," I say, "you'll get the hang of it. Let me explain the routine. Half the hour is speaking with the teacher or other native speakers from the community and the colleges, many of them students. The other thirty minutes is computer work with language lessons or watching things like videos in Spanish. I can show you some cool videos I watched last year that might help you catch up with where we are. You'll be amazed how quickly you pick it up. Besides, we can practice during soccer."

The class flies by, and soon we're on our way to our math/science block.

"How did English/social studies block go this morning?" I ask as we walk to class.

"Great. We got to talk a lot. I had a ten-minute conversation with this really cute girl, and it didn't seem awkward or forced or like I had to pretend to be somebody I'm not. People at this school seem so real, not fake. They're interesting, thinking about things in ways that never occur to me. And did I mention she was really cute?"

I laugh. "I got it, Sean. You can use our next class to figure out what chemical reactions happen when a boy is attracted to a girl!"

The classroom we're in for this block has seminar-style seating for forty students, with an adjacent lab room that we share with another science class. I recognize the technology teacher from a ninth grade computer elective class I took during last period that year. The other three teachers, sitting at one end of the seminar table, introduce themselves with their specialty: chemistry, calculus, and special needs.

The chemistry teacher announces that students will introduce themselves this period through a "Stump the Experts" game created by the four teachers. It goes like this: A student will state an interest that is significant for them. Then the teachers will relate that student interest to the discipline of chemistry.

"See, Sean, I got you all prepared to share your interest!" I say, jabbing him with my elbow.

Sean flushes. "Knock it off."

"Is anyone new this year at Stone Creek High, so not familiar with the 'interests' approach?" the chemistry teacher asks.

I find it funny to see Sean squirming like I do in unfamiliar settings. I point toward him before he has a chance to raise his hand. A girl also raises her hand.

"Change is our school-wide theme for this quarter," the

teacher says. "We will all help the two of you to quickly grasp our project-based learning approach for understanding. No memorization or repetitive practice of formula implementations." Moving toward Sean, the teacher continues, "I am a scientist. That means I have been trained in the scientific method. Thus, I am required to be a keen observer. I see you are wearing a surfing T-shirt. Is that a significant interest of yours?"

"Yes, ma'am," he says.

Sean's formality is *really* funny, but I can't laugh. He's already so nervous it looks like he might puke at any moment. Only a few quiet snickers escape my hand, which I'm using to cover my mouth.

"I hear your use of the local southern form of address to those in authority," she says. "It's fine with me if you prefer to leave off the 'ma'am.' Would you mind kicking off our game by being the first player?"

"I'm not feeling too confident about this," Sean says, so pale you wouldn't be able to see him if it weren't for the freckles on his face.

"As long as you have a sincere interest in surfing, you'll do fine," she says. "Okay?"

"Okay."

I try to give him a reassuring look, but he's not having anything more to do with me.

"Thank you. So, what is your name?"

"Sean."

"Sean, have you actually surfed before, or is this an imagined interest?"

"I surfed from age eight to fifteen, when I lived in San Diego."

"You have many years of practical experience. Great. And has your surfing led to a particular affinity for the ocean?"

"Definitely."

"So you have a feeling for the character of the ocean, its nature. That connection is important to you as an individual, but also important to all of us because the oceans support the greatest abundance of life on earth. The general chemical makeup of the sea, as you probably already know, is water and salts. The eleven salts are listed in the periodic table posted on the wall over there.

How the ocean's chemicals interact illustrate significant concepts and principles of chemistry. So, I think it is fair to say chemistry can further develop one of your interests."

She turns to the other teachers. "Someone else?"

Sean looks at me like, *Are you kidding me? More!?*

I try to think what Cora would say. She calms me down all the time. Too late . . .

"Many people are concerned with the growing imbalance in the ocean's chemistry related to fossil fuels and global warming," the calculus teacher says. "Mathematicians working for NOAA, National Oceanic and Atmospheric Administration, are using calculus to develop ways to measure ocean contamination."

"If you wear a wetsuit," says the special needs teacher, "it is probably made of a fossil fuel–based rubber and, thus, not biodegradable."

"I just read recently that Patagonia has been instrumental in the development of a wetsuit made from a biodegradable natural rubber, derived from a desert shrub," the technology teacher adds.

The chemistry teacher looks at Sean. "You be the judge. Have we satisfactorily demonstrated that your interest involves chemistry and calculus?"

"You have," he says, blushing. "Does that mean I'm more likely to be successful in this class?"

Everyone laughs.

"Good one," I say.

"Absolutely," the teacher says. "If you start to lose a sense of passion, talk to one of us. Okay, let's move along to the next person . . ."

"Sorry," I say to Sean in a quiet voice. "I got a little carried away at the beginning. Guess I was nervous watching you be nervous. But you were great, and I actually found the whole ocean chemistry discussion pretty interesting myself."

All of the teachers at Stone Creek use a project approach to learning, based on student interests. So I am used to this kind of demonstration. But Sean is blown away, and he hangs on every word said by teachers and students during the rest of the demonstrations.

The pace picks up and class goes on, the teachers making sure they get around to everyone, so it isn't boring. These two-hour blocks give us time to kind of relax and settle in. And the teachers are getting better at planning fast-paced activities that don't drag. When introductions by interest are completed, the math teacher distributes a handout describing a project for us to complete using calculus in a work situation we select. He and the other teachers will help us go through the process step by step. At the end, we will share our results, drawing out key concepts of how calculus works.

The project choices include: an architectural engineer designing a sports stadium; a medical researcher; designing a mountain road race route; business manager for a credit card company; graphic artist for a new video game; a physicist designing an SUV; or any other interest we declare.

Sean selects the architecture project and I pick the business manager one. We begin working on Step 1, using details provided in the handout to write a narrative of what measures are needed for the task ahead of us and why.

After class, Sean hands me a piece of saltwater taffy.

"Man, these teachers are working hard," he says. "In my old schools, they just told us to read pages whatever in the textbook and answer the questions at the end. I'm going to have to get more sleep if I have to do all this thinking."

"Lighten up, Sean. You're gonna do fine at this school. Trust me. Besides, it's playtime: soccer!"

We head outside to the soccer field. The soccer teacher, who the rest of the day is an English teacher, tells us our main agenda for the day will be to form the teams we'll play on for the rest of the semester.

I propose the language groups idea first thing. "It will give us language practice while we play," I say.

The teacher looks surprised. "That's very different from last year's emphasis on diversity of skill levels and social backgrounds in forming teams."

"Well, Chief did announce this morning that this quarter's theme is 'Change.' So how about we try something different?"

Other students don't seem to care much about how to form teams, but they do feel strongly about this being our time to play, and that students should be in charge of making decisions. After only a little more than a year since the shift to students being in control of learning at Stone Creek, it has become the bedrock of what we care about, because we've seen what a difference it makes when our teachers treat us with dignity, expecting us to take responsibility for our lives. The other soccer students begin speaking up in favor of my approach.

"Okay, Daniel, we can try your idea," the teacher says. "Let's agree to reassess in a few weeks and decide whether this idea is as good, or better, than the previous team formation process based on diversity."

The result is three Spanish-speaking teams, three English (Brits, Aussies, and US), one French, and one German. A smattering of students from other backgrounds—Chinese, Vietnamese, Indian, Sierra Leone, and Guinea—randomly join the eight teams. One of the Spanish teams is primarily Mexican-American students, with a few other students originally from Guatemala, Honduras, and Nicaragua. Another Spanish team is about two-thirds African-American students. The third Spanish team, the one I end up on, is all white natives.

I'm loving how all this is coming together so easily. But Sean hangs back, not participating in the process. "This doesn't feel right," I hear him mutter.

After school I go straight to the town newspaper office to see about the status of my application.

Several women are working behind the front counter of the office, but only one looks up at me.

I greet her in my cheeriest voice. "Good afternoon. What a beautiful day out."

No response.

I try a different tack. "I've never seen roses this color. Did you grow them?"

"No." The stare continues.

"I'm following up on an application I submitted two weeks ago." She has me so flustered, the last three words turn into a question.

"Name?" she mumbles.

I'm used to people talking down to me because of my age, but this is downright rude.

I give her my information, and she replies she will let the Human Resources Manager know. Without an invitation to do so, I sit in a chair near the door.

After what seems hours, checking the clock to see that a minute has passed, I am sweating, my hands twitching, and the dizziness is starting. From experience I know the difficulty breathing will start soon. I also know attempts to control these reactions will fail. It is just a matter of time before I have to bolt from the threat. If people who refer to me as confident, sometimes with the "over" modifier, could see me now, they would see my fear of being judged by people who have power over my life. Then again, they probably wouldn't see anything; I've become pretty good at hiding my panic reactions.

I researched all this on the Internet and learned that anxiety is quite common among teenagers. Makes sense, with all the stress we're under to make something of ourselves. I'm hoping it is just a temporary phase I'll grow out of when I have more freedom to direct my life. I hear Chief in my head, saying, "Use your freedom now, make decisions, and learn from them."

A woman older than God's dog comes out. No hello, no handshake, no "come back to my office." She looks at my application—not at me. I wonder if she even read it before this moment.

I take the initiative. "I'm hoping to work after school and weekends—"

"Do you have any newspaper experience?" she snaps.

"I'm working on my school newspaper staff."

"How long have you done that?"

"This is my first year. I will be responsible for interviewing—"

"We don't need you right now," she says, finally looking at me, "but you can check back with us this summer."

I bolt. Away from the injustice of what just happened, toward a spot that allows me to wallow in my worry. I follow Crooked Creek, a stream that meanders through town, to where it runs into Highland River, headed east and ultimately to the sea, hundreds of miles away. Where creek meets river there's a small cliff overlook, invisible to even purposeful observation.

I've never seen anyone here at my private spot, never even heard anyone nearby. This is my go-to place in times of extreme stress; here, I don't have to do anything, meet any expectations, I can just listen to the sounds of nature and hope the worry will subside. I hear the constancy of water moving, sliding along rocks and dropping effortlessly, leaving smooth surfaces, revealing order and comfort. I listen for barely perceptible punctuation of the movement, rhythms of more or less. My mind becomes tuned to the movement . . .

"Hey, kid, what are you doing in my spot?" a serious, deep voice booms out.

Mega-startled, I jump up and turn in the direction of the voice. I know this guy . . . from where? *Is it . . . ?* He is dressed so different, but it's my weed dealer. I think. Am I dreaming?

"What are you doing here?" I ask.

He cracks up. "Relax, I'm just kidding with you. I discovered this spot a few weeks ago. It's pretty special. I was looking for a new place to meet customers. The place where I saw you last has gotten unsettling. You come here often?"

"Sometimes." I gesture to his clothes. "You look out of place here in the woods in business dress."

I was introduced to this guy over the summer and made a couple of purchases from him. He appears to be college age. Not dressed in the usual style of feigned coolness characteristic of wealthy students—T-shirt broadcasting a fraternity logo, designer flip-flops, immaculate haircut grown out until parents' weekend, no shave since last Friday night. This guy's haircut and shave are definitely from this morning, linen shirt and creased slacks straight from the dry cleaner, finished off with a classy looking leather belt and shoes that I'm pretty sure are Italian.

"Yeah, I should definitely scale down, like running shoes and sweats so that brambles don't matter," he says. He studies me for a moment. "You look pretty upset." His tone is one of genuine concern. And confidence. He didn't ask how I'm feeling, he stated it.

"Yeah, my plans to make money for college just came crashing down," I say.

"I can relate. I had to finance my ticket to success. I learned early, high school age like you, that I had to rely on myself, create my own small business rather than rely on others."

"I don't see me starting a business—I have no capital, only small cash reserves." I try to sound businesslike, rather than like a green teenager.

"It doesn't take a lot of money if the demand is strong."

"Are you an economics major?" I say to test his credentials.

He laughs again, confidence seeping from him. "No, I'm a second-year law student. I learned what I know about managing a business from experience—over six years now. Starting in high school, I was able to finance my undergraduate degree, along with a little help from grants and scholarships. Now I'm in the most prestigious law school in the South, and the goal is to finish in the top 5 percent of my class. Not bad for a boy from inner-city Chicago."

So, add smart to confident and independent. Wouldn't I love to be in his shoes.

"What's your secret?" I ask.

"Provide a high-demand product in a professional manner. College students are away from home and away from their suppliers, so they are desperate for a discreet, reliable seller. And here you've got a perfect storm: large numbers of users from two colleges, a small town with limited options, and a state where weed is not yet legal but will be soon. People don't see it as a crime anymore."

"I'm glad it will be legal soon. It really helps me deal with stress."

"That's a big reason—stress relief—for the large demand among young people."

"But I'm afraid of getting caught." I think how that would really sever any hope of my stepfather, the lawyer, agreeing to pay for my college. "Aren't the college students taking a big risk using weed? What if they got caught?"

"For many of them, alcohol is illegal too," he says with a shrug. "It's convenient for the colleges to look the other way for tuition-paying students, not like with high school students. By agreement, the county police stay off the university grounds. The county police don't want any more problems than they already have. And the campus cops look the other way as long as things aren't out in the open. You know, we are on campus grounds right now. We're just not out in the open."

He tells me there is another way back to civilization, not the way I came, and I should leave that way so customers who are due here soon don't see me. He describes where to go—around the next rock outcrop, down the hill, following a line of old cedar trees surrounded by new-growth woods. It feels like he is dismissing me from class. I kind of respect his take-charge approach, and the fact that he's being straight with me about what he's doing, so I don't really mind him telling me what to do. Anyway, the sun is down to almost dinnertime level.

"Keep in touch," he says, all respectful-like, as I head off to explore the new path. It is a path definitely not suited for flip-flops; I'm glad I have on my already scratched up sneakers, not the brand new Nikes Mom bought me for the first day of school. It's weird, but sometimes it takes me months before I feel comfortable wearing new clothes.

I can't figure out where this path is going to come out. It's only when I step out of the trees that I realize I'm right behind the law school. My stepfather's first-floor office is easily in view.

Don't think I'll drop in.

✧   ✧   ✧

Mom greets me with a big hug when I get home. Her hug dissolves much of the remnants of my anxiety. I tell her about the town newspaper rejecting me. She says I'll get plenty of newspaper experience working on the school newspaper, and I can try again next summer.

"But I want to save money for college," I say, and it's almost a whine. My guard comes down only with Mom.

"Daniel, we have plenty of money to do whatever we want now, not like the old days."

"*We* don't have plenty of money. *He* does." I keep my tone neutral. The idea of being in conflict with Mom, the one person I totally rely on, makes me very uncomfortable.

"Honestly, can't you two call a truce?"

"Talk to my stepfather, not me."

This discussion topic goes back four years, to when they got married. He has never really cared for me, and vice-versa.

My real father left when I was three. I still think about falling asleep nestled in his lap. Mom worked the night shift at the hospital at the time, and would put me to bed right before she left—but I would stay awake, waiting for my father to come get me for storytelling on the sofa. Only at this time of night would he turn off the TV and put aside his Jack Daniels. (My mom says that is NOT where I got my name.) He did not read from a book; instead, he told me his own stories, looking into my eyes and holding me tight. I can remember the stories always involved a plane, what you could see happening on the ground. His quiet voice, full of sadness, seemed to never stop.

Other memories from that time are not so good. Like when he would drink during the day, often, and he and Mom would end up screaming at each other.

When Mom got home after the night shift, she would have breakfast with me and then walk me to my preschool so she could sleep during the day. I hated her leaving me again so soon. One day I threw a tantrum at preschool, literally throwing things, and saying unintelligibly, through missing teeth, "Don't want new clothes." Mom used to say she had to go to work so she could buy me things like new clothes. I just wanted her. But we didn't have enough money to live without her working. My father couldn't keep a job.

And then he left. I worry all the time that I'm the one who caused my father to leave.

After he left, Mom still had to work, so I slept—not well—at the next-door neighbor's. I couldn't be with Mom because of money. I couldn't be with my father because he couldn't make money. I couldn't sleep because nobody was there to hold me. Still can't. The nightmares of them screaming continue into the present, relived endlessly.

Now, my stepfather screams at me for one minor infraction after another, but never in front of Mom. After his raging events, his calm exaggerations and lies to her about what I did bear little resemblance to reality. It seems he wants me out of the picture and is doing his best to undermine Mom's unconditional love for me. When I try to explain to her what is happening, she thinks I am the irrational one. She never sees him lose it. What she does see is him being such a good provider. Money trumps everything again.

Dinnertime tonight is, as it always is, a strain of silence, the only sound in the room the ice hitting the sides of my stepfather's many glasses of vodka Collins for most of the meal.

My mom asks about my first day back at school and I share highlights. She beams with pride. I conclude with my triumph in the new system of forming soccer teams.

My stepfather says, "But you don't even know how to play soccer very well."

"I used to play on the community teams when I was younger," I say.

"You mean at the age when all the little kids just chase after the ball and don't even know how to play positions?" He's starting to slur his words badly—"just" sounds like "zhust," and positions sounds like "pozishuns."

I look at Mom. "Daniel will learn to play better by taking the class," she says.

"Have you ever made a goal? In your whole life? Can you run fast enough to keep up with the other guys? You're not tall enough to get headers, so what position could you play?"

The slurring is so bad now it's hard to even translate what he's saying. I don't respond.

"I asked you a question . . . many questions! Answer for yourself. What have you got to contribute to a soccer team, for Christ's sake?"

"Leave me alone!" I shout. I get up from the table and take my dishes to the kitchen.

Mom follows. "He's had a bad day, Daniel. Don't take it personally."

She has an appointment to pick up one of her paintings that's been hanging, unsold, in a small gallery downtown for a month. Her leaving is a signal for me to retreat to my room.

I thought my stepfather was already asleep in his La-Z-Boy recliner. I was wrong. He follows me upstairs and enters my room. He has never come in my room before—my safety space. He stands near the door, blocking my exit. I'm trapped.

The look on his face shouts disgust. I have done nothing, so the disgust must come from inside him. I've learned from previous episodes like this one not to say anything. If I'm quiet, not calling attention to myself, maybe he will leave.

Not this time.

"Why didn't you answer me when I asked about soccer?" He screams this so loud I think, embarrassed, the neighbors might hear. "You treat me like a freak in front of your mother. But you're really just a sniveling little pussy when it's just you and me."

He has never actually hit me—yet. But I know things are headed that way, since his physical intimidation is escalating. He pushes me down into my desk chair and stands there towering over me, bringing his face closer and closer, his expression turning darker and more evil with each insult he spits at me. "Weasel . . . girl weasel . . . think you know it all . . . let me tell you, she doesn't even like you—she thinks you're a sniveling trouble maker." His voice is increasingly harsh and loud. "Somebody has to teach you a lesson. I'm going to forget to give you your allowance for a while. You say anything to her and I'll make things worse, I swear. You could trip, fall down the stairs. Just an accident—"

"Stop it!"

My stepfather turns, and we both see Mom in the doorway. She's trembling as she approaches me; her eyes are fixed on him.

"Leave Daniel's room right now," she says.

My stepfather leaves without a word.

When he's gone, she starts crying. "Daniel, I'm so sorry for not believing you about him in the past. What if I hadn't forgotten my car keys?"

We hear him slam the door on his way out.

I can't sleep tonight, as usual. This time anxiety focuses me on listening for his car, or the house front door unlocking, or the opening of the liquor cabinet. All I hear is my obsessive thought, *What have I done?*

Mom will be penniless again. And alone when I go off to college. I'm afraid for the changes I have caused.

I should be glad his terrorizing me is out in the open. Looking at things logically, he has confirmed my conclusions about him. I should not doubt myself anymore.

Instead, I feel guilty. First I chase away my real father with all my crying. Then, even when I try to stay quiet, invisible, I can't get the second guy to like me, or to stay.

He stormed out the door just now, but the fear remains. He'll be back. Then what?

I wake to screaming, this time my alarm. I only got forty-five minutes of real sleep. It feels like cotton's stuffed in the space where my brain is supposed to be. A shower doesn't help much.

I hear Mom on the phone: "You can be here in thirty minutes to change all the locks? I'll see you then."

Good! I should have thought of that. She is stronger than me in all ways.

Next call, she leaves a message for an attorney: "I really need to meet with you today. The situation is urgent. Please return my call as soon as possible."

How will I ever make this up to her?

When I come into the kitchen, she puts her arm around my shoulders, pulls me to her, and says, "We'll be okay, Daniel. Nobody can come between us. I'll make things up to you."

I'm so choked up I can't say anything. I leave the house as soon as possible. I walk rather than ride my bike so I have space to think. Mom's right, nobody could come between us. But she's wrong about who needs to make it up to whom. I'm the one at fault. Why couldn't I just humor him, for Mom's sake?

He hated me so bad, humoring him would not have worked. He would have found a reason to not pay for me to go to college. I knew that on one level, but wanted to believe there was a realistic chance of me affording to go. That's probably where all this was leading. He was trying to push me out of the house or into exploding so he could justify not supporting me or my dream.

But at least Mom could have gone on with her life. Her painting is just starting to take off. *What have I done?*

Chapter 6: Success?

Once upon a time, I met a great challenge. With all the daring of youth, I searched for triumph over doom.

DANIEL

I don't even remember that I was supposed to hang out with Sean later in the afternoon yesterday until I see him this morning.

"Hey, Daniel," he says, "everything okay? You never showed up at the park yesterday."

Whoops. "Oh. Hey. I went to the newspaper office to check on, eh, my job application. Then . . . and then I was bummed because I didn't get the job."

"Hey, sorry, man."

"Yeah, I'm pretty depressed."

There's my script for the day. I won't have to do any more explaining.

Wrong. In morning block, each of us is asked to share a sentence or two from yesterday's writing on what school means to me, what I want from my school experience. In a small group, which includes Cora, I read a passage about the necessity of attending a reputable college and meeting people there who can assist me in launching a successful business career.

The girl right next to me asks, "What kind of business do you want to be in?"

"I'm open, as long as it is highly competitive, successful." I project a vibe of conviction.

A dude I recognize from Spanish asks, "What do you enjoy in school now?"

When I hesitate, Cora says, "You're on the journalism staff. Is that something you're considering as a career?"

"I'm not thinking of journalism as a career because it doesn't pay enough," I say, a little annoyed by the questions. Cora knows I'm committed to a business career. Why did she ask? "I like journalism now because I like listening to stories. I like to see what makes people tick. But a career choice is something different."

The teacher in the group says, "Your writing, Daniel, raises an important distinction many people make about whether any activity is an end in itself or a means to an end. Work can be an end. Like, work as a fulfilling way for someone to express themselves, or be with others, or contribute to a community. Along those lines, we can ask ourselves if school is an end in itself of growing in many different ways. Or is school only a means to a later end—college, a specific career? Also, which is money, an end or a means?" She lets the questions hang in the air for a moment, then says, "I hope y'all keep in mind how successful our counselors are in finding money for students to attend college. And for the record, I personally know many non-wealthy people who are anything but ordinary and very happy in their life."

I want to continue the discussion, to argue that money controls everything, but I don't trust my current emotional state.

I don't have to sit with my rocky self for long before we leave for a scheduled meeting with the librarian. As we leave the classroom, Cora says, "I think you have a lot to say, and journalism is going to be a way for you to have a voice."

I'll get paid a lot more for my thoughts in business!

✦ ✦ ✦

There's no newspaper meeting today, so I hang out in the cafeteria, text my mom, and wait. No response. She must be meeting with the lawyer. When the bell rings, I put my phone away with a sigh and head to science/math block.

We are working on the calculus project today. I try to work on mine, but I can't concentrate. Ten minutes into class, I flag down the technology teacher.

"I'm going to the cafeteria to call home," I tell her.

She nods. "Okay, see you back here after."

That's the policy. We don't have to ask permission to leave. It is to our advantage to stay in class, where there is assistance from teachers when we need it, to do our work rather than bringing it home and doing it alone. But we're under no obligation to use that advantage. Of course, if someone was leaving the classroom all the time, a conference with a counselor, and maybe a parent, would be scheduled. Phones are to be used only in the cafeteria—or, in the case of teachers, in the teacher's workroom.

Walking to the cafeteria, I remember my first year here, when students raised a big concern over past instances of being spied upon by security cameras in the hallways. Staff said the cameras had been installed for security and worries about an outside intruder. Students then did extensive research on the history of school shootings and found out that almost all had been shootings by current students, not outsiders. There was still a need for security from random outsiders, but the number of those happenings was quite low. The whole debate turned into a school service project assigned to the senior class at that time. Their job was to make a recommendation to a group of administrators, teachers, parents, and community members after reviewing all the information.

The seniors' recommendation was approved without revisions. The security cameras were moved to outside entrances, with constant monitoring of those cameras. Concern about internal security, which had originated from a student, was addressed in ways experience showed would be more effective than security cameras: Training for students and staff to show that speaking up about concerns prevents school shootings and gets help for those who need it. Establishing an effective system of referring students to high-quality mental health services. Setting up a Conflict Resolution Council to deal with problems in the school before they become major. The first two things were done right away. The last step, the Conflict Resolution Council, is scheduled to begin this quarter, with students as the majority of members.

I call Mom the second I get to the cafeteria, and she answers on the first ring.

"Daniel, I'm so glad you called. I've been worrying about you. You have to know this whole situation is not your fault, or mine. I promise to quit thinking of you as my little boy . . . and listen to you better. We're a team, right?"

"Yes. Thanks, Mom."

"Our attorney is already in gear for the challenge of opposing your stepfather. The fact that he's a high-powered member of the law school faculty means it won't be easy, but things are going to be okay, Daniel. You should relax and throw yourself into a new school year."

I trust Mom totally, but the anxiety that engulfs me today won't allow for relaxation. Mom's attorney may be able to get her financial support for day-to-day life, but no way would my creepy stepfather agree to pay for my college. And I can't believe my counselor here can pull off me getting enough money to attend the kind of high-quality business school I want to go to. Bottom line, I can't dump my worries about college money on Mom, when she has more immediate problems to get through.

Mom doesn't expect me home right after school, since I usually stop off at the student park gathering. Today, I need alone time for thinking, and walking works best for me. The familiarity of this small town is comforting, allowing me to focus inward. I wouldn't call it "thinking" as much as "obsessing," going over the same ground and beliefs over and over.

Stumbling on a fallen branch causes me to come to. I'm again following Crooked Creek up to the secluded cliff overlook. I look for signs of foot traffic and the weed dealer. Not seeing him, I sit at my spot, not relaxing but waiting for him to find me. He does.

"You look worse than yesterday."

"Yeah, I am." I take a deep breath. "And I need a job."

"I was worried you might blow my cover and new location. But then, I seem to be the least of your concerns."

Today, he has lost the Italian shoes and other upscale dress, and looks the part for the terrain.

Rising to the challenge I've been planning out, I say, "I'm hoping we can help each other. I can expand your customer base, find a lot of high school students who—"

"No, that's too risky," he says.

I wasn't expecting that comeback. My central bargaining chip tossed away, I begin to rack my brain for another idea . . .

"And, it's not necessary," he says. "I have more customers now than I can deal with. All the college students are back for fall term. But I could use some help."

Yes! "I really need money," I blurt out, unable to contain my passion.

Looking serious, he says, "That's not a great skills appeal to a potential employer. And in this job, desperation can encourage stupid mistakes. If you can't think on your feet, we could get into trouble."

He said "we."

"I need to be able to trust you," he says.

I launch into my confident persona, good posture, strong voice, penetrative eye contact. "I know about trust. I just got my whole world turned upside down because someone didn't trust me. What do I have to do to prove myself to you?"

"Well, that's a start. I like straightforward; seems honest."

A long interlude doesn't jar me from my game. I learned last spring in negotiation training for Model UN that you can't push people. You have to give them room to feel your sincerity, integrity.

He ends the long pause with, "Okay, we'll start slow and see how it goes."

Has he missed the boiling blood streaming through me? Or is he so confident that he thinks he can teach me to control the panic?

I don't have much time to ponder that, because Godfather, as I'm now calling him—he grew up in Chicago, and yesterday's outfit fit the bill—begins my job training right away, going over prices, quantity, what to say/not say, and record keeping. All transactions entered electronically, equipment supplied by him. Salary will be based on commission, but under no circumstances am I to engage in drumming up business. That's too risky; he will handle marketing. To start, he will mentor me, and later transition responsibility to me for completing the transaction. A few weeks of joint (pun) distribution should reach most of the current customers and ease me into their confidence. Final training is how to pick up on clues of surveillance and what to do in an emergency. Critical to the latter is the escape route, which nobody else seems to know about, ending at the back of the law school.

I'm impressed by his clear thinking and solid plan.

I make it home in time for dinner, expecting a quiet night in, but when I get there Mom says we're going to Sean's house for dinner. She ran into his mom today and ended up telling her what was going on. "Sean's mother was so understanding and supportive when we talked," she says. "It's good to develop friendships with people who aren't friends of your former stepfather."

I like the way that "former" sounds.

When we arrive at Sean's house, it is obvious he has been told what is up with the former stepfather. We walk out back to the creek.

"You know," he says, "you can count on me if you ever need anything. I mean it—anything."

I don't know how to respond to that statement. In my Mr. Mayor persona, I have lots of people who joke around and swap stories with me. But I have never had what you could say is a close friend. Nobody I believed I could count on. Cora is starting to break through to my real core, but it has more to do with what she is all about, not that I have developed any trust in myself to be out there. And I definitely pick up these vibes from her that she worries about me sometimes, which is uncomfortable for me and makes me want to bolt.

All I can think of to say is, "I'm okay, Sean. It's my mom I'm worried about. I hope your mom will stay in contact with her."

Dinner is quite lively, with Sarah relieving any lingering tension through stories of her preschool escapades. It is her second year there, and she seems to be thriving. Today's highlight was a field trip hike to the top of Black Bear Mountain, starting about three-quarters of the way up, from a public parking area. Halfway through the hike, one kid starts jumping all around, saying he sees a bear. Other kids scream and run to the teachers. Sarah says she stayed put and calm and saw a bald eagle, a "real" one.

I have vague memories of when the world did not seem like such a threat. Those memories slip away more each day.

Mom asks Sean how Stone Creek is different from the Hilltop.

"In a word, totally," he says. "Hilltop was like a fish tank—and we were the fish, kept apart from the real world of natural waters, glubbing around in circles, until we almost believed it was normal. But at Stone Creek"—Sean's voice gets lighter now—"people are enthusiastic, look you in the eye, move with a sense of purpose, and yet are patient, willing to stick with something until they figure it out. Helpful to new people like me. No shrill bells! Everybody can tell time and get themselves to where they need to be. In the classroom, people use normal speaking voices, not overly inflating them or whispering secrets. There are quiet areas for people who want that to concentrate. And iPods are allowed for people who concentrate better with music. I'm treated like an individual, like I matter."

"From Sean's descriptions of what goes on at Stone Creek," his mom says, "it sounds like the students are more mature than I would expect from teenagers."

Today in morning block we wrap up our review of US literature and history resources in the library, choosing what book we want to read in our area of interest.

The technology teacher helped me with Google searches in my area, industrialization. First, I focused in on the big tycoons—Carnegie in steel, Rockefeller in oil, Gould in railroads, and the banking guy, Morgan. There seems to still be controversy about whether they were good guys or bad guys. There's no doubt, though, about their wealth. Then I read snatches about Henry Ford, the assembly line, and updated teamwork approaches coming from the Japanese auto companies. That kind of related to the topic of theories of management.

Apparently, the most famous writing on the impact of industrialization on the average person is Upton Sinclair's *The Jungle*. But that sounded pretty gross to me, meat-packing warehouses in Chicago. It would be interesting to learn about the impact investigative journalism can have; honestly, though, the "good life" of the wealthy is more intriguing to me. So I've decided to plunge into an account of the lifestyle of the rich and famous, the payoff from hard work—I'm going to read *The Great Gatsby*, by F. Scott Fitzgerald. The librarian says it is a good choice, and she's excited to talk with me about it when I'm done.

Back in the classroom, the English teacher tells us our report on the reading we selected is to be written in the form of a short tale. "You know, 'Once upon a time,'" she says. "The major decision for you is when your tale begins and when it ends. Thinking in terms of a tale will help you look at events from a big-picture perspective and lead you toward a 'point.' Spend some time reading your source, or sources, before formulating a focus. You will be reading on your own in class for part of several days. Your written tale is due a week from today."

An arts teacher who specializes in drama agrees to come to our class to do a dramatic reading of the Gettysburg Address. It's only 272 powerful words long. I time her. It takes two minutes and three seconds to deliver the most famous speech in US history.

The history teacher then takes the lead, asking the question, "If iPads had existed when Abraham Lincoln was alive, how would things have been different for him and for our country, then and now?" We are asked to write a paragraph response.

I usually have an answer for these kinds of questions within two seconds, a lame one, but I'm trying to learn to slow down and take time to think. Today, my mind flicks around to other things, making it hard to come up with something good.

The group discussion is interesting, with lots of original ideas. We discuss big-picture concepts like change, perception of time, and key social institutions in society. The main conclusion we reach is that technology has brought many changes to our lives, but it has not substantially changed the character of the way we work, go to school, live in families, and govern ourselves. Like, we still work as many hours now as we did fifty years ago, even though technology has majorly increased productivity.

Starting to read *The Great Gatsby* relaxes me, I guess because it allows me to focus on something other than my jumbled personal life. 'Focus' is one of the main skills I work on at Stone Creek. I've always liked to read on my own, but in school I used to just go through the motions, quickly pulling out a few tidbits related to whatever topic I was told to focus on. The rest of the time, reading was pretend, sort of zoning out, only to realize I had no idea what had been said in the last paragraph I read. Now that I am not forced to read some particular selection to find some particular point in school, I try to take in the author's perspective and just go with it. I'm getting better at losing myself in a good story.

At the lunch newspaper meeting, one of the student editors hollers across the room to me, "I have an assignment for you, Daniel. Interview Chief about him sitting in on classes the first week of school."

I tense. Interviewing Chief sounds interesting, but she could have asked me rather than assigning it to me. Since I'm new to the newspaper work, though, I guess I have to prove myself. I bite back my annoyance and e-mail Chief. We agree to meet Monday during club time.

Right after I get that settled, the same editor, in the same hollering voice, says, "The events schedule posted on the school website lists a speaker for 9/11 in your US history class, Daniel. Would you like to write a story about that?"

Better. She asked. But the hollering? I get up and walk across the room to where she's working. In a soft voice I say, "Thanks for asking this time. Sure, I'll do it."

I can see my club time doing newspaper interviews and write-ups is likely to take up all five days of the week. My Investment Club idea seems to be crashing. Oh well, the newspaper work will be my cover for the fact that nobody else seemed too interested in investments—and doing it by myself would not be as much fun.

Today in soccer is our first opportunity to actually play. The last few days we've done organizational stuff and skills drills. Today, our all-white Chilean team is playing the Southies, as in "south of the border." Each match, fifteen minutes per half, has one teacher referee and one student referee recruited from among players on the community competitive team. Neither referee speaks Spanish. The Southies are using slang that many of us Chileans don't understand. I get a good bit of what they're saying but don't like them making fun of our mistakes so I choose not to engage with them. Sean, who knows some street Spanish from living in San Diego, likes the bantering back and forth and the constant laughter.

The Southies look like naturals, while we are struggling to gain control over the ball. Most of the action is us trying to defend against the superior offense of the Southies. Frustration rises with our profound lack of skill in comparison to theirs.

"Daniel, do something," one of my team members hollers. "You're our captain."

"Time out!" I call out loudly.

The Southies keep playing and score another goal.

Dodging Southies, many of whom are now on the ground in hysterics, the teacher referee comes over to me. "There is no such thing as 'time out' in soccer," he says, loud enough so all my teammates can hear him.

Humiliated, I say, "I know, but we just needed some planning time to get our strategy straight."

"That should happen before a match," he says. "What did you do yesterday in your team meeting?"

A free kick is awarded to the Southies.

The constant chatter from the Southies, their gestures towards us, and their incessant laughter, leads to me and a few other teammates losing any remaining cool. We start shoving and tripping Southies. Sean walks off the field, looking disgusted. Play is stopped every few seconds due to rule violations by our Chilean team, with yellow and red cards being thrown out with abandon. Mercifully, the end of the half comes before we lose all our players to penalties.

Some of my teammates glare at me.

"I thought this was supposed to be fun," one of them says.

The teacher calls both teams over to the sidelines. "We need to take a real break and figure out what's going on here," he says. "I want each person to pair up with a player from the other team that plays your same position. Spread out for private conversations, and the two of you talk about what happened here."

Calling us back after about ten minutes, he asks for reports of what we think happened.

"Male machoism unleashed," one guy says. "All the girls are on other teams."

"Is it any surprise the girls don't want to play with us?" says another.

"Okay, let's reserve the comments and discussion for later," the teacher says. "For now, let's just hear what all the pairs came up with. Is there a volunteer to take notes?"

"I'll do it," Sean volunteers.

Good, I think. He can understand the Southies' heavy accents better than the rest of us.

"Thanks, Sean. Okay, let's go around and hear thoughts about what happened from each pair."

"Somebody could get really hurt out there with all the roughness going on."

"We got mad because we felt ridiculed."

"Us Southies were just playing with you. It was really funny."

"There was no real competition, only a slaughter."

"We don't know most of the players on the other team very well. I only know one person. We worked together on a project in math class last year."

"I couldn't understand the Spanish words the Southies were using. I'm not sure I want to know what they were saying about me."

"I would like to get better at soccer, learning skills, rather than just playing at my same level."

"We also talked about getting better. Maybe the Southies could help the Chileans with drills and stuff like that."

"That will happen only if Chileans want to learn. Isn't that the way this school works? You can't teach somebody anything they don't want to learn?"

The teacher looks around to see if anyone else wants to say anything. "Okay, I compliment you guys on the maturity in your comments. The school's emphasis on problem solving, saying what you really think first, seems to be paying off. Sean, since you are new, it might be easier for you to be more objective about this problem. How about if you come back tomorrow, or rather Monday, with ideas about where we could go from here?"

Thank goodness I didn't get asked to do that assignment. My afternoons when school is over are consumed with my new job. It's making me super tense. Maybe my career choice isn't the best for someone with anxiety issues. Between that and the stress of having to be "on" every minute while I'm doing it, I get home every day feeling totally wiped out.

✧   ✧   ✧

Word got around school quickly about intramural soccer. On my way home, I got a text from Cora: "How did y'all manage to destroy positive relations between different ethnic groups in fifteen minutes?"

My response: "That's a long conversation."

After not getting the newspaper job and now the soccer fiasco, two big failures in the last few days, I was feeling pretty shaky about doing my first newspaper story, the Chautauqua book club meeting. I sent another text to Cora: "Will you show up a little early tonight to help me do a good job covering your book club?"

Her text back: "It's easy. Use quotes from what book club members say and then just write a concluding comment to wrap things up. The book we read is *My Beloved World*, Sonia Sotomayor's autobiography."

I arrived to this meeting feeling nervous, but I don't have much time to worry, because, as usual, Cora drives right to the heart of the matter. "I was so surprised that Sonia Sotomayor, a US Supreme Court Justice, thinks that the Latinos of the Bronx she grew up with are as important to her success as her Ivy League schooling at Princeton," she says.

Others in the group agree that Sotomayor's sense of community and Puerto Rican heritage assists her ability to see the world through a multifaceted lens.

A middle-aged woman says she has lived in this county all her life, but the sense of family and community here has changed. She says her experiences in school were all about social life, time to be with others her age. Now she has two young children who hate school, mostly because of all the pressure around testing. One has developed stomachaches and begs to stay home every morning.

Funny, I used to get stomachaches when I was in first and second grade, too. I had to take pills every day, and they eventually went away. I never drew a connection between the pressures of school and those stomachaches until now.

"At Stone Creek, we learn a lot from other students," one student says. "Just like Sotomayor learned from the Princeton students instead of envying them."

A man I recognize from the law school where my former stepfather works talks about Sotomayor's victories as a New York City prosecutor and how she stresses that fairness, not winning, is the end in our system of law. Sotomayor felt she could not try a case if she had to lie to the jury. Truth was more important than her own ego. I had a hard time listening to this guy at first, putting him in the same basket with the *former* stepfather, but I realize I like what he has to say. I guess nobody, not even lawyers, should be put in basket categories.

I write the story as soon as I get home from the meeting. My conclusion: "Growing up is about deciding what values are important to live by."

My weekend with Mom was much-needed relaxation time. Watching a movie with her on Saturday night and reading *The Great Gatsby* on Sunday night helped me let go a little bit. But I forgot to prepare for my interview today with Chief, and now it's too late, because it's time for us to meet.

Chief and I sit at a table in the cafeteria for our talk. He's eating a salad he made at the salad bar; I'm having fresh bread and a pear.

"That pear is locally grown, you know," Chief says as I take a bite. "I'm hoping to get more local foods in the cafeteria. In fact, the FFA club, led by Jake, is spearheading the idea of forming a Community Supported Agriculture (CSA) project in the county where individuals, and places like the school, can purchase food grown in the area."

"That's a cool idea," I say.

"Some older farmers don't much like the idea, seeing it as a communist plan that will be bad for family farms," Chief says. "The discussion Friday night at the Chautauqua was pretty lively." He chuckles. "But you want to talk about me visiting classes. Best part of my job. They are really inspiring. The bottom line for me is whether students are actively engaged, relaxed, and spirited."

"What was the best class you visited?" I ask. This lame, third-grade-level question is embarrassing. I definitely need to prepare for interviews and come up with better questions in the future.

"That's easy. I had the most fun in the class where they invited me to participate. You know I like to talk. A senior physics class asked me to talk about the seminar I participated in over the summer with Elon Musk, the CEO of SpaceX. Students wanted to know about the latest rocket launch and the progress that's being made in getting the rocket stage to land on a platform in the ocean so it can be reused. I also got to tell them what Musk thought of our school, and how he dropped out of Stanford graduate school because he didn't want to be an academic. Musk made a bunch of money as a cofounder of PayPal, invested it in Tesla, the all-battery car, and then started SpaceX. He likes our approach to cultivating individual student initiative and our three core values of openness, inquiry, and compassion."

He's telling me about meeting Elon Musk and I don't even have the decency to come up with thoughtful follow-up questions. *Get it together, Daniel!*

Chief misinterprets the look on my face as boredom. "Sorry, Daniel, I'm not a good subject to interview because I go on and on . . ."

"That's okay, Chief, I'm new at this interviewing thing. What else should I have asked?"

"Maybe why I visit classes at all?"

Duh, that's a no brainer. So why didn't I come up with it?

"Good one. So, why do you visit classrooms?"

"Seeing classes gives me energy to do my job better. I love witnessing the excitement that happens in the classroom and then sharing that excitement with other people in the community."

"Can you give a specific example of something you shared with community people this week?"

"Good question, Daniel." Chief gives me an approving smile. "I spoke with a minister about our school approach to how the universe began. Some people in our community would argue a religious origin. I told him we teach the science part and leave the religious interpretations up to students. We are clear that science and faith are different ways of knowing, and both exist in our society."

What I take away from this interview is Chief is a kind and patient teacher and I'm going to prepare better for my next interviewing job. In a few days, the 9/11 speaker is coming to my US History class. He's not really speaking so much as being interviewed by me. I want to be respectful to somebody taking the risk to come talk to us about his personal, very difficult, experience. Tonight I'll start coming up with questions.

"My goal for our soccer playing is mainly to have fun, plus get to know new people," Sean says.

We're back in intramural soccer; time to figure out our next steps.

"If you want to have fun, *relajarse* with us. Try the moves our way. Don't act afraid of us or like you're better than us."

Sean stands up, walks over, and gives him a high-five. "*Vamos a jugar,*" he says.

"Let's divide into teams by mixing up," one of my teammates says.

Other ideas are thrown out.

"Let's go recruit some girls."

"People who know the rules explain to the rest of us as we go."

"Teachers could act like coaches, giving tips to individuals."

The tension is gone. Except from me and a few white guys standing next to me. We have no idea how to save face in this situation.

"Daniel, your idea of learning Spanish in a natural way was a good one," Sean says. "Now we have all these tutors who can help us."

I feel like I have lost control of my idea. But it's clear I am in the minority. Better to join in than continue fighting a losing battle. If I go along now, maybe nobody will remember when I lost my cool the other day. That's probably how someone in the business world would handle the situation. Besides, I've got too many other battles going on in my life to invest in another one. I nod to Sean in agreement.

The teachers seem to reach a similar conclusion, like, let the students work it out. "Sounds good," they say.

"Daniel, are you going to the park?" Sean asks after soccer. "People ask about you."

"The newspaper stories are keeping me busy and I want to do a good job so maybe I can get a real job for the summer at the community newspaper," I tell him.

"Don't drift away, man. You got to have some fun too."

"Later," I say, with the tiniest of smiles and a good-bye salute. Then I head to my real job. Everything is going smoothly on the surface, but I'm still constantly on edge.

When I arrive at our spot in the woods, Godfather is already there.

"I won't be here tomorrow," he says. "I'll leave the bags of weed in the waterproof box and you leave the money collected for the afternoon in the box when you're done."

At today's newspaper meeting at lunch, I am surprised to see the local publisher of the community newspaper walk in. Our newspaper teacher/club sponsor walks over to greet him, and soon they are huddled in the corner, talking intensely.

The two student editors call us over to a large seminar table. "Sorry we forgot to mention he was coming," they tell us. "Actually, we're not totally sure why he is here. But I guess we're about to find out."

Mr. Peyton heads our way, still talking with the teacher. Finally, she introduces him and thanks him for agreeing to her request to meet with us.

"I'll be honest about why I asked him to come," she says. "I need help in communicating standards of high-quality journalism. I believe that some of you are not open to that kind of input from me and would prefer the paper be entirely student-run. Since the newspaper is a reflection of our school in the community at large, however, Chief and I both believe it must be held accountable to certain standards. I'm not saying accountable to Chief, to me, to the whims of community beliefs, or to any particular student who is editor for a year—I mean to standards y'all agree upon. Mr. Peyton, as a career publisher, can help us develop the parameters we want to use in holding ourselves accountable. I know y'all are already very busy writing stories for the first month's edition, but I think it is important to devote the time necessary to agree on what the newspaper should be."

This is the first time I've heard this teacher say much of anything. I'm not sure I get all she means about standards, but it seems like she has, like me, noticed the arrogant attitudes of the student editors.

One of the editors asks in an accusing tone, "What's wrong with what we've done in the past?"

Our teacher doesn't take the bait. "Before anyone can answer that question," she says calmly, "we have to agree on the purpose of our paper and how to uphold that mission." She's looking around at everybody in the room, not focusing only on the editors. "Perhaps the fault is mine in not insisting we establish those ground rules before publishing. I thought they would emerge over time, but that hasn't happened. That's not to say that we haven't published some great work—we have, and we can use those big successes in establishing what we want to do going forward."

"I think that is an excellent way to establish standards," Mr. Peyton says, pointing to the student who asked what's wrong with what we're already doing. "Look at what articles have 'worked' in your minds, and *why* they worked will be a standard. The same could apply to good articles in other newspapers—figure out why they 'work,' and use that standard for your newspaper."

From the back of the student cluster, I say, "That would help me think through how to cover a story or do an interview. Like, 'What does a reader want to know about the Chautauqua book club?' or 'What does a student in US History want to know about 9/11?'" If Cora or Sean could see me right now, they might think I'm just sucking up to Mr. Peyton, knowing how much getting a job at the community newspaper would mean to me. But I really believe what I'm saying.

I can tell by the dismissive looks of the senior leaders that my point of view is not popular with them. A few sophomores and juniors are giving me encouraging looks, but they are not about to say anything.

One senior who rolled his eyes at me a minute ago says, "Maybe not everyone knows what to do, but the experienced students can help them along. Clubs are supposed to be student-run." He adds an exclamation point to his statement when he crosses his arms across his chest.

Our teacher has had struggles with this guy in the past, but she always tries to get him to see the value of what she is saying rather than pulling a power play. "That is true," she says, "clubs are supposed to be student-run. That's why I am asking y'all to come up with these standards yourselves. Mr. Peyton and I are offering to be consultants to you in that process, but you'll be leading it."

The tension in the room is coming from the older students who obviously think they know how to do everything and the teacher should just get out of the way. I'm comfortable just watching things play out. But others are starting to fidget.

Another junior says, "If we spent some time thinking and researching on our own, we could bring specific ideas to the group so it wouldn't take so long. Maybe we could have an end-of-October deadline for the standards, and start using them after that."

"I brought a few articles with me written by professional journalists," Mr. Peyton says. "They might help get your creative juices going."

Finally, a sophomore has the nerve to say something. "I have wanted to be more involved but didn't know how. This sounds good to me."

"I'm going to talk with Chief about this," says one of the editors.

Ah, the old appeal-to-authority power play. I think I'll talk to Chief, too, and tell him how these older students are trying to maintain control . . . but to what end? Chief always says to focus on the goal of what you're trying to do and everything else will fall in line. I guess my goal is not to be a gopher for these seniors with attitude.

I meet Sean in the hall as he is leaving Math Club. "So, you're joining the braniacs?"

"I'm checking it out for now. There are enough newbies so I'm not too intimidated." He shrugs. "Speaking of not having much experience, my group is doing our presentation in Calculus today. I hope I don't get asked any questions."

"You will, sorry man. But they'll go easy on you since you're new."

Sean's group presents the sports stadium project. Their task was to figure out the amount of space below the dome for seats. First, they have to state in clear English what the question is and then translate the question into mathematical terms of change, since this is Calculus. They tell us how they cut the area underneath the dome into pieces to find out how it changes, then joined the pieces together to find out how much space there is. As different students describe the process, the teachers ask leading questions to expand their explanations, drawing out calculating principles. This is how we have learned math for the last two years, and it makes it seem alive—so much better than getting lectured about dead facts, working out the answer, and having to memorize processes we'll all forget in a couple weeks.

Sean does fine. I can tell by how fast he talks, using his hands to gesture, that he has thrown himself into the project and is feeling like he "gets it." A teacher even asks him if he'll go over the group presentation tomorrow with a student who is absent today. He's so shocked he can barely squeak out a "yes."

Sean seems more animated today than I've ever seen him, including at soccer. His fun-loving spirit is obvious when we're on the field, but in here, grappling with this math problem, he showed an intensity and determination to clearly explain what was a challenge for everyone. This place is bringing out a whole other side to him. I like math for its precision and logical steps, but Sean's passion to figure things out is different.

Inspired by Sean's enthusiasm, I spend the evening focusing on the 9/11 interview I have coming up. All I know about our guest is that he's a local firefighter who went to New York City immediately after the Twin Towers came down, as firefighters from all over the country did, to help look through the wreckage for any signs of life.

What do I want to know? Was he angry at the terrorists? Has he been back to the new Ground Zero Memorial? Where was he the day it happened? What does he want to tell our generation? Did he support the wars in Afghanistan and Iraq? Is he glad we killed Osama bin Laden? Did he know anyone who died on 9/11? This is probably not the right order for the questions, but I'll let him direct the discussion and ask a question when appropriate. I'm going to record our discussion, too, so I can go back and listen to it again before I write my story. I really want to be able to focus on not just what he says but how he says it—I want to capture his feelings during his experiences in my story.

After an evening of thinking about 9/11, I remember a TV documentary I watched a few years ago where people told stories of family members who died. I can still remember some of the details: a woman's call to her teenage daughter from the second tower just before it collapsed; a voice mail left by a man on the plane right before they charged the terrorists; bagpipes playing at the funerals of the Irish police and firefighters; survivors of the Pentagon explosion; President Bush's expression when he found out what happened; the ABC news reporter who broadcast an interview with Osama bin Laden saying years before 9/11 they were coming after us.

Listening to stories has always been the source of my ability to tune into events and recognize what's important through their impact on people. I tend to connect with strong emotions in a situation more than I do with distant analysis of geopolitical debates. I wonder how the people featured in that documentary are doing now.

I can't turn off the thoughts and my on-guard emotions, maybe because I've been stuffing down my own feelings since the blowup with "former" last week. My existence consists of swallowing over and over the fear for my future and Mom's flat expressions, numbness, and exhaustion. We haven't really been able to talk about it. I'm afraid to bring it up. Her deep sadness seems my fault. She keeps saying it isn't, but I can't absorb her words.

I can't lie here any longer. I resort to my obsession of straightening my room, even though it doesn't need it. I pace and ritually review everything in its place. Memories associated with pictures of me and Mom flood my mind. I take down the one lone picture of me with my father and carry it around as I roam my room. No pictures of "former" in sight. My space feels safer.

One picture seems out of synch: me as Mr. Mayor, looking ever so likeable at the park after school. Where did that persona go? An act, true enough, but it was one that made me feel secure and on the road to success.

Finally, I lie in bed—covers pulled up, iPod ear buds in, eyes closed—and let myself escape into the music.

This evening is a repeat of last night: I feel overwhelmed, anxious. I try to sort out the day's events and what might have pushed my buttons. Nothing was off about school today. Godfather was back at work with me this afternoon, and he complimented me on the job I did yesterday when he wasn't there. He was back to his usual position behind the large rocks while I handled transactions, there to support me if I needed it, but otherwise out of sight.

Still, I worry I've missed something important. I know the

anxiety I'm feeling is about the frat guy who got a little agitated today when we didn't have as much weed as he wanted, apparently enough for the whole fraternity. After the guy was gone Godfather described the way I handled the situation as "smooth." He even laughed about the guy's uptight manner. I didn't laugh with him.

"Man, you look all stressed out," he said. "Why don't you knock off early."

I'd only been there about forty-five minutes, but it's true, I was really agitated.

Once an anxiety cycle is geared up in me for a few days, I can't stop it through imposition of will. I get more and more desperate. Weed works—I bought some from Godfather this afternoon—but I can't risk disappointing my Mom, so I stashed it when I got home without smoking any. If she finds out I like to get high, it will devastate her.

Not thinking or deciding anything, I find myself drifting downstairs to her study. She is reading. She stops and smiles when I come in.

"Will you tell me a story, to help me go to sleep?" Like I'm three years old! But at this point I don't care. I have to stop my racing heart and twitching eyes, and the fear pushing on the linings of my gut.

Mom doesn't make me explain. Actually, she seems relieved to be needed. "Sit here next to me on the loveseat," she says, reaching out her arms for me to lean on her shoulder. "I was thinking about your father, how handsome he looked in his uniform when he left for war and how beaten down when he returned. Have I ever told you the story of how we met?"

She has, but I don't mind hearing it again. It's not the content of a story I care about now. I need to hear the love in her voice when she talks about my father. And the love I feel wrapped in her arms. To stop her desperate searching in my eyes to see if I am okay, I close them, pretending to listen to the story of their meeting, but really I focus only on the softness and caring in her voice. It fills my brain and carries me away from panic.

Thursday morning, 9/11, I am mentally prepared but an emotional wreck. To really focus on the firefighter, I need to relax my demons. I leave the house early, with my personal supply of weed. At the cliff, I focus on the water sounds while smoking a joint. I store my leftover weed in the empty hidden box, along with a note to Godfather in case he gets here before me this afternoon. By the time I arrive at school, I am ready for a stellar day.

In English/history block, the firefighter is accompanied by a woman who is introduced as Superintendent of Schools. She says the firefighter is a member of the School Board. We have all kinds of visitors come to our classes, but this seems unusual. Even that can not rock me from my pot-induced sense of calm, however, and the interview is amazing—this guy is so easy to talk with. Many students ask questions. The firefighter is so into it he stays the whole two hours.

I ask the concluding question: "What do you think is the most important thing we should remember about 9/11?"

He thinks for a minute and then says, "War is always about 'us' versus 'them.' Nobody can ever win in that fight. Spend your energy reaching out to 'others' to break down barriers."

The room is absolutely still. Then our history teacher stands, walks over to the firefighter, gives him a hug, and says, "Thank you for all you do."

The superintendent comes up to me afterward and says, "Daniel, you are a keen observer and have a knack for drawing people out. Well done!"

Who knew I could pull this off after my time in the pits last night, before Mom brought me back? I think I'm turning my Mr. Mayor skills into something useful.

"Great interview yesterday," my English teacher says when I walk into class today. "You really know how to put people at ease, and you did a wonderful job of hearing the emotions at work in the stories he told."

"Thanks," I say, grinning. "I hope you see similar positive things in my History Tale paper today."

Introducing class today, she talks about "voice" in writing and we read some passages from short stories that use first- and third-person voice. She suggests we may choose to revise our "Tale" papers—to first-person narration, for example—after she gives them back. For those of us reading novels, switching voice from the original is required to ensure our tale is our own thinking. When we get our papers back tomorrow, we can revise them any way we want, but an additional assignment, due in a week, is to add back story for the main character in our tale. The finished product will take weeks, with our teacher adding new requirements as we go along.

If we follow her feedback, she says, the final papers should be quite good. I think so too—I'm actually really looking forward to seeing how mine turns out.

I arrive to work early today, out of a sense of heightened responsibility—Godfather will not be here today. In exchange, I'm getting the weekend off. He left today's supply of weed in the box. Also in the box, I find a note from him saying, "You're doing great!" The note is attached to my first week's pay: $400, twice as much money, for half as much time, compared to my summer job at the country club!

I should feel happy, right? But instead I feel guilty. Ripping off the system the day after three thousand people died in 2001 doing the right thing, being good people. Am I lacking in morals? Weed is legal in many states, just not here, I remind myself. Why should I have to abide by stupid, arbitrary laws?

But if I believe that, why do I feel so bad? It's no mystery, really; all I have to do is think how disappointed in me Mom would be.

Business for the day starts with a customer I've dealt with a few times already. She's all business, no chitchat, and gone. The next two customers exchange a few pleasantries. It's like being Mr. Mayor again. Then the climate changes radically. The frat guy from the other day appears—the one who was mad because he couldn't get as much weed as he wanted. I explain again I can't sell him that much. I try to be charming, but he's not having it. I sell him the few bags I have in my pocket and he stomps off, angry.

Minutes later, I am jerked into awareness by hairs on the back of my neck standing up, literally. Godfather told me when he was first training me, "Pay attention. Your body will scream at you if there is danger." I remember laughing and saying my body screams at me a lot. But this is no time for laughing. *Think.* The guy is mad. The box is in its hiding place, with a substantial amount of weed left for sales later today. I move to the far end of the clearing, in the direction of the downhill escape route. I hear a dried leaf crack, from the direction of the path coming up.

That's it! I bolt down the secret route through sticker bushes until I reach the stand of evergreen trees below; luckily, they provide heavy cover, even for someone running in a panic.

Coming out at the law school, I force an amble so as not to arouse attention. My heart continues to hurry. I take a route from the law school that's used very little this time of year, as it leads down to the baseball field. I circle through neighborhoods with little pedestrian or automobile traffic and eventually make it home, to safety.

"Hey, Mom," I call when I walk through the front door, startled to be brought back to home base after the total immersion in fear I've just experienced.

Crossing the living room to me, concern in her face, Mom says, "You're home early today."

I will myself to get a grip on my anxiety, and I sound almost normal when I say, "Yeah. I'm kind of tired from a long week. Think I'll take a nap."

But I guess I don't sound that normal, because Mom persists. "You okay, Daniel? You're breathing so heavy."

"I'm okay, really," is all I can get out as I make tracks for the stairs heading up to my room.

In my bedroom, I add my pay for the week and payments from today to the envelope I keep in my desk. Then I collapse in my bed and make myself go over any possible loose ends. The personal bag of weed I bought two days ago is hidden well in my closet and there are no leftover bags from today on me. I have no way to get in touch with Godfather to warn him. I didn't run into anyone along the way home that would raise suspicion, so I should be okay there. The angry guy could identify me. But it would be his word against mine. And he would be admitting to a crime.

My breathing's coming so fast now, dizziness overtakes me—I can't grab another thought. I'm so tired, but can't sleep. I count each time the second hand on the Luke Skywalker clock my father gave me clicks. I try to ignore my rumbling stomach.

She needs me to be okay. I want to go back to the past, when we were all together—but I can't. He's not there. He would be, if I could control my life, win the carousel's golden ring.

A bell rings. The clock's second hand rhythm becomes "go away," "go away," "go away . . ."

A bell rings. This round of fighting is over. I'm beaten . . .

A bell rings. It's dark. Can't see the clock. Foreboding voices.

I drag my body out of bed, clothes and hair rumpled, and lumber down the stairs.

Mom, standing at the open front door, turns to me. Her eyes of terror are so far past the disappointment I feared.

The police support her, like the brave ones from 9/11, so she doesn't crumple.

I hear a muffled, "Daniel, we're detaining you and taking you to a Juvenile Detention Center."

Then I hear nothing.

Chapter 7: Drive

Once upon a time, a student of life learned conflict is the path to truth.

CORA

Perfection defined by the sound, like no other, when the club hits the ball. Body motion aligns with the principles of physics. Knowing achieved by intense focus on how movement feels to my physiological sensors, success stored in the synapses of my brain.

Not a bad rationalization for a person who lives in her head a lot yet spends all afternoon enjoying hitting a little white ball down a field of precisely cut grass.

The golf course sits on top of the Blue Ridge Mountains range, far from human crowds, home to many charming furry and feathered critters.

Stone Creek's intramural golf class teachers drove vans of students up the mountain to participate in this voluntary Saturday outing. In addition to free transportation, we also receive a huge discount for course fees, unlike the local city country club, which bars us from taking up valuable weekend space on their course.

I like individual sports rather than team sports, with outcomes totally determined by me, within my control. Doing well as an individual makes me feel I can count on myself.

As I'm walking to the second hole with the rest of my foursome, my cell phone tone interrupts my concentration. It's a text from Sean: "Cora, call me. Daniel being held in Juvenile Detention Center."

I can't believe it. Why did he have to go and do something stupid? It can't be too serious, because Daniel's not violent or dumb. Why now, interrupting "my" time, on a perfect outdoor fun day?

I know these are not the right questions. I should feel empathy, concern about Daniel, gratitude that Sean reached out to me. Nope. I just feel annoyed—a polite translation for angry.

Much as I might want to ignore the call to retain my golf state of mind, there is no way I can shut out that news. I think of a compromise. I text Sean back: "In the mountains. Reception not good. I'll call when I get home this afternoon."

True to the reality that compromises often meet nobody's needs, my drive on the second tee is horrible. Clearly, it's due to lack of focus. I can tell the rest of the day is going to be a bust; I'm just going through the motions without being really present. Such a waste.

Since golf immersion is not going to be successful today, I figure I might as well shift gears and get to know more about my new friend, Maria, part of today's foursome. She is also in my math/science block. I've been surprised in these first few weeks of school how easily we talk and hang together. Her family just moved to our area a couple of years ago.

I catch up to her as we're walking to the next hole. "Maria, how did you learn English so well, so quickly?"

"Teachers picked up fast that I was a good storyteller. That's how people in my village in Mexico would spend evenings," she says. "The teachers thought it would be an easy transition for me to develop a love of reading. They were right."

"I like to read novels and I'm in a book club," I say. "We could share books we like with each other."

She nods. "That would be great. What is your background, Cora?"

A polite way of asking if I'm black. "My parents grew up in Alabama, down south. My dad is black and my mama is white.

Interracial mixing is not welcome in the Deep South, so after they finished college, they moved here."

Maria looks confused and says, "I see less difference between black and white Americans than Mexicans and Americans."

"I guess when you grow up one way, you see the differences clearer," I say. "We'll have to point out to each other markers that highlight the divides as they come up."

Maria looks confused again. "What do you mean?"

I think for a minute. "Okay, I'll give a big example for me and my parents. I don't have any brothers and sisters. When we moved here we went to the traditional Black Baptist church at first, but Mama was not well received by the women of the church. There are strong feelings, still, about white women who 'steal' black men. Between wars and prejudiced over-sentencing of black men to prison, men are in short supply in African American communities. After a while, my parents switched churches."

"I bet your mama felt bad," Maria says. "For my family—there's seven of us—language is the big issue. My mother learned English quickly and became a teacher's aide at a church preschool. My dad got work at a lumber mill and didn't need to speak much English there, so he still hasn't learned. Where do your parents work, Cora?"

"Mama is a pediatric nurse at the hospital and Daddy works for the US Forest Service."

The rural country club where we're playing today uncovers the bias of backgrounds we deal with, color and money. I have it easier than Maria, since my parents have more middle-class jobs, but they also are still paying off college loans. More infuriating than color or money today are the patronizing comments I'm hearing, supposed to be funny, about women golfers. There's lots of focus on dress and appearance rather than golf swing from the boys we play with. I've been aware of that kind of stuff all my life, and have tried to let go of caring about my large breasts, hips, and butt. When I was younger I used to wear extra-large clothing, but now I try to give myself permission to wear the right size, clothes that show it all. But I'm still very aware of what other people see, beyond the "beautiful face."

My dress today is pretty conformist: stereotypical knit collared shirt and golf skort. But my shoes reflect the practical judgment of walking shoes rather than golf shoes with spikes. Walking, in general, is my thing, with club and ball secondary. People know me as the girl who wears walking shoes everywhere.

It's late afternoon when I get home. I call Sean right away. "What's going on?"

I'm not reassured by his grave tone. "Daniel was detained by the cops for dealing weed. His mom already has an attorney, and she's telling them not to worry. I haven't talked to Daniel yet, but his mom says I can go with her tomorrow morning when she visits him at the detention center." This all comes out lightning speed, not typical of Sean. I gather I'm the only person he can talk to about this.

"Wait!" I say. "I'm still stuck on your first statement. Daniel smokes weed?? Did you know that?"

"No," Sean says, slowing down. "But I don't feel like I know him very well in general. We've only been talking to each other the last few weeks. And he's been pretty preoccupied, going through a lot lately."

"Like what? Not getting the town newspaper job?" I sound judgmental here because I can't believe he's been dealing weed.

"Yeah, but more. Family stuff. I don't know if Daniel wants me telling his private life issues."

I sigh. "You just told me Daniel was in juvie. What can be worse than that? Besides, he and I go way back."

I've known Daniel since middle school days. Then we became closer in ninth grade, when he organized a cheerleading corps for the girls basketball team I played on. He had such fun organizing the cheerleader group and traveling to away games, it never occurred to me until now he might have done that just because I asked.

We became pretty close friends, pretty open with each other.

At least, that's what I thought at the time. But we were never a girlfriend/boyfriend item; in fact, I fell in love with a senior who was a musician when we were in ninth grade, and Daniel was well aware of my infatuation, because we both would drop into Ms. Jordan's room at lunch to hear him play jazz.

The musician was my first real love, one-sided as it was. But while I was thinking about his good looks and beautiful ebony skin when we were together, he was thinking of me as a "sister." His lack of interest in me as a girlfriend caused me to pull back and pretty much become a loner.

Daniel witnessed all my pain but never mentioned it, or my dramatic shutdown. He has been a consistent friend to me, as I have to him, but we never dig down to a vulnerable level. Still, I thought I knew him better. I never would have thought he'd become a drug dealer.

"I know you and Daniel are friends," Sean says. "I'm trying to figure out how to be a friend to him, because I know something that just happened and I'm sure he doesn't want other people to know about it."

It's hard to contain my disappointment in Daniel. With a flattened voice, I say, "The ball's in your court, Sean. You have to figure out what's right."

"Okay," he says after a long silence. "The other thing I know is that Daniel's parents are getting a divorce. They split up a couple weeks ago. Turns out his stepfather was an asshole toward him, bullied him badly. Daniel seemed pretty on edge the last two weeks, at least to me. Then, yesterday, his stepfather sees Daniel leaving this wooded area outside his law school office. When he finds out cops are milling around and onto drug dealing, he tells on Daniel."

I am so confused I can't recognize any feelings or thoughts. I can hear the fear in Sean's voice. Maybe it has something to do with the trauma he went through last year at Hilltop over Adrian's suicide.

I exhale. "Thanks for telling me. I don't know what to say, or do."

"Yeah, me either." He sounds completely deflated, no air left. "I guess part of me wanted to reach out to you because last year I learned talking with Chelsea helped me figure out what I needed to do."

"Well, I'm definitely happy to listen," I say. "If you want to call back later, do."

No response from Sean.

"What will you say to Daniel tomorrow?" I ask.

"I don't know."

I want to be encouraging. "It doesn't really matter what you say. He will know you care, and that's huge. Give him a hug for me—would you call me after?"

When we hang up, I wonder if I should have been more helpful to Sean. He sounds miserable. I remember my Sunday walks and conversations with Chelsea when she was all tangled up about Adrian. Mostly, she did a lot of soul searching about why she and other students had not reached out to him before he died. She was plenty angry at the school—she felt the environment there encouraged that kind of problem—but she felt personally responsible, too.

My talks with Chelsea helped me learn I can't solve other people's problems—and anyway, they don't want that. They just want someone to listen, understand, and care. Chelsea never asked me what I thought, and neither of us offered each other advice. It was more showing concern and drawing the other person out, not by asking questions but by giving each other space to say more what we were thinking and feeling, exploring where our own thoughts and feelings were taking us.

I learned how to do that when I got to Stone Creek; ninth grade was all about learning communication skills. The listening skill just seems to come naturally to Chelsea, though. When I was with her on Sundays, I never felt different, just normal and accepted. She talked for years about getting away, finding out who she is. I understood, and she felt better about herself knowing I understood. She was gone most of the summer, and now she's at UVA. I miss having someone here who hears me.

I message her:

Yo, Chelsea. What's up? Miss our talks—so here's a substitute for your Sunday morning pleasure, assuming you are out on the town now for a rocking Saturday night. True, I'm not. No particular reason except old ruts. Today, I played golf— stop laughing! It was great until I got a text from Sean saying Daniel was arrested and in a jail for juveniles, for dealing weed. Anyway, ruined my "perfect" day and now I'm feeling guilty for feeling sorry for myself. Sometimes it's just so damn hard to be there for yourself and others at the same time. You and I have all this trust built up, but how did we do that, like open up to each other? Maybe I need to learn to trust I'll be okay no matter what and risk trusting other people just because they're people, like me. Guess I'm just not there yet, not strong enough. So, are you meeting all kinds of amazing people? Tell all. How's college life? Expand my horizons . . . Love you, Cora

Pretty lame. I'm feeling the two-year age difference a lot more now that she's at college.

Since Chelsea left town, I don't go to church on Sunday mornings anymore. My parents kept going for a while, but then they quit too, preferring to spend all morning reading the Sunday *Washington Post*. Me, I like spending my Sunday mornings doing schoolwork.

Today I get to work on my history tale. The title is "Freedom." The inspiration for my thinking is Sue Monk Kidd's *The Invention of Wings*:

Once upon a time, black Hetty, "Handful," was the property of the Grimke family living in the city of Charleston, South Carolina in the early 1800s. Handful's mother was her security and role model for freedom. She taught Handful being free inside was possible, even if you were bound on the outside.

The opposite was the situation of the white Sarah Grimke, free by color and economics, even if not as a woman. When she is eleven, Sarah is "given" Handful for her birthday. She and

Handful become close friends. When the white family discovers the friendship, Handful is whipped and Sarah is banned from her father's library of books, Sarah's source for dreams of becoming a lawyer. Sarah escapes to Philadelphia and becomes an abolitionist.

Handful, meanwhile, lives a horrendous life of physical captivity. Through the inspiration of her mother's love for her, showing the origins of who she is in a quilt story, Handful learns to be a free spirit. Eventually, Sarah and Handful invent their freedom through a courageous escape from Charleston, headed north.

And they all lived free, ever after. Happy?

What is freedom? I'm not a slave, but am I free? Is it about freedom *from* something? Or freedom *to do* something? Being free inside or outside? Those are my questions from reading the book.

What a great book, even if it is partly fiction. Building in emotion to the stories helps me understand the past. I love how I feel after finishing a great book—this openness to new possibilities.

I am restless all afternoon after finishing my homework, waiting to hear from Sean. I drift out to the backyard to practice my golf swing with whiffle balls. I have to first unlearn those swings from yesterday, propelled by tension. That requires immense focus on breathing, relaxing muscles, body alignment, and seeing the ball from hit through flight. Gradually, the in-sync feel of driving returns to me.

Mom hollers out the back door, "Cora, your cell has been ringing for the last hour. I didn't want to interrupt you, but it may be important."

I run inside and pick up my phone. "Sean. Sorry I missed your calls. I was outside. How is Daniel?"

"Really shook. He's not so much worried about himself, but he's all wound up with guilt about adding to his mom's burdens. He looks awful—all washed out, red eyes, doing the bouncy leg thing he does, and he seems to only hear about half what you say. And oh, the answer to your question is, he started smoking weed this past summer—not all the time, but when he feels anxious. He says it helps. He wouldn't talk about the details of what he did, or the arrest. His attorney told him not to talk with anyone but her about the situation. She says the first thing is to get him out of juvenile detention. There will be a court hearing tomorrow. The attorney will call Chief today to ask if he will come and support Daniel." All this comes out in one big rush.

"Take a breath, Sean," I say calmly. "Seeing him there obviously freaked you out. Not that a guy would admit to that."

Sean responds to this with a half-hearted chuckle.

"Seriously, though, can we do anything to help Daniel right now?" I ask. "Can I do anything to help you?"

"I don't know. I think he's really ashamed and worried what everyone will think of him. I realized this afternoon that despite his Mr. Mayor role and everyone liking him, he doesn't have any real close friends besides you and me. And I don't even know him all that well, yet. But I'm definitely going to stick with him through this. I guess just acting normal toward him will be a relief for him. I don't know if this will become public. That would be harder on him, I think."

He knows Daniel better than he thinks. "Okay, so let's make a pact. We're going to be there for Daniel, no matter what. You're already being a great friend, Sean, in the support you've given him. It sounds like today has taken a toll on you too. Call me later if you want to talk more."

"Thanks, Cora. Thank goodness I can share this responsibility with you."

When we hang up, I compose a short text to Daniel: "You are a dynamite person and will get through this bump in the road. I'm here for you. Cora."

I wanted to say "Love, Cora," but people are so weird about that word. To me, it means I care deeply about your welfare. Not a Cupid thing or mushy girlfriend/boyfriend thing, and certainly not carelessly said.

A Facebook message from Chelsea pops up:

Cora, great to hear from you. Warning, my emotions are kind of out there these days. A whirlwind here. Rather than dealing with all the new stuff, I'm stuck back in making sense of Italy. I told you how great my Aunt Lucia was in supporting the waif of me as I tried to escape from my parents and my drifting life. But I soon realized I have no rudder for deciding what to do with myself. I've learned lots of what I don't want, but have no clue what I do want. Example: it is fraternity and sorority rush time and I know for sure I have zip interest, and lots of disgust for, that whole scene. They're like Hilltop cliques on steroids. But what do I want? I'm tired of being a loner, present company excepted. Also, excepting the closeness I felt to Jake when we were kids. Sean and I were tight last spring, but the distance, like with you, is hard. So I've got to grow up quick and figure things out here. No place to run to now. I heard an expression in one of my classes the other day that jumped out and tackled me—emotional anorexia. I see it in my relationship with my parents, only getting emotional crumbs, and therefore learning to only want that. Starved for deep acceptance, all the while telling myself I don't need them. When I asked them if I could go to Italy, their response was they would reward me for achieving at Hilltop and choosing UVA. In other words, they'll love me if . . . One other thing about Italy, the dig I got to participate on. It was good practice in concentration, looking through the dirt for hours on end. Unlike my kid play days, I was not building but was uncovering, a preserver, asker, listener to buried life. I don't know what those thoughts mean but they keep coming up when I think about what I want to do for the rest of my life. From your mixed up friend . . . . . Free willing, Chelsea

✧   ✧   ✧

Sean catches me at the end of first period. "My mom talked to Daniel's mom late last night," he says. "The attorney thinks they will release Daniel today until a later court date. Do you want to go to Daniel's house after school?"

"Yes," I say, "if Daniel and his mom want us there."

"I think it would be good for Daniel to see us acting normally, so he doesn't try to hide under a rock."

"I agree, but it needs to be Daniel's call," I say with conviction.

Second period seems entirely different without Daniel there.

At lunch Sean tells me, "I reached Daniel's mom. He was released this morning until a court date in a couple weeks. She said it is okay if we come by after school."

Sean seems more nervous about going than I am. Interesting. Maybe it's because he actually saw Daniel yesterday.

Yep, I am totally taken aback when I see Daniel, who seems so frail he looks more like a five-year-old than a teenager. Daniel's mom looks to us and back to him compulsively, registering shock in every glance. I break the tension in stereotypical female fashion, giving Daniel a big old bear hug.

"Did Sean deliver the hug I asked him to yesterday?"

Daniel looks confused.

"Sorry, I couldn't," Sean says. "We weren't allowed to touch at the detention center."

With that comment, Daniel's mom looks like she might lose it. Looks like I'm the one who has to control the direction of this interaction. With a knot in my stomach, I forge ahead.

"I missed you in morning block today, Daniel, but you can catch up easily. We turned in our history 'Tale' drafts and talked about how suggestions for revision would be made. Mine sounds like a seven-year-old wrote it, but it's a starting point. I really loved the book I read. I'll let you read what I wrote if you want. Have you finished your reading yet?" I'm babbling on purpose, giving everyone time to breathe.

"Yeah," Daniel says, "I finished *The Great Gatsby* last week and started on my write-up, but the whole world looks a little different now."

"I bet," Sean says.

Daniel's mom reaches out and pushes Daniel's hair out of his eyes in that classic, loving manner moms have. "It will be good for you to stick to your school routines, Daniel. You love Stone Creek and it is good for you." Turning to us, she says, "Chief was there in court today and came up to us afterward with very kind things to say."

Taking her lead, I ask, "So what is your view of *The Great Gatsby*? I saw the movie but haven't read the book, and I know the books are always better."

"Well, I originally read it for inspiration, like what it felt like to live a wealthy lifestyle in a time that was exciting. But Gatsby, and actually everyone, seemed pathetic, unhappy, really screwed up." Daniel raises both shoulders with arms outstretched in a "go figure" pose. "The poor people are really beaten down and the wealthy people seem hollow inside. They just hang out all day drinking, sleeping around, talking about how terrible the world is, and paying no attention to their kids. Gatsby just lives in the past, wanting everything to go back and turn out differently, hoping this woman he loved in the past will leave her husband for him because he's become successful. But all his bundles of money are from illegal alcohol and stock trading, and he doesn't even enjoy the money. And the woman he does this all for is dishonest and a coward; in the end, she's responsible for Gatsby getting killed."

A black hole of silence sits in the room, everyone sitting stiffly, no eye contact, expressionless.

Daniel looks around at us with a bewildered look on his face. "What?"

Only his mom has the courage to say, "So success, defined as lots of money, and made illegally, didn't bring happiness."

✧ ✧ ✧

Sean and I constantly remind each other of our pact to not allow Daniel to slip away into shame, isolated and alone. I'm glad his attorney made an appointment for him with a therapist. As is bound to happen in a small community, the appointment is with Sean's therapist. There are other therapists in town, but this one specializes in assisting teenagers with anxiety. Apparently, teenagers with anxiety and fear have a harder time than children or adults in learning how not to be afraid. Who knew? It certainly doesn't fit the legend about teenage years being the "time of your life."

In an effort to stay more connected with Daniel, I've been texting him in the evenings, but he doesn't respond to my texts. So I took a different tack the other night: I started writing down thoughts, about anything, in a spiral notebook, then handed the notebook to him in morning block the next day and asked him to give it back to me the day after with something he wrote. It isn't always a dialogue—more like two three-year-olds playing right next to each other and saying things that occur to us independently of what the other just said—but that's okay. I'm not trying to just reach out to him just about his issues, I'm trying to be real about what's going on with me too.

My last entry in the spiral notebook expressed my rage in this time of Black Lives Matter. Trayvon Martin shot by a neighborhood watchman in Sanford, Florida, followed by a white man shooting a young black man in Jacksonville over loud music. Police shooting young black men, for no apparent reason, in Ferguson, Baltimore, North Charleston, and Cincinnati. A young black woman dying in her Prairie View, Texas jail cell after arrest for a traffic stop. And as of now, I see seventeen more incidents listed on the website. We know there are many more, of course, but the press have just recently gotten onto it.

What would I do if I lived in one of those cities? Violence and white against black just goes on and on. Truth is I would be seen as singularly black in one of those cities. Stupid, arbitrary definitions! That's the kind of thing I write in the spiral notebook.

The first thing Daniel writes in the notebook is, "I am panicked I will no longer be in charge of my life, trapped in jail, my future ruined. I will not get into a good college with a police record, and I've ruined my chance for scholarship money. What an idiot I am, jeopardizing everything. The hardest thing of all is facing Mom, seeing how worried she is about me. And I worry about her being alone. I put this whole disaster in motion and am helpless to stop it."

I'm channeling my anger about racism out there in the world into learning how to resolve conflict. We all hear in first period details about the new Conflict Resolution Council (CRC) that is being set up, with ten students from different grades and nine adults from the community, as well as the school. We are told the national trainers are looking for people who are not afraid of conflict and can think "outside the box."

I fill out an application and go through an interview. I am asked to describe: a situation when I was open to new information different from what I thought previously; an example of a problem that is best thought of beyond just an either/or choice; and the most important outcome from resolving a conflict. My answer to the last one is that a good outcome for conflict is for all sides to get what they need, not necessarily what they want coming into the conflict.

A few days go by, and I find out I am one of three juniors who has been selected to be trained and serve on the CRC.

Training is incredibly interesting; we work on realistic conflict situations in a high school, role playing, looking at issues from different points of view, practicing listening and restating concerns, avoiding personalizing problems, and using creative brainstorming.

The job of the CRC is to listen to people in conflict whose concerns do not fall into other groups' responsibilities. Like, the soccer team should solve their problem, conflicts on teacher teams should be solved by them or the administrator assigned to them, and confidential problems should be addressed by student counselors.

The first case brought before the CRC involves a student-teacher conflict. Both sides have agreed to have the case heard before the CRC, actively participate, and try to follow the recommendations of the CRC. The student initiated this hearing as an alternative to complaining to the principal. She thinks she will get a "fairer" hearing from a group that has a majority of students. The issue is about progress reports from her art teacher that will be on her record and forwarded to colleges.

We are in a large meeting room, and everyone seems on edge at the newness of this whole thing. CRC members are asked to sit in a large circle of chairs, surrounding three chairs facing each other in the middle of the large circle. A school administrator selected as one of the members of the CRC will act as a discussion facilitator when needed. She sits in one of the middle three chairs. The discussion will be between the student and teacher, sitting in the other two chairs. Those of us on the outside circle are to remain quiet and not interact in any way with the three in the middle. I saw this demonstrated in the training and it is amazing how, after a bit, the two people discussing their issue forget about the people in the large circle surrounding them, though they do sometimes look to the facilitator sitting in the middle with them.

The student's name is Kaitlyn, and she's a junior. The art teacher's name is Mr. Mitchell. I'm pretty psyched to be a part of all this.

"Thanks to both of you for being willing to test out our new council for resolving conflicts within the Stone Creek High School community," the facilitator says. "The expectation is that this will be primarily a discussion between the two of you, but I can help if you get stuck at some point. Later, comments will come from the other council members sitting in the large circle around us." She looks Kaitlyn, and then Mr. Mitchell, in the eyes. "We're not looking to wrap anything up today, only to make a start. So, Kaitlyn, will you initiate the conversation by stating your concern?"

"Last year I took Drawing from Ms. Nicely," Kaitlyn begins. "She wrote great reports about my work and improvements. This year I'm taking Painting from Mr. Mitchell. He has not written a formal report yet for the first quarter, but comments he has made show it will not be favorable. I am concerned about how colleges will view this, since I want to have a career in fashion design."

She has been looking at the facilitator, or sort of over her head, but now turns her gaze in the near proximity of Mr. Mitchell.

"It is accurate that I have tried to get Kaitlyn to open up and be more free-flowing in her drawing and painting," Mr. Mitchell says. "Less snapshot reproduction, and more expressive. She has not acted on any of my suggestions, or asked for my assistance in any way. So, I'm not sure what she expects from me."

"I do all my assignments, I don't mess around in class, and the decision of how I express myself should be mine." Kaitlyn's voice rises a little, sounding stronger.

"I am not trying to force you to do anything," Mr. Mitchell says, with a somewhat stiff manner. "Merely recommending a variety of art strategies and techniques that you might want to try, to tap into your creativity."

Kaitlyn shrugs. "I prefer to stick with what works for me."

"If you want to do traditional fashion design, your approach may be perfectly acceptable. But if you want to do art or explore a range of ideas of beauty, then you will need to grow in different ways, try new things."

I make a note to myself—perfectionist? From her appearance, might be. She looks like she just walked down a fashion runway, the height of her platform shoes outrageous but trendy. Bet she expects a perfect job, perfect home, perfect husband and kids. On the other hand, Mr. Mitchell isn't sounding all warm and fuzzy, or like he gives a crap what she decides.

"What if I'm not good at what you want me to try?" Kaitlyn asks.

"Then you'll get better—if you keep trying rather than shutting down because you're afraid of being judged," Mr. Mitchell says, a bit more passion in his voice now. "Sometimes you don't make things happen, you just let things happen. Aren't you curious what else you might be able to do?"

"I had a 5th grade teacher who stomped on my confidence about art." Kaitlyn's voice is barely audible. "I have been careful ever since, rather than curious."

"You have the rest of your life to be careful. Right now, let your adventurous side come out. What is the world you see?"

I think he's asking a lot from her, to trust him. How can he build that trust? It's like this is the first time they've talked about all this. I want to believe in him, he's African American and there aren't many teachers at Stone Creek who are, but seems like he hasn't really reached out to her much. Why am I noting he is black? That is irrelevant to the problem here!

The facilitator intervenes. "This has been a great start to an important conversation. And the conversation will need to continue before the two of you reach a comfortable resolution. But I'm thinking now perhaps we could give some feedback that might encourage a continued conversation. Would that be okay?"

They both nod yes.

One of the teachers on the council starts things off. "Mr. Mitchell, I have had the opportunity to see some of your work as an artist and been very impressed. I hope your students have had the same opportunity, and more—to ask questions about your techniques, for example, and how vulnerable it feels to produce a work of art."

"Perhaps working on a project together with students would create an atmosphere of more open interaction," a parent says.

"Kaitlyn, it seems like you need to give yourself a break and allow your curiosity to come out more than worrying if you're gonna do it right," a student offers.

"Is there an opportunity for students to critique each other's work, with modeling from you, Mr. Mitchell, of how to be constructive in feedback?" asks another student.

"I think we can't overlook how difficult it is for students to unlearn messages they have received in the past, particularly regarding creativity and the pressure around grades," a teacher says. "We adults need to be sensitive to those fears."

"I think it is great you had the courage to bring this topic up, Kaitlyn," a parent says. "It shows a lot of maturity on your part."

"Mr. Mitchell, I think there is no one way to magically open up," a student says. "If you come to understand Kaitlyn's interests, strengths, and talents better, maybe you can suggest how to build on those in a way that won't seem so threatening to her."

"I think that was well said," Mr. Mitchell says. "Today has helped me to see how Kaitlyn and I can keep working on this together, with the rest of the class, and not stay stuck in a stand-off. Honestly, some of us teachers slip back into old patterns from the past; I worked in a bureaucracy for years, where my job was defined in a narrow box of judge, grade, and certify students as "employable"—disconnected from any individual. I sometimes forget what the purpose of us being here is: to be a learning community where everyone grows. I also want to say that I remember as an art student the excitement of letting go of the fear of judgment by others. I should share those feelings with students."

Wow, just talking can actually get someone to open up, even though they don't know each other very well. I can't wait to share this with Chelsea.

"Great comments, everyone," a school counselor says. "I'd like to make a comment about our school in general. In the same way we have tried to normalize failure as a step on the road to success, we have to say that it is normal to feel discomfort, anxiety, and loneliness in a learning environment. 'Fear is a natural reaction to moving closer to truth.' That's a quote from someone I greatly admire, Pema Chodron. Learning means there are unknowns. That's scary. So, the ultimate goal is to develop the courage to be uncomfortable, still growing."

"Kaitlyn, Mr. Mitchell, I hope you will come back and let us know the resolution you reach," the facilitator says. "Thanks for being great guinea pigs!"

On the way out, I hear one of the parents say, "I wish my boss had been here. My workplace could use this kind of approach."

It's hard not to be self-centered, thinking about the discussion. Like, I really related to Kaitlyn's shame of being defined from the outside. Like, what would colleges think of her? Like, what do people think of me as a black person? Yet the only way for Kaitlyn to stop the shame is to not buy into the outside definitions. Every one of us can take the defining power back. We just need to figure out how.

✦ ✦ ✦

At dinner, I ask Mama and Daddy when I first became aware of being mixed-race. Daddy looks at Mama and she says, "I guess it was when you first went to school and after a parent meeting, you pointed out the other kids were always the same color as their parents, but I was different from you and Daddy. My response was I was no different from you and don't ever forget that. "

I get up and walk around the table to hug Mama. "I didn't forget."

This conversation gives me the courage to pursue another topic I often think about.

"Mama, what exactly happened between you and the women of the first church we went to? They weren't very nice, were they."

"I didn't think so at the time," she said. "But your dad, and then some of the women I got to know later, helped me understand a custom for growing up black where the elders purposefully toughen up the younger ones so they'll be able to withstand the challenges they will face in life as black men and women."

"I felt bad I had not thought to prepare your mama for the sensitivity of black women to white women marrying black men, plus the bantering that goes on to toughen people up," Dad says.

I've had it wrong all this time. I thought the way those women at church treated Mama was all about jealousy and competition from the short supply of men due to serving in wars and aggressive jailing by police. That might be part of it, but it looks like it's not the whole story.

"I thought they were mean to you, Mama."

"You didn't really see any of it. I guess you got that impression from how upset I was right after," Mama says. "But in the years since, I've become close friends with two of the women from that church through work at the hospital. To show you how close we are, we all laugh when one of them refers to me as not only white-skinned but thin-skinned."

It's hard for even us to talk about race. I wonder how much

my wrong interpretation of what happened to Mama has influenced my standoffishness to blacks at school, particularly girls.

"Good conversation," I say. "I need some alone time now to think." I head to my bedroom.

Rejecting outside definitions means making yourself vulnerable. But that's not a bad thing, because you learn what and who you can trust by being open. I think that's why my parents have such a great marriage: they totally trust each other. And they trust each other because they accept themselves, who they really are, and are open with each other. Like Handful in *Invention of Wings*, I derive inner strength from my mama.

During the conversation between Kaitlyn and Mr. Mitchell, I was thinking in old, therefore comfortable, stereotypes—perfectionist young girl and black man—outside definitions kept alive inside me by my fixation on them. My perceptions are different now, though, and they come from the conversation between them that actually started building a connection, where Kaitlyn could ask, "What if I fail?" and Mr. Mitchell, despite being a proven artist, could say, "No big deal." The point was not a past bad experience or definitions of one's future but the present. Right now, open up and try. I'm glad people told Kaitlyn she was brave. She was. And Mr. Mitchell was brave, too, saying he could be more understanding.

Inspired, I pick up the spiral notebook Daniel and I share. Reading his entry from last night stuns me. I have never heard Daniel speak of his father, his real father, before. Also, the old Daniel, pre-arrest, would have endlessly obsessed about his legal problems, ratcheting up his level of anxiety with each thought about his situation. This is different.

Should I try to find my father? Now that I'm not so perfect either, maybe we could revive our close times. Not judge. Not think about me driving you away, wanting all the yelling to stop, wanting my mom to stop crying. Looking for you now might hurt Mom more than what I've already done. Make her feel like she is not enough. She is. She's everything to me. But she would want me to open up to others, wouldn't she? Probably not you, though. If I could take a risk with you, maybe I could take a risk with others. I'm starting to learn to be real with Cora, and Sean's like a dog with a bone. He's not letting go of me. They make me feel better about myself, the real me, which I can see by letting them in.

What amazing insight from Daniel. All my friends, and there aren't that many of them, seem to be lurching forward in personal growth.

Maria and I spend some time on the golf course today. As we're walking to the second hole, she tells me about her launch into a new endeavor, encouraged by teachers who have been pushing her to take a risk. Maria is combining the risk idea with a guy she heard on *Oprah* last Sunday morning, talking about a "curiosity" project he invented. The goal is to meet a new person every day.

"Cora, isn't that a perfect way for me to come out of hiding?" Maria says. "I've been sort of unthinkingly invisible. You are the only person, Cora, who knows I am undocumented. I have to keep that hidden for my family's safety, but it doesn't mean I have to shut down all of who I am."

"You're up to tee off, Maria. What's the project all about?" I ask.

Maria says, "Just to have a real conversation with people I don't know well, which is pretty much anyone but you."

Her drive is the best I've ever seen from her. Everything must be in alignment for Maria today.

Not counting my parents, people I know well would include Chelsea and Daniel and starting to know Sean and Maria better. Maria counts me as the only person she knows well. What does that even mean?

My drive at the second tee results in a shank to the right, ending up in the woods.

Walking down the fairway, Maria continues, "What I've

learned so far is I need to start things by saying something important to me, not start right in asking somebody a question. That puts people off, makes them think I'm pushy, like getting into their business. So yesterday at the grocery store there is this check-out person who goes to our school, I've seen her around, and I said to her, 'I just got done with my golf intramural class. It is so nice to be outside and I saw a wild turkey for the first time. There aren't many turkeys left in Mexico, where I'm from.' Then she starts being interested in me, asking questions, but not like judging me. Today I saw her in the hall on the way to morning block and she says hello, all friendly like. I felt more a part of the school."

"I mainly make small talk with people in stores," I say. "Or, in school, I just talk about schoolwork. I guess I don't see those kind of encounters as going anywhere, so why open up?"

Maria has a good lie and her long nine iron shot puts her a ways from the cup on the green. Me, I get lucky from an awkward shot that ends up close to the green on the fairway. Joining up, we head toward our balls.

"For me, I don't know to start with who might be a friend," Maria says. "And people don't think of me as a possible friend if I don't open up to them. Here's what I did today: I was early for the bus coming out here to the golf course, so instead of huddling down waiting for you, I struck up a conversation with the bus driver. Turns out he met my dad one day at the lumber mill. He said, 'One of the Mexicans.' I said right back, 'We're not all alike.' And he said, 'You're right. Your dad was the funny one, had everybody laughing.' I can't believe I had the nerve to say that to him. But he didn't think anything of it. I amazed myself, saying what I really think for a change."

"Wow, Maria, that took courage." How would I have acted in that situation? I probably would have thought the bus driver was just prejudiced and shut down.

My chip shot over a sand trap makes it on the green, but I'm still far from the cup.

"You know what, Cora? It didn't seem brave. I just felt like I was respecting myself as someone other people would appreciate knowing, but only if I acted by who I am on the inside."

Maria hits a long putt that curves in line with the slant of the green and goes in the cup for a 1-under par birdie. A perfect read of the trajectory.

"You may become my mentor in social outreach, Maria!" I say. "Seriously, I always feel like I'm on a mission, so I don't take the time to just chat with people, relax, and enjoy their company." Maybe it's the "mission" idea I have, the belief that I have so much important work to do it keeps me from taking a risk to be right there in the moment with the whole me.

This is not my day for golf. My two putts result in a one over par bogey.

Chapter 8: Judgment

Once upon a time, Judgment Day came to pass. Is the soul lost or found?

DANIEL

Court day, and I am a mess. Consistent with my usual compulsion to be early to guarantee being on time, Mom and I arrive at the courtroom way early. She advised against coming so early but I insisted on sticking with my pattern, not even thinking about why she might be right.

The extra time I have to observe all the formalities reinforces how Serious, with a capital "S," this is—guards with guns, no talking, no reading, hard pew seats, stand up when the judge comes in, no smiles. I have to concentrate hard just to keep my leg bouncing to a mild roar.

Mom motions to me to look behind me. Sean and Cora sit a few rows back. Their terrified expressions are not reassuring.

As the judge enters, she looks at me with a totally neutral expression. Neutral is not what I'm looking for—maybe kindly, or something along those lines.

Mom leans over and whispers, "Daniel, I love you."

My concentration shifts from controlling my leg bouncing to stopping any tears from appearing.

The Commonwealth's Attorney rises and says, "Your Honor, an agreement has been reached with the Defendant."

My attorney supports my arm, indicating I should stand up with her and face the judge.

The Commonwealth's Attorney continues, "The Defendant agrees to plead guilty to possession of marijuana, a Class 1 misdemeanor. He will be sentenced to eight months in a Department of Juvenile Justice Group Home. During that time, he will receive therapy for anxiety disorder, based on a recent assessment provided by a psychologist. The Defendant will attend his current high school under the approval and recommendation of the school's principal. The Defendant will return each day, and on weekends and holidays during the eight months, to the DJJ Group Home."

Thankfully, I have had some time in the last few days to think about the agreement proposed to the judge. It could end up much worse if the judge does not approve the agreement, which drops the distribution charge. Distribution is a felony and would mess up my chances at college acceptance and scholarships. There was evidence at the sale site, but it turned out my former stepfather didn't want to testify about seeing me run that day. He would have been asked in open court about his previous threats of violence toward me. I fantasize how rewarding it would have been to glare at him and watch him squirm as others shook their heads at his behavior.

The judge asks to hear from the psychologist. She says she will not ask any personal questions about me in open court since she has his written report for the record.

Dr. Lewis takes the stand. We haven't spent a lot of time together yet, but I like him, and at least he doesn't look scared like Cora and Sean do.

"I am interested in hearing your analysis of the prevalence and effect of anxiety disorders among teenagers," she says. "That could help with my judgment in this case and many others that come before me. My first area of interest for your comment, Dr. Lewis, is the remarkable increase in anxiety and fearfulness during the teenage years you noted in your report. You wrote that around 20 percent of teenagers experience a diagnosable anxiety disorder, and many adults diagnosed with an anxiety disorder trace it back to their teenage years. Why do you think this is?"

Dr. Lewis first looks at me and gives me his usual gentle smile, his open and clear eyes assuring me all will be okay. Then, turning to face the judge, he says, "Your Honor, thank you for your interest. As with any question about human beings, there are always two answers: physical factors and social experiences. Brain research has confirmed what we thought we knew for many years about adolescents: that maturity is uneven during the teenage years. The amygdala, the part of the brain that processes fear, develops way ahead of the prefrontal cortex, the source of reasoning in, for example, assessing and responding to fear."

Dr. Lewis explained this stuff to me in our last session, but I couldn't take it all in then. And I'm focusing a million times less right now. Mom looks like she's not doing much better, fidgeting every two seconds.

"The reward center of the brain also matures earlier than the prefrontal cortex, driving much of the risky behavior of teenagers," Dr. Lewis says. "This is a very serious matter, since the top three reasons for death among teenagers are accidents, homicide, and suicide. The relatively steady prevalence of both anxiety disorders and risky behaviors suggests the contribution of biology is significant."

I turn around to scope out who is in court. Not many people. A few rows back, Cora looks intent upon what Dr. Lewis is saying; Sean catches my eye and smiles at me. Godfather is here too, sitting in the very back. I didn't know he would be here. I'm glad he is.

"To summarize, the teenage brain is hard wired for both heightened perception of fear—anxiety—and heightened engaging with fear, or risk taking. At the same time, there is lack of reasoning to assess the fear and risks. All this suggests a learning approach is critical to balance out a developmental disjunction."

"Thank you, Dr. Lewis, for that amazingly clear description of what I am sure are quite complicated physiological interactions," the judge says. "Could you provide as clear a definition of 'anxiety disorder'?"

"An anxiety disorder is prolonged, intense anxiety affecting daily life. Of course, all of us experience anxiety, or fear learning, alerting us to possible danger. But if the experience is intense enough or keeps coming back to us in memory or triggered associations, the fear is hard to unlearn, even once the apparent danger is gone."

Geez, this is like being in a movie theater. And I am the main character!

"Examples of specific forms of anxiety disorder would include PTSD, panic attacks, phobias, and OCD," Dr. Lewis explains. "Symptoms of anxiety disorder might be excessive worry but avoiding talking with anyone about it, trouble sleeping, restlessness, trouble concentrating, separation illnesses, substance abuse, and bodily adrenaline alarms like difficulty breathing or shaking. By the way, I should also say medication can sometimes interfere with unlearning the association of fear with certain experiences."

"Thank you, Dr. Lewis," the judge says. "I would now like to hear from Mr. Shepherd, Principal of Stone Creek High School.

Chief approaches the witness stand with the usual jovial bounce in his step.

"Mr. Shepherd, it's highly unusual for a principal to want someone in a detention facility to remain enrolled in their school, not to mention attend regular classes rather than an alternative program."

Smiling broadly at the judge, Chief says, "Your honor, we think of our school as much more than a series of classes and activities. We work on building community every day, first period, first priority. In my mind, you don't throw someone away if they do something wrong."

As Chief shifts his gaze to me, I imagine me taking on the look of a big old teddy bear, flopping freely now rather than sitting with the stiff back I had a few seconds ago.

"Don't you think there is a time to stop, reflect, and take stock?" the judge asks.

"I absolutely think that, and the time for it is every day," Chief says. "That's what learning is to us. Students asking questions and getting answers from adults who are trained to listen and respond in a caring fashion."

"Mr. Shepherd, your school's approach has not been very effective in this case," the judge firmly asserts.

Uh-oh, she's out to discredit Chief and Stone Creek. I squirm around in silent protest.

"Your Honor, I see the difficulty not in what was learned at Stone Creek but rather what had not been unlearned from previous messages Daniel had received. Dr. Lewis just spoke about the difficulty in unlearning fear messages. Schools, traditionally, have done a lot to flame the fire of fears."

Cora has talked to me before about this idea of unlearning. But Chief is explaining it better.

"I know," Chief continues. "I've been there. We push kids along like machine parts, saying the reward will come 'some day.' And you can recognize the reward by its dollar worth. In fact, your integrity as a person will be defined by that outside measure, regardless of who you are, really. High school should help students find their real self, their power to inquire and decide, joy in working as a part of a community, and the magic of what can be accomplished. As Dr. Lewis explained, many young people are conflicted about those issues, either because of their past experiences or the value-less messages of our culture. It's time we listen to young people, give them the power to direct their lives, and help them instead of saying, 'We know what's best for you, and it's the same for you and you and you.'" Chief chuckles. "Sorry about getting up on this soap box, Your Honor. What I should say is, this young man is part of our community and we want—no, we *need*—to be there for him. Please allow that."

The judge lets a smile slip out. "Mr. Shepherd, I would enjoy going for coffee with you one day."

I want to applaud. Then I catch the eye of the bailiff and his look sobers me right up.

Chief returns to his seat. The courtroom is pin-drop silent. The Judge is reviewing the papers in front of her. Everyone watches every move she makes. I think about how Cora described

Sotomayor, the power of a judge, and my desperate need to be understood.

The judge looks up, straight at me, her expression still neutral. "Daniel." My attorney rises, pulling me up again by the elbow. "If you make this work for you for the next eight months, I'll dismiss the charges and your record will be cleared." She pauses. "Do you have any questions?"

I look at my attorney. She says nothing. Then I look at Mom, who beams at me. "No, Your Honor. Thank you."

"I'll see you in eight months." The Judge rises to leave, and so does everyone else.

After leaning on my Mom for the longest hug ever, I shake my attorney's hand, barely able to get out a thank-you.

When I finally make it to the courtroom door, I struggle to open the massive door, made of heavy, once extinct, American chestnut. Stepping onto the marble entranceway floor, I hear thunderous clapping break out. Nobody tells people to stop the noise. Even the guards smile.

Godfather is nowhere in sight, but I don't blame him for not wanting to call any attention to himself. Cora comes over and surprises me with a big hug. Sean offers a fist bump and a smile as wide as an ocean.

Mom, our attorney, and I go out for a lunch celebration. The attorney wants to make sure I understand what will happen next—schedules, transportation, appointments with Dr. Lewis, and endless more details, which Mom is, thankfully, writing down.

As soon as we have eaten, I say, "Mom, I need to go to school. I need to be there today, not let this whole day be about court."

She looks at the attorney, who smiles and nods yes.

I arrive at school just in time for soccer.

I've never felt such a need to run and run like a wild man, a happy wild man. All the good poured into me today came out in joy multiplied—the kind of joy you want to share with others. My own laughter surprises me and stimulates laughter returned from others. People come up to me for no particular reason and slap me on the back. It seems as if they just want to be close to the source of this new bundle of joy.

I leave school still feeling buoyant, and the feeling doesn't leave me as the evening goes on, even though it's strange to think this is my last night at home; tomorrow, life at the group home begins. It's late now, and I'm still too keyed up to sleep. I open the spiral notebook Cora and I have been writing in and scribble my entry for the night:

> *Make miracles by paying attention to my life. The only way forward is the door opened by the present moment. Don't serve time, let time serve my needs. Grow aware. Decide.*

I'm learning change doesn't happen in a straight, upward line. There are ups and downs. Several weeks after my court success, I run into Chief.

"How are things going, Daniel?"

"Not so good, Chief. I beat up on myself a lot for my stupid mistake."

"What if you had lived sixty more years thinking life was all about success through money?" he says. "Many people do. You are lucky you failed in that belief early, so you don't waste your whole life."

Some days are amazing. I'm thinking of how much I'll relish the opportunity to pass on this Chiefism one day as I join Cora in a quiet section of the cafeteria for lunch.

"I can't stop thinking about what Dr. Lewis said in court," Cora says. "I want to know so much more about brain research. But neuroscience is complicated, and to really learn about it would require a commitment of so much time."

"What else are you going to do with your time?" I say. "Random activities that fill up your life?"

Rather than answer me directly, she shifts focus. Cora does this a lot.

"Seems like you've been thinking about time."

"Kinda, in the reverse, like how much time I have for thinking." I say. "At the group home, if you don't cause any trouble, the staff pretty much leave you alone. Plus, I am finally able to sleep because of the meds I'm taking to key down my anxiety. And I can remember more about my father now." I decide to bite the bullet and let her know what is really going on with me. "I asked Mom what the nighttime flying stories my father told me were all about. She said probably his experiences as an Air Force bomber pilot. She said he never recovered from the horrors of the genocide in Kosovo in the late 1990s. The reason for his drinking was to forget. I think maybe I picked up on some of my father's anxiety."

Cora literally gasps. I've never seen that kind of reaction from her before. "That is scary, Daniel. But I'm kind of like you in not liking surprises and wanting to know the source of problems."

In the past, a statement like that would have thrown me. But I've had a lot of time for myself to think lately, and I don't feel defensive. "I don't blame my father for anything. I hope he has gotten past his anxiety, gotten peace somehow, because it sure is miserable."

A pause in the conversation. The old me would feel nervous about saying all this stuff to someone. Then it hits me: "Cora, have we graduated from the spiral notebook to actually having a live dialogue with each other? You know, give and take over an important issue, opening up to each other?"

She looks startled, again. "Well, good for us, huh?" she says. "Since we're on a roll, can I bring up something that has been nagging at me about your weed venture? You've never said anything about the drug dealer who got you in trouble. How did he get you to trust him?"

Lunchtime is over and people are leaving the cafeteria. We look at each other and nonverbally agree to stay at our secluded table.

I shrug. "He was Mr. Confident, wore expensive clothes, was in a prestigious college, and was nice to me. He was everything I wanted to be. And I think he wanted to help, maybe saw a lot of himself in me. I gave him the nickname 'Godfather' because he was from Chicago and wore expensive Italian clothes. Thinking about it now, it's pretty ironic that I thought of him as some type of 'father' figure. I don't blame him for what happened, even though he feels pretty guilty about it all."

"You still talk with him!?"

"Yes, but that's a secret. You can't tell anyone. Will you promise?" With amazing force, the anxiety returns in an instant. Dr. Lewis has talked with me about the problem secrets create, feeling shame. But this secret has to be kept, at least for a while.

"I can see I've hit a nerve," Cora says, suddenly formal. "I'm sorry for intruding. Anyway, if you're doing something illegal, I don't want to know about it."

"No, that's not it. He's not dealing anymore, or doing anything else illegal either."

"You know, Daniel, I'm not good with trusting others. And you haven't been so good with trust in the past either. That's what puzzles me about you and this guy."

In the past, Cora would have just walked away from the table, literally. In staying, she's saying she is willing to go with me to try to understand what's going on for me, and maybe for her and the issue of trust.

"Godfather and I have spent a lot of time talking since my trial," I say, choosing my words carefully. "He's in law school, and the group home where I am is actually a project he devised for one of his classes. He visits and talks with three of us, individually, several times a week."

I dig in my pocket for my wallet and find the picture I'm looking for—of Godfather and some of the other guys at the group home. "He's the one in the sweatshirt, no fancy clothes anymore."

"He's never been caught for dealing?" Cora asks.

I lean forward and lower my voice to impress upon her the need for confidentiality. "No. Some strange story about a customer saying the last buy he made from Godfather was a controlled buy set up by the county cops. The guy said he wouldn't testify against

Godfather if he paid him a chunk of cash. Godfather told the guy he'd think about it. Then quit dealing until things cooled down. After my court date—he was there in court, by the way— he decided to stay quit for a while. Then Godfather read about the guy in the local paper . . . you know they have everyone listed who is charged with a crime, except juvenile's names are left out. Anyway, Godfather read about the guy being charged by a grand jury with distribution of cocaine. There went credible testimony for the cops against him. But he hasn't gone back to dealing. He thanks me for turning his life around."

"This is blowing my mind." Cora frowns. "Aren't you angry with him? Don't you want to get back at him?" The volume of her voice increases with each question.

"No, I'm not angry," I say. "But it sure sounds like you are. I appreciate you caring about me, but I don't think anger at God-father will help me. Like I said, it was my decision, a bad one. Godfather was actually trying to help me out in his own way. What I need is to understand how I got myself to such a point, how to deal with the shame I feel, and how I can trust myself. I think my anxiety was part of the issue, but now I've added shame over being a drug dealer to that." I lean forward. "Let me ask your advice. I'm thinking of trying to talk with our English/ social studies class about everything, to help with getting past how ashamed I feel."

Cora throws herself back in her chair, shakes her head, and looks at me, speechless. I'm not sure I've ever seen her speechless before. "Wow, Daniel," she finally says. "I suggest getting advice from Dr. Lewis on that idea. My question is, where are you getting all this bravery from?"

"It doesn't feel like bravery. More like something inside me died. Like I lost the identity of Mr. Mayor, but I found something else. People besides you who know what I did are really supporting me. Did you know that Sean's dad comes to visit me every Satur-day? He's a history teacher at the college, so he talks about people like Martin Luther King writing letters from the Birmingham jail and Nelson Mandela taking the time, twenty-seven years, in jail to think and grow, and later becoming president of South Africa. Can you believe he talks about those guys in the same breath as me?"

She still looks shocked and her arms are crossed tightly across her chest, but she says, "Really? Okay, I'm going to stop worrying about you. Truth. Maybe I can learn some things from you about me not trusting others."

"Better learn quick, because my upswing today could be a downturn tomorrow," I say with a grim laugh. "Seriously, Cora, I need to ask for your help. My rock of support comes from Mom. But I worry about her. She has had to deal with as much as I have. Since you're not going to spend time worrying about me anymore, how about you visit Mom once in a while?"

"Deal!"

Sealed with me reaching out and hugging Cora's steel-tight body.

Chapter 9: Looking for Me

Once upon a time, confusion reigned. Questions of either/or yielded nonsense answers. History made more sense.

CORA

"Cora, help!" Chelsea says in her Facebook message to me. Seems she has a new boyfriend. He's in a fraternity (yuck!), good looking (Chelsea always had good taste there), and scaring her to death (he wants to zoom in close, fast, and apparently has a lot of practice at that).

"I don't know how to love," she writes. "My withdrawn parents, their shutdown of my life with Jake, and my joy with the dogs are not sufficient examples. Plus, add sex to the equation . . . I don't trust myself to know what's best for me."

Chelsea always goes back to her parents breaking up her relationship with Jake. She also describes her parents as emotionally distant.

My parents definitely show they love me and vice-versa. But that hasn't helped me avoid the "in love" quandary. I now see my falling in love with the musician in ninth grade was a fantasy. I didn't really know him, he didn't know me, and I didn't know myself or what I wanted. It became clearer to me what happened after listening to Ms. Hoffmann, my counselor, speak in first period a few weeks ago. She said many students she talks with confuse intense emotions between people (love) with a physical act (sex). The students say the physical act without emotional connection makes them feel used, lonely, and hopeless that they'll ever experience "true" love. Ms. Hoffmann recommended focusing on learning to listen to the person you want to be in love with, recognize your own emotions, and speak honestly.

She wasn't talking about hookup culture, casual sex where the only meaning attached is demystifying the physical act or meeting someone else's expectations, usually women pleasuring men. Emotional connection is not a prerequisite for this sex, nor is it expected during sex.

Ms. Hoffmann helped me understand why I have been avoiding sex. Hookup sex seems like treating other people, particularly women, like objects. On the flip side, I don't feel like I can feel emotional closeness with someone my age unless I figure out myself, my own emotions, first.

My talk with Daniel helped me realize how I'm generally distrustful of other people. I think it may come from people putting me in boxes, not seeing the "me" inside.

I remember a couple experiences with boxes when I was younger. At six years old, my heart was broken when my teacher said I didn't have the right body type for ballet. I did not even know what that meant until Mama explained my inherited genes.

The end of fifth grade, all of us from different elementary schools took a standardized test to place each of us in sections for sixth grade at the middle school. Class sections one through four took a foreign language, along with advanced math and English classes. I was in class section number eleven of thirteen, considered to be in the remedial category. When I asked the teacher, "Why?" she asked in return, "What's your address?" I was too ashamed to mention it to my parents. I was learning. But I got even, becoming an overachiever in school so nobody could put me in the bottom boxes anymore.

My Conflict Resolution Council training defined box thinking as either/or, black/white, student/teacher, male/female, mind/

body, etc. In reality, we need to think both/and, which leads to new directions and understanding.

Chelsea's dilemma came to a head with the boyfriend last night when he accused her of being in the lesbian box—as in, why else would she not want to have sex with him? Chelsea's room-mate is the proposed transgressor. Chelsea says her roommate is a lesbian, and they are close friends, but she's furious at the bully approach her boyfriend used, like she has no say in whether there are romantic feelings. She said to him last night, "So, do you think I practice bestiality because I love my dogs?" That comment was so far beyond the norm, the boyfriend thought it was hilarious. Then Chelsea tried another tack and asked him, "Are you jealous of my feelings for my roommate?" He responds, "No, I'm not. In fact, it's kind of cool, if you know what I mean."

Chelsea was so stunned, she didn't know what else to say. It didn't help that she was a little drunk at the time, too.

Chelsea writes that several cups of Starbucks' Dark Roast led her to conclude, "What it means is, for him, it is all about the sex. Am I a prude for being offended at that?"

My response to her:

> *As your Free Willing friend, I think you're feeling offended he only wants sex and not something more. Like appreciation of the whole you, as a really neat person, who can't be bullied into doing something on someone else's terms. But, then, the sex part is out of my realm of experience. Trust your gut. It'll be okay. Cheer in the struggle!*

I go to bed thinking about her conundrum, and wake up in the morning to another message from her. This one has a very different tone, though, urgent and full of fear.

> *I woke up this morning, and my first thought was, "I could have been date raped last night." Then the fear set in. What am I doing?!?! My second thought, really a feeling, was anger. The entire day I've been trying to sort out, anger at him or anger at me?*

Obsessing works sometimes. It hit me finally. The reason I was attracted to this guy was he reminded me of Jake in a superficial way—his long, wavy, coal black hair. But nothing inside him was remotely like Jake's sure-footed, beautiful, trusting nature. I could go on and on, but the short story is no more dates with the creep. Thanks, Cora, for your confidence in my gut.

Thanksgiving brings a focus on our school-wide project, joining other community service groups, to distribute food in the community so everyone can have a good holiday. The last two years I helped pack baskets along with my parents. This year I've signed up to be on one of the teams that distributes baskets because I want a person-to-person experience. Today, the Saturday the weekend before Thanksgiving, our team is delivering baskets in the city, in residential neighborhoods just outside the city, and out in some of the mountain areas with gravel roads, farms, country stores, and—always—a church.

When we arrive at each house, I make sure I'm one of the group actually knocking on the door and greeting the family living there. As we're pulling up to one house I see a classmate from school out back. She quickly disappears into the house and is not part of the group who greets us at the door with many thanks for the basket.

I am surprised that our team is delivering to so many black families, so I start keeping a count. I text Sean, who is on one of the other teams, and ask him to keep a count also. I ask our team leader, who is older and says he has done this for eighteen years, if the proportion of blacks to whites this year seems the same or different than previous years. He says it is about the same every year. I determine that about one in three deliveries go to black families. I know from a research project last year that about one in eight people who live in the whole community are black. Sean reports the same numbers I'm seeing from his team, and says his team leader also says that's typical of past years. Knowing the food baskets are for people of low income, Sean and I conclude a disproportionate number of black people in the community are low income. If I had been told that in a classroom and shown a statistics sheet, it wouldn't have had the impact of meeting, even briefly, so many charming and hungry black people.

Right after Thanksgiving we started our junior class project for the year. We decided to follow the recommendation of a local minister to pair up with a student from one of the five elementary schools or two middle schools in the county to be a mentor. Together, we came up with a common approach of focusing on how younger students can start recognizing their interests and acting on those in school classes.

What I learned from my first month of mentoring, but already knew from my own experience, is that younger kids are very shy with strangers and try to hide significant things about themselves. Like when I was encouraging a second grader, who I had been laughing and talking with for weeks, to ask her mother to read to her at night, her friend told me the girl's mother had cancer and was in the hospital. I couldn't fathom why but the girl clearly wanted to hide that information from me.

I've started to see a pattern in my recent experiences that raises some hard questions for me to think about. Would a black teenager have had as positive an outcome with the justice system as Daniel? Why don't I want to hang out with the Stone Creek political action club of black students? Why did a large share of the Thanksgiving baskets for families in need go to homes of black people in our community? How many of the elementary students I've met through my junior class project feel like they also have to hide, like Maria, for various reasons—because they're undocumented, black, gay, fat, poor, have a dying parent, on and on?

I see Chief walking down the hall and impulsively ask, "Can we walk a bit? I'd like to ask you a question."

Slowing his long-legged pace, he says, "Sure. What's on your mind, Cora?"

"Why are there all these boxes with labels defining what group people are supposed to fit in?"

"Boxes, huh? Give me some examples of labels you're thinking about."

"Black, criminal, poor, slut, things like that."

"Well, when we don't know people very well, seems we take one thing about them we do know and believe it is an essential characteristic of who they are. That, of course, is wrong, because the essential things are the same for all humans, as science tells us."

I literally stand in front of him so he can't keep walking. "So why do we focus all the time on differences, Chief?"

His face grows serious. "These are great questions, Cora. You realize I'm just giving you off-the-top-of-my-head thoughts. I guess the differences are interesting, one way we learn new things. But then differences are scary too. People your age have grown up in a climate of fear, as fallout from 9/11. Our country's reaction to being attacked by terrorists was 'get the bad guys.' Going to war spread the circle of who was considered bad guys and expanded the fear. And then there's fear of immigrants, poverty increasing in the Great Recession, and some police targeting young black men."

"And now here I am, growing up in a climate of fearing people I don't even really know."

"Ah, Cora, that's an amazing thought." Chief takes out a small notebook and writes something. "I want to be sure to remember that one." Then he starts saying out loud, word for word, what he is writing. "If we did really know them, and if we really knew ourselves, we wouldn't fear them."

"I'm one of 'them,' Chief."

Chief puts his hand on my shoulder, "Are you? Who do you see when you look in the mirror? Do you feel like a 'them'?"

During winter break, my parents and I drive to Alabama. Recent US History class discussions of slavery and the Civil War have roused both my curiosity about and wariness of the Deep South.

The farther south we drive, the more displays of the confederate flag on trucks, houses, and businesses I see. Our class talked about the flag as a symbol of rebellion and regional heritage, both of which speak of violence toward other human beings. How can anyone take pride in that? How can other people trust a culture built on violence? Of course, you could say all of US society is built on original violence—to Native Americans.

The last time I saw some of my relatives was six years ago, when they came up to Virginia. Last time I visited Alabama I was five years old, so my memories of the place are scarce. My parents talk to relatives on the phone all the time, and we get a few letters from them each year. My grandma, Dad's mom, sends great presents—things she makes by hand, like stuffed animals when I was younger, and for my birthday this year an awesome knitted sweater, which I brought to wear on the trip.

I vaguely remember the cabin she lives in: it sits on a stream, and large and impressively beautiful old water oaks define the spacious yard. The many acres of woods on either side of the cabin were walking grounds for Daddy when he was growing up. The line of red tick hounds he started when he was a teenager remains, in their latest rendition, though now their mating arrangements expand all the way to surrounding states.

As we pull in the driveway at Grandma's, Daddy's uncle CJ leaves the porch and comes to greet us. "Welcome!" he says. "You made good time. What time did you leave this morning?"

Funny, I've only heard that greeting in the South, usually followed by, "How long are you going to stay?"

We find Grandma in the kitchen, making final adjustments to the smells of dinner.

"Y'all sit right down while the meal is hot," she says, making her way around for a big hug from each of us.

Conversation must wait in line behind everyone helping themselves to abundant dishes. "Grandma, fried chicken never tasted as good as this!"

Mom chimes in, "The mashed potatoes literally melt in your mouth."

Grandma has not even started to eat, too busy taking in all the praise.

"What are these?" I ask. "I've never had them before, but they seem kind of familiar tasting."

"Those are acre peas," Grandma says, looking amused.

"Daddy, can we get these in Virginia?"

"I've never seen any fresh, Cora. I've also never seen you so into food. Is that a comment on your mama's and my cooking?"

Uncle CJ and Grandma entertain us with accounts of local people and events. They really know how to tell a story. I don't remember ever being around people who open up so easily. Grandma tells about a fancy wedding she went to last weekend, "not sweet and moving like yours," she said looking at Mama, with a warm smile coming from way down deep.

"Cora, what do you like to do when you're not doing homework?" Uncle CJ asks.

"Actually, I like reading novels and reading for research on projects, and those are the only kind of homework I have. This year I am taking US History, and I read a story based on the Grimke sisters from Charleston and the oldest sister's friend, a slave owned by the family. I thought of you, Grandma, because the slave girl's mama stitched a beautiful quilt that told the story of the girl's family history going back before slavery. I'd like to know more about our family history, starting with you and Big Daddy."

"Well, Big Daddy worked his whole adult life on fishing boats in the Gulf," Grandma says. "Growing up in the Depression, hard work was driven into his whole being." She pauses to pass Daddy the plate of chicken. "He was lucky to get that good job, from a buddy he fought with in WWII. Big Daddy came home from his job every weekend, and for a month in the winter. A whole month! We spent every second together when he was here, appreciated each other more than if we were together all the time." She holds her napkin to her mouth and giggles. "We could happily make it on our own during the week, but those weekend times together, they were beyond happy. I got to know the soul of that man, a good man."

"What did you do during the week, Grandma?"

"Well, keeping up the place and taking care of your daddy and his older brothers and sisters kept me busy until your daddy went to school. Then I had more time for my stitching work. Built up a good business. Everybody wanted something knitted, tatted, or sewn."

Uncle CJ gets up from the table, goes into a back room, and returns with clothing folded up in plastic bags. "Here's some of her handiwork. She wins prizes all over the county."

"The white customers mostly want clothes," Grandma says. "Quilts are the biggest thing our black friends want. I charge whites three to four times what I charge blacks, always have, because they can afford it. I design the dresses and such. Never used any store-bought patterns, and I won't make anything tacky that the people might dream up. If someone doesn't like what I made, I won't sew for them anymore. I say, 'I'm too busy right now.' They get the message and spread it around to all their friends. Never hurt my business any, and it's made my other customers more agreeable-like."

Stroking the sleeve of the sweater I'm wearing, I say, "I love this sweater you made for me. It really is beautiful. How did you learn to design clothes?"

"Practice. But more important was I had a gift, an eye for beauty. How colors went together. Used nature as my guide for images of what would work. That sweater you have on, Cora, is straight from the sea. Blues and greens swirling together in movement like the waves."

Grandma gets up from the table. "Time for blackberry cobbler."

"With homemade ice cream?" Daddy asks, a huge smile on his face.

"Of course," Grandma says.

"I'll help," Mama says, and she starts to clear dishes. Uncle CJ gets up to help her.

I follow Grandma into the kitchen. "Did you spend a lot of time at the Gulf, Grandma?"

She nods. "Once your daddy and the others were old enough

to leave alone, weekends I would often go to the Gulf to see Big Daddy and stay with friends of his there. So many hours of walking together on the beach set aside for black people. There always were new things to see, and so much to say to each other. My heart remains full to this day thinking of him and our love for each other."

Big Daddy died when Daddy was twenty and still in college. Lung cancer was what did it. Seems smoking was a major pastime during lulls on a fishing boat. He was fourteen years older than Grandma.

"Sounds like a wonderful, easy-going life," I say as we carry dessert back to the table.

Everyone laughs, but before I can take offense, Uncle CJ jumps in to explain.

"Cora, truth be known, times were very tough," he says. "Your grandma and my brother just made the very best of it that could be made. My life was different from my brother in that I never found the love of my life, and things in this community were tough compared to floating in the Gulf. Tough economically—lots of people left to go up North for jobs. Also, tough between blacks and whites."

"Tell her about the Klan, Uncle CJ," Daddy says.

"The Klan was *here*?" I blurt out.

"All over the South, and some beyond, Cora," Uncle CJ says. "Here, led by this young white guy who the Army had rejected because he was nutty. So he starts looking for people here to fight with. Gets in barroom brawls for a while but then decides to organize a local chapter of the Klan. We got word of it. My grocery store was the center of all black gossip in the county. Some of us decide not to quiver in fear but come up with a plan to counter the mounting talk. It was early July, and the biggest thing that happens in this community every year is the 4th of July parade. We decided that would be the perfect time to, as they say about wars these days, 'win the hearts and minds of our enemy's people.'"

Daddy has obviously heard this story before. "All the black men dressed for the parade in US uniforms—army, navy, air force," he says. "Even two black women wore their WAC uniforms from WWII."

I wonder why Daddy's never told me these stories before. Was he trying to protect me somehow?

"Not everyone wearing a uniform actually served," Uncle CJ says, "but they were representing someone in their family who did. I wore your Big Daddy's army uniform, which included a medal of honor."

Daddy says, "Look here, Cora." He's pointing to a framed picture on the mantel of Big Daddy in his uniform.

"That July 4th, marching behind the US flag, they all looked just as handsome and dignified as Big Daddy in that picture," Grandma says.

"We figured that would give people something to chew on," Uncle CJ says. "And it did. The other part of our plan was for after the parade: while people were milling around, everyone in uniform had to speak with at least five white people—a real conversation, not just a hello. And it was beautiful, the genuine interest by the whites in where we served and what we did. We also made sure we spoke with every police officer there. We knew how much they could come to our assistance at various times if we made friends of them."

"I wasn't born yet for that July 4th parade, but I remember the Black Eagles organization, first started to plan the march in uniforms at the parade. Black Eagles still exists to protect blacks in this community from terrorism."

"Terrorism, Daddy? I thought terrorism was between countries."

"The USA has our own personal history of terrorism," Uncle CJ says. "Against Native Americans and Black Africans, mostly. Surely you know about the lynchings of more than four thousand black people between the Civil War and WWII? That was a way of controlling blacks in the Jim Crow South, which whites could justify with their belief they were a superior race. But the Black Eagles had a way of fighting back against terrorism. We paid attention. When we heard something, we talked among ourselves."

I think about Black Lives Matter. These days it's the police who are targeting black teenagers.

"One time we heard the Klan was targeting a black teenager," Uncle CJ says. "Bad thing was our ally—the white Chief of Police, a friend of mine—was on vacation. So we sent the boy away to a remote lake to go 'fishing.' Everyone claimed not to know where he was, just that he was 'fishing.' When the Chief of Police returns from his vacation, the teenager comes back home, with lots of fish. We get with the Chief, he talks with the Klan leader and tells him if anything happens to that boy he'll be after the leader himself and put him away, maybe in a loony bin—and that was the end of that story."

"Why was the Chief of Police different from other whites?"

Uncle CJ laughs. "Another story. A funny one. You want to hear it?"

"I love hearing all your stories," I say, nodding eagerly. "You make me feel like I'm a part of history."

"CJ, make this the last one. It's getting late," says Grandma.

"Okay, okay," he says. "Well, when the Chief was a young boy, I scared off a black bear that he thought was about to have him for dinner." Uncle CJ can't continue until he's able to stop laughing. "The boy didn't know black bears are very shy and intimidated by people. Truth is, given a chance, they almost always run away. But to this day, the Chief gives me credit for what was in the bear!"

Hearing more stories, good and bad, over this week has made the inside of my head hurt. I'm so confused. The stories seem still alive yet also from days gone by. Violence, guns, separation, and people believing this thing called race was real . . . and at the same time, the so-called "race" on the bottom of the power ladder was full of people living happy, productive lives. And where does all that leave me, stuck in the middle of black and white?

We leave Grandma and Uncle CJ reluctantly, knowing how hard it is to keep in touch across the miles. But it will be easier for me now, because they have given me the gift of spirit; for the first time in my life, I feel truly connected to these brave and loving people.

I also understand now where Daddy got his ingrained tie to nature, among the lure of the mysteries in Grandma's woods. Every day this past week he walked those woods from dawn to dusk, returning excited to tell his experiences of new acquaintances and old friends among the species thriving in the depths of those woods. When I'm older and return home, I wonder what will connect me back to my roots.

Next stop is Tuscaloosa, Alabama. The biggest thing in the town of Tuscaloosa is the University of Alabama, where both my parents went to college. This is where Mama grew up. I read up on the town a little as we drive. The European conquest of the area was achieved only after they fought a variety of Native Americans—Creek, Alabama, Chicksaw, Choctaw, Koasati, and Mobile—for the land. The University of Alabama campus was burned in the last weeks of the Civil War. In 1963, Governor George Wallace blocked, literally, the entrance of two African American students into the university. Federal marshals arrived and Wallace stepped aside.

My mama wasn't born until 1970, but according to her, the legacy of racism never died in Tuscaloosa. She says her parents were different, though. On the drive there, Mama decides to tell me a story she says her parents would never speak of with me.

"I was born in the home of a midwife in the black community. Your grandmother was seventeen, unmarried, not sure who the father was, and hiding her pregnancy from everyone, including her parents, who were strict and racist. Grandmother intended to give the baby up for adoption, but after seeing me, she just couldn't do it. She convinced the midwife, a very loving woman, to keep the baby until she could get married and come back for me. The midwife said she would do it if your grandmother would visit once a week. That arrangement lasted for over a year. Finally, your grandmother got married to your grandfather, he welcomed me into their home, and your grandmother was disowned by her parents as white trash. I never met them."

"That's crazy," I say. "If you hadn't been born, or had grown up with other people, I might not have been born."

I try to focus on what I know about Grandmother and Grandfather. They are not warm and fuzzy people, but they're kind and decent folks who live a simple lifestyle. Grandmother always seems to be hiding, like she has a big secret. (And I guess she does!) Being pushed away by her family most of her life and Grandfather's people not being close, living spread out and far away, it's like they are on their own.

Mama has tried to get them to travel up to Virginia but they won't. And I can tell it is very uncomfortable for Mama to visit here where she grew up. Not that anything bad happened—there's just lots and lots of silence in her parents' house. The funny thing is, at home, Mama and Daddy talk all day and night. Mama's parents act friendly to Daddy, but in that same standoffish way they are with everyone, including Mama. And since they don't talk much, they don't tell stories.

It's our second day here and I'm snooping around Grandmother and Grandfather's small, 1920s-style city row house, curious to learn more about them. I see this picture of a white guy who looks like a young version of Grandfather with his arm around the shoulders of a black man the same age. In the background, there are old cars I've only seen in history books. The sign above their heads says it is a repair shop.

Grandfather comes in and says, "That's me and Henry, my best friend. Going on fifty years, we've worked together five days a week and fished together every Sunday. I know him better than anybody, and vice versa."

Holding the picture in his hand, Grandfather says, "Henry brings out the gumption in me. I've fought with hospitals, drug stores, and insurance companies about the way he has been mistreated. He has the sugar, diabetes. I've also stood up to our boss about finding other things for Henry to work on since he can't see too well or stand for very long anymore. Henry is smart, even though he didn't go far in school. But when he is not feeling good, he just doesn't have the energy to fight for himself. Besides, the boss is white and the higher-ups in health care are white. The idea of race still matters around here, the way businesses and such are set up."

I'm thinking about the importance of Henry in Grandfather's life when he totally shocks me by saying, "Cora, how does it feel to be in between?"

I'm used to being the one who asks questions. Nobody has ever been so straightforward with me. And there's not one bit of judgment in his voice—just a simple and caring interest in me.

Because of that, it seems natural and easy to be truthful. "Like I don't know where I fit," I admit. "And it makes me mad I feel I have to fit in some group. I push everyone away so I don't have to choose. Well, not everyone. But I make it hard for people to get to know me."

"Like your Grandmother?" he asks, his voice quiet. Grandmother's constant companion isn't a person—it's church. From what Mama says, Grandmother takes her shame to church every Sunday and Wednesday night. Her shame from sleeping around looking for love, not standing up to her parents, not being able to love Mama, who rejected her when she returned for her, and pushing Grandfather outside the trust border because he knew her too well. For her, shame means trusting nobody, not trusting herself, not knowing herself.

"I don't know. I'm not ashamed or anything," I say. "It's more that I want to be just me, the same individual, no matter where I am or who I'm around. And that's hard. So I guess it seems easier to just be on my own. Except for Mama and Daddy—they're great. But I'm getting older, and I need to find my own way."

Grandfather puts his arm around me and says, "It's good you're thinking all this through when you're young. I know me standing up for Henry, putting myself out there to be took down, has made me stronger. I wish I had learned that when I was younger. Not to be afraid. If you don't take a stand out in the open, then it seems to make you feel ashamed inside. There's nothing worse than feeling shame."

"Like Grandmother?"

He goes quiet for a minute; then he says, "I love her, I truly do. But the shame has crippled her. She thought once she told your Mama her story, she would be released from the pain she'd felt all those years. But it was too late. In her head she knows she doesn't deserve to suffer, but her heart has become too rigid, unforgiving—not of other people but of herself."

"Thank you for being honest with me," I say. "I'm struggling with who I am, and it helps to hear how others, family, have grown through the challenges they've faced—and how they've gotten stuck." I surprise myself by turning toward him, arms wide open, and giving him a bear hug. I'm even more surprised when he hugs me tight back.

"Grandfather, do you think racism is dying out? That young people are more aware now?"

"Many whites I know think they are not racist and try to treat people with respect. But they don't see the way traditional beliefs like 'whites are more intelligent and hard-working' have become built into workplaces, schools, and politics. Groups are more separated now, like in neighborhoods, churches, voting districts, and schools, than they were before the big school desegregation case the Supreme Court decided."

I learned about that in school. "Brown vs. Board of Education."

"Right. Anyway, change is slow when you got to change not only people's minds but their livelihoods, habits of trying to get ahead by buying more and more things rather than standing up to people at the top of businesses and government."

"People my age I talk with think racism is gone."

Grandfather shakes his head. "Things look different in my world. Seems like young and old today are still buying into that idea of climbing to the top using whatever is to their advantage, race being one example. Their attention is taken up with the climb to the top, so they don't speak up when some redneck says he's going to start a race war by doing something crazy, like shooting nine black people in the Charleston Emanuel AME Church."

"Do you want to go for a walk?" I truly want to be with Grandfather, just talk and get to know him as deeply as possible before the looming, long drive home. In his presence, I feel my life matters.

"I'd love that," he says, and I feel warm all over.

Walking must be in my bones and heart. Grandma and Big Daddy strolling the beach, loving more with each step, listening to the roar of approval from the surf; Daddy's passion for life in the woods; me and Chelsea going through our paces of growing-up questions; and even golf for walking meditation.

Grandfather knows the real me. That's love. And I know Grandfather now too. He trusts me to open up, like I am mature enough, worthy. That's love.

During the drive home to Virginia, my brain is running on high speed. Walking is not an option, so I employ reading, my second-best calming strategy. I need to finish a book and write-up before school on Monday anyway. Our English teacher played an audio tape of Toni Morrison reading a section of her book *God Help the Child*. Four of us decided we wanted to read the whole book and talk about it together. My ticket to get into the discussion is a short written description of events in the book I would like to explore with others. There are amazing parallels in the book to encounters I've had on this trip, so I'm feeling inspired and start writing.

God Help the Child *is about a beautiful young woman who grew up too black to warrant her lighter-skinned mother's love. Her mother would not even touch her, hold her hand. The father left, assuming the child, who was so dark, could not be his.*

The young woman's lover is a deep thinker, stalled in growth by his brother's murder as a child at the hands of a molester, for which he blames everyone else—even, mistakenly, his current lover. Neither one knows about the most significant experiences of the other.

Her identity, as an adult with a new name, is the surface characteristic of stereotypical beauty, playing in shallow form to her blackness, for attention and admiration. His identity is perpetual mourning of his brother, unstated and unresolved, while feeling superior to everyone else. "Black is just a color" is his response to her defining blackness. There is a clear, fundamental connection between them, but not enough trust for them to be open to themselves or each other. Their heartbreak as children has not been mended but stuffed down, and it comes out in the untruth of silence and secrets.

Hope is suggested by new awareness of each one's deeper self.

My parents have never abused me and no twisted events happened to me during my childhood. Just the opposite. But I've always felt an inner large black hole of absence when it comes to the question of who I am. I have only been able to answer the question in socially defined categories, like "black" or "white"—not "neither," which is the answer on the down deep human level. I need to be able to answer, "Who am I?"

Everyone on this trip—except Grandmother, who is not at peace with who she is—was so welcoming and easy to love. I want to learn how to be that way.

Before I actually realize it, these last comments about our trip are tagged onto what I've written about *God Help the Child*. It will be interesting to see the response of my English teacher. We never get papers back marked up with "corrections." She puts an "SP" when she thinks something is spelled unconventionally, so the student can decide what they intend; a sentence bracketed with a "G" means she thinks there is a grammar issue (we have to figure out what it is); and a "?" means she is not clear what you mean in a given section. It feels better that she raises questions rather than taking a "wrong" approach. It also means more thinking on our part to figure out what would be better in our writing. Bottom line is I write more, rather than holding back so I won't be judged or misjudged.

I'm lucky to be in a school that doesn't shove me into a box of right/wrong, either/or, black/white, rich/poor, young/old, or smart/dumb. Instead, we learn to think both/and. Both are real, and truth is a bigger picture that holds both. Otherwise, if you're not on the "right" side, you live in shame. Shame based on being defined from the outside. Not based on inner awareness of the real me.

Back home, the Alabama trip a shadow still with me, I am inspired to write an entry for the Forensics Club competition, which other schools in the state also participate in. In the "Original Oratory" category the purpose is to persuade, and I can pick any subject I want. The tricky part is that what I've written is not a traditional speech, it's more a back-and-forth with the audience. So, when I submit my entry, I assure the reviewers that I have tried out my approach and found that it works and stays within the time limit. They allow my entry, I think because they know Stone Creek is kind of weird but we come up with interesting stuff.

Friends help me prepare by being a guinea pig audience. They push me to think more clearly and applaud my growth through the rehearsing. Sean even travels to the competition with me. Right before I go on stage he says, "Don't think of this as a competition but a chance to show who you are. They will love you."

And then it's time.

Unlearning

"At my school, we sometimes struggle to unlearn things we used to believe were true. I plan to demonstrate how unlearning works, with your help. I'm sure all of you have filled out a form that asks you to identify your race. If you were me, what would you answer?"

A handful of people answer:
"I would skip it; none of their business."
"Or irrelevant."

"If it was a college application, I would be tempted to check a minority box so they would give me additional consideration."

"Be proud of who you are. Say 'black.'"

"It's hard to be proud these days if you're 'white.'"

"I see hesitation to speak among many of you. Why is that?"

Again, people shout out answers:

"Race is a touchy subject. I don't want to offend anyone."

"I felt confused. Being 'white,' the question never posed a problem for me before. Looking at it from your point of view was a new experience."

"I wasn't sure what the right answer was."

"I was taught not to talk about race because it just ends up in bad feelings."

"Thank you for speaking out. Let's come back at the end of our time together to these issues of why it is hard for us to talk about race. By the way, please understand that anyone here is free to leave at any time without judgment. . . . Is race an important factor in our society? Social science research shows it is. I'll give three examples from research:

- Those of you who perceive me as black will more likely experience me as different. Even if you are black, you will notice differences in shades of black.
- If you perceive me as black, you will more likely think I am a 'bad,' as opposed to a 'good,' person.
- If you think I'm black, you are more likely to see me as angry, particularly about how blacks are treated."

Some murmurs from the audience.

"So far we know three things. We experience race as a part of daily life and see the issue of race differently. Race is an uncomfortable subject to talk about. And third, our idea of race matters in how we see each other. Okay, now let me share with you the answer I would put on the form asking me to identify my race. I would answer 'none.' I'm not saying there is no box that fits my race; some forms do have 'mixed race' or 'other race.' But even if there were these options, I would still answer 'none.' I would not skip the question, as in it's none of their business; I would answer affirmatively, 'none.' Why do you think I would do that?"

This is clearly a confusing question to many in the audience, and there are few comments:

"How can there be no race? That's ignoring the issue."

"It would be like saying your heritage doesn't exist."

"You don't like labels?"

I laugh at the last comment. "It's very true, I have a hard time with labels. I feel like people try to define me by putting me in labeled boxes instead of letting me show them what's inside me. However, there is a more universal reason I answer 'none.' Science has been clear for over sixty years that there are no sub-species among humans. In fact, humans are more genetically alike than many other animals in nature. In other words, there is no such thing as 'race' among humans."

I look out at the audience. They're with me.

"History tells us how important believing in 'race' differences was to the founding of the United States. Labor was needed to build economic prosperity. We turned people into slaves, justifying the action by saying they were an inferior 'race' of people, physically—not just culturally—different and inferior. The impact of our history is why it took US scientists an extra thirty years, compared to the rest of the world, to state publicly that there is no such thing as so-called 'races' among humans."

Someone from the audience raises his hand and stands up at the same time. "Why do you want to deny your heritage? And deny the heroic struggles of blacks in America?"

"I am denying neither. I am proud of my black heritage, including fighting our way out of slavery. The way I refer to my background is that I belong, in part, to the black ethnic group in America. Ethnicity is a cultural term to indicate heritage or social standing, like religion, economic class, gender, etc. To say I belong to the 'race' of blacks in America is a lie. Again, there is no such thing as race. Remember, the form did not ask me for my ethnic group but for my race."

An older woman in the audience stands. "Why is the term 'race' as opposed to 'ethnicity' so important to you?"

"Thank you for asking that very direct question. There are two main reasons. The first is I want to be perceived as 'human,' not as an inferior sub-category that is scientifically nonexistent. The second reason is I want to be perceived as defining my own identity rather than being shoved into pre-defined boxes. I will define what my identity as a woman means for me. I will define the role money plays in determining my sense of success. I will choose my friends based on trust and respect. How I communicate these depends on shared language between us. Ultimately, I am saying that language and precise thinking are important."

A young black woman from the audience rises. "We'll never get to that shared communication if we don't fight racism."

I applaud her, literally, to stunned stares from others. "Yes, that is our current tragedy. Race does not exist, but racism does. And that, I believe, is why we had such a hard time at the start today talking about race. I believe, in our guts, we all kind of know race doesn't exist but people are being hurt by pretending it does, that it matters. *That's* racism."

The girl who just spoke seems satisfied by my response; she sits down.

"In conclusion, if you have not unlearned the belief that race exists, then you are not alone or unusual. Unlearning, another word for change, is hard. We see racism every day, people acting as if race exists and people across races are different. I struggle every day not to be racist, whether I'm filling out government or college forms that ask my 'race' or wanting to cheer for the all-black basketball team. But soon we will get past racism in the same way fewer and fewer people now claim global warming is a hoax."

The last thing I see, before tears block my vision, is Sean hooting and hollering in the back, the loudest of the applauders.

Chapter 10: Reality Check

Once upon a summer, a youthful dream met the power of Mother Nature.

JAKE

A marker that I have grown up, possess social status defined by law. That's the sense of it. Not any actual achievement. Sixteen years and three months, the requirement for me to exercise freedom of movement. Today, the first time I am allowed to drive, alone, the ten miles from home to school. No matter that I have been skill-fully driving vehicles in my farm community for years. The license represents my first legal sanction of adulthood.

At age sixteen I can also legally drop out of school. One of the smartest people I know, my dad, left school at age sixteen. He was bored and belittled there. He's a whiz at math but because he wouldn't always use the teacher's method to solve a problem, he received no recognition for often thinking correctly, but differently, for himself. The youngest of ten, he rose from extreme poverty and has done well for himself. An early career in construction funded his dreams of owning his own land and farming. Empty time—particularly winter evenings since my mom died—he fills with reading and talking history of this area. I swear he knows every person and every piece of land from hundreds of years ago to now, in his head. That's a sharp mind.

I would need his permission to drop out of school now. I can't see that happening. He has seen the world change from valuing what a person knows or can do to caring only about degrees. Employers now require higher and higher levels of schooling just because they can, without any need for all that education to do the job.

Honestly, I'm not really thinking about dropping out of school anymore. I used to feel bored and belittled, like Dad—but then Chief came to Stone Creek as principal, and school started to feel different. I have learned a ton more about what I want to know. I am just as committed to farming as Dad, and he has taught me everything he knows. But I have also learned that to survive in my chosen field of work, I'll have to do it differently than he does. Exactly how, though, I'm not sure.

Students in the Future Farmers of America (FFA) Club at school share my background, unlike the city kids, but not my drive for new answers. I push for answers to questions they don't have. They seem comfortable in a future of part-time work on their farms, almost like a hobby, with a real paying job doing something else the rest of the time. As we share what we learn in our classes related to agriculture, I keep raising my questions, which others see as unrealistic. They see what I'm dreaming of as big change, not something you can do with just one small farm here in the valley.

Crossing the Stone Creek parking lot, a little awkward in stiff leather, I hear, "Hey Jake. Look at those fancy new boots."

"Hey, Sean." I look down at my boots—pristine, not a bit of mud on them. "Yeah, I'm celebrating my first day of legal driving. Got these for my birthday a few months ago, but decided to keep them nice a while, save them for special occasions."

You wouldn't know it to look at these boots, but they are very expensive—well made and totally waterproof. Dad wears plastic grocery bags over his shoes when it's wet out. He says it's his idea of recycling.

"I'm still biking it for a couple more months, until I'm a grownup too," Sean says, looking a little bummed about it.

We walk into first period and head to our customary spots.

I sit on the left end row with some of my FFA friends, while Sean sits on the right end row with his soccer friends—Daniel and some other guys—and Cora.

Sean and Daniel's soccer friends are immigrants from south of the border. Actually, I'm not positive exactly where each of them is from. Sean told me a big issue for many of them is that they lack legal documentation to be in this country. Meaning, for instance, they can't get a driver's license, whether or not they're old enough for one. Yesterday at the DMV, I had to show my social security card as proof of "legal presence" in the US. Many of the parents of these kids get paid under the table for the work they do on farms, in restaurant kitchens, and at sawmills.

Cora, Sean, and I have been hanging out a lot with Maria, Cora's friend from golf. I'm guessing members of her family are undocumented, but I would never ask. Even though we're friends, it's kind of like "don't ask, don't tell." The stakes are high, with the threat of possible deportation hanging overhead like a constant cloud.

Our three junior class counselors are talking today about how we should visit colleges to see what they have to offer for each of us. I lean over and ask Sean whether undocumented residents can be accepted to Virginia State colleges.

"The guys say colleges don't make an issue of it, but money is the real issue," he whispers. "Like not being eligible for federal Pell grants."

Funny how you can see people every day, even joke around with them, but not really know them.

Arriving at our English/social studies block class, we are greeted by a parent Sean recognizes as the helicopter mom of a guy in the student jazz band who lives down the street from him. Sean says the guy complains about how his mom hovers, texting him constantly and trying to control his life in many other ways. When class starts, she tells us she will be observing us today. I see forms on her clipboard, the ones teachers and students approved last year for parents visiting classes to provide feedback about what they observe. Parents are encouraged to visit classrooms their own children are not a part of. The jazz band student is not in our class, but Sean says he has our same teachers in afternoon block.

At the end of class, I hear the parent say to one of the teachers, "Seeing your class helps me understand what my son is doing every day, how he is growing. Maybe I need to loosen up and quit pushing him."

"His counselor, Ms. Hoffmann, is scheduled in a few days to do a review of his portfolio and my quarterly evaluation for this class," the teacher says. "I'm confident she will be pleased by the progress he has made."

The counselor job has changed over the years. Now there is a big emphasis on communication skills in ninth grade English classes—making friends, resolving conflicts, expressing your thoughts and feelings in writing, speaking publicly, stuff like that—and that groundwork helps prevent many problems, freeing up Stone Creek's counselors to work one-on-one with students on other issues. Ms. Hoffmann, for instance, had the time to help Sean transition into Stone Creek after attending two other high schools. They worked together to develop an Individual Student Plan for him based on teacher assessments of his skills. A few teachers set up specific review activities for him and monitored his progress. He worked hard and did fine on exams at the end of first semester. His dad the professor still wants him to do better, but he did admit to Sean that he had made quick progress.

Ms. Hoffmann has helped me a lot with confidence. Us country kids go to school with kids much wealthier than our families are, and I'd always had a chip on my shoulder about that, aggravated by their privileged assumptions about life and the fact that I came up short when I compared myself to them. Like, how I talked, what I wore, never having traveled out of the state, and how much they already knew coming into elementary school. Ms. Hoffmann grew up here among farm families, and she knew how to get me to see my strengths. She encouraged me to dig into things I wanted to know, and kept reinforcing practicing those communication skills. It must have worked, because now my dad teases me by calling me Mr. Professor.

I'm still debating about going to college. The staff all assume everyone will, at some point in their life, need to go to college, but I'm not so sure.

The last time Ms. Hoffmann and I talked, she said, "College can help you with farming. Agricultural science, economic markets, and business management classes—"

I raised my hand in a stop motion. "I agree college can help, but I can also learn a lot through firsthand experience, online research, and social networking with other farmers. I'm not interested in wasting time and money taking a bunch of required college courses that are not in my area."

"Taking courses outside your interests broadens you as a person," she countered.

I had to think about that one for a minute. She had not brought that argument up before. Finally, I said, "I prefer the direct experience approach rather than always taking classes. I taught myself to play the bass. I'm not great at it, but I play in a band and we have fun. I'll probably play the rest of my life." There's something nobody else knows but me. I guess I trust her enough to tell her. "Please don't spread it around, but I have also gotten into writing poetry. Again, I'm not great, but a college class probably wouldn't make me enjoy it any more. The teachers here inspire me plenty."

She didn't keep pushing, but we both know the topic will come up again.

I am enrolled in a computer programming class this semester. I chose this class over intramurals since I get plenty of physical activity at home working on the farm. And the arts, like playing the bass, I'm doing on my own. I hear the community college will be offering a new class in sustainable agriculture here at Stone Creek next year. I definitely want to take that course.

I walk with Daniel over to the vocational and computer wing, as usual. At the end of first semester, he switched from soccer to a business management class taught by the community college instructors. The comfort we've grown into with each other after doing these daily walks together for months gives me the courage to ask, "How are things going at the group home, Daniel?"

He looks surprised I've asked the question, but not mad or embarrassed. "Pretty quiet," he says, "but that's not a bad thing. I'm changing in many ways. The big challenge is to keep the best parts of me and let other parts go. One of the things I'm wrestling with now is whether the idea of a business career suits me. This class is helping me sort through the question, too."

It surprises me that he doesn't act bitter about having to live in the Group Home until the end of the school year. I don't know if I would be so cool about it.

After school Sean and I head to our usual hiking spot along the Appalachian Trail. Sean says he wants to hike in celebration of my new status as an adult. The surprise is that Cora and Chelsea, who's home for spring break, join us.

As we hike, Chelsea and Sean describe the walk on this trail last spring in memory of Adrian. They display a close connection with each other. Something about their closeness, hugs and all, makes the hair on my arms stand up. I don't know if I've ever been jealous about anything before.

My piercing look at Sean may account for him stopping and saying to all of us, "If it weren't for Adrian, I wouldn't have found the courage to change schools. I looked up to him for his determination to be himself. He also made me realize I don't know what goes on in other people's heads and made me want to learn to reach out, know people for real."

"Adrian's dying frightened me so bad I froze up, turned even more inward, wandered around Italy, and then off to college, hoping it would change my life," Chelsea says. She bends over and picks up a rock, getting to know it by turning it over and over in her hand. I think she might say more, but it seems she's done talking for now.

Cora and I exude quiet; the only sound we make is with the leather walking shoes and boots we wear on our feet. On both sides of the trail, the mountain laurel are already budding. Above, the canopy of trees absorbs the sound of our voices. Breaks in the natural growth and boulders reveal vast views of our valley below, encouraging us to see a bigger picture of our life.

Chelsea reports she visited Hilltop Academy yesterday, mainly to say hello to Ms. Carter, the school secretary.

"Ms. Carter told me the new principal was friendly and easy-going, but little has changed in the daily life of students. I also chatted with a few students, now seniors, who confirmed the lack of change. Between their comments about continued boredom at Hilltop, I asked if they ever think about Adrian." She sighs. "They said, 'Who?'"

We continue in silence for a bit. Then I ask Chelsea to tell us about college life at UVA.

"The number one best thing about college is the freedom from dreadful routine," Chelsea says. "A professor was telling us the other day that changing up your routine, according to neuroscience, promotes the brain to reorganize perception, get insights, and discover new things."

"Sorry to interrupt, Chelsea, but would you ask the professor for the source of that information and send it to me?" Cora asks.

"Sure thing," Chelsea says, flashing her a smile. "The other main difference from high school is there's a ton of reading—but you learn how to read for the big questions, not every little detail. Of course, from what Cora tells me, you guys have more of that at Stone Creek than I had at Hilltop. I got so little exposure to learning to think on my own in high school that college classes have been really hard for me, even though I made good grades at Hilltop."

Sean points to himself. "It's been hard for me at Stone Creek because of that too. You have to be able to form conclusions and back up your thoughts with reasoning. Nobody tells you what to think, you have to figure it out for yourself. It takes some getting used to."

"Do you get to decide what courses you want to take?" I ask Chelsea.

"Not so much for the first two years," she says. "There are lots of required classes. I can see where it would be just as good to go to a community college for the first two years, especially since you're guaranteed admission to any of Virginia's four-year colleges as long as you make C's or higher in all your courses."

I frown, thinking. Community college is a lot cheaper than a university; still, I'll have to take the same boring required courses either way.

Cora impatiently rolls her hand, as in "fast-forward." She says, "Come on Chelsea, tell them the really hard stuff about your social life at UVA."

Chelsea looks at me, then takes a deep breath. "I don't even know where to start. I've had a really hard time. I didn't want to do the Greek thing, but didn't know where I did fit. So many people, and 99.99 percent of them, I don't know. Country me didn't really know how to interact with different people. I had zero confidence. Mainly I hung out in my dorm room, and only got to know a few people on my floor the first couple months."

Chelsea stops walking. I'm feeling nervous for some reason.

"Then I made a big mistake with a guy, getting in way over my head fast. It was terrifying, really. An article in the UVA newspaper said one in three women on college campuses experience unwanted sexual contact. I was on the brink of that. And it affected my studies. I couldn't think straight until I sorted through the fog of fear I was in."

I watch Chelsea starting to walk again. The idea of Chelsea having a boyfriend bothers me. Bad. And not just because of the sexual aggression.

"I've been thinking a lot about what you shared with me during the year, Chelsea, and I've decided my first choice of a college for next year is Howard," Cora says. Seeing the blank looks on all of our faces, she continues, "It's in DC, and it's a historically black college. First, I've decided I want to go to a city, and DC seems great for both a large black community and an international community. Howard has about ten thousand students—it's smaller than UVA." She puts her hand on Chelsea's shoulder to turn her around to face her. "But beyond the size, there is a real sense of community and belonging, and sense of safety there. I'll be among people like me."

"Whoa, Cora," Sean says in a voice louder than usual for him. "What happened to your prize-winning forensics speech about there being no such thing as race?" The question is punctuated by his hand brushing his hair out of his eyes, as if he doesn't want to miss seeing something.

Cora, raising her voice to the same level as Sean's, says, "My speech was about how race is not supposed to matter, but it *does*. In this country, anyone who looks slightly black is black. I have moderately black skin, so I am definitely black in the eyes of others. It doesn't matter if that perception is not based on scientific truth. The social preference for whiteness is still alive. That racism is wrong, but I have to learn to deal with it. I think Howard would be a supportive environment to do that in."

"Where did you learn about Howard, Cora? Online?" I ask a neutral question to tone things down.

"I did check it out online. But that was after hearing how it felt being at Howard from Ta-Nehisi Coates. He wrote a book to his son about growing up black. He talks about the remnants of slavery that still show themselves in the US through fear of blackness. He writes about having lived in four big cities in the US, and then Paris, and says the last was the only place he did not have to be black. The American Dream, Coates says, is built on prosperity through slavery, bodies for sale, accepting black bodies as currency."

Cora is talking very fast, not looking at any of us. "It's no surprise black bodies are disproportionately being shot by police, thrown in jail, and sentenced to death. People who believe themselves to be white excuse themselves from responsibility by saying

'it's not me.' 'Black Lives Matter' shows it's a whole system thing."
Cora gestures with her arms above her head, rounded like a globe,
with her stern face at the bottom. She looks at Sean. "I ended
my speech a few months ago by saying I'm struggling to learn
how not to be a racist. I could benefit from being exposed to the
experiences of many others in my same situation. This was clearly
evident to me last week at the Chautauqua book club meeting
discussing Coates's book. Members of the book club reached little
understanding with each other. The separation line was clearly
confusion by people who believe they are white versus frustration
from people like me, who appear black . . . or brown, or red, or
Arabic . . ."

Sean walks over to Cora, so close that their shoulders are
almost touching. "I have learned so much from you," he says quietly. "The most important you've taught me is to not look at things
as either/or but as both/and. Can't both sides have some truth to
the way they see things?"

"Theoretically, that's true," Cora says. "But people who
believe they are white seem to have little motivation to work
through their confusion. That's what I mean when I say I could
learn more from people who've had my same experiences."

"But then you wouldn't hear the other sides' 'truth,'" Sean says.

Seeing Cora's face become tight again, and how she moves a
few steps away from Sean, I take a different tack. "Cora, you're so
smart, you could go anywhere you want and be okay."

"What if I want to be beautiful as well as smart?" she
demands. "Beautiful looking black. At Howard, I would feel that
and relax."

"*That* I understand for sure," Chelsea says. "Is Howard the
only place you think you would feel secure in that way?

Cora shrugs. "I did pick out two other schools in DC that
could be possibilities. Georgetown is rated as 'most selective' in the
country, but they guarantee meeting the financial need of everyone
who meets admission standards. I don't think I can get in, but I'm
going to apply because financial aid is extremely important for
me. Then there's George Washington, which is very expensive,

but again, I think it's worth seeing what financial aid I can get. And, I am going to apply to UVA because at least I would have one good friend there." Cora puts her arm around Chelsea's shoulder.

"That's what I wanted to hear," Chelsea says, grinning.

"You should talk with Ms. Hoffmann," Sean says, back to his normal voice. "She told me to talk with my parents about finances since my dad may have money allotted for me from the college where he works as a benefit of being a professor there. I found a college that has a major in marine science, with very few extraneous courses—Maine Maritime Academy. It's right on the Atlantic coast. They have their own ships, winter break in the Caribbean, about the same number of students as Stone Creek, they offer a high school teaching certificate, and they're called the best public college in the nation for the dollars according to *MONEY* magazine. I thought that last thing would help sell it to Mom and Dad. But Ms. Hoffmann said the Academy's small size will make it hard to get into, so she suggested that I come up with some alternatives to keep in mind."

I raise my eyebrows. "Maine?"

"It's not such a crazy idea," Sean says. "There are mountains in the west for winter skiing, and the school is literally right on the ocean." Sean shoots me a look. "Okay, Jake, what you got?"

"I'm going to take Sustainable Agriculture next year, the new community college class that will be offered at Stone Creek. We'll see how that goes. If I do well for two years at the community college, I could transfer to the Ag School at Virginia Tech. But I'm not going to take a bunch of irrelevant bullshit."

All conversation stops as we reach the stone memorial to Adrian, mostly still intact. Chelsea tells us the wonderful day of tribute to Adrian was pretty much singlehandedly organized by Sean.

"Bet y'all didn't know he's such a leader," she says. "He keeps it pretty hidden until all of a sudden he's needed."

Again that flare of jealousy.

Hiking back down to the trailhead, Cora and Sean seem to want to mend the harshness of their discussion earlier; they throw themselves into catching up on news about Daniel. Daniel's mom and Sean's mom have become good friends. Daniel is on a mission to find his father. I'm not sure why this is significant, but Sean and Cora think it is a courageous act for him.

After a bit, Chelsea and I hang back. I've been wanting some private time with her, so it feels good that she seems to want that too.

"I've thought a lot about you and our early years together over the past year," she says. "I wish things had not changed between us."

"I never really understood what happened," I admit. "I thought it was me being too young for you—I figured you were moving on beyond childish things."

Chelsea shakes her head. "I only changed as a result of my parents' pushing. That's what kids are supposed to do."

"Sometimes I wonder if I would care so much for the farm if I had a life outside of it," I say.

Chelsea stops walking and waits for me to turn and face her. "Farming is you, Jake, regardless of anything else. Don't let anyone take that away from you."

After a long, comfortable, welcome silence, I say, "I learned not to miss you. Now, I'd like to unlearn that. You always listened to me and knew me better than anyone. And yet you still thought I was an okay person."

"I still do, Jake. More than okay. Here's your birthday present." She puts her hands on either side of my face, lowers my head to her level, and gives me a quick kiss, our first. We join hands and walk side by side, synchronized in familiar step.

I don't know what else to say but don't feel a need to say anything. We stroll along while the red sun's rays pierce the clouds floating over the mountains to the west. Being with Chelsea, I feel complete somehow. Like, I could maybe care about her as much as I do about the farm. I wonder if that's what Cora means by both/and?

✧ ✧ ✧

Cora approaches me at lunch today and says, "Can we talk? You are the closest to Chelsea I can get at the moment. Daniel knows me best, but he's not here today, and besides, a fresh perspective would be helpful."

I'm a little startled by her request. "I can't believe you want to talk something over with me," I blurt out.

Cora frowns. "Why? Don't you know how much people respect your grounded thinking?"

"What?"

She shakes her head as if my question is ridiculous and simply says, "So I talked with Ms. Hoffmann about my college plans. She gets it about diversity. Did you know she is Jewish?"

"No. How does that relate?"

"Like the problems blacks face now, you know Black Lives Matter, for her it was the Holocaust, knowing what her ancestors endured, and what she faced as a continuation of their suffering. But she said her inner self is only partly about her Jewish family, friends, and synagogue. She said her life as one unique human being has been the harder journey. She told me my identity is not a carbon copy absorbed from the outside, that I am writing my story to reflect my own range of experiences—a story that includes my views as a woman, a child of economically comfortable parents, an American, living as an infinitesimally small part of the Earth, uncontrollably curious, with eyes wide open. She said, 'Be assured there is never either/or. The path forward is always more complicated.'"

Cora is usually deliberate and contemplative in her speech. Today everything is just tumbling out of her head. "She sounds like you, Cora," I say slowly, trying to make sense of everything she's just said. "With the either/or thing, I mean. I'm not sure I even get that. But I do know I don't see you as part of some group. You're Cora."

"And who is that, Jake?" Cora folds her arms across her chest and sits back in her chair like she's waiting for me to prove my last statement.

"You're someone who thinks deeply about everything. Not just school stuff. Life is a mystery for you, and you're out to solve it."

"Then why am I always confused these days?"

Cora, confused? That I have never seen. "Maybe because you see the truth in how complicated everything is."

She relaxes a little. "If you were me what would you do about college?"

"I would lose the pressure of feeling like I might make a wrong decision. I would make a list of what is important and look at colleges through those lenses, go visit, talk to the students there."

Sounding beaten down, she says, "What if I still can't make a decision after all that?"

"Won't happen. At some point, it will pop out at you and you'll say, 'That's it!'"

Cora nods and seems to stop in her tracks, even though she wasn't going anywhere. "Yep," she says, "that's why they call you salt-of-the-earth guy."

Tonight I'm getting a break from my usual farm chores. Dad agreed to do them for me so I could go over to Sean's for dinner.

Boy, his house is much livelier than mine. His sister, Sarah, a bundle of constant energy, sees reality exclusively through the lens of her kindergarten world. The events of her day revolve around adventures in the books her teacher reads to the class, math discoveries made while manipulating different colored and sized wooden rods, and the ever-present social challenges of the playground. She can really entertain during a lingering dinner meal, without help from anyone else—but Sean's mom and dad are working on getting her to develop interest in other people's activities, and tonight I'm the guinea pig.

"So, Jake, what are your interests?" Sarah asks.

"Farming. My whole life has been about life on the farm."

"Can I come visit? I've never been on a real farm!"

"Sure, Sarah. See that ear of corn? That comes from a farm, and it grows on a plant taller than me."

Her eyes widen. "What's your favorite thing about life on the farm?"

Ah, the perception of a clear mind. She reminds me of a poster in my science classroom that reads, *"In the beginner's mind there are many possibilities; in the expert's mind there are few."* It's a quote by Shunryu Suzuki. My science teacher constantly prompts us to let our minds be free to discover fundamental curiosity about ordinary life, and to remember that the way to learn is by each person being in control of their own practice.

Coming back to the present moment, I say to Sarah, "First sun, bringing all life on the farm into soft awareness."

"That's pretty," she says and gives me a big smile.

Sean tells his mom the woman down the street observed our first block class a few days ago. "She thought Jake was terrific."

"I can see why," his mom says and smiles at me. "I feel so welcomed when I go into Stone Creek, comfortable in that environment to be open and appreciate other people. Daniel's mom says the same thing. She is so thankful that part of Daniel's life is stable and nourishing. Not that the group home is bad, but at school Daniel feels free to explore and be new, starting over rather than paying for past mistakes or being told to be patient for some future life."

"You know, Sean, we couldn't see how your spirit was withering away when you were at Hilltop," his dad says. "The only hint was at the end, when you came to life planning the EarthWalk event for Adrian. And now, as we see you growing into your own more every day, I think, how could we have been so blind?"

What different experience from dinners with Dad, who spends most meals recounting stories of life in the county. Sean's family seems more interested in reflecting on their own lives and what it all means. Sean's dad pretty much admitted he was wrong about what was good for Sean, and he shouldn't have fought Sean about transferring from Hilltop to Stone Creek. My dad would never admit he was wrong about something.

Maybe that's where my growing interest in poetry comes from. It's something I can do on my own, to express how I see things. Often the perspective is different from my dad's. After dinner at Sean's, this pops out:

Not observing the morning sun at a distance.
Seeing sun up close in every form on the farm.
All things alive with sun.
Sun encompassing us all.
Not one thing, sun.
Not two things, sun and us.
Both sun and us inter-are.

In science classes over the years, my focus has been relating everything to the farm. A few years ago, I started following developments in the movement for sustainable food. There's a national leader whose farm is in the next county, about thirty miles away, just east of the Allegheny Mountain Range. I've read a lot about him, and also saw him in the movie *Food, Inc.* My science teacher this year keeps saying I should go spend a day with him. Teachers encourage every student to get out in the real world of work, to learn from the people doing something of mutual interest.

"Interest" is a mild word when applied to this farmer. I read a newspaper article where he referred to himself as a lunatic. He also calls himself a Libertarian, which to him means keeping the government out of farming. I guess we'll get into that next year in government class.

For now, I'm more interested in how he does farming differently. And recently I finally got it together, on the courage front, to get in touch with him and set up a day to visit his farm. Today is the appointed day, which is why I'm currently driving up the narrow, dusty road that leads into Joel Salatin's farm.

He's standing out front when I pull up. I jump out of the car, feeling nervous, and walk up to him.

"Hello, Mr. Salatin, nice to meet you."

"Call me Joel, Jake, so I don't feel so old," he says, smiling.

He doesn't look so old, with his funny straw hat, though he does have a grown son who manages a good bit of the farm. But the main thing that makes him seem young is how he gushes over the animals, the grass in the pasture, and the marvels of nature. Other farmers I know in his generation seem hardened, hopeless about any positive landscape ahead; he's just the opposite.

It's one thing to read about the ecological symmetry of pigs, and cattle, and chickens in the pasture and its wooded edge. But it's another thing to hear him explain "Let a chicken be a chicken" for thirty minutes, with me hanging on his every word (though I have no clear idea what many of them mean).

"Where did you learn all this?" I can't bring myself to call him by his first name, yet.

"Getting a master's degree in English helped me learn to think and express my feelings, but it was my father who introduced me to the long tradition of environmentally conscious farming," he says. "Also, available land in the family presented an opportunity for years of experimentation. It all started with growing grass in healthy soil."

He delivers another thirty-minute lecture on the science of grass—the importance of its height, the critters living in the soil, and the contribution of animals in the pasture.

The tour ends with him showing me the outdoor area where the chickens and turkeys are processed, right next to where people come to the farm to buy fresh items once a week. He also sells at a farmers market and directly to restaurants in the area. Buying groups in towns organize for one person to make the drive to the farm and pick up what people want.

"The 'distribution' organization takes a lot of time and planning," he says. "Thankfully, my wife helps with that part of the operation."

He tells me about other farms in the area who are converting away from the industrial food system of tilling, nitrogen-based fertilizers, feed that's not good for the animals or the humans who eat them, and taking cows to markets that send them west to be processed before they're returned to the local grocery store, resulting in a $500-per-cow profit loss to farmers.

"That's corporate agribusiness for you," he says, taking off his straw hat and drying his forehead.

"I'm having a hard time convincing farmers in my area to try a new approach," I say. "They don't seem to believe it can be more profitable." I point to the crowd at his farm stand. "I mean, it's clear that more and more consumers want healthier and fresh foods. It seems like what happens in the distribution system is beyond the farmer's control, except for farmers' markets, which the farmers I know aren't interested in."

"Yeah, there are lots of things to figure out yet, which is why farmers need to be smart and get a good education," Joel says. "But I think it comes down to a moral issue of having a feel for the earth and every living thing. Believing nature has inherent value. I'm optimistic that young people your age have turned the corner toward sustainable agriculture and will be the ones who lead us in the right direction."

I've never thought of this approach to farming as being a moral issue. Dad always talks about the economic issues. Me, I just love the work. I guess you could say it is a moral thing, humans tending the land.

This visit with Joel is a real shot in the arm of enthusiasm—and I needed it. At the last Chautauqua meeting, I was argued down around the idea of getting farm-to-school food for our cafeteria. On the school end, Chief got funding from the local schools foundation for more refrigerators in our cafeteria, to replace the many freezers serving as coffins for dead food to be thawed and heated. But those refrigerator dollars are pending the Superintendent convincing the School Board to expand the number of cafeteria workers to cut and cook even more fresh food, planned largely around what is in season at the moment.

On the farmer end, they want up-front school commitment to guarantee amounts of dairy, produce, and meats the school will purchase. That way they can be safe in planting appropriate amounts of crops and making the expenditures on feed and livestock. But the school food services director says they are not allowed to buy from exclusive sources and have to get the best price at the moment, so they can't make the farmers any guarantees.

These arguments seem to me like technical issues. I think

what is really lacking is both sides seeing their mutual interests and taking a risk to do things differently, and I said so at the meeting. It didn't seem to convince anyone, though Chief did seek me out afterward, saying I did a good job making my case. He also told me he's been meeting with farmers individually, and has been impressed with how many times they've described my dad as a strong, quiet force.

My gloomy prospect around change is very personal. I have not been able to convince my dad to plant produce crops beyond the family vegetable garden we've always had. He keeps saying that the change would mean hiring workers to do the planting, tending, and harvesting crops, and that would mean him losing money on the deal. Plus, he says, you can't find reliable farm workers these days.

On the drive home from Joel's place, it hits me. I will propose to Dad we try growing crops just for the summer. I will find and manage the farm workers, and he can continue with his summer routine of haying for the cows for next winter and doing small construction jobs on the side.

Today in first period, I tell Sean, "I saw a farm just like what I want to do. Sustainable agriculture, and the farmer has people coming to the farm to buy food. I'm not sure about that last part, but I'm going to try to convince Dad to let me expand our farm and hire some helpers for the summer."

A couple of Sean's soccer player friends overhear me.

"Hey man," Jorge says, "I'm good at farming if you're going to hire workers for the summer."

"Me too," Amelio says. "We both have experience in crop planting, weeding, and harvesting."

"If you guys do it, I will too," Sean says. "It would be fun working together."

"Great!" I say, feeling galvanized. One big obstacle solved easily. I bet Dad never considered hiring immigrant workers. It's nice to have friends that will help me out and want to work with me.

Tonight, Dad and I hammer out a plan for the growing season.

"I'm willing to help you do this because I figure you need to experience all the pressures firsthand to see it isn't possible to make a go of small-scale farming these days," he says. "The high prices paid to FFA kids at the County Fair for the animals you raise is about farmers being supportive of young people, but that's not the way it works in the real world."

Our plan is to grow only produce that will be mostly picked by the time school starts in late summer. Dad will move his cows to a neighbor's field for the summer so we can use our fields of rich dirt, free of previous pesticides. He will also help me behind the scenes with each step of what needs to be done, and when. I will be in charge of managing the work with my crew of three, and maybe four at harvest time—though I'll have to figure out who that fourth person will be. With the exception of a tractor, all the work will be done by hand.

I insist the workers be paid minimum wage, $7.25 per hour, even though their young age and the total number of employees only requires a $4.25-per-hour wage for farm work. I suggest that Dad pay me at the end of the summer, and then only if there are enough profits to pay my salary. Starting in March, weekend workers will be in the greenhouses, setting up beds and mending fences part time. Dad will front the costs of all seeds and other supplies needed.

When Dad goes to bed, I call Sean to fill him in on our plans.

"Sounds awesome," he says. "And hey, I have your fourth farm worker! Cora. She can't work until harvest time, but that's perfect, right? The early part of the summer she'll be at Howard on scholarship in a science program for rising high school seniors. Ms. Hoffmann helped her get in."

Everything is coming together. I can't believe how well it's all going. "That's great for all of us," I say. "Cora will get to see if Howard is the college for her, and we'll get more help just when we need it. You're right, the timing is perfect."

I didn't expect to get all this help. Dad and his friends help each other out at times, but nothing like this. I better not get cocky, but I've passed the first major test in Dad's eyes for a summer he is betting will be a failure. I really needed this boost in confidence. Thanks, guys!

Wait, is that sexist?

Tests of the usual standardized type are taken at Stone Creek at the end of each year. My dad is much more interested in these tests than he is in my summer farming test.

He told me one of the Stone Creek counselors came to last night's Ruritan meeting to talk to them about giving scholarships to graduating seniors. She asked them to make financial need a priority in awarding scholarships, so all students get a fair shot at going to college.

"Charlie Parker asked her to explain all the tests that go on and are required by colleges," Dad says. "The counselor lady gave us a handout she went through because the testing craze has made things so complicated. She said there are three types of tests, most not required by colleges."

From here on, Dad is reading from the handout, shaking his head the whole time:

> The first is state-required tests, which all Stone Creek students take to justify class credit for graduation and are not required by colleges. Second, some Stone Creek "Saturday" students voluntarily meet during the year to prepare for: SAT tests they may or may not report to colleges; AP tests for credit from whichever college they eventually attend for a Stone Creek class they take with regular students during the week; and Dual Enrollment tests for college credit through the local community college. The third type of test is for all Stone Creek students—the PISA exam. This test is the one widely discussed in the news comparing the US to other countries. The PISA focuses more on

*skills like critical thinking than do typical standardized tests,
which ask for recall of information from memory. Many colleges
prefer to see high school teacher recommendations and results of
the PISA than other tests or information. Stone Creek teachers
prefer project portfolios to assess student growth over tests.*

"It seemed to us this testing malarkey is a mess," Dad says.
"What do you think?"

Finally, something we agree on. "I think you're right. All tests
do is make people nervous and feel like idiots. I know students who
score well on tests and yet they cannot say things clearly or solve
simple questions that come up in everyday life." Not so many kids
brag about their test scores anymore, of course. They've been shot
down too many times by those of us who know better.

"Why doesn't the school change things?" Dad asks.

"Chief is trying, Dad. I bet he would appreciate support from
the Ruritans."

"I got you to worry about. That's enough."

"You don't have to worry about me, Dad. I'm doing fine,
test or no test."

I switch the conversation topic to plans for the summer. Dad
passively listens to me talk about all my ideas for the farm, and even
though he's very helpful in explaining the nitty-gritty of what needs
to be done, he is not excited, or even mildly interested, in listening
to my outside-the-box ideas about future farming. My real partner
in dreaming is Chelsea, who actually listens to all my thinking
out loud about how farming has to change for new times. She
says listening is what she has always done, but I'm the first person
who has ever really listened to her. I feel the same way about her.

Sean, Jorge, and Amelio are easy to work with. Despite their play-
ful approach, I've already realized from our spring weekend work
just how much Jorge and Amelio know about the details of farm
work from past experience. They've already rescued me several

times when I misunderstood my dad's instructions. Dad's not long on words, and since he stays away from our actual work, I have to rely on his clipped explanations—not always the best formula for success.

In one of our downtime chats this weekend, I learn that the name "Amelio" means "hard-working," which fits his style. Jorge says his name is the same as "George" in English.

"That's my dad's name," I say.

Jorge laughs. "You must have smart grandparents, because the name means farmer."

"The name 'Jacob' means to replace with something that works better," I say. I googled my name long ago to see its origin and meaning, but thinking about it now it could be prophetic, making farming work better.

"Okay, don't laugh," Sean says, "but my name is the Irish version of John and supposedly refers to a people person—likable and optimistic. You think that's me—or 'mise,' in Gaelic?"

"No way!" I say, just as Amelio and Jorge both say, "*Ni hablar!*"—which I take to mean the same thing.

Then Amelio adds, "Well, maybe in a goofy kind of way," as he grabs Sean and kisses the top of his head.

Our conversations get pretty silly, but when we're working, it's all business. All three guys have amazing concentration; we like to work while singing along with loud music projected from an iPod, an unsupplanted source of energy for the rhythm of farm work.

One Saturday afternoon in mid-May, as we wait for a rain shower to pass, Chelsea appears in the greenhouse.

"Are you ready to hear my report of the CSA outside of Charlottesville?" she asks me.

I stop what I'm doing. "Yes!" The Community Supported Agriculture farm I asked Chelsea to check on is supposedly the most successful one in the area.

"The farm has been around for about five years, financed

by a wealthy person who lives in New Jersey," Chelsea says. "The CSA has five hundred members who pick up their allotted produce at a central location once a week. It is a mid-size farm, around twice as big as yours, Jake."

"Tell us about the important part, the workers," Amelio says.

"You're right, that is the important part, and the workers aren't too happy. They have about ten workers, all of them recent UVA graduates, and they're earning about $10 per hour. A few are paid by UVA as interns related to agriculture careers. Most are not experienced farm workers because there's substantial turnover every year. They're growing primarily vegetables. One of the workers' complaints is that a lot of food is wasted because the owners say people won't want the vegetables if they don't look perfect. That relates to major concerns from the workers that they have little say in how things are done on the farm and just feel like hired hands. On the upside, they're all young people who have a lot of camaraderie in the strenuous work."

I ask Amelio and Jorge, "How does that compare to places you've seen?"

"The main difference is the pay and exploitation immigrants experience," Jorge says. "If you have a work visa it's specific to one farm, and you can't legally leave to work someplace else."

"That sounds like the days of indentured servants and slavery here," I say.

Jorge nods. "The boss treats people badly, withholding from their pay, say, $200 per week for horrible housing on the farm, five people to a bedroom. The workers make minimum wage, which after deductions is not enough to pay off the money they borrowed to get to this country. Many do not speak English and have no idea what their rights are. Most end up leaving to work somewhere else."

"Sounds like a real change in farming is going to require changes in laws for immigrants and farm workers," Sean says.

I heave a sigh. While I know Sean's right, this all seems overwhelming to me right now.

✧   ✧   ✧

Our labor each day is physically hard, and sometimes we have to work long hours to be a step ahead of things like coming rain. Other days, we hang out in the greenhouse together, waiting for the rain to pass, even though I tell the guys they're off the clock during the down time and can leave. Nobody gets antsy or anxious about our lack of control over the weather. Instead, we accept and adapt to what Mother Nature sends our way. Sean and I are learning a lot from the spontaneous activities Amelio and Jorge engage in. We've all become pretty good at hacky sack. I'm the worst with my gangly frame, providing much laughter at my expense. If the humiliation gets too bad, I suggest the serious game where I excel—poker.

Sometimes friends drop in, rolling up their sleeves to help us weed or move irrigation drip hoses or whatever. Farmers in this area have a strong connection to the land from past farming days, but little present activity, maybe just a small herd of cows and a few chickens. My FFA friend, Will, from over the hill at Blacks Creek is our most consistent drop-in. Sean says he seems more like my dad than I do. I think, but don't say, *Except Will is black and my dad doesn't have any personal relations with blacks*. That's a battle Dad and I have had over and over again. I refuse to let any instance of his racism go by unnamed. He doesn't even get offended anymore, just says, "You're damned straight."

The other day, Daniel stopped in to do a story for the summer edition of the school newspaper. He recently wrapped up his stay at the group home.

"Chicos!" he boomed to Amelio and Jorge when he arrived.

"Daniel!" Both guys went over to shake his hand. They got to know each other pretty well after the start-of-the-year soccer fiasco was over.

Daniel was blown away by photographs Sean had taken of both our serious work and our antics. To add to the antic photos, he took a shot of Sean on top of a pile of hay bales in surfing stance—knees bent, arms spread to the side, his very sun-bleached hair gleaming in the sun.

Today I get a text from Daniel telling me to look at the spread on the school website. I show it to the guys on my tablet. In youthful style, the story on the website is more about our antics than it is a serious discussion of what we were up to. There are already dozens of comments from students about the story and photos. The photo of surfer Sean has a caption that reads, "Recognize this surf farmer?" A bunch of the responses to the photos of Sean, Amelio, and Jorge are emojis for things like "hot."

Amelio blushes when he sees the comments. Jorge looks smug.

"Of course, my strong brown body should be appreciated," he says, flexing.

The rest of us groan and then burst out laughing.

I think I should take Jorge to the farmers market with me next week. Maybe his outgoing personality will help me sell more vegetables.

Mid-July we celebrate Cora joining our ranks with an evening around the fire pit. She seems unusually quiet and reflective, not telling us much of anything about her month at Howard.

"That's just how Cora is," Sean whispers to me. "She needs alone time to think things through."

She's giving our get-together a very different aura than the silly days of our past month have had.

With the fire blazing heat in the cool night, after all of us have adjusted our mood to hers, Cora says, "I am so glad to be away from the hustle of civilization and back to the comfort of the country."

"What about the longing for big-city life?" Sean asks.

"I'm not sure," she says. "I definitely did not feel afraid in DC, mostly out on Howard-sponsored activities. But I also did not feel independent and confident like I do here. Right now, I just feel exhausted."

I hope the exhaustion doesn't last too long. We've got work to do.

✧   ✧   ✧

It came as no surprise that it didn't take Cora long these past few days to begin responding to the fun-loving Jorge and his sidekick Amelio, with Sean and me as their biggest fans.

Our regular late-afternoon guest is Chelsea. She and her dogs walk down the hill from her house just about the time the others are headed home. That timing works for me, because then I don't have to share her, particularly with Sean. He seems to get it and does not hang around or strike up one-on-one conversations with Chelsea, which is a relief.

The weeks before Cora returned, nobody said much about me and Chelsea hanging out. But Cora, not the silent type, asked on day one if Chelsea and I are an item now. I didn't have to say anything: Chelsea answers Cora through her daily appearances. My answer is a lightness of being whenever Chelsea is around. She and I have spent many evenings, and a few nights, together these past couple months. Of course my dad has no comment.

Chelsea's folks are traveling abroad for most of the summer. Chelsea says better them than her. She loves being home and answering only to herself and her girls, Ayla and Lily.

A couple of weeks ago she told me, "I am still so angry at my parents for separating us as kids, not taking our feelings for each other seriously."

In a strange way, her anger made me feel proud, like she would fight to keep us together now.

"They made me doubt myself," she said, "like I was wrong that our friendship was special. Eventually, I came to not trust their judgment, or mine, about anything."

Fortunately, I've seen a change in her spirit now that she's started working from mid-morning to early afternoon as a cook's assistant at a Quaker camp for teenagers. She told me a few nights ago, "My life was transformed today. A Sufi, who is also a whirling dervish dancer, taught 'turning' to the kids and me."

I must have looked confused, because she said, "It's like dancing meditation. Obviously, I have to practice and practice, like any art. But today was enough to give me a glimpse of an inner me I've never felt before."

Since then, she's been spending all her free time watching videos of whirling dervish dancers, practicing, and researching teachers who might come through our area.

"Is this like a cult?" I ask as we're walking to her house this evening.

"Just the opposite. It's all about connection to others, the world, from an authentic me."

Her words don't dispel my worry about this new interest. But when we have sex tonight, the way we fit together absolutely confirms Chelsea's opening up to the world and a budding, joyful spark.

Our idyllic pastoral life has been abruptly interrupted today by a surprising event: a category-five hurricane that's bearing down on the western Virginia mountains from the eastern coast. It's unusual for a hurricane to head so far inland. True, the strength and winds have died down some as it's crossed overland, but its swift movement during the middle of the night means that we'll have only this one frantic morning to try to harvest as much as we can before the damaging rain and flooding hit.

Before sunrise, I text media-wise Daniel and ask him to post a help request in every way he can think of, for people to come ASAP to the farm to harvest crops. My dad uses a more traditional approach, communicating through the local volunteer firehouse system to round up help.

Huge numbers of young people show up looking like they just rolled out of bed. The country folks who heard about our need through the firehouse show up with their whole families, and tools also. For a very long second I just stare at the onslaught of people jumping out of trucks, cars, and one school bus. I hear soft-spoken Amelio whisper, "Milagro."

Clearly, organization has to happen immediately. I start creating teams, pairing experienced farmers with green young people, to work here in the east uphill field. I turn to Jorge and Amelio and ask them to each take one of the downhill fields, form teams of workers for their field, and direct them to what needs to be done. They stare at me like I am nuts.

"Just do it," I plead.

Jorge and Amelio look at each other, shrug, and walk to their appointed fields. I yell to newly arrived people to follow Amelio and Jorge. They do.

A group of Blacks Creek farmers who heard me head off for the lower fields; one pats me on the back as he walks by and says, "Good call, Jake."

Another group of young, muscular white guys look at me as if daring me to ask them to mix with people "not of their kind." These are guys who stayed in the county after high school, spending a good bit of their time in the parking lot of the local bar, leaning on their confederate flag–draped pickups. Low-key Sean seems just the thing for them.

"Sean, would you show these guys where we left off yesterday up here in the west field?"

Just as I expected, walking determinedly along with Sean and the toughs is Cora. That's my idea of a compromise.

Dad's buddies take orders from him, hurrying off to collect tools to distribute to all the fields.

In the upper large field, I organize smaller kids to carry baskets for the produce to the pickers who need them. Young teens serve as runners, hauling baskets of picked produce to the greenhouse, where they will be protected in the storm.

While time flies by with the wind, the storm slows a bit when it hits the Blue Ridge Mountains. Seems the national forecasters aren't too used to a hurricane path like this one.

We pick for hours, until we can hardly feel the tips of our hands. Early drizzle has created mud that attaches to our boots and requires more effort from already exhausted leg muscles. I'm one of the fittest people here, and I have to hold back the tears of exhaustion and force myself to go on.

And now it happens: I can hear the storm bearing down on us. There's only enough time to make an all-out run for the house. And the closeness of the storm, signaled by screeching wind and the pop of limbs breaking, makes even the house destination questionable. Adults are quick to grab up youngsters, hold them close, and comfort their fear of the power of the wind. Strong young adults hang back to assist older workers, making sure everyone is accounted for. Just as the rain begins to come down in large drops, making vision almost impossible, the last of us tumble in through the basement doors.

Fortunately, our large, finished basement can accommodate the crowd of more than fifty exhausted bodies. The young collapse to the floor, leaving the furniture for their elders.

Dad's friends seem most at ease in this scenario. One of his buddies shouts to him, "Hey, old man, empty out the refrigerator and food cabinets."

Laughing, Dad obliges with quick reconnaissance missions up the basement stairs to the kitchen. Me, Sean, Amelio, and Jorge help bring the food and drinks he finds downstairs and start handing it all out.

Teenagers who live in town are super interested in our sturdy, built-by-hand log home. Not a speck of rain or wind pierces the exterior. I see a couple of them asking Dad questions about how he built it when he comes back down from the kitchen.

Then the ritual storytelling starts among the quiet of people gratefully chewing. The oldest farmers compete in "top me" stories of storms gone by. Kids ask lots of questions, egging on the stretching rights of the storytellers. Pretty soon, an entire history of the area, recounted through the storm theme, is cast.

Next thing I know, the sun is coming out. I guess that's the nature of a hurricane: fast and furious.

It was Sean's idea to call Chief and ask if we could haul all the vegetables to the high school cafeteria and set up a sort of farm stand there. I'm grateful for his quick thinking; I was too overwhelmed by the sight of all the pummeled produce remaining in the fields to come up with my own plan.

All our volunteer helpers load up produce and truck it to the high school.

When we're through organizing the produce on cafeteria tables, our presentation couldn't compare to something you'd see at Whole Foods or the local groceries, yet, to me the squash, corn, peppers, cucumbers, tomatoes, and greens of many varieties are an array of inherent beauty.

Shopping at our unusual farm stand becomes the after-hurricane thing to do. Word gets out to the university communities thanks to Sean's dad, and my dad lets the firehouses across the county know. Daniel, mister master organizer, even manages to get musicians to show up for an impromptu jam session.

Near the end of the evening the manager of the healthy foods co-op approaches me.

"Would you like us to take what's left of all this produce to the co-op store and sell them tomorrow?" she asks. "We'll pass along the money to you for the sales."

"Thanks, neighbor," I say. "You really live the cooperative spirit."

I get home late night, but despite the hour—and my total exhaustion (of the worry kind, not the physical kind)—I force myself to calculate total sales for the summer. My strategy for distribution and sales over the summer has been a weekly farmers market and also selling to the permanent produce stand guy, who pushes my vegetables as "local" but does not pay me close to what I charge at the weekly farmers market. The loss from the hurricane isn't going to mean so much since people buying vegetables at the school were very generous, many saying "keep the change" as they paid with large bills. And the free picking will help as well.

Dad has not been forthcoming with costs for supplies. I think it's his way of being supportive, not pressuring me to factor in that cost. It must have been very hard for him to shell out money for wages every week with nothing coming in.

I've been pretty tight with the labor costs, telling everyone not to come in on rainy days and saying they can leave early for afternoon rains, even though they usually hang around for free and hacky sack or poker. Now, the hurricane means they're losing the chance to get paid for the last two weeks of the summer. They seem to be okay with all that; it helps that they know they are being paid a higher salary than other farm workers (except the subsidized CSA). Also, they've all told me they felt respected in the day-to-day work, involved in the decision-making process. They also respect the fact I work so hard, including on weekends. They tease me that it's just an excuse to spend time with Chelsea, who was often my weekend free helper this summer, but really they know I'm busting butt. Cora's getting the worst deal of anyone, since she has only worked two weeks, but her mind seems to be elsewhere, and she probably won't care about not working these next two weeks.

I find Dad to go over the results of my calculations.

"Not good news," I tell him with a sigh. "Through today, it seems I'm short about $2,000, subtracting sales receipts from what you've paid out in wages. If I had been paid $10 per hour, that would be another $4,000. And I owe you for seed and other supplies."

"Well, Jake, you're out $4,000 of labor you don't get paid for. I'm out $2,000 in excess wages paid to your workers and about another $2,000 in supplies. Seems to me we're even. Both our losses are not too high a cost for you to learn, before you get in way over your head, that farming today is a losing proposition, money-wise, for a small farmer. Make going to college an attractive alternative?"

My calm, businesslike start to this conversation is punctured by Dad jabbing at the heart of the matter for me: my future. My only defense is to make clear what's at stake.

"No," I say, trying to control my temper. "I loved farming all summer. Not to make money. It's just . . . it's just who I am. Hard physical work, figuring out problems as they come up, making decisions with help from you and the guys, getting up early and watching the first rays of sun bringing everything to life, plants popping through the soil, getting to know how they're all different in the way they grow, feeling like this land is where I belong, and realizing I can count on a community to help me when I get into trouble—in part because of your friends and their respect for you."

"I hear how you feel about farming," Dad says. "I felt the same when I was your age. But time has passed us by. We have to adapt."

I can't just adapt to a life that kills my dream. I can't even imagine that, I can't even . . .

"Dad, there must be ways I can do things differently." *Please help me Dad, instead of just saying it's all over.* "My biggest problem was what to do with all the produce after it was picked. That's when things left my control. Small farmers have no system for easily selling their stuff. That's another whole part of the process that's messed up. Like, people are making money off selling the turnip greens *I* grow."

Dad gets a sharp edge to his voice. "You're talking about losing money on turnip greens. I lose $500 on every cow I take to market because it is shipped off somewhere and fattened up with stuff none of us should eat, and by the time it gets back to town I'm paying the store for all that stuff that happened in between."

"But if we expand into food distribution like the sustainable farmers are doing—selling directly to restaurants, buying clubs, and members of CSAs—then we're in a whole new business of marketing I don't want to do," I say, shaking my head. "There has to be another way, Dad. We need a more direct connection to consumers where we don't take on more responsibility. Something that's just as convenient as grocery stores for the buyers. Like, how many working people have time to go to a farmers market at a set time one day a week to buy fresh food? And how many farmers can take the time to go to the farmers market to sell their food?"

These questions would make sense if I was talking with someone at school about this whole problem. Why can't I get through to Dad?

"I know all this is hard for you to accept," he says. "But that's reality. I know it's your dream. That's why I wanted you to have a chance to experience reality, before it's too late."

I've experienced your reality, Dad, but my reality is just starting. Failure means looking for another way forward. I'm only sixteen. There's no way I'm resigning myself to "it is what it is."

Still riding the high of the hurricane day, Chelsea, Cora, Daniel, Sean, Amelio, Jorge, and Will decide to celebrate our summer's end with a late-night bonfire at my fire pit. Only Chelsea knows how down I am about the financial results of the summer. For everyone else's sake, I need to be in a positive frame of mind. I want to celebrate their hard work and loyalty.

First order of business is, of course, roasting marshmallows to put on graham crackers with chocolate bars. Among a small group of friends, chocolate is more satisfying than alcohol. That's a law of nature—google it.

The next best thing is laughter. Sean and Jorge accommodate this need by acting out vignettes of disaster, such as how to chase a cow out of the pasture before she tramples the vegetables. The slapstick is the real humor.

Chelsea points to the stars, set in an ebony sky, and says, "There I am—Libra, my birth constellation."

"I've always had a thing for Aquarius, the water-bearer," Sean says, pointing. "But it is always so faint and pretty much impossible to find. Then there's the idea we're entering a new age—you know, the hippie song, 'The Age of Aquarius.' Supposedly, peace and love will guide the planets."

"You do know, don't you, that the idea of the New Age, when Jupiter aligns with Mars, is not scientifically precise?" Cora says, gazing up at the sky.

Sean shrugs. "I don't need it to be precise. Still, combining the poetry of peace and love with science, I wonder where we are now, in the big picture."

"I like the Carl Sagan statement, 'We began as wanderers and we are wanderers still,'" Cora says.

"That's awesome, Cora." Sean grins. "I like thinking of

myself as a wanderer, combined with adventure. Maybe we're the generation of grown-up *Star Wars* bearers of the force," Sean says, escalating in excitement with every sentence.

"Let's go around and answer this question posed in my sophomore science class," Cora says: "What word best describes your self-defined identity as a being in nature? You can only answer with one word, no explanations of why you picked that word."

Starting with Cora, we go around the circle:

CORA: "I think of myself as *human*."

CHELSEA: "I feel things really shifting for me. Lately, I've been preoccupied with the word *mammal*."

JORGE: "Nobody will be surprised if I answer *male*."

AMELIO: "My answer is *brown*."

SEAN: "You're a man of few words, Amelio, but they're always powerful ones. I choose *cetacean*."

DANIEL: "My experiences this last year have resulted in a deep dive into how I see everything in the world, including myself. My identity is an *animal*."

WILL: "*Dark*."

ME: "*Dreamer*."

"Next, we try to guess *why* each person chose that word," Cora says. "We keep guessing until we get the right reason."

Some people's words are somewhat easy to guess about, since most of us know each other pretty well. One identity factor is obviously ethnicity, with Cora saying "human," not "race," and Amelio being proud of his "brown" heritage. We all wrongly assumed Will was referring to his black ethnicity; when we ask, he explains that he chose "dark" because he is fascinated by darkness, night, and mystery. It took a long time for us to guess his reasoning, showing that even though I knew him best, none of us know him well. For Jorge, male machismo rules with girls. My word, "dreamer," was also cultural, like ethnicity and gender.

The rest of the "whys" turn out to be more related to nature. Chelsea explains her newfound desire to have children, which has prompted viewing herself as a mammal who will birth and care for children. Sean's spirit is tied to life in the ocean.

The most complex explanation comes from Daniel, who, of course, has spent this past year in deep soul searching. His conclusion is that humans think of themselves as exceptional, better, within nature. People build up artificial things that end up hurting other animals, nature, and ourselves. Daniel thinks remembering he is "only" an animal will keep false journeys in perspective. And as an animal within the huge planet and cosmos, he is nurtured by our awesome home.

What Daniel says really hits home for me. That kind of thinking is what underlies my love of the farm. The events of the summer have given me that understanding about myself, even as they've forced me to confront the overwhelming practicalities of living in a world that hasn't yet catapulted to where I dream.

Beautiful as Daniel's statement was, though, the truth is I am stuck in the vision of Chelsea as a mom.

Chapter 11: Freedom Fighters

Once upon a time, a band of friends battled a corn king.

JAKE

Driving into the Stone Creek parking lot for the fall opening day of school, I park my truck, sit back, and, as I often do, take stock of my dream failure. What pops into my head is the first time I met Sean, when he told me I was lucky to know what I wanted in life. Turns out I only knew part of it—the farm.

The community's support before and after the hurricane was like a passing down of the baton from my father's generation to mine. Personal support like I've never had before came from friends who I knew would be there for me through it all. Most unbelievable for me was the summer life Chelsea and I shared, and our sense of certainty with each other.

Chelsea almost decided to drop out of UVA this summer. But then she found a Charlottesville group engaged in learning to "turn" from a Sufi whirling dervish teacher who comes to town several times a year, and is in the direct line from Rumi. Chelsea says her goal for the year is finding a bigger self. Bet that's not in the UVA curriculum.

I miss her already, but then I would be embarrassed to see a "poor Jake" look from her as I wallow in self-pity every day, obsessing about my summer failure as a farmer.

The walk from my truck to the school building, surrounded by majestic mountains, reminds me of Daniel's campfire vision of our nest in nature. As I open the front door, I have to laugh at the big "no fear zone" sign.

The first person I see is Cora. We give each other a big hug, and then walk together to the library, the senior first period home.

Chief leads the opening activity. "You folks started here in ninth grade, the same year I first came to Stone Creek," he begins. "I believe we've been bringing about change here every day since. I think we've been adjusting how we see school toward a different paradigm. Let's test out my belief. Everyone close your eyes and visualize the organization of Stone Creek. What do you see? What's in the frame of your picture?" Chief waits a considerable amount of time, until people start shuffling. "Okay, shout out a description of your picture when I point to you, and your three counselors up here will write what you say on a flip chart."

For every shout-out, the counselors look at each other and decide who will write it on their list. By the end, one list has picturing words, like the parking lot, principal's office, the science and math classes on the first floor and social studies and English classes on the second, and students cutting off their phones and heading to class. The second flip chart list has people going to their lockers, a kid glued to a computer screen, and a teacher writing notes at his desk. The third list has friends waving for another person to come join them, a lively debate at circle time that begins class, a group of students laughing, and a teacher helping someone with a project.

Chief points to the first flip chart. "Seeing the first list, we could say it is a view from the outside looking in. There's a principal and a student, two different roles for people in the school, and they are related to each other by the hierarchy of their role, me on top." That comment gets lots of laughter. "The student is turning off a phone because . . . right, that's the rule. So we have a picture of power structure, roles, and rules. That's the definition of a structure that is a bureaucracy, or, visually, a pyramid."

I've never thought of Stone Creek as a power structure. I suppose you could think of any setup, like family or work, in power terms. But it seems to me the "I've got more" thing just gets in the way of relationships and accomplishing things.

"Okay," Chief says, moving over to the second flip chart, "this second set of pictures looks like people doing things individually." He moves to the final chart. "In the third set of visualizations we see friends, welcoming, emotion, fun, and helping. This third vision is where we want to be, correct?"

Finger snaps, sounding like a hoard of insects, signal out our answer. Last year our class switched from the practice of clapping to finger snapping.

"I think we have been labeling something incorrectly for the last several years, and that is holding us back in fully reaching this last paradigm," Chief says. "We have talked at length about 'individual interests.' That's a misnomer. No interest is truly individual. Many people—scientists, artists, writers—share your interests. We should have been saying 'personal' interests, emphasizing that these interests come from within each of us and yet we want to connect with others around them."

It feels like Chief is talking directly to me, where my head is at this morning.

"This last view of connections looks like a circle, or overlapping circles, or webs of connection, the links between us strengthening over time," he says. His delivery is getting louder and faster, so you know he's getting to his main point. "The circles, or webs, represent a new paradigm. That view explains why teachers want you to 'circle up' for discussions in class, right? They don't want to stand at the front of the class and dispense information to you top down, right?" He reaches his finale: "Scholars describing strong interconnections among people say they are based on acceptance of each individual as a whole person, in the present, and are often hard to describe in words. You can recognize that interconnection when you feel calm satisfaction, in sync with all around you. How's that vision for a life worth living at school this year?"

I don't know. He lost me at the end. I get the strong interconnections idea, like my life over the summer with Chelsea, Sean, Jorge, Amelio, Cora, and Daniel. Also, ever since the campfire night, I've been thinking about Daniel's vision. It helped me realize something important. I never felt anger toward the hurricane. Nature is. Humans are interconnected with all of nature. We just need to figure out how to be a part of the bigger scheme of things. There's a strange kind of security in that understanding, even though disaster happens.

Morning block is government/rhetoric with Sean, Daniel, and Cora. Question of the day: "What is freedom?"

"Doing whatever I want," one student calls out.

Ms. Jordan, our government teacher says, "Like, using your cell phone in school?"

She receives a rousing chorus of, "Yes!"

"What if I presented credible data from brain research showing there is no such thing as multitasking?" Ms. Jordan asks. "You can't do two things at once, like texting and driving, for instance."

"I can," says a guy who's into drag racing.

"I would love to see research results from you that demonstrate your belief," Ms. Jordan says. "What I've seen from neuroscientists is that the brain cannot function that way." She continues, "Let me give another example. If one of you is using your phone right now, you are saying to the rest of us that what we are doing is unimportant to you, an example of disconnection." She gauges our response to this statement. "Okay, I'm sure many of you are still skeptical, so let's switch gears. I would like for you to free-write one page expanding on the following statement: *If government ceased to exist, my life would be different because . . .*"

When I look up from my writing, I see many students are writing more than one page. That kind of pushes me to go deeper. When most of us have wound down, Ms. Jordan suggests we form small groups and share our answers.

My small group gathers under the window on the carpet, using pillows as seats. We are surprised to find a lot of similarity in our writing. The lead sentence for several of us is, "If government ceased to exist, I would not be in school, a government requirement." From there, however, we have gone in many different directions, describing life amid lawlessness and survival of the fittest expressed with weapons, all the way to "Armageddon." Looking around our comfortable environment, this conclusion is mind-boggling for me.

The other groups report similar scenarios. When conversation begins to peter out, Ms. Jordan brings us back from our small groups to huddle back together in one large group.

"So, we could think of freedom not as freedom *from*, in this case government, but freedom *to* establish security through each person's involvement in deciding rules for the common good," she says. "Deciding together would require establishing trust in working with others, despite our differences. That's the modern idea of democracy: government by the people, each person having a vote."

"That sounds like the connection with others Chief was talking about this morning in first period," one student says.

"So school should be a democracy?" another student asks.

"It has to be if we're going to learn to make decisions for ourselves," someone else says.

"I agree with you," Ms. Jordan says. "We all act within the previously established rules, but those can be changed if people see the necessity to do so. For example, you are all taking required classes commonly accepted as providing a broad foundation of knowledge of our current world. But each of you see that field through a lens of your personal—not individual—interests."

When nobody jumps in to say anything, she says, "Okay, what do we call government rules we must all go by?"

Various answers are called out: "laws," "regulations," "court rulings," "what the president decides," and "what adults tell kids they have to do."

Whew. This class is going to be a challenge for me.

"What are the rules bigger than all the things said so far?" Ms. Jordan asks.

More answers flow forth: "religion," "love," "survival of the fittest," "money," "the Constitution."

"Bingo," Ms. Jordan says, and stops for a dramatic pause. "The United States Constitution. Examining the Constitution, we'll see how those other values you mentioned are reflected."

"What about other countries?" someone asks.

"Remember our Model UN work? There are treaties countries sign."

"Also we have agreements directly with other countries, not through the UN, like trade agreements and military alliances," a student says.

"So all this discussion is the foundation of government," Ms. Jordan says. "Next I'd like to suggest we switch gears to illustrate what we've already said by talking about your personal politics, conducting an examination of your stand on current issues in the US. You don't have to declare your stand publicly if you don't want to. What's important for our analysis is the range of views represented in the room, from 'liberal' to 'conservative,' in political terms. As we discuss issues during the year, we will want to make sure we include a wide range of views. That will increase understanding for all of us. And if we're really going to focus and listen to each other, that means no cell phones on during class. If you have an emergency, you may go to the office or use your phone in the cafeteria. See? A good rule exists for a reason, and has necessary exceptions."

Uh-oh. I have no practice in political conversations. My dad doesn't like to discuss politics. When something comes up, he tends to rant about the government being involved way too much. As for me, I have no clue what I personally think about issues. But I bet Ms. Jordan is going to insist I figure out my views. In some ways, she sounds like a science teacher. They always quote Socrates, saying we have to walk around a problem, seeing the various perspectives, connections to other problems, doing things to reveal the complexity, until understanding emerges. I get science pretty well, so maybe I'll just try to remember the circling-around-it method when things confuse me in government class.

✦   ✦   ✦

At lunch, Sean comes to the FFA club group with Amelio and Jorge. Along with Will, we talk about the hurricane day, which some students want to know more about. Probably because Sean is so friendly and outgoing, the FFA students warm up to Amelio and Jorge, and vice versa.

At one point Jorge says to Sean, "Hey, man, I hear you're running for Senior Class President. Why do you want to do that?"

"To make sure students are heard by the adults," Sean says. "The four student class presidents meet with one teacher, one counselor, and one parent at least once a month. Everyone expects the group to surface issues not being dealt with and inform Chief. Then Chief farms the issue out to the appropriate working group, always made up of representatives of students, school staff, and community members, to decide needed changes."

"Sounds like a lot of extra work," Jorge says.

"I'll make sure it's fun, too," Sean says.

"How will you be able to do that without me?" Jorge says, elbowing him.

Sean laughs. "I'll survive somehow!"

We head to Spanish class after the meeting, and Sean tells me, "Amelio and Jorge will be working some this year as conversation leaders for a Spanish 2 class. So you can shine in ways other than just having fun, right Jorge?"

"I hope you aren't going to miss too much of Spanish 4, 'cause I need your help!" I tell them.

"Not after the summer, man," Jorge says. "You're good to go."

We walk into class and find seats next to Daniel, who just came from a newspaper meeting. As soon as we sit down, he turns to Sean.

"One of your opponents running for class president filed a complaint with the Conflict Resolution Council," he says. "The student, Izyan, is new at Stone Creek. He moved here over the summer from Turkey because his father teaches at your dad's college. Apparently some students have been calling him 'ISIS' outside of adult hearing range. A few students have tried to intervene on his behalf, but the harassers refuse to stop."

"That's awful," Sean says.

The rest of class, it's all I can think about.

When I tell Dad about the conflict with Izyan at dinner, he brushes it off, saying, "The new kid needs to toughen up and adjust to where he's living now." Then, switching the topic away from politics, he says, "Word on the street"—meaning his Hardee's friends—"is coaches are ticked off with the school. The football coaches complain the kids are not motivated and aggressive like players in the past. Like winning is not a big deal. Apparently, players are asking the coaches to tone things down and talk to them rather than yell . . . can you believe that?" He snorts and shakes his head.

"What's the big deal about that?" I ask.

"Get this," Dad says, "the guys on the team even want to be able to give more input to the coaches about what plays are working and which aren't. Can you believe that? Is that the stuff they're teaching you kids at school?"

I know it's useless to argue with him, so I say, "We don't play football at school, Dad."

He drops it too. I guess both of us are tired of fighting these battles.

I don't usually think much about sports, but the topic has been on my mind since last night's conversation with Dad, so today I ask Jorge and Amelio why they don't play soccer on the competitive team.

"We don't like to call attention to ourselves," Amelio says.

Of course, I think. It's dangerous for them to stand out; it's a threat to their family, increases their likelihood of being deported. I'm guessing the "we just like to have fun" thing from Jorge is a cover for the pain he feels in having to hold himself back in so many ways.

I'm still thinking about it later, as Cora and I walk to class together. In a different twist on the topic, I ask her, "How do you know how to talk with people over touchy subjects? My dad and I love each other, but we can't talk about things we disagree on."

She tells me she's learning a lot being on the CRC. "It's about not choosing one thing over another; it's about trying to see both sides and coming up with not a compromise but a way forward that encompasses what both sides want. We've met our biggest challenge yet with this 'ISIS' thing. I'll let you know how that all turns out."

I don't get the idea of not choosing one side over the other. Clearly the new kid shouldn't be hassled.

A few days later, Cora tells me how things are unfolding. First, the CRC couldn't meet to hear the conflict because only Izyan agreed to the approach. The harassers did not. They said ISIS was a major threat to the United States and has beheaded US citizens, and Izyan has refused to denounce Islamic extremists. Izyan said he was not an extremist and the students had put him in that category based on his religion alone, which has many different groups of followers.

"I told the CRC that was like someone from another country calling me a KKK member because I'm a Christian," Cora says, rolling her eyes.

I'm impressed. "That's a good comeback!"

She also tells me one of the American students wants to eventually be in the CIA, and he sees this as a test of his loyalty. His father is retired CIA and supports him.

"What do you think about the guy saying it's a loyalty test?" I ask her.

"I don't buy that reasoning. But I'm trying to figure out what the common ground is here."

The CRC facilitator, one of the oldest members of the faculty, told Cora and the other council members her guess was that many students have questions around this whole issue, just as many people had strong feelings about communism when she was growing up. Also, in college she was involved in various movements, like for women and civil rights, and she said their strategy was to have a "teach-in," where students would skip classes and come discuss the issue in a "free speech" area.

Cora loved that idea and proposed we try it for this issue at Stone Creek. The CRC agreed and recommended to Chief that a "talk-in" be scheduled during first period. Students can voluntarily, or not, participate in small group discussions about what is going on in the Middle East and how it affects the US. A teacher will be in each group, primarily to listen, but also to provide information when asked. All students will be told we now have a student whose home is Turkey.

A teacher who can provide information to people in a group—I like that part. I have no idea what's going on in the Middle East.

Cora told me Chief agreed to the "talk-in" and spoke with Izyan about his right to file a complaint with the School Board if he continues to have concerns in the future with how he is being treated. "And get this, Jake, I looked up 'Izyan' to see what the name means. It means 'one who possesses wisdom.' We'll see what we can learn from all this Monday first period."

After first period Monday, I saw Izyan in the hall several times throughout the day, always surrounded by a group of people. It's like he has become an instant rock star. I'm glad people have opened up to him; besides it meaning that he has new friends, it also means the hasslers are keeping their distance.

Sean was pretty good about not panicking over his election prospects with Izyan's new popularity. The whole thing forced him to better articulate his qualifications for being president over someone who is new to the school. And today he won the election 59 percent to 41 percent, with the other candidates having dropped out.

Seems to me it's a win all around. Izyan is now a part of the school, Sean learned to not take his skills for granted, and a lot of people like me now know a whole lot more about what is going on in world politics. Maybe I can get the hang of government class after all.

When I walk into science/math block on Monday, my physics teacher says, "Jake, I know about your passion for farming. What do you think about the Fresh Food news?"

I have no idea what he's talking about. "What Fresh Food news?" I ask with a frown.

"My wife works for the county planning commission, and she heard a presentation from a large agribusiness, King Corn—they're a subsidiary of Planet Oil—about plans to come into our area with a spinoff called Fresh Food," he says. "They've already gotten pledges of support from our representatives in the Virginia General Assembly, the current governor, and both the candidates running for governor in November. Based on extensive market research, they plan to develop local agricultural potential by capitalizing on consumer desire for local, fresh food."

I do some online research during class and find out that King Corn plans to buy up a lot of farm land in this area and grow food for their regional distribution center in the county, yet to be built. They say this will mean an efficient system to replace many national suppliers, as well as the scanty hodgepodge of small farm producers of everything from beef to cheese to apples to honey to corn in the area. The local produce and meats will go from the distribution center straight to local grocery stores, restaurants, schools, hospitals, prisons, etc., eliminating the need for local businesses to deal with national or regional food supply corporations, and for consumers to make special trips to farm stands, farmers' markets, and food cooperatives.

Armed with this information, I go back to my physics teacher. "Why are they going to the county planning commission?" I ask. I don't understand that part.

"Because King Corn wants all kinds of tax breaks, regulatory exemptions, and government infrastructure, like water, sewer, and utilities for the regional distribution center," he explains. "In exchange for this local support, King Corn provides economic development opportunities for the county, like jobs."

I smell a rat. Why should this corporation get tax breaks and exemptions local businesses don't get? How is this going to help local farmers?

At dinner last night I told Dad about King Corn and their Fresh Food model for here. He scoffed at the whole idea, saying, "That idea doesn't make a bit of sense."

But a day goes by, and at tonight's dinner, Dad has a different tone.

"The guys at Hardee's say it might be true," he says. "Some of them are actually thinking they would like to sell their land to someone who would farm it. They're too old and they don't want to see a subdivision where their farm used to be. It would also help the community with jobs. Not only for farm workers but for people who could work at the distribution center, which would have a large USDA slaughterhouse and food processing plant."

How can he do a 180-degree turn in twenty-four hours? Why didn't he trust what I told him last night and want to discuss it with me?

"What do *you* think, Dad?" I demand. "What about me and my FFA friends who want to farm?"

"Jake, I'm sorry, but I thought you learned this summer it's not a realistic idea for your future."

He's back to rubbing my nose in failure. I'm fuming now. "But King Corn's plans are realistic because they have a lot of money?"

I ask this in a shout, unable to hold back. And once the words are out I don't wait to hear his answer; instead, I retreat to my room, where my anger turns to feeling depressed and very alone.

I need to quit exploding at my dad. My dream is destroying my relationship with him. I can't lose him too. I don't know how Jorge and Amelio find the inner strength to let things roll off their backs.

This morning I find it impossible to concentrate on school details; my internal rudder feels broken. I gravitate to the only other people in the building who seem as passionate as me about our food future: the cafeteria staff.

"Ms. Goodbar, how are things going?"

She slices a warm piece of fresh bread and hands it to me. "Hey Jake, sorry I missed your hurricane sale. I was out of town, visiting my daughter in Kentucky and meeting my new grand-daughter. Things go well for you over the summer, other than the hurricane?"

"Not really. Seems farming for my future comes down to money. I hate that."

She puts her arm around my shoulders and as we continue talking, she gently rocks me sideways. "Well, I've seen people start-ing to come around," she says, her voice soothing. "There are a few local farmers taking a risk to meet our requirements. But I agree, it does come down to money. If we have to keep paying the prices farmers want, we'll have to charge more for lunches, and that's when the school board will balk."

"What can I do to help?" I ask.

This conversation feels so different from the one with Dad. Both Ms. Goodbar and I are trying to work out a problem, together. Her always-positive stance helps pep me up too.

"Well, you could try to win over our head of Food Services for the schools. She's used to the old days, when the school board didn't care about food and expected her budget to be in the black as top priority. She's not even a nutritionist, but she does have a business background; she's the one who deals with budget numbers."

"Maybe I could find other schools doing more than us and ask their food person to talk with ours."

"That's a good idea!"

There's the encouragement I needed.

Ms. Goodbar continues, "The Food Services lady keeps saying we can't do this and can't do that because of Virginia and USDA regulations. If other people are doing things, they could help her see how."

Chief happens to be walking by, and I call him over. After catching him up on our conversation, I say, "Chief do you know of any other schools buying locally?"

"I've talked some with a Harrisonburg high school principal, but I don't know details," he says. "I'll find out who their food services person is and you and ours can make a trip up there. I would like you to focus on state and federal regulations and how Harrisonburg deals with that, because sometime soon somebody on our school board is going to ask me about the issue."

This is great; two short conversations, and not only am I being listened to, I'm being helped to do something about my worries. And as a side advantage, I now have a government class project. My mood is improving, being able to throw myself into something I care about.

The trip to Harrisonburg is very educational, not only regarding learning regulations and ways to frame farm-to-school issues but also regarding what is required for change.

Despite everything the Harrisonburg food services person is sharing with us about their successes, Stone Creek's food services person asks every negative question she can think of, mostly about costs and prices. I try to remember Cora's mantra, "You have to see both sides." Seems my agenda is to address the cost stumbling block.

One aspect of farm cost must be addressed: wages for farm workers. I find an ally in Daniel, who has chosen to do a big-picture look, journalism style, at US government through a contemporary issue, immigration. Apparently during his time in the group home he built a close friendship with a guy living on the margins as an immigrant.

Daniel's research presentation to the class involves explaining our complicated government system. He shows us a circular diagram, with points on the circle for "we, the people"; the US Constitution; the legislative, executive, and judicial branches; the fifty state governments; and life decisions outside of government. He tells us an aspect of the issue of immigration, and we tell him where it fits on the circle diagram. Many issues involve multiple points on the circle. Examples he throws out include:

- Requirements to be a US citizen
- Eleven million undocumented people are living in the US. No path to citizenship
- All children, even those without documents certifying them as legal immigrants, are allowed to go to school
- Recent government action to defer deportation against people who arrived in the US as children, as well as their parents
- Despite passage of laws, poor working conditions for immigrants; one large area of work, two million farm workers

Many sub-issues and sub-parts of our government come up under each big topic. Even though I am mainly interested in farm workers, I see how everything ties together. Like, large agricultural employers get away with violating wage and hour laws because penalties are cheaper than abiding by the laws, there's little active oversight of laws by Congress, and government representatives are pushed by businesses and their money (like for election campaigns) to not take strong actions.

Boiling it down in my head, farm workers need to be paid a decent wage and have a stake in their work beyond money. Can that be done despite the standoff between our representatives in government?

✧ ✧ ✧

In Spanish class, Sean and I brainstorm about all this.

"Where would the money come from to raise salaries for immigrants?" Sean asks me.

"The small- and even medium-size farmers are barely making it," I say with a sigh. "The money is in the large agribusinesses, which includes not only corporate farms but also feedlots, slaughterhouses, and suppliers of farm equipment, seeds, pesticides, and stuff like that."

Our instructor, who is from Spain, overhears our discussion and asks, "Have you guys heard about Mondragon?"

Sean and I immediately start researching it. Short story is Mondragon is an area in the northern region of Spain where in the 1950s they started worker cooperatives. The idea was to stem the negative effects of industrialization on workers. Basically, workers are member/owners of the business, and each member has one vote in how it is run. They even elect their managers. Sounds like the self-government Ms. Jordan talks about, but in the workplace. Mondragon cooperatives have lasted over the years, and now have 147 companies and 80,000 workers.

Sean and I look at each other and say in unison, "Why not here?"

"It will take a lot of researching to figure out how something like that could work here," I say.

"How about a field trip to Spain?" Sean says.

Worry turns to hope for me.

Word about Fresh Food has gotten around fast. The five elected Supervisors who run Stone Creek County set up a meeting for the corporate representative in charge of Fresh Food to speak, and the community turnout tonight is even larger than it is when the supervisors talk about tax increases. Missing are college people, like Sean's dad. The meeting is on familiar turf for me, the high school auditorium.

The first interesting thing to me is that the corporate rep is black. Around here you don't see many minority people in positions of power. I'm sitting next to Cora, and she is visibly squirming in her seat. This must be a real conflict for her between black as good and black as a potential threat to her community. This guy speaks with a Boston, Kennedy-style accent not typical of Midwest agribusiness locations. He's clearly identifiable as an outsider by his pinstripe suit and silk tie. No warm and fuzzy "glad to be here," and such.

He starts with an announcement: "King Corn sent letters this morning to landowners with farms in the catchment areas of interest to us. Each letter contains a specific offer amount for the land parcels identified. This initial offer is quite generous and will be the highest offer put on the table. Failure to sign a contract by the date specified will result in subsequent reduction in land price offers."

So that's what power looks like in action. Sign or else. No negotiation.

"Second, I have already secured land for the distribution facility and filed information to the County Supervisors for needed assistance in infrastructure, expedited regulatory approval, and negotiation of tax abatements. The USDA and Virginia regulatory bodies have committed to speedy support and required approvals. Finally, King Corn is committed to the success of this cutting-edge business approach to growing and distributing fresh food on a regional basis." He sits down.

Daniel leans over to me. "That last statement means they expect to take a loss in the start-up to underprice local competitors, while making it clear to national suppliers that they're taking a non-compete stance."

I stand up and move to a microphone, feeling like David about to be squashed by Goliath. "I would like to ask if your plans include undercutting current arrangements between schools and local farmers for purchase of food."

King Corn corporate guy looks totally annoyed at having to answer a question from a kid. "Son, we at King Corn are committed to an efficient business model that offers all our customers, including schools, the best price for quality products. A contracting process is already underway with one local college, and another is anticipated to sign since it is a state-supported college."

When I return to my seat, fuming, Daniel says, "I researched King Corn's Board of Directors. One of them is also on the Board of Trustees for Sean's dad's college. Bingo!"

The rep drones on for a while longer, and then a few other people speak. After the meeting is over, Sean says, "We should organize the farmers to not sell their land."

"I think some will see it as their only choice," I say, shaking my head. "We need to be able to offer another choice." I can't muster much enthusiasm after my battering at the microphone.

"Like Mondragon cooperatives?" Sean asks, his eyes opening wider.

"Something like that." I feel a flicker of hope, but I can only sustain it for a moment before it dies out.

When I come home, angrier than I have ever been, I avoid Dad, who did not go to the meeting, and head straight to bed. No relief emerges; I get more exhausted with every toss and turn. I have to learn to stand on my own. This is my dream, my life.

About midnight I get a text from Cora, "Check Facebook message."

Her message:

Daniel and I talked after the meeting. I decided to talk with the King Corn corporate representative, using what I've learned in conflict resolution training. I told him I wanted to explain the point of view of a significant part of the community he may not have heard. I also said it was to everyone's advantage that the development he proposes be a positive one.

He said, "I'm creating opportunities for people in a dying former farming area. Farmers can make good money, residents will save money on the cost of food, and new jobs will be created."

I responded, "In order for farmers to decide to sell their land, they need to feel they can trust you. Now, you are perceived as an outsider. They don't know you. Perhaps you could spend some time getting to know people and speak to your values beyond money and the values of your corporation."

He said, "This is a business deal, young lady, not a community social. Farmers will come around because it is the best financial choice they have at the moment."

I said, "People here think in the long term. They have seen how new businesses coming in work. The cost of food will stay low until all the small farmers and local food businesses are put out of business. Then, with no competition, prices will be raised higher than ever. The good paying jobs created will go to people brought in from out of town, with the hard labor jobs done by low-wage workers, probably many migrants. Meanwhile, you will be promoted and move on to some other community to replicate what happens here."

He says, "You think you're pretty smart, don't you? I advise you to focus on schoolwork and go to a good college so you can get a successful job like mine."

I say, "I don't want a sell-out white man's job. If you knew me, saw beyond the presumptions of my appearance, you would understand that. And, you won't get what you want from this community with your view that money motivates them. They care deeply about the land and their neighbors."

Laughing, he says, "We'll see."

My strategy didn't work, Jake. It's like the CIA-identified student who refused to engage in resolving the conflict with Izyan. We have to figure out how to get this corporate guy to pay attention. I'm all in for the struggle!

"I told Sean's dad about the guy on the Board of Directors of King Corn and Board of Trustees of his college, and he promised to put in some discreet inquiries," Daniel tells me at school today.

He and Sean's dad have become very close since Daniel's group home days, when Sean's dad visited him every Saturday. I guess not having a father can be as hard as trying to separate out from one to gain independence.

"That's awesome, thanks for doing that," I say.

He gives me a slap on the back. "I gotta run, but I'll catch up to you later," he says and heads down the hall. Sean walks up just as Daniel is walking away, his brow furrowed.

"Mr. Corporate would pay attention if Chief came out against Fresh Food," he says, shaking his head, "but he won't do it. I told him his friend the newspaper editor will write in opposition to King Corn. The school board members are influential, too, and they would back him. Parents would listen to him too. But he said no, it's not his job to take sides on community issues. 'I will defend your right to question and take a stand,' he said, 'but I advise you not to create enemies, sides, or victims. Stand for yourselves and all in the community.'" Sean kicks the ground. "I feel totally betrayed. Doesn't he even care?"

I put a hand on his shoulder. "Look, we have to calm down and be smart about this. There's too much at stake to be hotheads. Let's go hole up in the library and think this through."

And we do just that, going over and over every aspect, but we're making no headway.

"Tell me again what you shouted at your dad at the dinner table," Sean finally says.

"I'm ashamed for yelling at him." I look down. "I'll apologize tonight."

"No, no, you said King Corn's plans are realistic—"

"Because they have a lot of money."

Sean jumps up from his chair and points at me. "Jake, that's it. Our plan can be realistic with what we've got—not money but a whole community that already knows how to cooperate. We don't have to convince people here about cooperatives like Mondragon, because we already have cooperatives all over the place. It's one of the first things I noticed when I moved here: the Farmers' Co-op, the Electric Co-op, the Free Clinic, Stone

Creek Conservation Council, Food Co-op, Stone Creek Artists' Co-op, Volunteer Firefighters, Stone Creek Solar Co-op, and I'm sure more I'm not thinking of. Co-ops where there are member/owners who make decisions about how to operate to provide services as nonprofits. Some of them, like the Farmers' Co-op, have been around for a hundred years. But they're out of practice with how to be a real cooperative and not just another version of an Ace Hardware. We have to unlearn the corporate model and go back to self-management, like the principle of our government—which isn't working all that great now either, but I guess that's another conversation." Sean sits down and slaps the table like it's a done deal.

I pace around. "So we would have a regional distribution center run by a farmers' cooperative. The co-op would supply grocery stores, restaurants, schools, etc. without making a profit off the farmers or the consumers. The co-op would serve as a direct farm-to-community link. We would have our own USDA-certified slaughterhouse, super fresh fruits and vegetables, and processing equipment to get the food ready for stores and restaurants and so on. We could also distribute items from food artisans like makers of cheese, bread, jams, etc."

"Should we be writing this all down?" Sean moves to pull out a notebook.

"Are you kidding me? Now that we have the big picture, the details just pop out easy." I'm practically bouncing up and down now, I'm so excited. "Anyone who knows farming would get it."

A huge wave of relief rolls over every part of me, taking away my burden of failure. "If we'd had a working cooperative this past summer, we could have made it financially. Think how much would have been saved on not having an intermediary like the farm stand guy, not to mention a whole company that buys, resells, and ships stuff all over. Then there's farmer time—not having to sit at a farmers market or drum up contracts to sell the produce. The seed and other supplies would cost less from the Farmers' Co-op, with an emphasis on non-profit, unlike now, where the co-op is no cheaper than anyplace else."

"We don't have to be a big corporation to survive," Sean says, "we just have to be connected, like Chief's web."

I see Daniel walking by the library, and I motion for him to come in.

"You guys missed morning block," he says. "What's up?"

We tell him what we came up with, so excited we both are talking a lot at the same time.

Daniel looks just as pumped as we are when we're through. "You're right, Jake, once you see the big picture, the rest just flows. Amazing work, guys! I'll talk with Godfather, my law school friend, to see if he will help us understand how a cooperative non-profit works—legal structure, bylaws and such." He glances at the clock. "Okay, I gotta go to a newspaper meeting. I'm editor this year; have to set a good example, right?" He winks.

"Don't tell anyone about this idea until we figure out next steps, okay?" I say.

"Sure thing," he says before heading out the door.

Cora comes rushing into the library seconds later. "I saw Daniel in the hall and he told me to come see you two."

After hearing our idea, she, too, thinks it is a great one.

The more we talk about this plan the better it gets, with new details added. Our level of excitement increases each time too.

"When conflict resolution didn't work the last time, President Sean, we held a 'talk-in' for all students who wanted to participate. Why don't we organize a Chautauqua 'talk-in' for the whole community where you can lay out your plan and compare it to the Fresh Food plan?"

"Great," I say. "I can get the FFA club members to help me flush out the Farmers' Co-op plans more and then they can be the small group facilitators at the Chautauqua."

"Meanwhile, you can get Chief to approve putting this on the agenda for the Chautauqua in a few weeks, Sean," Cora says.

Sean looks miserable, Cora puzzled.

I laugh and explain, "Sean's not too fond of Chief right now."

✧　✧　✧

I take off for FFA club meeting to get their help in fleshing out the co-op idea. I'm glad to see Amelio and Jorge there.

"It may take you club members being leaders and convincing your parents and other older farmers that we, the younger generation, are excited about not only continuing the farming tradition but actually expanding the amount of farming," I tell the group.

"What about farm workers?" someone asks. "We will need a lot of help."

"What do you think, Jorge and Amelio?" I ask.

Without hesitation, Jorge says, "Build it and they will come. Treat them right and they will stay."

Amelio nods his head yes.

I see the other FFA members getting excited at the prospect of help working their farms.

"I never thought change like this could happen," one guy says. "I thought farmers in this country would just become extinct, appearing only in history books."

I thought I had an individual dream, but with possibility, others stand up.

Publicity for the Chautauqua was easy. In the previous few weeks, the community has talked of little else besides the "offer" letters received by farmers from King Corn. Insult is pretty unanimous, based on the lowball prices offered for the farm land. The letter also reinforces the bully approach that this offer is the highest farmers will receive and if they do not sign on within thirty days, the number will go down dramatically. In a move to divide the colleges from the farmers, King Corn also sent letters to the colleges saying that in exchange for preferential pricing, they would like Fresh Food to be their exclusive provider of local food in the region.

That caused a shift in Sean's dad from discreet inquiry directed to the Board of Trustee/King Corn Director to all-out advocacy for farmers. Obviously it helps that he can now present our co-op alternative, which would mean lower costs for the college.

Previous Chautauquas have always gone directly to subgroup meetings and activities, but this Chautauqua is scheduled to start with a key note speaker: Sean. Chief spoke with the other group leaders and received their agreement to postpone their agenda until the next Chautauqua, allowing everyone to participate in the local foods issue. Sean claims the key note idea is Chief's punishment for his acting rude to Chief, but I think it's because Chief knows he'll do a great job. I'm speaking too, right after Sean.

From my position on stage, as people file into the auditorium, I see Daniel with his arm around his Mom. She's beaming with pride. I quickly turn away from the scene before the tears come.

Daniel spoke to all of us seniors in first period a week or so ago. The title of his talk was, "I Learned to Fail at Success, and I'm Glad." After explaining the events of his life for the last year, he said he believed we all carry shadows with us that are trying to tell us something important about who we are, our true self. He said he felt lucky to have, with a lot of support, become aware that monetary success will not prove his love for his mom, bring his dad back into his life, or make him feel secure. He said, "My life now is a maze of unexpected turns, with no pressure to go in one particular direction, only patience and cheer in the openings in my life."

As we stand on stage in the auditorium, waiting for the Chautauqua to start, a bunch of community people come up to chat with Sean. When I look at him, puzzled, he says, "They are people I met on my bike rides when I first moved here." He gestures to a group of seats to our left. "See that guy in the fishing hat, sitting behind Sarah?" he whispers. "He changed my life. People I met on my bike rides taught me what you already knew, Jake, to recognize the importance of having a sense of place and community. I learned mountains and fields can be as grounding as the ocean."

At this moment, the only thing I can imagine imparting is a sense of fear. I'm terrified. This night means everything to me.

Sean must be able to read my thoughts, because he says, "Jake, you have to know the nature of fear from the inside to be fearless. My experience with overwhelming fear came when a massive wave pulled me under and I somehow knew relaxing and letting the ocean have its way with me was my salvation. You will overcome the fear you face now because you know the stakes from the inside."

There is no way I can wrap my brain around that statement right now. But Sean's calm and assuring aura does make me feel a little better. "I'm going to try my best."

"Yoda said 'Do. Or do not. There is no try,'" Sean says, grinning.

Star Wars? Really? At the most important moment in my life thus far?

But I don't have time to respond, because Sean is already walking to the microphone to deliver his speech.

Over the next few minutes, he talks about the value of having a sense of community, and how we can't just assume it will happen. "We have to be actively involved in directing what we want to happen for our community," he says. "That involves each person making decisions for what they see as the common good."

With Sean's last phrase, I see Ms. Jordan's big smile. She is listening closely to his words, in rapt attention.

Starting in ninth grade, all of our teachers at Stone Creek require us to speak up constantly, including making prepared speeches. This year's rhetoric class has been the most pointed in terms of how to make a persuasive speech. While we were prepping for tonight, Cora also impressed upon Sean and me the importance of speaking with emotion and appealing to our community's shared values, not just logic. She got that from Sotomayor's book.

Hearing Sean's self-assurance as he speaks, my nervousness subsides. I have practiced speaking on so many occasions, and I have experienced success many times. Realistically, I know I will not have great influence on anyone's opinions tonight; it's just that for the sake of my dream to farm, I want to do my very best.

I have an advantage over Sean: the FFA club prepared a handout outlining the idea for a Farmers' Co-op that's a true cooperative to accompany my speech. The characteristics listed, which come from the International Cooperative Alliance, are: voluntary, open membership; democratic member control; member economic participation; autonomy and independence; education, training, and information; cooperation among cooperatives; and concern for community.

I talk about the cooperative movement being over a hundred years old in the US, now with 30,000 organizations. In the last twenty years, places like California have revitalized the movement and placed greater emphasis on strong labor policies.

"Farming is not defined by money but an appreciation of the magic of our earth and our desire to share our bountiful harvests with our neighbors, here and around the world," I conclude before walking off the stage.

After my talk, the audience leaves the auditorium to break into small groups, with an FFA member in each.

Sean's dad must have been busy recruiting these past couple weeks, because there are a lot of college people here. I see members of the Hardee's group leaving the auditorium together, all appearing in good humor, even my dad. He always seems more together when he is with his friends.

Daniel interviews people as they leave the auditorium. There is a logjam at the back due to interest in a large, student-produced painting on bulletin board paper with the title "Natural Limits." The painting shows a field of tears, screams, bug-eyed plants full of fear, animals with elephant heads and donkey behinds, and bodies (plants, animals, and humans) buried under a mound of dollar bills and plastic rulers. A strong, rich man is on top of the mound, while small, distraught people carrying golden rulers walk into a school, backs to the field.

I see the King Corn corporate guy and Cora talking. She tells me later her parting comments to him were, "It's too bad you didn't learn real leadership from the civil rights movement leaders like Dr. King, Diane Nash, and James Baldwin, among others." He apparently had no comeback for her.

He does have a comeback for the collective excitement in the crowd, however. Someone else tells me later that they overheard him in the parking lot calling the governor.

"You better see this principal is fired by tomorrow," he shouted into the phone. "He could make the whole deal fall through, and you can't afford to lose King Corn and all our resources."

In small-town fashion, word spread fast.

At the end of the night, Sean and I go to Chief to thank him for supporting us.

"I hope you won't feel any pressure from big-wigs for the support you've given us," I say.

Chief laughs. "Any pressure I'm getting just demonstrates how effective you folks are. Don't worry about me. But I do worry you-all aren't prepared for as big a fight as you've initiated."

Next battle: the County Supervisors Board meeting, with Fresh Food on the agenda.

Community leaders like the newspaper editor, the CEO of the only local bank, Dad and the rest of the Hardee's group, college officials, and members of other cooperatives in town all show up. The Board of Supervisors will vote on whether to approve the various tax and other concessions King Corn wants.

Word on the street is the Governor quit pressuring the Supervisors to support Fresh Food due to a close governor's race in a few weeks. His successor-hopeful, who's from the same political party, needs all the votes he can get.

Lots of people speak at the meeting, making for a long and tense marathon. One County planner mentions there are USDA grants that might help a non-profit cooperative and also "Virginia Farm to Table" grants. The community college president promises assistance from their newly formed Sustainable Agriculture initiative. The local bank CEO says he is behind the farmers with, as always, low-interest loans.

The last speaker didn't know you have to sign up on a speaker's list before the meeting starts. It's the King Corn corporate guy.

The Supervisors allow him to speak anyway, but he has nothing new to say—he just forcefully repeats past themes.

The Chair of the County Supervisors announces they will retire to an anteroom to consult with each other about their decision. "I promise we will not take long, so please wait," she says.

The King Corn guy stands in a corner, arms folded in front of him, flipping through his phone messages. I sure would not want such an alienating job— nobody wanting to have anything to do with him, investing all his energy in places he doesn't care about, not living in the present moment, only to repeat the same agenda over and over again.

His dour face, a stark contrast to everyone else's around him, reflects the accuracy of my assessment. Neighbors are joking with each other. Newspaper reporters are also interviewing students, particularly the ones with FFA jackets on. The TV station from forty miles away is here filming and interviewing some of the speakers from earlier.

In the midst of all the celebration, I become nervous. What if we're just being dumb hicks? Is this going to be a throwback to how I was treated most of my life, before the change at Stone Creek?

Just as I'm spiraling, the antidote for my mood crash appears, puts her arm around me, and rocks me gently. "Look what you did, Jake."

I lean into her. "Thanks, Ms. Goodbar. You're the one that got me going a while back, just when I was ready to give up." How does she manage to send all those good vibes through a simple hug?

The Supervisors return to their stage. I'm afraid to look at them, so I look at Sean, who emotes confidence. The Chair announces the vote: there will be "no concessions" to King Corn, including no waivers of required approval from several planning committees. That will slow down any go-ahead by at least six months, probably a year.

The King Corn guy leaves so fast all I see is his back in the doorway. I take this as a victory.

I begin jumping and jumping, no stopping. Friends gather around and we form a large circle, arms around one another's shoulders, swaying back and forth, looking deep into each other's eyes, finding a universal "can you believe it?"

It doesn't take long to hear via news reports that King Corn is retreating from our town and going in search of another, more receptive, location to try the Fresh Food model.

Here, high energy about the cooperative is catapulting many how-to ideas throughout the room.

Even Dad seems buoyed by the energy in the room. "Your dream started a whole movement of change back to fundamentals," he says, clapping me on the shoulder. "Life sure is mysterious."

Chapter 12: A Life Worth Living

Once upon a time, Socrates said, "The unexamined life is not worth living."

DANIEL

Jake has his dream still intact. My old dream, as I see it now, was about running to a nowhere called Successville.

I didn't know how to listen to myself. If I had known how to ask myself where I was running to, I would have heard, *It's what I'm running from that's key.* Now, though, I'm strong enough to let some of that pain and confusion through. *I hurt so much after you were gone. Why did you leave me? Was I a bad son?* Those questions get easier each time they resurface.

My involvement in journalism these last two years has taught me to listen, and then to ask the next question. Often, people in the middle of an event are so caught up in immediacy they aren't able to see through to what's next.

For a long time, with everyone except for Mom, I functioned as a stepped-back kind of person, removed from the depth of personal connection and the intensity of events in a moment. It was because of Sean and Cora and Godfather, and eventually others, like Chief and Sean's dad and some of my teachers, that I finally learned to open up to people and know I can rely on them.

Some people say you have to do the step-back thing to be objective as a journalist. I disagree. A journalist has to be able to go back and forth. First, connect with a person and truly listen to what is at issue. *Then* step back so you can help the person see the next question. The people involved in any event tell me the story. Then I write it in a way that will make it possible for other people to hear and relate to the story too. So, as a journalist, I get to hear stories all the time and retell them. It's a job of building connections between people.

I recently finished writing up a more in-depth story of farmer Jake and his friends last summer, including Sean's pictures, all the way through to the King Corn drama. While I was working on it, I read an article in *The New York Times* about a school in South Carolina and the issue of graduation rates versus grade inflation. Before reading the article, I clearly identified the school's problem just by looking at the pictures. Of the four pictures in the article, two are of students sitting in desks in a classroom, staring straight ahead with blank expressions. No animation, no interest, no life, no learning. Another photo shows a student completing a math assignment with pages full of questions like, "Based on the equation given, find the position function of the particle." That explains the motionless, bored looks in the other two pictures. The last picture captures a principal standing in the hall outside the cafeteria, his hands held out in front of him like a traffic cop. This article convinces me how seeing can accentuate the words in storytelling.

Several of my teachers helped me with the King Corn rebellion story, and they encouraged me to submit it to Mr. Peyton, the editor of the local paper. He remembered me from the meeting early last year with the school newspaper staff, and said he has been following my stories in the school paper and thinks I am improving with each one. He agreed to run my King Corn story. Then he asked if I'd thought about writing about my experience in the group home. Even though I have come out to everyone about my history, I was still a little thrown by his question. But the more I thought about it, the better I felt about the idea—and about myself. Not only is he complimenting my writing ability, I feel like I'm free to be the person I really am, even with important people who I don't know very well. *That* is a milestone for me.

Based on the positive reaction to my King Corn article in his paper, Mr. Peyton asked for my permission to send it off to the *Washington Post* for their consideration. He also offered me a job at the local newspaper after I graduate, if I agree to take a college class or two every semester in addition to my reporting. He says he would be proud to mentor me in investigative journalism.

It's an amazing opportunity for me, but lately I have been thinking about how much I enjoy doing interviews "live," like with the firefighter who came in on 9/11 last year. I also interviewed a local businessperson in first period the other day about his company making military uniforms and equipment for our government. He has instituted many progressive approaches to running a business, including employees having a say in overall business objectives and how to meet them. His motto about decision-making is to always ask "why" first. I followed that statement with asking if he and his employees find it difficult when they think about *why*, since the ultimate purpose of their work is to equip the military to fight and kill people. He didn't flinch, obviously having thought a great deal about the question before. I really respected how honest and straightforward he was, and he seemed impressed that I had the guts to ask.

The excitement of that interview—thinking quickly on my feet and maintaining a positive relationship with the person I am interviewing while still asking tough questions—all that felt like what I am supposed to do. And students listening to the interview got to see the story live, which is even better than seeing pictures in an article in a newspaper. Of course, that experience could have been a lucky shot. I should probably get more experience in the basics before setting my sights on TV reporting and interviewing.

I am not anxious to leave town after graduation like some of my friends are. For one, Mom and I are really enjoying life right now, both individually and together. Also, I'm adjusting to another big change in my life: With Mom's help, I found my father. He's now living in the Midwest. Our two phone conversations have been pretty awkward, since we don't really know each other or where to start. But we both seem okay with taking things slow and starting to fill in the gaps, mainly talking about what each of us is doing now. Every once in a while he'll mention something related to his continuing PTSD. In our last conversation, I told him about my work in journalism and he said, "I used to be the storyteller. Now you are."

That connection alone is enough to keep a warm light shining in me for some time.

CORA

I posted comments on Stone Creek's website about a recent event, with the title "Black Lives Matter Goes to School," while the whole King Corn controversy was going on:

The black high school girl, South Carolina again, thrown violently across the room by a police officer assigned to the school. Some wonder what the girl was doing before the three videos shot at the scene. Turns out her crime was not giving up her cell phone to the teacher. Do people then wonder how much she had been asked to give up previously in her life? Could the police officer, assigned to protect young people, not imagine there might be something legitimately important at stake? No. A black person is not entitled to human complexity, only obedience to authority, conveniently still overwhelmingly white.

James Baldwin wrote, many years ago, "The question of color, especially in this country, operates to hide the graver questions of the self." He argued that is why the question of race is so tenacious in American life, and so dangerous.

The post went mostly unnoticed, since the King Corn thing was taking up most people's attention, but a few people wrote responses in the days that followed. Mostly favorable, but not the deep reflection I need. Then I received a private message from Jake.

Cora, I read "Black Lives Matter Goes to School." I want to tell you how much I admire who you are. You are brave every day, taking responsibility for defining who you are—not a finished product but alive, with sense of purpose for whatever comes along. I know you have been struggling with where to go to college, so I'd like to offer my thoughts for you to consider. To think you need support in college to grow is to doubt yourself. What you need is the challenges of a lifetime, which will allow you to expand your own platform of support for yourself. Your platform foundation has the experiences of love of family, friends, and Stone Creek High School. Now, broaden your horizons and free your inner spirit to soar. Don't doubt it's already there. Sometimes I look at the dirt under my fingernails to remind me where my purpose lies. If you need reminder of your purpose, reencounter your portfolio of beautiful writing, deep questioning, analytical mind, and passionate values. It's also okay to ask for hugs. I still imagine, in my hardest moments, rocking in my mom's lap. Love, Jake

Jake is right. I have been afraid of being terrorized by others defining me as black. I hate the idea of being judged from the outside. That's what's been going on with the college thing. My resistance to judgment of colleges, to the idea of them deciding if I am worthy based on ridiculous criteria like tests. How did that power get shifted? It should be my decision what college suits me; it shouldn't be based on irrelevant criteria like tests or so-called race. The consumer, the student, should get to decide if they want to purchase the college's educational product.

Today at school, I walk up to Jake before first period and give him a bear hug like I gave my grandfather last year. "Thanks, Jake. It's nice to have friends I trust enough to listen to them."

"And for you," he says, smiling, "I have a gift for your future. Chelsea gave me one of these brochures and asked me to give you the other. I'm not ready to go down this road, but you may be."

I take the brochure home with me and pore over it in my room. It is about the Echols Interdisciplinary Major at UVA. The program is founded on student self-motivation and intellectual creativity. That's an academic way of saying you get to take courses from different areas and call it a major. How fabulous it would be to combine areas like neurobiology, developmental psychology, and cultural studies. Not either/or but all three/and. Stone Creek has prepared me for a program like this. I'm confident I could talk my way into the program, which starts sophomore year, by showing them my high school portfolio and proving I am capable through my college freshman classes.

Chelsea attached a sticky note that reads:

> *I don't even have one interest yet, much less a program like this. I could see Jake combining agricultural science, natural ecology, and cooperative organizational structures. But I understand why he wants to continue working with the new Sustainable Agriculture department at the community college. They have him suggesting what speakers they should invite for an upcoming regional meeting. And, mainly, he is already putting in every spare minute to reforming the current Farmers' Cooperative. Both of you attending Stone Creek as a background, plus practical experiences, would likely get you accepted for the Echols program. Meanwhile, I'll work on getting some direction for my life. The Sufi dancing somehow allows the authentic me inside to bubble up sometimes. Funny how my teenage years were spent listening to everyone else but me. One new development here—a psychology professor wants me to take an independent study class with her next fall, reading in my areas of interest and talking with her. I can't wait! Also look forward to you coming here next year . . . maybe??*

An unsettling thought hits me. I might have taken an entirely different direction. My involvement in the farm cooperative idea prevented me from having time to decide among colleges and apply for early acceptance like I planned, not even knowing about this UVA program. I can't technically apply for Echols until after my first year, but I bet my interest in it will help me get accepted to UVA and also get financial aid.

I message Jake:

Yes, it's true I'm over my self-doubt phase, thanks in part to you. I think my crisis in confidence was coming from the fear of leaving my parents, not realizing they would always be with me. Also, my close relationships with Chelsea, Daniel, Sean, and you helped me learn to accept myself as I am. Leaving Stone Creek will be hard, too, because I have felt so comfortable here. But you were right, and my time in the science program at Howard this summer helped me realize I'm ready to throw myself into more demanding challenges.

Saying to Jake how comfortable I've been at Stone Creek makes me wonder if I haven't been too comfortable. Maybe it's time to add action to the thought of spreading my wings.

SEAN

I applied for early acceptance to the Maine Maritime Academy. Dad managed to get an exception to the early decision deadline for me, and they gave me an in-person interview after the County Supervisors made their decision about Fresh Food. Mom and Dad fret over my appearance to the college people; my hair is now super long, uncut since last summer. I didn't let them talk me into cutting it. It's a badge of honor to remember who I am, with sun-bleached hair. And my confidence apparently came through louder than my shaggy hair: the interview went well and the Academy people seemed impressed with my leadership role in the King Corn invasion. I heard pretty quickly I was accepted.

Weird, and a little scary, to think I'll be going to another academy. I hope it is nothing like Hilltop. Based on advice I received in first period sessions at Stone Creek, I knew to investigate what life is really like at the Maine Academy when I went in for my interview: I talked with many students, not just the ones selected to tour prospects around, visited freshmen classes, and talked with professors in the science department. It seems like a great combination of being adventurous and challenging, and yet chill (no pun) in atmosphere—probably since it is so small.

Dad seems more relieved than I am to have the whole thing settled. He is now deep into planning a family summer vacation to Ireland for the four of us. I did some online research to see what I might be interested in doing there, and I found a couple marine ecotourism outfits to check out. That would be a fun job.

Since Chief arrived at Stone Creek, senior pre-graduation activities have been planned by students. The senior class president, me, forms a planning committee to decide what day-long special activity we want to do for the senior class, typically something like a water park. The committee also needs to decide senior activities the four days before graduation—sometimes things like a talent show, although the graduating class the first year Chief was here actually decided not to come to school for some of those days. Seems like they were into the "freedom from" mentality Ms. Jordan talks about.

The closer we get to the end, the more I want to make the most of every minute, particularly spending time with people I've come to know, getting to know other seniors better, before it's too late and we all part. Since many of us will also be leaving the community, at least for a while, I think we ought to go out with a bang, give the community something to remember us by. And it's my responsibility, as senior class president, to lead the effort.

At our first planning committee meeting, I get a wake-up call. People on the committee quickly come to agreement that planning a senior activity day and last week of school senior activities pales in comparison to what they want: a non-traditional graduation ceremony. No monkey suits and boring speeches. *Gulp, seems pretty radical to me*—that's my first thought. But my second reaction is to ask myself what Chief would do in my shoes.

The group discussion so far has focused on trashing the usual graduation ceremonies, with some pretty wild alternative ideas getting thrown out.

"Okay, guys, I get what you don't want," I say. "Let's focus on what you *do* want. We're going to have to convince Chief and parents what we want to do. So let's come up with some real ideas."

Further committee discussion focuses on a few main conclusions:

- We want to *do* stuff to show our parents and community we deserve to receive the official sanction of adulthood.
- We will create small groups around interest themes for student presentations at graduation.
- We will use the week after senior tests and before graduation for the small groups to plan details and practice presentations.

"These are great ideas for our graduation ceremony," I say when the list is complete. "The more we talk, though, the more I realize the whole senior class needs to approve what we've come up with. After all, it's their graduation, too."

When we present our recommendation, we hear lots of positive feedback. Comments like, "It sounds like a whole senior class talent show for our parents."

Then people start asking each other questions that don't seem to have an answer, like "How will the interest groups be formed?" and a shift in mood occurs.

I hesitate, not knowing what to say. We didn't think that out in our committee.

Another person jumps in. "Weren't y'all supposed to plan our senior activity day? What about ideas for that?"

"We focused on graduation and didn't get to senior activity day," I say. "Do other people on the planning committee want to answer these questions?"

No response. I'm in the center of this mess alone.

"I suggest a student-parent meeting for students to present an alternative idea for your graduation ceremony," Chief pipes up. "Any students who are not speaking up now but would prefer a traditional ceremony can attend the meeting and speak to their preference. Graduation is extremely important to family after all the years of support they've provided to you. They deserve a chance to consider any change."

Even though nobody is expressing disagreement with the graduation ceremony idea, the lack of forethought by our committee is causing general restlessness and twinges of anger in the crowd.

Daniel is in reporter mode, walking around with a notepad and a camera around his neck. He comes over to me and whispers in my ear, "Form three more groups so the agitators can get in on the action."

Of course! Wish I could think on my feet as easily as he does.

"I propose we solicit volunteers from among everyone here to come up with a process for forming the small performance groups based on themes of interest," I say. "Second, other volunteers who want to make decisions about our senior activity day can come up with where we go and what we do. Last, some of you can commit to attend the parent meeting and speak for our graduation ceremony proposal. Those of you who disagree will also commit to attend the parent meeting and speak up. Agreed?"

Thank goodness there is finger snapping and not booing.

I find Daniel at the end of first period. "Hey, man, you saved my ass," I say. "Thank you."

"You would have thought of the idea later. A little later? Much later?" His last question barely audible as his words drift over into giggling.

My reply is a hard fist pop to his left bicep.

I go to each of the subgroup meetings, and I think it's going to take a lot of my time and energy—but not so. Right away, the groups form their own structure for working together and I become a resource person, not a director, modeling our teachers! I guess this thing wasn't entirely my responsibility as president after all. Just like teachers can't make us learn things, my job as class president is to encourage fresh ideas and let my fellow seniors organize in a way to make it happen. I'm still learning. It's not my show, just like it's not Chief's show. I bet he gets nervous like me, worrying whether graduation will come off well.

I am reassured when I attend the theme groups planning meeting, hearing all the creativity and excitement flying around. I also overhear several students make comments like, "I didn't get what Sean and the planning group meant, so I was kinda against the idea. But now I'm loving it."

In the end, it's decided that senior activity day will consist of an end-of-year field day at the two local middle schools. It's something a lot of seniors remember as being the highlight of middle school—but they also remember thinking they could have done a better job of planning the fun. Now's their chance. Of course, I wasn't here then, so I have little to contribute.

The big test is the meeting with parents about the graduation ceremony. A lot of parents show up since they have learned any meeting called by Chief will have meaningful decision-making involved. Sprinkled among the parents are a few students who are presumably for a traditional approach, since they are not sitting with the large group of seniors here to present the alternative graduation ceremony idea. Chief has asked his friend, Pastor Moore, to facilitate the meeting.

I'm standing at the back of the meeting room, too nervous to sit down. I think it is more nerve racking to have to just listen to a debate over something you really care about than to be able to speak up. I don't think I would have thought that a couple of years ago. I would have preferred silence.

The first issue, thrown out by a dad, is, "What will an alternative graduation do for the reputation of this school among colleges?"

A student looks around to the group to nonverbally ask to address that concern. She stands and says, "First, thanks to everyone for coming and taking our proposal seriously. My understanding is that college administrators are concerned about student performance in high school as reported by teachers and then student performance at the college as reported by professors. I would be surprised if a college even bothered to inquire about the graduation ceremonies of individual high schools. But if they did, I believe they would view what we've planned as a creative initiative, and I think you will also."

Another student asks Ms. Hoffmann to speak to the dad's concern. She says, "I believe the previous comment about college perspective is accurate, and I'll also add that based on rumors I've heard, I can't wait to see the performances."

A first step success; many parents in the meeting room clap in support of Ms. Hoffmann's statement.

A mom says, "All our relatives are coming from far away to see my child graduate. It's a big deal to us."

A guy I recognize as a lead actor in many of Stone Creek's drama performances stands to respond. "I think you will be proud to show your relatives the level of student ability in this school. We are not taking this challenge lightly and are not aiming to be silly. We have already put in a great deal of effort during non-school hours and plan to put in a lot more to deliver polished performances."

A parent in the audience yells out, "I can vouch for the work they're putting in, gathered at all hours in my basement."

A student sitting with her parents stands and says, "We only get to do this once in our life, so I want a lot of the extras, like nice graduation announcements and a picture of me on the mantle at home in a cap and gown like my brothers."

An art whiz student jumps up. "I have already made personal graduation announcements to send out. They look very professional and are specific to our school, with a photo on the front. I would be happy to share my design, and to come up with other designs, and it is simple and cheap to get them printed."

Another student says, "That's a good thought, about a graduation photograph. We could have traditional caps and gowns available for photos before and after graduation. And I know a professional photographer who would probably agree to be here too. Parents could ask for what they want."

With all this good input, our ceremony can be even more awesome than we were thinking.

The mood in the room is changing from tense to more relaxed problem solving. Still, there is a detectable uneasiness in the air.

Cora—who else—says, "I suggest we try out an alternative graduation ceremony for this year since this year's seniors are so committed to the idea. It doesn't have to be a permanent, for all time, decision." She's told me before that this is another principle of conflict resolution decisions: because people fear forever obligations, thinking what if they make a mistake, it is better to make short-term decisions with evaluation built in.

As the tension eases, Pastor Moore asks for a show of hands regarding Cora's suggestion. Her proposal is accepted. I feel the exhilaration of validation, almost like this meeting is our real rite of passage, and looking around the room, I can tell a lot of my fellow seniors feel the same way.

✦   ✦   ✦

CHELSEA

It's end of the second semester of my sophomore year of college. I've amassed mostly required credits and gotten sufficient, if not spectacular, grades. I feel like I'm about a half centimeter emerged from a cocoon, coaxed that far out by my psychology professor. It all started when I mentioned my whirling dervish training and how the turning helps me center my awareness on me, but a me without boundaries that separate me off from what's out there. Somehow we get to talking about my high school and I told her about my names, first "Country Girl" and then "Listener."

She laughed and said, "Sounds like you have a calling to be a therapist."

I told her about Adrian and how far off I was from being present, off doing backpack interviews. She was a good listener as I talked about Adrian and the impact his death had on me.

"Sounds like a wakeup call for you, one that you're still not sure what to do with," she observed.

After uncomfortable silence—I wasn't sure how to respond—she asked about the backpack research I did, saying it was a unique approach to capturing an important stage in adolescent development.

"Why don't you do an update interview, two years later, and listen to what they say about their lives now?" she suggested.

"You think that would reveal anything?" I asked. I was thinking, *Reveal something about them or me? Is she thinking I'm a mess?* It didn't seem like it. She seemed so easily open, whereas I still second-guess myself a lot.

"You won't know until you ask," she said.

Talking with her like this struck me as a 180-degree difference from my experiences at Hilltop, and the many messages I received there that nothing I thought or did was real. Last summer with Jake was the first time I received confirmation that what was inside me as a child was real. Sure, college is supposed to be different from high school in this way, but why does high school say they are preparing us for college if it took me two wasted years to be open to what college has to offer?

The more I think about re-interviewing the students I talked to two years ago, the more exciting it becomes. But I decide I'm not going to try to find the Stone Creek students. I didn't know them, and it would seem weird to ask them to meet at a coffee shop or something. Besides, Stone Creek probably has rules about giving out confidential information like people's home addresses or telephone numbers.

So, first stop, Hilltop Academy to see Ms. Carter. Hugs, of course, then a tear in her eye where the footprint used to be. Maybe I just imagine that. After I ask how she is doing, and receive reassurance she is okay, I ask, "Why did Adrian commit suicide?"

"I knew you'd be back someday to ask," she says. "I almost told you when you came by last spring, but you seem much stronger now, like things are going better for you. It's a hard story to hear and live with, but I believe in truth, as soon as someone is ready to handle it."

"I think I'm ready," I say, bracing myself.

Ms. Carter nods. "Well, first of all, the gun Adrian brought to school was not a real one, but it did look very real. He achieved his objective in frightening the three bullies who had been bothering him, and who in that last month had escalated their taunting and shaming. One of the boys, the son of the college president of one of the Hilltop sponsors, calls home, terrified, after the incident. The principal gets a call from the boy's father and searches Adrian's backpack. He finds the toy gun, and suspends Adrian, threatening that if he says anything about the incident, Adrian's father could lose his job at the college. Rumors start flying around about a student bringing a gun to school, and the principal quickly institutes the backpack search policy to show precautions are being taken, even though there was never a real gun to begin with."

"So it was all the principal's fault," I say.

"No," Ms. Carter says. "Because the story doesn't end there. What happens next is, the two college presidents meet with Adrian's parents, apologize for the handling of the situation by the principal, and say they are willing to force him to retire. They also offer to pay Adrian's tuition at a private high school in an adjoining town that provides daily van transportation. They pitch this as an opportunity for Adrian to start fresh and remind Adrian's father of his professor employee benefit for college financial assistance for Adrian—assuming a suitable resolution of this incident."

"That is so mean, Ms. Carter."

"Yes, very mean. Adrian's mother, who told me all of this, objected to Adrian having to make a major change in his life while the bullies got off with no punishment. The presidents responded there was no proof of bullying and Adrian had never made any accusations. A private attorney confirmed to Adrian's parents it would be hard to prove there was bullying."

"So that's why Adrian did it? Because he was upset that after what those other kids did, he was the one being forced to change schools?"

Ms. Carter shakes her head. "Like Adrian's mother, I do not believe he committed suicide."

My mouth drops open. "You don't?"

"I don't," she says firmly. "I guess we'll never know what really happened up on that trail, but I do know that months earlier, Adrian had been questioning his sexual identity—things like his hatred of violence, which he thought was a feminine trait. His psychiatrist helped him understand that was a cultural definition, not a biological one. After that, Adrian actually got happier and excited the world was more complex and there were lots of gender choices of how to be. He was upset about moving schools, though. He felt that nobody was standing up for him and it would be just the same at a new school."

I think he was probably right; chances are, transferring would not likely have gotten him to a better place. My renewed grieving for Adrian follows my former pattern of anger.

"The new principal this year was informed last week that Hilltop Academy is done. Attorneys of the two colleges decided there were too many liability issues in running a high school, and advised the colleges to close it at the end of this spring term. How about that?"

Seething, I say, "So the public never knows the truth of Adrian's death linked to being bullied. And the schools are not held accountable as petri dishes for growing bullies, hatefulness, and ignorance. The pyramid tomb of Hilltop Academy will live as a scar inside survivors who all knew, even if they did not want to talk about it, what was going on." I sigh. "At least the next generation can grow up at Stone Creek."

I tell Ms. Carter I need to sort through how all this affects my view of life. I still think it might help to re-interview the three students in my graduating class. I ask her to provide contact information for them.

All three students I reach out to graciously agree to a re-interview, this time with no scripted questions, just a natural conversation. This is what they tell me:

Glitz Queen

"Immediately after graduation my boyfriend joined the Air Force. He had been talking about it for years, so it wasn't a surprise. But, in a way it was, because I had not thought through the reality of what that meant, my dreams being put on hold and all. He has loved being in the Air Force, learned a lot, and plans to go to college to study engineering. Funny, when I first met him, we were both juniors and bonded over hating school, this small town, and wanting to get away. The difference being, I was thinking getting away together and he, in the end, not so much. His senior year at Stone Creek, life really started changing under the new principal. He began taking himself more seriously, trying to figure out what he wanted to do with his life. Before it was just, like, go into the military to be supported and get away. His Counselor at Stone Creek got him to think, 'Okay, so what do you want to *do* in the military?' He had always loved toys like remote control cars, rockets, etc., along with his brothers. His last year at Stone Creek, he got into robotics and figured he could follow up in the Air Force. He hasn't gotten to do as much learning as he hoped, but now they will pay for college so he can do engineering."

I get the feeling she has never told that story in its entirety before. I feel a little honored that she's sharing it with me. "What about you?" I ask. "What have you been up to?"

"At first, when he left for the Air Force, depression kept me from doing much of anything," she says, looking down. "I didn't know what to do with myself. In high school, I had focused only on him. I hadn't really thought about me, what I wanted other than being married to him and having kids down the road. My mom pushed me into getting a job, which brought me out of my isolation and depression ditch. I started as a hostess at Healthy Choices Dining, which had just opened up at the time. I've moved up to waitress and made new friends."

She adopts a less robotic, more intent voice. "I ended up hanging out a lot in the kitchen, watching the chef. He noticed my interest and ever since he's been awesome, teaching me all kinds of things about the nature of different foods, how they go together, how to bring out the flavor, on and on. Next fall, I'm starting at the community college in their chef program." Looking satiated, she says, "Enough about me. What are you doing these days, Chelsea?"

"Well, I have a boyfriend who's a senior at Stone Creek and wants to farm and refocus the Farmers' Co-op to a real cooperative and expand it to distribute local farmers' products. I'm living in Charlottesville right now." I want to be "real" with her, not just share the superficial stuff. "My most exciting activity is learning to dance, whirling dervish style. UVA classes haven't been too motivating, until the last month. A professor is encouraging me and I'm developing an interest in psychology."

Glitz shows no interest in the whirling dervish stuff. "I heard about the whole King Corn thing," she says. "Good they were chased out of town. My friend the chef is very excited about the new possibilities of fresh food from local farms, sold at a reasonable price and conveniently delivered. As for you, psychology is not a surprise. At Hilltop you were always so good with people, helping them by listening to them."

I couldn't even help myself; how is it possible I helped anyone else? Laughing, I say, "You know, the big joke is people major in psychology to figure out their own problems."

"It would have helped us both to do some of that figuring out in high school, huh?" She sighs. "I have one more thing to tell you."

My fear antenna goes up. I have no idea why.

"After graduation I ran into a girl who dated a jock at Hilltop when we were there," Glitz says. "When the girl realized what a self-absorbed loser he was, she broke up with him. Before that, though, he was really high one night and started crying, mumbling some story about a queer named Adrian. He said he and a couple of buddies followed Adrian and his golden retriever one day when he was hiking on the Appalachian Trail. At an overlook they caught up with him. After hassling him, one of the other bullies grabs the dog's collar and Adrian lunges toward the guy, trips on a rock, and falls off the ledge. The dog jumps off the overlook after him and lands next to him way below. The three bullies panic and run, saying nothing to anyone."

I'm holding my breath for a long, long time.

Star Tech

"I was accepted to MIT and roomed with my best friend," Star Tech tells me first thing.

"Sounds like your dream come true," I say.

"That's what everybody says. But, lately, I'm not so sure."

"Why's that?"

"I haven't really told anybody, even my best friend, but I'm not really happy."

I'm surprised. "What's going on?"

"The classes at MIT are really hard. Turns out I'm not as smart as I thought I was. There's a lot of pressure, constant work. And for me, it gets confused with my personal life. I really want to look good to my friend. What he thinks of me matters, a lot. He thinks I just get lazy sometimes and pushes me to snap to. But I'm not as good as he is, can't do what he can. And, lately . . . I wonder if I really want to be in the circuit of next-stage elite computer design. Maybe it's not for me."

"So, you're taking some space to figure it out?"

He shakes his head. "Not enough space, or time, or focus. I've developed pretty bad stomach ulcers."

"Ouch! You remember Adrian? He felt confused in high school. Hilltop just boxed him in more and was no help to him. Seems like maybe you're experiencing that at MIT."

"You mean the gay guy who was constantly bullied and committed suicide? I'm definitely not like *him*."

North Face Dude

"Hey, Country Girl, heard you're at UVA. What sorority?"

"I didn't pledge."

"Too bad." He looks genuinely disappointed. "My KA brothers are my world."

"How so?"

"They've got my back. Help me with everything, like meeting girls, knowing what the ladies like . . ." He lifts an eyebrow. "Also, how to totally chill, into a zone of totally letting go—induced by the spirits, of course, and sometimes uplift via script."

"And academics?"

"Oh, yeah, they help with that, too. We have huge computer files of previous tests, organized by professor, for most every class.

Also, notes taken by frat brothers in previous years, so we don't even need to go to class."

"Your grades . . . ?"

He rolls his eyes. "They're fine. Not super, but I get by. Besides, that's not the important thing for my future. I meet KA alumni who are successful in all kinds of businesses. They tell me I have a job at their firm, if I want, when I graduate. I am all set."

"Is there a particular area of business that interests you?"

"Not really. I'm flexible. Management jobs are pretty much the same, regardless of type of business."

He had no questions for me beyond the tribe I pledged.

After those interviews I revert back to patterns I thought I had out-grown. Like holing up in my bedroom at my parents' house eating a quart of cookie monster ice cream in one sitting. As always, my dogs comfort me in my pit of despair. They're much better than pills, cuddling up to me, letting me pet them until I realize the numbness in my hands has dissipated. I can only hope the numb-ness of my heart will dissipate soon as well.

I want to talk with Sean about Adrian and what Ms. Carter and Glitz told me. But I'm not ready yet. I need to feel more cen-tered first. Not just regarding whether I think what Glitz said was true or not but in terms of how Adrian impacted both of us.

I make a special trip to Charlottesville for a "turning" lesson. On the drive there, the radio station plays that iconic high school graduation time song, "Time of Your Life." I always hated that song because to me it sounded so nostalgic for the good old days in high school. Listening carefully to the lyrics now, however, I realize the depiction is full of conflicts: changes and choices vs. time directs you where to go; don't ask why—lessons are learned in time; unpre-dictable things happen that are out of your control so just make the best of things; there are the good memories of friends but also the scars you keep from the experience. I couldn't hear or understand any of that when I was in the fog of Hilltop, but it resonates now.

It's a relief to arrive at the Charlottesville community center and be among my grounded whirling dervish companions. In the midst of dancing, I feel a tingling at the back of my skull and hear myself silently saying, "Uncover goodness and love everywhere."

Remembering the moment, driving home, I think, *But I don't know how.* Shifting to beginner's mind, I realize, *I can learn. I now have a purpose.* Not unlike my young days building a community by peopling dirt villages and caves or, later, uncovering past civilization in Italy and signs of meaning in their lives. I am a listener who wants to find the goodness in me and help other people find it in themselves.

CHIEF

First Tuesday in June, graduation week, I have to deliver the hardest message of my life. Actually, there are no have-tos in life. I choose this approach in order to earn respect for what I preach. I need to be open, for my benefit as well as that of this graduating class, which has brought such joy into my life—not through their antics but their courage to grow into themselves.

As I approach the auditorium stage to address the seniors first thing Tuesday morning before graduation, I hear music from an ad hoc band of seniors—they're singing "Hail to the Chief." Everyone stands, laughing and finger-snapping. Then comes a chant of "S-C-H, S-C-H, S-C-H," to the rhythm of the more traditional "U-S-A" chant. Okay, maybe it's their antics too. They have such a profound aliveness.

I step to the microphone grinning. "How can I top that welcome? Maybe by saying, you got it wrong. You folks are the ones to be hailed today, the rest of the week, and at graduation Saturday."

A trumpet plays a few bars of "Time of Your Life."

I laugh. "Seriously, I hope you've had an opportunity to analyze the lyrics of that song. It's a meme for growing-up conflicts in high school." I take a moment to look out at the sea of students before me, intentionally changing the mood in the auditorium. "On behalf of all the staff here at SCHS, I want to thank you for the time of *our* lives. We believed in you, all of you individually and together, and you demonstrated by rising to expectations that our faith was warranted. Your enthusiasm has revitalized us in our chosen profession. You have increased our moral certainty that young people want, and deserve, to take charge of their own learning and life."

The students all start finger snapping, and it goes on for minutes. Some stand and add a new gesture, raising a real or imaginary hat off their heads and gesturing toward me.

"I could go on and on with instances of your inspiration to us," I say when the snapping dies down. "As you know well, I often go on and on when speaking. Not today, though. So, let me just cite one example of your spirit inspiring an old man. Your recent field day at the middle schools showed your joyful compassion to those kids and warmed my heart. The force awakens."

More finger snapping. I motion hats off to them, in all directions.

"This is the last time we'll gather together, just us. I'll miss our time together. And out of respect for the openness you have displayed with me these last four years, I want to tell you directly some hard news. I have cancer."

Gasps and looks of alarm spread through the audience.

I blunder on. "It is a serious kind that can be treated, but will likely be terminal."

Now there is total silence and intense focus on me.

"For a time, I can continue on in the work I love. I wanted to deliver my news directly, honestly, to thank you all in person for making my life worth living during these years we've spent together. I definitely want to keep in touch with the great adventures you folks will have in the coming years. Please keep me posted." I feel tears coming, and I breathe a couple of times to keep them from surfacing. "I need to leave for a bit so I can tell the other classes my news. I want as many people as possible to hear it directly from me. But I'll be back in a little while to check in on what I'm sure will be a joyful planning for graduation day presentations."

I quickly exit the stage.

Later, I'm told by a counselor who remained at the senior meeting what transpired after my departure. Sean went to the microphone and suggested they all move to their senior "home," the library, so they could move around and be with each other instead of being restrained by auditorium seating. Some students went to the outside courtyard between the library and cafeteria. It seems the informal discussions, not entered by staff, revolved around sharing experiences students have had with me.

Many students asked teachers and counselors if they knew any more than I had announced at the assembly. The staff replied honestly, saying I had told them the exact same thing yesterday afternoon, adding only some logistics for next year. I will work half time with the two middle schools to align expectations for their students with what we are doing at the high school. Ms. Jordan is to fill in half time at the high school, assuming some of my responsibilities.

Sean's presidential advisory committee gathers and makes a decision for altering the schedule of activities for the rest of the day.

I return to the auditorium after speaking with the freshman, sophomore, and junior class meetings, and the seniors all reassemble there. Then they present me with a gift that has apparently been in the works for months. Seniors have been knocking on doors of businesses, the colleges, community organizations, and a few individual homes of people of means. The result of their work is an endowment for a "Chief" scholarship, which will be awarded each year to a graduating senior in pursuit of a dream.

Sean recognizes Daniel's special efforts, who trained seniors in salesmanship. Seems his major training advice was, "Speak from the heart."

Thunderous finger snapping.

Later, the seniors want to attend club/lunch, to show leadership in dealing with my hard news.

The seniors use the rest of the day, and three subsequent days and apparently nights, to work on their small group performances. I have a feeling, despite their pledge to finish class projects and senior tests before working on performances, they have been working on their performances via websites for months. That was one reason I made my announcement today, knowing they had compelling activity to throw themselves into.

Carol, the Superintendent of Schools for the county, drops by to see me this afternoon, aware of my agenda for the day. She recruited me for this job, knowing from a twenty-two-year friendship what she would get—someone driven to do the right thing for kids, negotiate through the difficulties, for little pay.

"Hey, boss," I greet her when she walks through the door. "You're a welcome sight at the end of a rough two days. Since you can't pay me more without an act of Congress, how about a hug from an old friend?"

The hug lasts much longer than usual.

I worry Carol may lose her composure. I rush to direct the conversation, saying, "You haven't dropped by in a long time. Let's see . . . the last time was during the King Corn drama. You told me to keep supporting the students, and let me know someone important had my back and was working to see I didn't get fired." I raise my eyebrows in "do tell all" fashion as I settle into my beaten-up but comfy office chair.

"You know I was working with the school board to prop them up," Carol says, taking a cue from me and sitting down as well. "If any firing was going to take place, they were the ones who would have to do it. I wasn't worried about them unless some other power really leaned hard on them—someone who could make it miserable for school funding or whatever."

The last statement surprises me. "Like state funding for the schools? The governor leaning on the school board?"

She nods. "The governor was wavering at one point. Want to know who came to your rescue? Our newspaper editor. Frank organized regional bigwigs in the governor's political party to say they would not support the wannabe guy running to succeed the governor unless talk of firing you stopped immediately. This region is too important in elections for a governor to bet against the local power brokers. But you know, Frank would never have stuck his neck out unless he knew he had a broad base of support in the community."

That comment gives me a deep feeling of accomplishment, sorely needed to keep me going in these difficult days.

"The real turning point in Frank's eyes was how you reached out to the Hardee's eight. Everyone knows those guys are die-hard traditionalists. And he was amazed how you brought everyone into the school—Pastor Moore inspiring students to do community service work; county people working on school planning groups; parents observing classrooms; the push for sustainable farming; and even getting Frank himself to advise the school newspaper staff."

"I think the whole community turned a corner standing up to the King Corn threat," I say.

Nodding strongly in agreement, Carol laughs and says, "I was amazed at how restrained you were in taking no position. Remaining neutral is not your usual style, my friend."

"Just proves I can shut up when required," I say with a laugh.

"Switching to a related subject," Carol says, "things are looking great with getting an expedited School Administrator degree for Ms. Jordan. She has impeccable academic credentials. There are a couple more layers of university bureaucracy to work through, but I'm positive it's going to work out."

"Thanks, Carol. Her leadership will be important for continuity." I lean forward in my chair. "The faculty reaction to my news yesterday afternoon was very supportive. Rather than panicking about their positions or the chaos that could ensue under a new leader, they were quick to reassure me they are never going backward. All the changes we've made here have brought their teacher instincts back to life. They expressed confidence in Stone Creek's future without knowing who might be principal down the road. Of course, my announcement that Ms. Jordan will act as principal half time hinted at what kind of transition will take place, and I'm sure that helped. They seem genuinely happy about her new role."

"I'm so glad people are responding in a compassionate way," Carol says. "You deserve it."

✧ ✧ ✧

CORA

"Welcome, everyone, to our senior graduation ceremony for Stone Creek High School," I begin. I was recruited by the performance groups to be the master of ceremonies for today. I think it was a kind of reward for clinching an agreement at the parent meeting. Initially, I was worried Sean might have wanted to do this, but he was one of the first to rush to congratulate me and make sure I accepted the group's offer. I almost cried when he hugged me. Not that I let on how touched I was.

"This afternoon's celebration is our tribute to all who supported us in our journey toward 'A Life Worth Living,' the senior class theme and nod to Socrates," I say. "First thanks go to our parents and families for our launch into learning from day one. Second, events this past year clearly show the interdependence of schools and a community in forging a shared sense of purpose and growth. The last group deserving our heartfelt thanks is our teachers, counselors, and administrators, who so acutely listened to us that we came to better understand our world and make decisions based on listening to our own inner voice."

Traditional applause rings out from students, some in the auditorium, some clapping and whooping from back stage.

"The large banner you saw in the hallway as you entered the building today lists eighty-eight different senior responses to the question, 'What one verb captures how Stone Creek High School contributes to learning for a life worth living?' Recognizing tremendous variety and overlapping meaning of some words, a few verbs stand out: 'decide,' 'understand,' and 'listen.'" I pause a moment after each of the three words, to give the audience time to absorb and reflect on their power. "Based on these key words, our senior class president and the senior class planning committee asked each senior to write three one-sentence descriptions of important lessons learned during their time in school here. The responses for each person are listed in your program in alphabetical order of each student's name."

There's a good bit of shuffling, as people are curious to see what individuals, particularly their kids, wrote. To show it's okay to look at the student answers for a minute, I quickly glance at a few:

Daniel

I expanded my greetings beyond "What's up?" and now actually want to know the answers.

Nobody else is responsible for my bad decisions.

I choose awareness as my measure of success and stories as my method of enlightenment.

Sean

Change brings you a broader perspective on life, as long as you can handle uncertainty.

Friends give you courage.

I proved to my dad that learning what I want every day can lead to high enough scores on standardized tests.

Me

I see the world on a different plane than either/or.

Trusting others is the flip side of trusting yourself.

I need more training to listen clearly to all that spins around in my brain.

Jake

I now understand the depth of the quote, "It takes a village."

The kernel of a dream starts young, but takes a lifetime to grow it into reality.

I need much more than farming—like music, poetry, love, friends, science, travel, and stillness.

Jorge

I don't need to be afraid of people who don't look like me.

My next adventure is training for next year's tryouts of the US national soccer team.

If that fails, I will learn the restaurant business from my uncle.

Amelio

The USA is a pretty neat place, but there's no place like home.
I'm moving back to Mexico with my family.
I plan to use sustainable farming methods I learned here back in
my home village.

"I'm sure you will want to review many more of the senior
statements," I say, "but right now we need to move along with the
student performances we have planned for you this afternoon. As
your program shows, we will start with four performances of ten
minutes each:

- Political Satire—Terrorism
- Inventions We Would Like to See
- Intergalactic Travel Slide Show
- Teaching Math to Elementary Students—
  Demonstration

"I hope you enjoy the show!" I say before exiting the stage.
  The first set of performances goes off without a hitch; when
the last one ends, I come back onstage and explain what is available
during intermission. "A twenty-minute intermission will allow you
to taste a variety of what we call 'New Eats,' which are both deli-
cious and healthy, and prepared for you by the student chefs serving
them. While you are enjoying those, you can meander through an
exhibit titled 'Stone Creek Au Naturel,' which displays photography,
painting, and fiber arts. The student who produced each work will
be stationed with it, eager to tell you about their piece and its signif-
icance to them."
  After intermission, I draw the audience's attention to the
next four ten-minute performances listed in their program:

- Concussions in Athletics Update
- Gun Control Debate

- Our Planet through Song and Dance, Original Music, Lyrics, and Choreography
- A Job I'd like—Preminiscences

The audience is still clapping for this last round of performances when I take the stage again.

"Thank you for your attention and generous applause for each group," I say in my concluding remarks. "The performances and demonstrations were intended to give you evidence of five criteria, listed on the back of your program, that we believe define the worthiness of a high school diploma: each of us understands learning is living, and living is learning; we have learned to learn through self-direction; we can deal with risk, uncertainty, and change; we approach learning with great interest and enthusiasm; and we have repeatedly experienced working collaboratively, realizing more heads are better than one."

Those five criteria are my favorite part of the ceremony. I wrote them in consultation with Sean and the senior class planning committee. I hope I never forget those words.

"Chief, could you please come to the stage to finish our celebration?" I say, scanning the crowd for his face. All students have assembled on the stage and in the aisles of the auditorium.

As Chief climbs the steps to the stage and starts toward the podium, he sees Sean on stage and winks at him. He gives me a hug and says, "Fabulous."

Leaving the podium, I see Jake standing on stage with his FFA friends, including Jorge and Amelio. I try to catch his eye, but he only has eyes for Chelsea. She's sitting in the audience with Jake's dad, who is so dressed up I hardly recognize him.

I join students in the aisle next to where my parents are sitting. They are in the middle of the row, so we can't hug, but Dad gives me a thumbs-up sign and Mom is beaming.

I notice Daniel standing in an aisle next to his mom and a young guy I recognize, from a photo Daniel once showed me, as Godfather. Daniel never ceases to amaze me.

Seniors throughout the auditorium all look as one, wearing our new senior class T-shirts, which have the names of every senior on the back, and graduation ball caps.

Center stage, Chief says, "By the power vested in me by the Commonwealth of Virginia, I now pronounce you graduates of Stone Creek High School. Congratulations!"

Caps fly in all directions amidst whoops, snapping fingers, hugs, and tears.

Acknowledgments

Thanks to all who have helped me listen to my deepest understandings, too many to name:

My brother protectors;

Sisters in struggle to claim our humanity, some who became lovers;

The young of age and heart sharing their journeys of hope;

The furry four-leggeds, my constant companions;

And always muses along the way.

This book project was fun, made me think about truths, and connected me to the puzzles of our times. One other person cared about this story from the start as much as me—thanks for your enthusiasm, Peggy. The women of She Writes Press brought the story to light, particularly my amazing editor, Krissa Lagos.

To the readers of *School Tales*, I hope it encourages you to make changes in schools that will support young people to grow into their own.

About the Author

Sharon grew up in the U.S. Deep South, trying to figure out why she was not the image of a white southern belle. School was no help in understanding that problem or any other, until a college professor finally taught her to think. After doctoral work in sociology of education, Sharon's passion for eighteen years became teaching, experiencing again every level of school, preschool through college. Related work experiences, managing community educational programs for thirteen years, revealed how change is possible through an "it takes a village" approach.

When not tending her Virginia mountain cabin or engaging in local political concerns, Sharon contributes to the school change movement by listening to current high school students speak about their personal needs and new ways school could help them. Interviews of youth by Sharon and others can be found at the website *schooltaleslive.com*. She loves to hear from kindred spirits who want to connect with the national discussion of school transformation.

Author photo © Claudia Schwab

SELECTED TITLES FROM SHE WRITES PRESS

She Writes Press is an independent publishing company founded to serve women writers everywhere. Visit us at www.shewritespress.com.

Class Letters: Instilling Intangible Lessons through Letters by Claire Chilton Lopez. $16.95, 978-1-938314-28-5. A high school English teacher discovers surprising truths about her students when she exchanges letters with them over the course of a school year.

In a Silent Way by Mary Jo Hetzel. $16.95, 978-1-63152-135-5. When Jeanna Kendall—a young white teacher at a progressive urban school—becomes involved with a community activist group, she finds herself grappling with issues of racism, sexism, and oppression of various shades in both her professional and personal life.

Vote for Remi by Leanna Lehman. $16.95, 978-1-63152-978-8. History is changed forever when an ambitious classroom of high school seniors pull the ultimate prank on their favorite teacher—and end up getting her in the running to become president of the United States.

Stella Rose by Tammy Flanders Hetrick. $16.95, 978-1-63152-921-4. When her dying best friend asks her to take care of her sixteen-year-old daughter, Abby says yes—but as she grapples with raising a grieving teenager, she realizes she didn't know her best friend as well as she thought she did.

Slipsliding by the Bay by Barbara McDonald. $16.95, 978-1-63152-225-3. A hilarious spoof of academic intrigue that offers a zany glimpse of a small college at a crossroads—and of the societal turmoil and follies of the seventies.

Our Love Could Light the World by Anne Leigh Parrish. $15.95, 978-1-938314-44-5. Twelve stories depicting a dysfunctional and chaotic—yet lovable—family that has to band together in order to survive